CATRIONA McPHERSON

Dandy Gilver and a Spot of Toil and Trouble

HODDER &
STOUGHTON

First published in Great Britain in 2017 by Hodder & Stoughton

An Hachette UK company

1

A CIP catalogue record for this title is available from the British Library

Hardback ISBN 978 1 473 63344 5
eBook ISBN 978 1 473 63345 2

Typeset in Plantin Light by Palimpsest Book Production Limited,
Falkirk, Stirlingshire

Printed and bound by Clays Ltd, St Ives plc

Hodder & Stoughton policy is to use papers that are natural, renewable
and recyclable products and made from wood grown in sustainable forests.
The logging and manufacturing processes are expected to conform
to the environmental regulations of the country of origin.

Hodder & Stoughton Ltd
Carmelite House
50 Victoria Embankment
London EC4Y 0DZ

www.hodder.co.uk

For Lisa, Patrick, Fred and Rupert Moylett,
with love.
And in memory of Frank.

I would like to thank:

Lisa Moylett, my agent; Francine Toon, Jenni Leech, Jessica Hische, Jim Caunter and all at Hodder; Marcia Markland and all at St Martin's; Sarah Brown; my family and friends; and, of course, Dandy's readers and fans. Your emails always arrive just when I need a reminder of why writing seemed like a good idea. Thank you!

Prologue

The walls, rough-formed from great black lumps of stone, ran dank and wet like the flanks of a sweating beast. Single drips and rivulets coursed the length of the stairway, three full storeys and more, sliming the steps and fouling the air.

Footsteps skittered down a half-flight's turn, then slipped and stumbled the next half to a respite at the dark landing. Terrified breaths filled the close damp, breaking into whimpers and sinking into groans.

When at last those ragged breaths were caught, into the silence came a second set of footsteps, the steadier tread of a pursuer advancing, no halting, no hurry.

'I'm sorry. But I have to.' The voice wavered, as though from a recent shock, still reverberating.

The voice that came in answer was flat and dead. 'No. *I* am sorry. But I cannot allow it.'

There was a scuffle, quick and grim, then a rush of unruly noise filled the tower: gasps and shrieks; scrapes and thuds. Last, a resonant *crack!* like a coconut, heavy with milk, raised and smashed.

Then nothing.

I

'I've heard stupider ideas,' was Hugh's pronouncement as I read him a snippet of the letter heralding the case we came to call The Cut Throat Affair. He did not look at Donald as he spoke. If he had tried much harder not to look, he might have sprained an eyeball.

Donald sank a little lower in his chair and inspected the dry inside page of the *Scotsman* as though it were the key to all mythologies. Or rather, since this *was* Donald, as though it showed a new picture of Claudette Colbert in her nightie.

My poor boy. He had come unstuck over the matter of some cattle during the winter. An unscrupulous breeder had beguiled him, against Hugh's advising, into the purchase of two truly enormous bulls, which were to strengthen and transform his herd.

I daresay had they been bought by a farmer in the gentle south or the temperate midlands, even by a north countryman with a breath of sea air across his acres, their pedigree would have counted and their promise been fulfilled. As it was, one Perthshire winter did for them both. They barely saw out autumn in the fields with their harem, but instead retired into strawed quarters, like Miss Havisham on her wedding day. After that, no amount of plugging draughts with bales or buying in expensive cake stopped their vertiginous descent from lusty health in late summer to puny trembling by Christmas.

Donald and his factor tied sacks over the two sets of shivering ribs and packed them on to a train headed for Devon

3

and a rosier future. Even that found disfavour with Hugh. A few pounds for their dead weight from the Pitlochry knacker-erman was sound business sense, he barked at Donald when the scheme came to light. Paying carriage for a trip to the seaside was . . . Words failed him and I was glad, since I had a strong suspicion that the *particular* words failing him were not often spoken in my drawing room.

It did not help that Teddy was home for the Christmas vac at the time and that, despite seeing the inside of more nightclubs than lecture halls during the Michaelmas term, he had reeled away from college with a respectable set of marks in his long essays and an indulgent set of comments from his fond tutors. It would be so much easier all round if my elder son sparkled and my younger was the . . . I did not finish the thought, for I love them both dearly.

Anyway, this morning's idea of middling stupidity was related by an old friend I had scarcely seen since we returned well-finished, from Paris. I had pounced on her letter to me, eager to hear her news, for she had always been the most tremendous fun. She had been, in fact, the great 'hit' of 1904, landing in the middle of the season with a splash and carrying off her beau before the ink was dry on the first round of invitations.

Minerva Roll. A lesser girl would have buckled under such a name, but Minnie made it seem part of her own cleverness to have been dubbed with something so extraordinary. All around, Annes and Marys began to hint that they were really Titianas and Mirabelles.

And it seemed she was as clever now as ever. She mentioned the wolf at the door, holes in the roof and the spectre of death duties; a familiar litany. She also mentioned, however, a novel plan to outwit the wolf, the rain and His Majesty's exchequer too.

★　★　★

. . . we are turning Castle Bewer into a theatre – open air, summers only – and putting on plays! As you can imagine, dear Dandy, we are a little trepidatious (is that a word?), about the hordes descending. Not just the paying public, although certainly them too, but the actors themselves and, of course, actresses. Can you imagine what our mothers would say? And stagehands, I daresay. At any rate, I would be much happier with a pal on the spot who could loom threateningly if someone starts looking with covetous eyes at any of our treasures.

Are you laughing at the thought of our possessing treasures, Dandy dear? We do, you know. Or at least we did. And we still might. It's all rather complicated and we have not quite decided what to do about it, my mother-in-law, my husband, and me. I promise to have the whole plan hammered out once and for all before you arrive. For now, think 'Treasure Hunt' and you will be in the right general area. Possibly. Or not.

More soon,

Much love,

Min.

'Quite a good spot for it,' said Hugh. 'I'll give them that much. But they'll never turn a profit if they're going to employ battalions of ancillary staff. Where do you come in, Dandy?'

'I'm to loom, I think,' I said. 'And perhaps hunt treasure too? Minnie's style was always more flowery than fluent. Anyway, I shan't charge her much. She's a pal.'

'Typical,' said Hugh, executing a swift volte-face. 'Roping in chums and doing it on the cheap.'

'I shall only be going at all if Alec fancies it,' I said, hoping to placate him. 'It's not really a case of detection, after all. And we are usually billed as detectives, aren't we?'

'You can't keep turning down paying jobs,' said Hugh.

How he managed to keep revolving like that without getting dizzy was beyond me.

I stood, dropped my napkin and clicked my tongue. Bunty, my puppy, still just about a puppy anyway, crawled out from under the table, shook herself thoroughly and sat at my heels gazing up at me, awaiting instruction. Hugh gave me a look with a long history and a longer list of ingredient emotions.

He had enjoyed despising me for the atrocious conduct of Bunty the First, throughout her happy life. Now here I was with Bunty the Second, brought up on the same indulgent principles and yet, miraculously, better behaved not only than the original Bunty but also than any hound or terrier Hugh had ever trained under his regime of shouts and thwacks. He ought to love her. He did not. We both pretended none of it was happening.

Donald spoiled the atmosphere of dignified face-saving a little with a tremendous snort as he watched Bunty and me leave the room, but Hugh had returned to the European news by then and even his wife had no power to annoy him.

'I'm coming over,' I said to Alec from the telephone in my sitting room. 'There's a sniff of a case. Well, a job anyway.'

'What's the difference?' Alec said.

'Anything your end?'

'Nothing you'd countenance.'

'Oh?'

'But it's a lovely time of year for a trip to the coast.'

I groaned. We had decided at the outset of Gilver and Osborne twelve years before that we would not sully ourselves with divorce work. Not for us the quiet hours in a corner of a seaside hotel lounge watching for some Mr and Miss, masquerading as Mr and Mrs, to mount the stairs.

It was becoming untenable. Even I conceded it. For one thing, there seemed to be a perfect epidemic of divorce taking hold. The lower classes were just about managing to make a vow before God and stick to it, whether too tired

6

from their labours to be getting up to mischief in the evenings or perhaps unable to foot the bill for all the resulting upheaval, but amongst our own set every *Tatler* brought news of another cabinet reshuffle and it was creeping down among the doctors, lawyers and even the odd schoolmaster. It was unseemly and extraordinary and lesser detective firms were making a nice living out of it, or so Alec never tired of saying.

'The difference between a case and a job,' I told him, answering his question, 'is that nothing has actually happened and we're to make sure nothing does. There's guaranteed entertainment too. I'll see you in half an hour.'

Alec lived just across the valley, his pretty little estate the next neighbour but one to mine. He inherited it from the grateful but grieving father of his late fiancée, after the solving of her murder, which was our first case. There he had lived for twelve years, looked after by an austere valet-cum-butler by the name of Barrow and a cook as devoted as my own Mrs Tilling. Every so often he murmured about a wife, the way Hugh murmured about coppicing the top plantation, or I murmured about turning out the attics one day.

This morning, I found him strolling down the drive to meet me, hands in pockets, pipe in teeth, with Millie his spaniel waddling along at his side. Bunty gave a single polite yip when she saw them and then wagged her whole body from just behind her ears to the tip of her tail. I slowed and leaned over to let her out of the motorcar. Millie was as blind as a beggar these days and the drive, where she could feel the hard ash under her paws, was about the only walk she could rise to on her own. With Bunty at her side, though, she was free to rush about as joyously as ever, trusting her friend to wheel back and collect her. As Alec climbed in, we watched them dash off in between two bedraggled rhododendron bushes to go adventuring in the woods.

'You should get a puppy of your own,' I said. 'As her companion.'

'If I thought I could use it during the day and let it sleep in the kitchen, I would,' said Alec, turning to me as the undergrowth closed and stilled behind the dogs. 'But I know myself too well. It would be nipping in front of her at supper-time and climbing into her bed at night to chew her ears.' He sat back and grinned at me. 'What's this entertaining job then, Dandy? Where are we off to?'

'We're to guard the treasures of Castle Bewer,' I said, giving it a bit of swagger.

'Against whom?' said Alec. 'The taxman's the only one laying siege to castles these days, isn't he? And what can we do about *him*?'

'The taxman has a minor role, it's true,' I said. 'But we needn't concern ourselves with anything so dull. It's faeries, dukes and queens for us!'

'What?'

'Awake the nimble spirit of mirth!' I added.

'*What?*'

'Shakespeare, darling. Actors. Actresses too.'

'And you scoff at lurking in a boarding-house lounge watching for adulterers!' Alec said.

We could not imagine then what we were shortly to know. A man and his mistress, off for a seaside liaison, would have been wholesome refreshment compared with what the castle had in store.

2

Our first glimpse of the place was not promising. It was one of those dour days in a Scottish June when the sky rumbles purply and the rain batters flat the straggling meadowsweet in the hedgerows. Only the midges are happy on such a day and we slapped at them tirelessly as we trundled along.

'How are the little devils getting in?' Alec demanded, not for the first time, running a hand along the seal of the window, checking for gaps.

'I've never been troubled by midges,' said Grant, my maid, from the back seat. 'I'm not to their taste.' She had told me this many times before in the twenty-odd years of our joint sojourn in Perthshire, that most midge-infested of Scottish counties with its untold burns and forests, its rivers and valleys. It was a midge's paradise and I a midge's feast. Nothing, not even the winter snow, not even the suet puddings, made me miss Northamptonshire more.

As to why Grant was *on* the back seat: truth be told, once I revealed the theatrical element of our current concern, it would have taken a heart of cold stone and more energy than I could muster to keep her away. She was born in a trunk, the daughter of travelling players, and although she left the company voluntarily at the age of fifteen to go into service, she never lost either the taste for it or a blithe assumption that she was an expert. If she did not get at least a walk-on part in the upcoming production she would sulk until spring.

Even Grant, who often sees romance where I see damp, fell

silent when we crested a little hill and the castle escarpments were laid before us. Castle Bewer was ancient – fourteenth century at a rough guess – built when marauders were a plain fact of life and to soften the landscape with trees would be folly. It was a stretch even to call its surroundings a park, for the land was flat, its boundary was a wire fence and a flock of blackface sheep were standing in it, up to their hocks in watery mud. It was, frankly, a field.

In the centre of the field was a puddle somewhat bigger than all the other puddles, and in the centre of *this* puddle, the walls rising straight up out of the brown water, was a roundish jumble of pink stone. Upon close inspection, one could see towers and turrets, pitched roofs and lean-tos, arrow-slits and escutcheons, crow-step gables and studded shutters. But at first glance it looked like nothing so much as a rather ragged dumpling floating in gravy.

'I've brought both your fox furs, madam,' said Grant when she had recovered the power of speech.

'We can share them,' I replied, as I turned my little Morris Cowley in at the farm gate and splashed through the potholes. The sheep raised their bony heads and gave us looks of practised ovine despair as we passed them.

'What do you think?' Alec asked, peering out at the bridge across the moat. It was not a drawbridge. The no-doubt-mighty studded planks that must have kept the castle fast in the bad old days were long gone and someone had knocked this one up out of packing crates, or so it looked to me. It was five feet wide with a generous eye, and made of plain unpainted pine planks, much patched and mended and green-ish-grey from weathering.

'It must be all right,' I said, looking at it dubiously. 'How else do they come and go?' For there was no track leading around the castle to either side and no garage or stable anywhere in the field. Still, I hesitated. Then, at the other end of the bridge, in the mouth of the castle itself, a stooped figure draped in a mackintoshed cape and holding a lantern stepped out of shelter into the rain and waved at us, cawing his arm to beckon us onward.

'Right-oh,' I said and took my foot off the brake. I saw Alec stiffen beside me as though trying to levitate and save the rickety little bridge the weight of his body. I would have laughed but I was doing exactly the same myself, holding my legs off the seat and stretching up out of my collar like a hungry chick when its mother returns to the nest with a worm.

'I could have walked,' muttered Grant and she sounded tense from clenching too.

The gusts of the three of us breathing out fogged the windscreen when my front wheels rolled across the cobbles of the gatehouse passage and I laughed as I leaned forward and cleared a patch with my sleeve.

There was a horseshoe of windows curving out from behind us to either side, reaching three and four storeys high above the gate but stepping down to just two, and then dribbling on to low sheds and outhouses at the ends of the horseshoe arms. Directly before us lay a long wide courtyard, open to the moat at the far end and flanked at either corner by the remaining two castle towers. The Bewers had evidently let one wing of the castle fall into ruins, perhaps for the view, but what remained was still a house of generous proportions.

The figure with the lantern was standing, arm aloft, about halfway down the courtyard, in an empty space between an elderly Crossley and a pair of rusted bicycles, and I deduced that I was expected to park there. I frowned. There was no nearby door and such was the aspect of the castle keep that it seemed to be raining even harder here than out in the field, great gouts of water splashing down and heavy curtains of drips falling from every overhang.

Still, it is well-nigh impossible to ignore a wet stranger swinging a lantern at one, and so I rumbled over and parked as indicated. Anyway, it was not as bad as I had feared, for leaning against the wall beside the Crossley were two enormous umbrellas and the caped figure held one out above my head as I stepped down.

With much shuffling and the inevitable fuss of sharing two umbrellas among three individuals, we struggled across the cobbles and in at an open door, twice my height and wide enough for a carriage. On the other side of it was a stone-floored, stone-walled, arch-ceilinged passageway that stretched without relief into darkness in both directions.

The lantern carrier pushed back his mackintosh hood once we were under cover and regarded us out of a lugubrious face with pouched cheeks and red-rimmed eyes. I had never seen a human face more like that of a bloodhound. He sniffed.

'Tea,' he said. 'Drawing room.'

Then he turned on his heel and left, taking the light with him. We made to follow, but he stopped, rather as though he had been shot, and without turning his head repeated: 'Drawing room!' very definitely before starting up again and beetling off out of sight.

'Ah,' said Alec. 'Drawing room. I see.'

'And what about me?' said Grant. 'Is that the butler? Am I to go with him? Who's getting the bags?'

'I think we should stick together,' I said. 'If we find this drawing room, Minnie can ring and get him back again.'

We looked along the passageway to the other end. There was not what one would call a glimmer of light in any definite sense, but we could tell where the end of the passageway *was* so at least we knew we were not about to step off into an oubliette without warning. Alec struck a match and by its glow we advanced. The stones were gritty underfoot and the walls were damp where they were not truly slimy. I breathed in deeply, hoping to catch a whiff of toast or muffins, or wood smoke or even floor soap; something that hinted at human habitation. All I smelled was cold stone. And all I could hear were drips, within and without. Alec's match burned down and he dropped it. It sizzled without being stepped on as he lit another.

At the end of the passageway, matters improved. Round a corner, we met with the cheerful sight – comparatively speaking – of an unlit candle sconce in the wall, a threadbare runner on the floor and, halfway along, a door.

When we reached it, I seized the iron ring that did service as a handle and wrenched it round, drawing back as the door fell open towards us and grabbing Grant before it squashed her.

Matters, on this peculiar's door's other side, improved again. Here was a room. It had no furniture and few features beyond a dark fireplace at either end, and its single window was shuttered, but it had a second door and around *this* door there was a faint yellow seam. We trooped across another threadbare carpet, which gave up coughs of mousy dust at every step. Alec, pinching out the latest match, lifted the latch and shouldered the door open.

'Dandy!' The woman who was sitting by the fireside leapt up and came forward, beaming, to hug me. She had iron-grey curls set in tight rows all over her head and was dressed in bagged tweeds, darned stockings and scuffed shoes of such remarkable dowdiness that for once I felt like a fashion plate. 'And you must be Alec,' the woman went on. 'Minnie. Welcome, welcome. Is Puff at your back?'

I looked behind me.

'Puff?' I said.

'Butler,' said Minnie. 'P-U-G-H "Puff". Don't call him "Pew" if you expect an answer. He was supposed to be watching out for you. But never mind. Here you are regardless. Come and sit down and warm up. It's not much of a day.'

She waved towards the fireplace where, in a pool of lamplight, tea was set out on a couple of low tables. For the first time I noticed that there were other people in the room. The chair pulled closest to the flames contained an elderly woman in a lace bonnet and a good number of shawls, sitting with her feet up on a little stool and blankets wrapped around her legs. She was holding a teacup close to her pursed lips and was firing a look of some malevolence at the three of us standing by the open door. Grant caught the look, deciphered it correctly and hastened to shut the door, kicking a straw-stuffed draught sausage back into place with an expert toe.

The armchair on the other side of the fire was exerting its hold on a gentleman somewhat younger than the old lady in shawls but a good bit older than Minnie. At last he managed to clamber out of it and advanced on us all. I searched his face for the pale young man who had danced every dance with pretty Minerva Roll and had sat whispering with her over supper, but could not find any. He had spent every day since then out of doors, in wind and rain and occasional sun, and was now the colour and texture of an unpeeled beetroot, his few strands of hair flopping over his forehead like the beetroot's wilted stalks. Not until he smiled could I see so much as a wisp of the man I knew.

'Bluey?' I said.

'What's left of him,' said Bluey Bewer, giving me a grin full of gleaming white dentures. 'And my dear mother. I expect you've been in the same room as her before now, Dandy, and might even have met, but all a thousand years ago, of course.' He walked over to stand by the other armchair and shook the old lady gently by one shoulder. '*Mama?*' he bellowed. I felt Grant start and noticed that a dog, dozing on the hearthrug, twitched in its sleep. '*Let me present some friends of Minnie's.*' The volume was impressive and his sustaining it even more so, for people usually drop their voices, even when yelling at the deaf. The old lady reached out to a side-table, put down her cup, and then with ponderous deliberation unfolded a pair of long-handled spectacles and held them to her face. Her eyes were greatly magnified by the lenses and between that and the lace round her cap she looked like a baby doll, peering up at us. '*This is Mrs Gilver and Mr Osborne,*' Bluey thundered. '*And . . .?*'

'Oh,' I said. 'Grant, my maid and assistant. We weren't sure of the floor plan. Could you ring for Pugh? Could he act as a guide?'

'Hm,' Minnie said, but did not elaborate.

Then, after clearing her throat as deliberately as she had exchanged cup for lorgnette, Mrs Bewer spoke. 'Are you front of house?' she said, in tones rather cracked but still commanding. 'You don't look like players to me. And that's not a trained voice you're piping away in, girl.'

'Don't mind my mother-in-law,' said Minnie. 'Sit and eat and tell me your news, Dandy.'

I sat, and I accepted a cup and a little plate of toast, but as to condensing the news of decades into a bulletin, I did not even try. Alec saved me by swinging into step as the perfect house guest.

'I'm Dorset,' he said to Bluey. 'And Cromwell pretty much did for the best of our houses. So this is all very thrilling. Exactly how old is the castle?'

Bluey nodded, catching on to what was needed, and proceeded to regale Alec with tales of battle, siege and scotched invasion. I followed politely for a bit and then turned to Minnie.

'Now then,' I said, quietly enough not to disturb the men, 'I am going to have to press you for quite a lot more details regarding what exactly Alec and I are doing here. Not – gosh, no – that it's not bliss to see you.'

'Very kind,' Minnie said vaguely. She shot a look at her mother-in-law. 'It's as I said in my letter. You know how things are, Dandy. Well, I assume so.'

'I'm working as a detective,' I reminded her and she shouted with laughter, before heaving a sigh.

'Can you believe it?' she said. 'We didn't know we were the end of it all, did we?'

I glanced at Grant, who was taking dainty bites of toast and prim sips of tea and looking around with her face like a mask. Knowing her as well as I did, I was not fooled by the mask. I knew she was listening to every word and I should send her away if Minnie was about to get down to business. But I also knew I would have to prise her off the chair with my fingernails and frogmarch her.

'Tell me all,' I said to Minnie and settled back to hear the sad tale of the Bewers that had brought us here.

3

'Have you heard about Mespring?' Minnie began. As I shook my head, she went on: 'It's opening to day-trippers.'

'Mespring *House*?' I said.

Grant forgot herself so far as to gasp. Mespring House was a Palladian marvel of unrivalled splendour, full of the fabulous collections gathered by generations on end of rich marquises.

Minnie nodded, enjoying our surprise. 'First Chatsworth, then Hopetoun, now Mespring. Open Tuesday to Saturday, charabancs welcome. And at first we were filled with envy. We got quite sour. "Just our luck!" we told ourselves. "Two miles along the road, putting us and our ancient towers in the deepest, darkest shade".' She dropped her voice a little further. 'I'm glad Bluey can't hear me. He's terribly proud of the old dump. But it's not even as if Mespring doesn't have towers of its own. The old keep over there is older than our curtain wall by fifty years. Or at least, their librarian is well paid enough to say so.'

I tutted sympathetically.

'No, no, Dandy,' Minnie said, sitting forward with her eyes shining. 'No need to commiserate. Because you see, in the midst of our gloom, we saw the light. We needn't carp and sulk about Mespring! We should thank our lucky stars! It's a few miles along the road and the only way to get to it is right past our door.'

Hugh is a great one for maps and our library is littered with them, so it was easy to bring the topography of the county to mind and confirm what she was telling me. The route to the Mespring House and its Italian Masters was indeed along the little road that abutted Minnie and Bluey's puddled field.

'But would people stop off, even at that?' Minnie went on. 'How could we make them? That's when we hit on our marvellous idea. The gaping hordes are only allowed into Mespring on an afternoon tour and then they're kicked out. We are putting on much more of a show. Literally, ha-ha! Every afternoon and evening except Sunday. We've got carpenters coming to knock up seats in the courtyard and the company arrive from Edinburgh tomorrow.'

'And you'll make enough on ticket sales?' I said. 'To cover the carpenters?'

'Not just ticket sales, Dandy.' Minnie put her empty teacup down and wriggled up out of the depths of the armchair to perch on its edge and regale me. 'We can charge the company rent. We can charge the actors for their digs in the West Lodging. We're going to have talks in the mornings – Shakespeare scholars and all that, you know. We'll serve tea after the matinee and late suppers too. We're going to let audience members, who're so moved, stay the night in the Bower Lodging and charge them a shilling for bacon and eggs in the morning. We're going to offer lifts from the station at sixpence a pop and if anyone brings his own motorcar, well then we ask sixpence for parking.'

Bluey, who had started listening somewhere in the middle of all this, now rumbled irritably.

'Talks, teas and tickets, yes,' he said. 'But my dear Minnie, if you think you can get a chap to hand over sixpence to leave a car in a muddy field you are on a flight of fancy.'

'We'll see,' Minnie said. 'Of course, what we've been hoping for – what we've all been praying for – is Americans. Pots of money and so *avid*. We've hooked a first catch of them, actually, and if these send picture postcards home to their friends, that could really put us on the map. What do you think?'

'I think it's brilliant,' Alec said. 'I think I shall neglect my duties here completely and go home to Dunelgar in the morning to start up in competition. How did you ever come up with it?'

'It started as a favour to our daughter,' Minnie said. 'Our darling child. The company are friends of hers and she's going to be one of our scholarly lecturers as well as taking a small part in the play. Did you know Penelope was stage-struck, Dandy? Lord, it's been the same since her first Christmas treat. Ballet, pantomime, dreadful dreary plays that make me want to scream. She nagged us into letting her go to drama school in London instead of finishing – can you imagine? We thought that would get it all out of her system, but it only made her keener than ever.'

'How unfortunate,' I said. I have often wished that one of my sons was a daughter but when I considered the horrors of steering a modern girl safely to the altar, avoiding the kind of nonsense Minnie was describing, I was thankful for Donald and Teddy despite everything.

'Then the tale takes a turn for the absurd!' Bluey said. I shot him an enquiring glance but he had said all he was going to; the details were Minnie's worry.

'Ghastly,' she agreed. 'Of course, we couldn't dream for a minute of letting her go traipsing around with a theatre company – all those "digs" and Sunday travel! But we knew a distant cousin of the Bewers happened to be theatrical. I thought he trod the boards in Glasgow which would have warned us, except that Glasgow has some fearfully proper merchants as well as everything else.'

'Fearfully,' I said. 'Alec and I were employed by one not too long ago and his daughter was practically Rapunzel in her tower.'

'Yes, well,' Minnie said. 'It's Edinburgh and no better for

that. Cousin Leonard, we discovered, was the actor manager of a small theatre there. And so we thought no harm could come to Penny if she went along for a while. She'd learn what a comfortless, miserable life it was – this was the idea – and come home.'

'I take it the plan didn't work,' said Alec.

'It backfired more roundly than I could ever have feared,' Minnie said. 'And the mother of a girl is a fearful creature. Anyway, Leonard's theatre is in a terrible district in the old town and he – or the backers or whoever it is who should have been paying attention – haven't been. They neglected the upkeep so badly that they all had to turf out over a spot of dry rot in the spring.'

'Bit more than a spot,' said Bluey. 'The place is falling down. Wet rot, dry rot, woodworm, slipped slates, pointing all gone to blazes, buckets everywhere. We mightn't be the last word in home comforts, but at least the roof is sound. The roof must be kept sound!'

'Hear, hear,' said Alec and I am sure that, a hundred miles north in Perthshire, Hugh was nodding along in his business room. The soundness of the roof is a topic of which he never tires.

'And so they needed a venue just when you needed an attraction?' I said. 'What's that lovely word for things like this?'

The door had opened without my hearing and the young woman upon the threshold now spoke. 'Serendipity,' she said. 'Is that the one you mean? It was the most marvellous seren-dipity, as it happens. After the shock, I mean to say.'

She was not what my imagination had conjured at the mention of a stage-struck child, being quite twenty-five for one thing, and having a frank, open face with a friendly smile, and being sensibly dressed in a thick fisherman's jersey, a pleated tartan skirt and gum boots. She did the rounds of parents and grandmother, dropping kisses on to each head and putting a smile on to each face as though her salutations were the touch of a fairy wand. Then she shook hands with Alec and me and dropped down onto the hearthrug beside the dog. One more kiss was planted on *his* head and then Penny Bewer set to removing her boots and socks, draping the latter over the fire rails where they steamed gently.

'And it *was* a shock!' she went on. 'Caliban went right through the stage like something from a pantomime. He actually disappeared! The audience thought it was an avant garde decision on the part of the director. There was a rustle of approbation from the posh seats, or so I'm told.'

I laughed and turned to Alec to share my delight in this pleasant girl and her story. Then I caught my lip. Alec, not for the first time, was dazzled. He was looking at young Penny Bewer, the way that Donald looked at picture papers, Teddy at bottles of wine, and Bunty at cold sausages left out on the kitchen table. The steaming socks and fisherman's jersey did not appear to trouble him.

'Did the show go on?' he asked.

'There was a wobbly moment,' said Penny. 'Miranda rushed on and bent over the hole, shouting "Are you all right, Davey, or do you need a doctor?", which must have killed the mood a bit, but Bess, the ASM, brought the tab down and they handed out free ices whilst making hasty repairs. Still, it's different once you know, isn't it? And the chap they brought in to price up the repair and check the place over had to lie down on a couch and have a brandy. Apparently it was only the carpet holding the upper circle together. The whole tier was ready to plummet at any moment and since that's where the school parties sit for matinees, the owner closed up and they've all been resting ever since. So this,' she waved a hand at the room around her, 'is most welcome.' Then she leapt up, grabbed her gum boots but left the socks, and stepped back over towards the door. 'Are we changing?'

'Of course,' said Bluey, getting a nod of approval from Grant.

'We can't change once the company gets here, Daddy,' Penny said. 'None of them will have a dinner jacket to his name.'

'Take Granny up with you if you're going, dearest,' Minnie said and while her husband and daughter were busy winkling the old lady out of her armchair and yelling into her ear that it was time for a rest before dressing, she added to me, 'I can't believe my girl might marry a man who hasn't the means to dress for dinner.'

'Marry?' said Alec. Minnie shushed him.

Grant had somehow got herself inveigled into the exodus, murmuring that she would help Mrs Bewer. I knew her game; she reckoned there was a headful of long hair under that lacy cap and she meant to have her way with it. Grant abhors my boyish shingle; thwarted by it and feeling her talents wither from lack of use. She avoided my eye as she swept out, even though all she would have seen was me shaking my head fondly.

When it was down to the three of us, Minnie took the matter up again. 'That's the bit we didn't tell you,' she said. 'Not only did Cousin Leonard *not* turn Penny away from theatre life with its cold realities but he actually stole her heart too. They are now betrothed, if you please.'

'But if he's a distant cousin,' I said. 'He can't be too beyond the pale, surely.'

'A second son generations back,' Minnie said. 'His father works for the railway. In the offices. But for the railway. It really is all quite over, isn't it? Our world, our ways.'

'But we shall do our best to save a corner of it,' Alec said. I looked at him speculatively. Was he thinking only of our brief here at Castle Bewer or was he thinking that Penny's heart so recently given could still be snatched back again. 'For instance,' he said, 'if you've got an eye on the accounting book, shouldn't you be keeping costs down? Why do you think it's worth a pair of detectives, or even just guards, on the pay roll?'

'And forgive *me*,' I added, 'but am I not right in thinking that Penny is your only child?' Minnie nodded. 'Then why don't you sell up and go to a villa in Spain? Is Bluey determined to see life out where he was born? Hugh's as bad but, Minnie my dear, if he didn't have Donald to add weight to his claim I'd be able to swat it all away for the nonsense it would be. And Bluey's a poppet compared with Hugh, isn't he?'

Minnie gave us each a grave look and then glanced at her wristwatch. 'Oh, close enough!' she said. 'Who's for a drink?'

There was a sideboard roughly the size and shape of a pharaoh's tomb sitting against the wall and upon it grew a forest of dusty bottles, half-empty and re-corked, sticking up from an undergrowth of mismatched glasses. Minnie selected one of the fuller ones, which happened to be sherry, and poured three healthy measures.

'In note form,' she said, 'Bluey can't sell up because he doesn't own the place.'

'Oh?' I said. 'Who owns it?'

'His father,' said Minnie. I frowned at her. Minnie was forty-eight like me and, as far as I could recall from that London season, Bluey was the perfect number of years older than her, making him in his late fifties today. His father, in turn, had to be well into his eighties or even nineties given the sorts of ages gentlemen settled down to filling cradles in those days.

'Why does the old boy want to hang on?' said Alec. 'Does he live here? Shall we be meeting him?'

'Heavens, no,' Minnie said. 'He died years ago.' Alec and I shared a glance. 'That is,' Minnie went on, 'I *expect* he died years ago. He'd be ninety-nine now if he was still on the go. But the thing is, you see, he left. He abandoned his wife when Bluey was quite a young man. Actually, at the time of our wedding. He hightailed it off to Beirut or some such outlandish place and he's never been back.'

The question that jostled its way to the front of my brain was why on earth I did not know the story. Gossip made the world go round and this was delicious gossip. It ought to have been the talk of the town when Minnie and I were girls; it ought to have hung around Bluey like a bad smell. Certainly, it ought to have stopped that darling Minerva Roll from getting mixed up with him.

Thankfully, I bit my tongue and it was Alec who spoke, choosing a much more diplomatic and professional question.

'But can't you have him declared dead?' he said. 'Seven years, isn't it?'

'And it's been thirty,' said Minnie nodding. 'Of course we could. But Ottoline, my dearest mother-in-law, doesn't want to. I think at first she was sure he'd come back. He wrote to her from all over the place, at least for a bit. Meanwhile she put about the story that he was at home in frail health and was living quietly. She was just cagey enough about what he'd come down with that no one visited in case they caught it. Rather clever, really. But that was the way of it with our parents' generation, wasn't it Dandy? An invalid not to be disturbed covered a great many sins.' She frowned quickly and then mustered a brighter smile than ever. 'Over the years, she got so *good* at the story I think it entered her soul. Do you know what I mean?'

Alec looked askance but I knew exactly what she was referring to. It was a feature of our mothers' generation, that talent for not knowing anything shocking and not seeing anything nasty. It allowed them to live lives of such quiet contentment. It was watered down a little in girls like Minnie and me, bashed by modern novels and careless talk in intellectual circles, but we had vestiges sturdy enough to get us through the war. I called on the spirit of my mother as never before while I was trapped with horrors in the officers' convalescent home those five long years. Nanny Palmer was quite done away with for a change. For, while she was starched to a crisp in day-to-day life, she had a sentimental streak and might 'come over queer' or be rendered 'all of a doo-dah' by extreme wretchedness. Holding a bowl while some poor chap emptied his gassed tummy into it would not have troubled her, but holding a bowl while a doctor filled it with the peeled-off bandages from another chap's four stumps would have been beyond her. I had kept a smile on my face and chatted to him about plays and concerts. My mother would have been proud of me.

'All passion's spent now, of course,' Minnie was saying, 'Ottoline is past caring what anyone thinks of how he treated her those long years ago. A quiet notice in *The Times* and it could all be over, with no more of a ripple than a few old acquaintances saying "hmph" and turning the page to juicier items.'

'But?' said Alec. He is a wonderful sniffer-out of buts.

Minnie gave him a fond smile. 'But now it's a question of the death duties. We simply can't afford to let Bluey's father die just yet. And it's bearing down on us like a charging bull. Hence this last ditch attempt to get in the black, once and for all. On his hundredth birthday this autumn he'll be swept away and we shall have to sell up to pay our bills. So, much as I love my mother-in-law – and I truly do; she has had a splendid life despite what that rotter doled out to her – I find myself hoping that she doesn't outlive Richard's allotted century and gets to die in peace in her own little bed with Bluey holding one hand and I the other.'

Alec returned the fond smile, as who could not? It is not often one meets with such simple goodness as this. 'And what about the other question?' he said. 'Why are we here? If you know the company through your daughter, can't you trust them with the run of the house? And couldn't you lock away all your loot while the audience is around? You're not giving them silver spoons to stir their tea, are you?'

25

The word 'loot' jogged my memory. I had been so swept up in the story of the play that I had, unaccountably, forgotten.

'Where does the treasure come in, Minnie? Have you made up your mind about whatever it was you were chewing over?'

Minnie shrank down into her collar and screwed up her pretty face as though to brace herself for a blow. She had always done it, despite our mothers' warning that any extreme expressions would see off our looks and wrinkle us like prunes. 'Promise not to titter, won't you?' she said. 'Castle Bewer, unlikely as it sounds, really does have a secret treasure. Richard, God rot him, blabbed about it on his travels. Perhaps he even sent emissaries back here to lay hands on it and deliver it to him. For whatever reason, we used to have a dreadful time with burglars breaking in. And we're just a bit concerned that some ne'er-do-well might use the opening-up of the castle to come and have a rummage. Illicitly, as it were. Do you see?'

'Um,' I said, 'not real— I mean, just about, I suppose. Can't you put it in the bank?'

'Or give it to a friend to look after,' said Alec, with a pointed look at me. 'You know, if you want to keep it quiet.'

'The trouble is,' said Minnie, 'that we don't know where it's hidden. If it weren't for the burglars that came a-hunting, I think we'd all have believed that the dastardly Richard took it with him. So, as I hinted in my letter, as well as lurking around being threatening and off-putting, I do also rather want you to find it. I'm almost sure that's what we've decided anyway. Pretty well certain we shan't go further than that. Because, you see, if we could convert it into hard cash before the day of reckoning, Bluey and I would be able to stretch to a little flat in Edinburgh and a cook-housekeeper, and give Penny a respectable pot as a dowry.'

'But why on earth do you think that would be troubling news?' I said. 'Why not just tell us in the letter?'

'Well there's another half-baked sort of a plan, we're

probably not going to . . . ' Minnie said. She was still wriggling as though in some discomfort. 'And I was afraid it would sound silly.'

'It sounds *thrilling*, don't you think, Alec?'

Alec's eyes were shining. 'Searching a castle for hidden treasure?' he said. 'Every little boy's dream.'

'And what is it?' I asked. 'This treasure?'

At that moment, with perfect timing, the door swung creakingly open and the sepulchral Pugh, now without his mackintosh cape, entered.

'Your bags are in your rooms, Mrs Gilver, Mr Osborne,' he said. 'And your baths are drawn. Follow me.'

4

The best rooms lay in a wing of the castle known as the Bower Lodging and Minnie insisted that Alec and I were to be billeted there, despite the fact that two more wealthy and romantic Americans might be persuaded to pay handsomely. I had been quartered in what Pugh delighted to inform me was the 'plague chamber' and Alec was destined for what Pugh delighted even more to inform him was the top tower room, known to its friends as 'Dead Man's Drop'.

'I'll see you at dinner then, Dandy,' Alec said, as Pugh pointed my door out to me before dragging him off up another round of the spiral staircase. 'But if you hear a splash from the moat, do say a prayer.'

I tried to smile. But the long tramp from the drawing room, through a succession of cold dark passageways, and then the long climb up the slimy staircase-tower had depressed my spirits. I have never liked castles. When I stepped into the plague chamber, it would have taken thick carpets and bright lamps to hearten me. As it was, I met with narrow windows, smoky candles, and a copper bath sitting on the hearthrug before a fire. The fire was leaping merrily up the chimney, it was true, but I felt my jaw drop just the same.

'Drawn!' I exclaimed. 'Pugh most definitely said my bath was "drawn". That means taps and a bathroom by anyone's reckoning, not . . . *this*.'

'I'd hop in while it's hot, madam, rather than argue,' Grant said. 'It's a long way from the kitchen.' She was busily laying out nightgown, cardigan jersey, bed socks and nightcap on the high mound of the bed. June or not, I agreed with her view of the temperature in here.

I shucked off my clothes rapidly and lowered myself into the water, which was not quite warm enough to feel pleasant and only minutes from actual discomfort. I slid down, nevertheless, searching for the angle that would get most of me underwater. I have never been able to decide whether shoulders or knees make one feel colder when they poke out, but I knew I had to get it right first time because any portion of the anatomy emerging wet into the air after a miscalculation would do away with all pleasure completely.

'Don't wet your hair yet,' Grant said, without turning, and I froze. 'There's another kettle on the way. Gilly wants me to alter her Sunday coat for her.'

This apparent non-sequitur made perfect sense to me. Grant had, once again, inserted herself into the servants' hall within minutes, making friends and trading favours. Gilly would go to church in a short coat with a low back-band made from the carved-off hem and a kick-pleat set into its newly-nipped silhouette and I would have warm bath water in return.

'Thank you, Grant,' I said. 'Anything to report?'

'You'll have heard about the treasure?' Grant said. 'It's hard to credit, isn't it? He snatched it right off her neck, you know. He sounds like a bad lot. He sounds – now I come to think of it – like something out of a three-volume novel.'

'A cad and a bounder,' I agreed. 'But no, I didn't hear about the snatching.'

Grant thrilled to tell me. The Bewer family had a few decent oil paintings, the requisite scrap of tapestry said to have been stitched by the usual suspect, and just one true marvel. A ruby the size of a plum, flanked by a dozen more rubies each the size of a cherry. One of the last torrid intervals in the stormy marriage of Richard and Ottoline saw him swoop down on his wife one night and grab the necklace off her throat, like a madman.

I had heard the next chapter already from Minnie but Grant's retelling still offered diversion. When Richard left at last – flouncing off into the night – the necklace was nowhere to be found. His wife heaved a sigh and called it a price worth paying to be rid of him.

'Five bungled burglaries later,' Grant concluded darkly, 'she had changed her mind.'

'But the burglaries stopped,' I said. 'So presumably the last burglar found it.'

'The housekeeper doesn't believe so,' said Grant. There was swoop in her voice and a veiled look in her eye as she spoke.

'Or, just possibly,' I went on, 'Richard died. Beirut was mentioned, after all. Hardly healthful. And once he was dead, he necessarily stopped sending thieves back to hunt for the ruby. I wonder if his letters dried up at the same time. That would be a good clue.'

'The staff have all been here for years,' said Grant. 'Pugh and Mrs Ellen and the cook, anyway. They'll know. After all, they know abou—' she put a hand up to the side of her face as though overcome by some strong emotion. 'No,' she said. 'I should let you hear it for yourself. And here comes Gilly now.'

I could hear it too, a heavy tread on the stone steps outside my door. Grant, sparing my modesty, held up a sheet as the door opened.

'Hut watter for your mistress,' came a gravelly voice, thick with the local brogue. It did not strike me as the voice of a girl who wanted a short coat with a kick-pleat.

'Thank you, Mrs Ellen,' Grant said. 'And since you've done the great kindness of bringing the kettles up yourself instead of sending a maid, I wonder if you'd be so kind as to take a seat – over by the window there – and answer some questions.'

Mrs Ellen, well into her seventies and work-worn to an extraordinary degree for a housekeeper, even given the usual plight of a domestic servant in a shrinking staff, clearly had better things to do, but, after setting down the two enormous copper kettles she had lugged up from the kitchen, she rolled down her sleeves and buttoned her cuffs, then sank onto an uncomfortable-looking little three-legged stool that stood beside a rustic spinning wheel in the turret window. I would suggest to Minnie that they would do more good in the bedroom of one of the avid Americans and that I should rather like an armchair.

Once Mrs Ellen was settled, easing her swollen feet out of their clogs and rubbing them together with delight at the unexpected rest, I started the interview. I affected not to notice the easing and rubbing for I only caught a glimpse of either on account of being crouched in a bath, at eye-level with the hem of her apron.

'I heard about the ruby,' I began, and she was off.

'Oh, it was a sight,' she said and laid one of her gnarled hands against her breast as though caressing it there. 'A beautiful sight and a terrible sight. I feared to see the young mistress with all that on her neck, like drops of blood across her shoulders and a puddle of blood above her heart. Like a slit throat, it was. Even before you heard its name you could see it. An unlucky thing. An evil thing.'

Out of the corner of my eye, I caught Grant smirking at me, watching me try to take this in my stride.

'There's a painting of the old mistress in it,' Mrs Ellen went on. 'But we don't keep that unlucky lady on show. And there's another of the young mistress in it too. She hangs it in her own room but she'll show you. Then you'll see what a terrible evil thing it is.'

'I-I shall certainly make sure to,' I said. Then I stalled. How could one follow that with plain questions about plain matters? Thankfully, Mrs Ellen went on.

'A cursed thing too,' she said. 'Cursed by the one who gave it to the old mistress. It was a wedding present. And it killed her.'

'I-I-I shall certainly be looking into all that very carefully,' I said. I shot Grant a dagger of a look. She was biting her cheeks.

'And if it's found it'll kill again.'

'Well, that's all very interesting and useful, Mrs Ellen,' I said. 'And thank you for the hot water. Now, I'll let you go about your busy day. Such a terrific lot of work there must be in this old house, especially with guests arriving. Thank you very much for making my bed so prettily and be sure to thank the housemaid for that extremely generous scuttle of coal, won't you? I'm quite modern, you should assure her. I shan't be ringing for my fire to be fed. I'm very capable with the tongs and can look after it nicely.'

Mrs Ellen scrambled her clogs back on and got to her feet, grabbing the kettles and making good speed out of the room with a brief curtsey. It is a skill I used to admire in my mother; that way of hounding servants into briskness without ever issuing an instruction worth the name. I was not aware of its awakening in me but, sometime in the long years, awaken it had and I was now a master.

Grant allowed herself a soft snort of laughter once the woman's footsteps had faded.

'What I don't understand,' I said, as I clambered out of the bath and wrapped myself in towels to keep warm while she got to work on my hair, 'is what makes any of them think it's still here. It's a large house and far from Spartan but they've had decades to search and have never turned it up. What makes them think it'll suddenly fall out of a cupboard into the hands of an actor by this time tomorrow?'

'It's not so much that they think it's likely, madam,' Grant said. 'It's more that they fear it, unlikely as it may be.'

'Because of . . . ?'

Grant nodded. 'The curse. I happened to dress Mrs Bewer's hair for her.' Of course she did. I knew she was going to. 'And she mentioned it. She wouldn't tell me what the curse is, though. She didn't seem to believe I was an assistant detective. Quite annoying. I'd be glad of it if you'd put her right, madam. You could visit her before dinner if you're quick.'

'I daresay you plunging in and setting about her with your curling irons didn't strike her as part of an investigation, Grant,' I said. 'You can't be all things to all men. Assistant detective or lady's maid. Take your pick.'

She thought about it for a long moment while working up the pump on her bottle of setting spray then, as she doused me in a noxious cloud like a gardener killing blackfly, she made her pronouncement. 'Lady's maid. It's a shorter step from there to dresser and I do so very much want to get in about the costumes. So I'll leave the detecting to you and Mr Osborne this time, madam.'

I said nothing but gave her a dry look and stood to let her help me into my frock.

Her successes as assistant detective are admittedly several, but Grant is a wonderful lady's maid. Despite its being June, she had correctly anticipated the temperature and humidity of a lowland castle and had packed a velvet evening dress with a high neck and long sleeves. My white fox fur lent a faint air of the music hall against the dark velvet and clashed a little with the cream lace in my headdress, but my mother was dead and could not be shocked, and I was almost cosy as I followed Grant, to be shown Mrs Bewer's bedroom door.

'There aren't any bells,' she said as we parted, 'but just wait. I'll hear from Pugh when you come back up and I won't be long. That's it over there, madam. And mind your head when you go in. There's a flying buttress lying in wait for you.'

I took word of the flying buttress in my stride. The passage-ways we had traversed between my room in the Bower Lodging and Mrs Bewer's above the drawbridge gate, in what Grant informed me was called the High Keep, had taken us up and down myriad little steps, often for no reason at all that I could see, and past ghosts of earlier walls or little wisps of long-vanished doorways. At least some of the curved ceilings had to be decorative rather than structural too, for the passageway was a mere four feet across and Hugh has droned me into a state of reluctant expertise on the question of barrel vaults and their best diameter.

I knocked, entered and ducked the buttress – actually the underbelly of an old staircase with no beginning or end. Mrs Bewer was sitting in another armchair, with another footstool, drawn close to another fireplace, but had been transformed from the bundle of shawls I had met downstairs into a grand old lady in satins and pearls. Her white hair would not have disgraced the court of the Sun King, for Grant had teased it into an enormous ball and studded it with jewelled pins like an orange stuck with cloves.

'Your girl's a lively one,' she said, peering at me again through her lorgnette. 'I haven't had this frock out of its bag for ten years but she talked me into it.'

I rather thought Grant had talked Mrs Bewer into some rouge and lipstick too. She would be blacking the old lady's lashes and sticking on patches by the end of the week.

'*You look lovely*,' I bellowed.

'I'm not deaf,' she snapped back at me. Then, seeing my look, she said it again with even more fervour. 'I'm *not* deaf. I pretend, so that I hear things. It's very useful and I recommend it to you for your own dotage if you end up living with your children.'

'But why have you just admitted it to me?' I said. 'If even your own son doesn't know.'

'I pay the bills,' said Mrs Bewer. 'Including the detective's bills, and so you are bound to me by confidentiality. I am your employer and you must tell me what you learn from Minnie and Bluey as well as everything else you might stumble on.'

Divorce work would have been less murky.

34

'Tell me about the ruby,' I said. 'The necklace.'

'See for yourself,' she answered, and waved at the far wall, beyond her bed with its brocade hangings. I stood and lifted one of the candlesticks from above the chimneypiece to take a closer look.

'Mind your footing,' Mrs Bewer said. 'The floor slopes sharply for a bit in the middle there.'

I had already found the spot, a ridge almost deep enough to call a step, treacherously masked by the blots of colour in a Turkey carpet. I padded on and raised the candle to study the portrait in its gilded frame.

She had been beautiful. Her hair was fair, her skin white and her dress the barest pink, like the last blowsy day of the apple blossom before it falls. And then there was the jewel at her throat, fiercely red and glittering. I leaned closer and peered at it.

'It's quite something, isn't it?' Mrs Bewer said from behind me. 'You know its nickname, I suppose? The Cut Throat.'

'Nasty,' I said. 'But apt.' It gave me the shudders to look at the picture and think of the name, for it was impossible, once it had been suggested, not to see those red gleams as drops of blood and that great red eye as a pool of it settled in the white hollows. 'And it was given to you as a wedding present?' I asked, remembering what Mrs Ellen had told me. 'Wait. No.' Mrs Ellen had claimed the gift's original owner had died.

'My mother-in-law, Beulah,' Mrs Bewer said. '*She* got it as a wedding present. From a neighbour.'

'Gosh,' I said. 'Rather lavish, wasn't it?'

'The neighbour was the Marchioness of Annandale,' Mrs Bewer explained. 'From Mespring, you know.' That made it a little less odd; the Annandales had been fabulously wealthy in their day, even if they were reduced to day-trippers now. 'But it wasn't a kindness. Bluey's grandfather had been promised to one of the Mespring girls, you see.'

'That would have been a—' I stopped myself before the words 'splendid match' escaped my lips. It was not diplomatic to remind a woman who had married into the Bewers that they were something of a comedown.

'Splendid match,' said Mrs Bewer, with a twinkle. She might be ninety and frail but she was still a pretty sharp twig. 'On paper, perhaps. But the particular Mespring girl selected for Harold Bewer was not likely to be found beating off an army of suitors. She was . . . Well, one doesn't like to be cruel.' She left a pause for me to fill silently. 'And so the gift of the ruby necklace was by way of a "dig". Suit yourself and God rot you, kind of thing. It made the bride squirm with shame, as you can imagine.'

I nodded. Of all the indignities associated with a wedding, the show of presents was ever the worst. The ranking of items by hard cash value, the suckings-up and snubs delivered in code by way of solid-silver soup-tureens and Sheffield-plated cake-forks, and then all the dowagers trooping through, nodding and smirking as they found out what everyone thought of the poor girl.

'Forgive me, Mrs Bewer,' I said, 'but someone mentioned, to my maid, the question of a . . . well, it sounds silly, but a—'

'The curse?' said the old lady. 'Good grief, you can't be as squeamish as that, girl. Yes, of course, the curse. I'm getting to it, if you'd let me.' She craned her head round the wing of her chair to take a look at the portrait, then sat back with a huff that was almost a groan.

'The card on the wedding present said something along the usual lines: to grace every party at Castle Bewer throughout your long and happy union. Or some such. You know what the Victorians were. Romantic tommy-rot came spilling out if you so much as nudged them. And, well now, you see it so happened that my mother-in-law did not go out in society much for a year or so after the wedding. Must I say any more or do you understand me?'

'Oh,' I said. I understood her perfectly. It was a variation of the 'invalid resting' story Minnie had mentioned. A fruitful honeymoon had resulted in a sickly six months' child which was coddled until it was bonny. Or rather, the baby arrived already bonny and too promptly by far, and the dates needed a little shading.

'Yes,' said Mrs Bewer. 'That baby grew up to be my husband, Richard. Well anyway, what with one thing and another, it was two Christmases after Richard's birth before the first time his mother packed her trunks and went off to a house party. Boxing Day shoot after a Christmas ball. And she took the beautiful ruby with her. She wore it to the ball – this was somewhere off in the depths of the Highlands. Rosshire.'

'What happened?' I asked. 'Do you mind if I shove a couple of bits of coal on the fire, by the way?'

'Yes, it still makes me shiver too,' Mrs Bewer said. 'By all means, my dear.' She took a deep mustering breath and went on with her tale. 'My mother-in-law dazzled at the party, so legend has it. She was wearing white satin and no other jewels at all. The next morning, she went out for a ride and tried to jump a narrow gate with briar roses on either side. She was whipped off her horse by a branch all caught up in ropes of ivy that snatched at her neck and practically garrotted her.' Her voice, I noticed, had turned into a singsong, as though this were a fairy tale.

'Her husband, Richard's father, saw her lying in the ditch, her white stock undone and her white neck laid bare and all the blood. Thirteen drops of blood, the story goes. And the note on the card came back to him. He said he heard it as if a witch were whispering in his ear. "To grace every party at Castle Bewer throughout your long and happy union."'

'Ah,' I said. 'It was never to leave the castle?'

'Exactly,' Mrs Bewer said. 'Harold brought it back the next day along with his young wife's body and it never crossed the drawbridge again.'

'And,' I began gently, 'forgive me, but what do *you* make of it all, Mrs Bewer?'

'Oh, do call me Otto,' she said. 'There is much I dislike about modern life but it's certainly chummier than it was in my day. And you don't need to step so carefully: I don't believe a word of it. I wouldn't have sat for that portrait with the thing around my neck if I thought it had killed my late mother-in-law. Would you? But my husband believed it. Oh yes, Richard mourned his mother until it became a kind of mania with him. And when I tried to show him it was all silliness and sentiment – I didn't say it quite like that, I should add – he became quite peculiar. So I gave up and went along with it. The Cut Throat stayed in its velvet box in the salt-cupboard in the gatehouse keep, with a stout padlock keeping it safe and the story of the curse keeping it even safer, as far as the servants were concerned anyway. But,' she went on, 'then came dearest Minnie.'

I had never been so agog since a nurse enthralled my sister, my brother and me with tales of headless horsemen in our night nursery and gave us all such horrid dreams that she was sacked and sent away.

'What did *Minnie* do?' I breathed.

'She lit up our lives,' said Ottoline. 'She's a darling. And, while I didn't care for the Cut Throat myself, it bothered me that she wasn't going to get to wear our treasure. It was Christmas time when Bluey first brought her and I could think of nothing prettier than the Cut Throat for her wedding day.'

'Hm,' I said. I like to think I am not a superstitious woman, but I tried to imagine a cursed ruby and a dead mother-in-law and Donald or Teddy's bride and I wondered if perhaps I might not have suggested a string of pearls instead.

'So I told Richard I would prove that the curse was nonsense,' Ottoline said. 'I would wear the Cut Throat to a party – Mespring House, no less, which struck me as poetic justice – and then, when no harm came to me, we could give it to Minnie as a wedding present and she could take it on honeymoon with her and enjoy it as I had never been allowed to do.'

'But he wasn't to be persuaded?' I guessed.

'He snatched it off my neck,' said Ottoline, confirming what Grant had told me. 'I was dressed and ready to go, waiting for the carriage, and he grabbed it and snatched it right off my neck. In the morning I shall show you the scar. It's just about still visible amongst my wrinkles in a strong light.'

'Poor thing,' I said. 'That must have been dreadful for you.'

'Oh, he'd been getting more and more strange,' said Ottoline. 'The wedding was bothering him. And the memory of his mother dying. Except of course, it wasn't a memory at all, because he was a babe in arms. It was his father's endless maundering on about it. Such silliness. Anyway, I'm afraid I wasn't very clever. I screeched at him that I would go for a walk round the field in it one morning, or I'd go for a carriage-ride into town with it hidden under a scarf. I really rattled him.'

She was rather rattling me so I could hardly scoff.

'That was our last contretemps,' she went on. 'Shortly afterwards he left me. Fled in terror of what I might do. I hushed it up. Of course, I couldn't keep it quiet from Minnie but that was a love-match.' I smiled, remembering. 'And she has never said a cross word on the matter. Nor has she ever complained that the crowning jewel of her portion – that fabulous necklace – had been lost all the years she's been here. Now I am a very old woman and I am past rubies. And Minnie is getting past them too. But while I'm alive I want to see Penelope at a ball in the Cut Throat. I want to see her wear the thing on *her* wedding day.'

'You really, really don't think it's cursed then?' I said.

Ottoline had been gazing at me gently, but at that she

unbent the handle of her lorgnette, held it to her face and fixed me with a piercing look.

'Do you?' she said. '*Curses?* I thought young people were too modern and scientific for that.'

'I don't believe it exactly,' I said. 'But something puzzles me about what you say your husband did. Running off like that.' She leaned forward and regarded me closely until I went on. 'Wouldn't it have been you the curse came down on? If he – I know you said I needn't pussy-foot, but stop me, won't you? – if Richard wanted to be free of his wife, wouldn't he have just let you go out in the necklace and then waited to be widowed?'

She stared at me, as still as a stone, and I guessed I had gone quite some way too far.

'Forgive me,' I begged her. The years of rolling theories around with Alec had evidently blunted my sensibilities.

'Not at all,' she said. 'You didn't offend me. You impressed me by cottoning on so quickly. Because of course the same idea occurred to Richard, once he was away. When he was no longer here in this gloomy place where his mother is buried and where his father dripped such misery into his young ear, he saw sense. He must have kicked himself that he left behind such lovely "portable property" as Mr Dickens called it. And so as well as some rather nasty letters to me, listing my faults and threatening to ruin me with scandal, he also sent henchmen – five in all, over a couple of years – to try to find the necklace and steal it away.'

'But you had hidden it?' I asked.

'Not I,' said Otto. 'And not Richard, before he left. Or he would have known where to look and one of his burglars would have found it.'

'What makes you think one didn't?'

'Because the last one was run off at the gate after being pressed to admit what he was and who had sent him.'

'Then who *did* hide it?' I asked.

'That,' she said, 'is certainly something of a mystery. But not the great mystery. You see what the great mystery is, don't you, my dear?'

'Well, yes,' I agreed. '*Where* is it?'

Before she could answer, a gong sounded deep in the bowels of the castle.

'Dinner,' she said. 'On you go ahead, you young thing. Gilly will come to help me.'

I left her and made my way, with only a few wrong turnings, back to the head of the staircase in the Bower Lodging. There was a dull ringing from overhead as male footsteps descended. They were slow and deliberate and I waited to see if it was the elderly Pugh or if perhaps a footman was carrying away heavy pails of bathwater, two at a time. When legs, then a body, and finally a head appeared, though, I saw Alec, walking as if stunned.

He stared at me. Even in the gloom I could see the whites of his eyes quite clearly.

'What is it?' I asked him.

'Valet,' Alec said. 'Told me the whole tale. At least I think it's the whole tale. I certainly hope so.'

'The Cut Throat was a wedding gift that killed a bride with a briar rose and is hidden in the castle where the curse lives on?'

'Masterful summary, Dandy,' said Alec. 'All this and Shakespeare too.'

5

Dinner was served in something called the sheriff's apartment, which was a long slog from our bedrooms and equally far from the cosy drawing room. I surmised that it was close to the kitchen and made life easier for servants charged with the delivery of hot food, for it had little else to recommend it, being so small and square that the long thin dining board had to be jammed in slantways to fit. The places set at either end were practically in the fireplace and out the door.

Bluey presided over another tray of drinks and offered us whisky, gin or a cocktail as we entered.

'Don't let him make you cocktails,' Minnie called over from where she was standing in the hearth to get close enough to a sulky fire to do herself some good. 'A little of everything that's open and a glug of bitters.'

Bluey gave her an affectionate look and poured us a couple of whiskies. Of the many features of northern life to which I have failed to cleave over the years, nothing brings me out in such a rash of goose pimples as the very thought of a hearty glassful of whisky, served without so much as a splash of water. Not the rim of cold fat on a slice of yesterday's mutton, not the suet grease seeping from under the crust of a beef pie, not even the nameless rebarbative morsels that survive the mincer whenever a haggis is made.

Thankfully, the arrival of Penny allowed me to put mine down unobtrusively in the shade of a bulbous plate warmer lurking on a sideboard. She stepped into the hearth to stand beside her mother, and I threw decorum to the winds and picked my way over the firedogs to claim the other side.

'Another telegram,' Penny said, plucking the thing from where she had tucked it into her belt and shaking it open. 'And surely the last. They'll all be here tomorrow.' She cleared her throat. '*M only choice.*'

'Marvellous!' said Minnie. 'Oh, it's all going to be so very pretty.'

'Jolly good,' said Bluey.

'M?' said Alec.

'*A Midsummer Night's Dream*,' said Bluey. 'We made a strong bid for it and we appear to have carried the day.'

'Despite Leonard—' Minnie began.

'Mother!' said Penny.

'Because Leonard—' Minnie tried again.

'The producer,' Penny said firmly, 'is an adventurous spirit. Ibsen, Chekhov, some of the Irish chaps. They've done wonderful things in Edinburgh. *A Midsummer Night's Dream* is rather tame for him, actually.'

'I thought you said they were performing *The Tempest* when the stage-floor fell in,' I said.

'The late plays are quite a different matter,' Penny said. 'I never thought Leonard would agree to a comedy.'

'I saw a Chekhov play once,' Alec said. 'It was in Oxford. One performance on a Sunday afternoon.'

'A Stage Society?' said Penny, in the sort of voice one usually hears being used to say 'a basket of puppies?' or 'a week in Monte Carlo?' 'Leonard was in one for two winters and did some thrilling work. Which play was it?'

Alec played for time by taking a long sip of his whisky but it did not help him. 'It might have been a chap's name,' he said. 'Which one would that be?'

'I saw Henry Irving as Othello once,' I offered up, by means of help. 'Gosh, it was terrifying. A whole matinee of nurses and nannies bolt upright with horror. Not a toffee wrapper rustling in stalls, circle or gods.'

Penny gave me a kind look. I was interested to see that I had graduated onto kindness. Ten years before, any theatre fanatic would have withered me for such inanity.

'Now, now, Penny,' said her mother. 'I see your thoughts as though they're painted on your face. The choice of play is a good start, but you must promise to help me with Leonard. We need fairies with gauzy wings and flowers in their hair. We need rustics with green beards and red cheeks. We need beauty and lightness and laughter. You must stop Leonard if he threatens to get peculiar.'

'But,' Penny began.

'We need a nice entertainment for the sort of people who'd like a picnic tea,' said Minnie.

'But,' Penny tried again.

'A delightful crowning glory to a day of lectures and country walks,' said Minnie.

'If you charge them theatre rent I don't think you can also expect to have a say in the artistic decisions, Mother. Leonard—'

'If Leonard wants to spend next winter with Norwegian housewives fainting all over his stage without falling *through* it,' said Bluey, 'he will need to spend this summer with pretty fairies flitting and rude mechanicals mugging and a jolly Puck. And being a businessman at heart he has seen that it is so. He has chosen well and will see sense about the rest of it if we present a united front to him.'

I was speechless. Bluey had just displayed a knowledge of modern and classical theatre unrivalled in any man of our set. Penny looked mutinous at the description of her beloved as a businessman, but since her grandmother chose that moment to totter into the room on the arm of a little maid, the awkwardness passed.

'Shepherd's delight out the west windows,' Ottoline announced. 'Good weather for carpentering tomorrow.'

In the murk of the castle, its shuttered casements and

44

arrow-slits as much lead as glass, I had forgotten that it was summer outside and it was hard to credit that there was a June sunset going on beyond these feet-thick walls. The dinner, when it came, did not strike a summery note either: brown soup, smoked fish, roast pork, mashed roots and fruit mould. I returned to the plague chamber gravid with it.

Waiting for Grant, though, I manhandled one of the shutters open and then managed to open the casement, bashing at the catch with a shoe until it gave. I threw the window wide, leaned out, and was charmed to see an almost full moon gleaming like a pearl in the hazy night and reflected softly in the stillness of the moat so that it looked, as I gazed down on it, like something submerged. I thought of a face looking up from deep underwater, its features blurred, and shivered.

'You'll catch your death, madam,' said Grant's voice from behind me. 'Come away.'

'How was your evening?' I asked her. 'It might be the last rest you have for a while, you know. There's much talk of fairy wings and coronets.'

'What's *that*?' said Grant. She had leaned out as far as she could stretch to pull the window closed and was craning over to the left where the track led across the field to the gate.

'What's what?' I said, joining her. 'Oh, yes. What *is* that?'

A pair of lights, small and dotting about like fireflies, were winking in the darkness.

'Do sheeps' eyes reflect the light like cats' eyes?' said Grant.

'Not that I've ever heard,' I said. 'No, surely not. Or driving through farmland with headlamps on would have been unnerving all these years in a way it hasn't been.'

'And it's the wrong colour for cigarette ends,' Grant said. 'Should we raise the alarm?'

'More of the famous burglars, right on cue?' I said. 'Rambling along the lane with torches lit?'

Grant shrugged and then tugged the window shut with a

sharp bang. In an instant, both little lights disappeared, leaving perfect blackness except for that pearly moon and the blurred face in the bottom of the moat.

'You've scared the fairies away,' I said, trying to make a joke of it and not quite succeeding. Grant, in turn, did not quite laugh.

'How are your quarters?' I asked her, to get things back to normal as I was undressing.

'More modern than these,' Grant said. 'A square room with plastered walls and a flat floor. I'm sharing with Gilly.'

Ordinarily she would have taken great umbrage at this. It was a mark of her reluctance to spend a night alone in a cursed castle that she welcomed the company.

'Gilly?' I said. 'Is that the child who led Mrs Bewer into dinner? She seemed a nice sort.'

'And she knows nothing of the history of this place and it's to stay that way,' Grant said. 'They've had maid after maid take the vapours and leave. They had to go as far as Carlisle for this one and she is not to be unsettled.'

Half an hour later, as I lay in my bed, high and narrow and hung about with curtains, I cast my eye around by the light of my candle and rather wished someone had decreed that no nasty stories were to unsettle *me*. I have never liked bed hangings. Nanny Palmer disapproved vociferously, of course, for fresh air was next door to a religion with her and sleeping inside a tent of cloth with spiders in the folds kept all air, fresh and stale, shut out. When I was small, though, and could not have cared less about fresh air, any more than clean nails and straight backs, all I knew was that Nanny disapproved of bed hangings for me. With the self-regard of infants everywhere I surmised that they put me in mortal danger. Add the thrilling tales that were read to us at bedtime, of pirates and highwaymen and orphans out in the cold, and I spent many a night shaking in a huddle under my blankets, sure that some ne'er-do-well was stalking the corners of my room and, if it were not for those hangings, at least I might be able to see him.

Back then, I was wont to put my fears from me by turning them on my little sister Mavis and delighting in her terror. Stevenson's verses were a great help and poor Mavis's temperament did its bit. Scoffing at her tears drove all memory of my own away.

That first night in Castle Bewer, though, I felt a few wisps of those early horrors begin to steal back around me again. The candle guttered, the hangings shook as draughts caught them and once, just once, a vixen barked out there in the quiet night. I sat up and hugged my knees, ready to give myself a stern talking-to.

It was a case like any other case. I looked forward to hearing what outlandish scheme Minnie was 'pretty well certain' not to pursue, of course, but there was plenty besides it to occupy me. Alec and I were to search for something lost and try to make sure no one else found it before us. It helped me to think of it that way: a lost item of high value. I cast my eyes around my bedroom. There must surely be floor plans of the castle. There must be a library amongst these lodgings and turrets and keeps. We could make a methodical search of the place from the chimneys to the dungeons and would either find the thing or report with confidence that it was gone.

Tales of curses would not help us in the task. We had to stick to the plain facts. We had to put ourselves in the mind of Richard Bewer all those years ago and intuit what had happened. I sat up a little straighter. *Something* had certainly happened. Between his hiding the thing and his sending his first dogsbody back to fetch it for him, it had vanished. We needed the residents of Castle Bewer from those days, thirty years ago, to search their memories and dredge up any tiny thing that might be a clue.

Methodical searching and a round of interviews, I thought.

Mrs Bewer herself, Bluey if he had been at the castle and not in London the whole time. Any servants of long standing. It would surprise me if Pugh were not decades into serving the Bewer family.

At last I felt sleep tug at my ravelled sleeve and I wriggled down into my bedclothes to let it do its work, feeling for the first time, equal to the task before me.

Morning brought another surge of confidence and energy. I woke in my favourite way, to the echo of an excellent housemaid who had laid and lit a fire, opened curtains and shutters, and then brought and set down a tea tray, but whose first sound loud enough to rouse me was her closing the door behind her on leaving.

The shepherd's delight of the evening before had borne fruit: it was a sparkling blue day with swifts wheeling joyously back and forth across my window and the cheerful sound of a cart pony clip-clopping along the lane at a steady trot. I got up and went over to feast my eyes on the view.

The sheep were steaming as the dew rose from their backs in the warmth of the morning and there were ducks making rippled darts in the moat far below. The pony harrumphed in a friendly way as its driver leapt down from the cart to lead it through the gate. I drew back a little, not liking to be seen in my nightie by a grocer's boy or a late milkman. Taking a closer look at the carter, though, I suspected that this was the vanguard of the theatrical players. He was dressed, it is true, in ancient flannels and a collarless shirt with a cotton scarf at his neck and a pipe in his mouth, but something about his swagger marked him out. Besides, on the other side of the high seat there still sat a brawny young woman dressed in a long skirt of something with a shimmer to it and a tight coat of the cut Eliza Doolittle had learned not to wear. She was smoking a cigarette in a long black holder and lounging back against the bulk of the cart's load.

'They're here!' said Grant, coming in at my door. 'The first of them anyway. The AM and the ASM.' She was dying for me to ask what those letters stood for.

'So I see,' I said, nodding out at the cart. 'Go down if you like. I can manage.'

Grant cast a critical eye over me, evaluating this claim, but in the end contented herself with laying out my clothes, forbidding me from making any changes and pressing my hair hard all over my head with her fingers until she deemed it satisfactory.

By the time I got down to breakfast, the flannel-clad man was sitting tucking into an enormous plate of eggs and bacon and the large, shimmering woman was nibbling a slice of toast. The shimmer was gone along with the tight coat and she was dressed in stout twill trews and a man's shirt, minus its buttons and held closed over her front with twists of string. More of the same string held her abundant hair in a kind of mop-shape on the back of her head, as though she had started to dress it and been disturbed early on.

'Mrs Gilver, this is Leonard,' said Penny, 'and Bess.'

'How do you do, Mr . . . ' I said. 'And Miss . . . '

Minnie tutted but Penny did not complete the introduction. At least the graceless manners of the two youngsters spared me having to account for my presence. They cared not who I was nor why I was there.

'Such a beautiful morning!' Penny went on. 'If it carries on like this, the opening will be a dream indeed.'

I noticed that Leonard gave a quick frown at her words but he did not speak. He might be a cousin but he had none of the Bewers' affability. On the other hand, he had escaped the Bewers' unfortunate colouring too; I did not foresee him turning to a beetroot as the years rolled by, for his hair was as black as a raven's wing, his skin milk white and his eyes as blue as the painted willows on Minnie's breakfast china.

49

'When *do* you open?' said Alec. He had finished his breakfast and was sitting with a last cup of coffee and his first pipe of the day, enjoying the sight of another prodigious eater at work.

'Saturday,' said Leonard. 'We're cast and rehearsed. The whole company off the book. We'll build sets today, tech and dress tomorrow, and Saturday night we open.'

'Gosh,' I said. 'One day to build sets? Shall you manage it?' I was imagining high wires set up for fairies to swing across above our heads and the many wooden trees it would take to turn the courtyard into a forest glade.

'We are no longer prisoners of the proscenium arch,' said Bess. Her tone was brusque to the point of rudeness.

'But, Penny my dear,' Minnie said, 'we *did* discuss this. You are having *some* scenery, aren't you? The paying public want to see a spectacle as well as listening to the poetry. We need to put on a good show.'

'We had a quick look round,' Leonard said, 'and really we don't want more than a doorway or two. This place is perfect already. If we can light some lamps in the open windows at either side of the stage . . . I mean, why make a paste castle when we're in a real one?'

'Castle?' said Bluey. 'Of course, it's been a while since I saw the play and tastes have changed but are you really setting it in a castle?'

'Oh,' said Minnie. 'I rather thought the audience would be up this way and you would build the stage at the other end where it's open to the meadow and the far wood. How will the people get to their seats?'

'Mother,' said Penny. 'They can come through the West Lodging passageway and out at the under-hall door. Really, you don't need to concern yourself with the minutiae.'

'We *could* move to the other end,' Leonard said. 'We have plenty willing hands. Everyone's gladly walking on as messengers and soldiers. And none would quail at the thought of picking up a paintbrush or a hammer.'

'Well,' said Bess. She had nibbled as much of the toast as she wanted and she set it down and dabbed her lips. I wondered how a woman got so Amazonian without eating. 'Don't ask Duncan to knock together flats. He's eighty if a day. And one of those witches is drawing a pension. As you'll see when they get here, Minnie,' she added, turning to her hostess and affecting not to notice the blink of astonishment Minnie gave at being addressed this way.

'Witches?' said Penny. 'Duncan?'

I think the truth broke on all of us at once, excepting Alec who has never been much of a one for Shakespeare.

'You think the castle will make a better backdrop than the meadow,' said Minnie, rather bleakly. 'And the walk-ons are messengers and soldiers. And the elders in the cast are . . .'

'Oh,' said Alec. 'Duncan and a witch!'

'We were supposed to be doing *A Midsummer Night's Dream*,' Penny wailed.

'What?' said Bess, with a snort. 'That romantic twaddle?'

'I sent you a telegram,' said Leonard.

'Telling me M was the only choice,' Penny cried, her voice rising.

'Yes. M,' said Leonard. 'The *Dream* would be D.'

'But this won't do!' said Bluey. 'We've been advertising a beautiful summer's evening with love in the air. We've all been mugging up on Puck and Peaseblossom.'

'We've painted bills to post around the village!' said Penny. 'Leonard, I'm surprised at you. I thought you had swept away all the hackneyed nonsense. I cannot believe you were too superstitious to write the word "Macbeth" in a telegram.'

'I'm not!' Leonard yelped. 'Good grief, Penny, what do you take me for?'

'Well, what in the blazes, then?' said Bluey. 'Were you trying to trick us into agreeing?'

'I was trying to save six letters at a ha'penny each,' Leonard said and his words had such a ring of truth and were so pertinent to everyone's concern in this escapade that they silenced the entire party.

It was at that moment that Grant, trying to be servant-like but made bold by her pride, marched into the room with a pair of gossamer wings held aloft.

'Behold!' she said. 'Silk-net with a silver thread through it. It's left over from that frock with the panels, madam, do you remember? I put the half-bolt I'd saved in my case on the off-chance. It's perfect, isn't it, and the wire frame is so light it can be held on with a couple of pretty ribbons.'

Never had one of her notions met with such unwelcoming blankness. She gave a quick dart of a look at the fairy wings and, unable to account for it, muttered a soft 'excuse my interruption,' then, crestfallen, left the room.

'So, *Macbeth*,' I said. 'It's very gripping. And I think it's shorter.'

With that, I sealed my fate as the resident Philistine. Bess, Leonard and Penny each gave me a withering look and never really took me seriously again.

6

Neither Minnie nor Bluey were fierce as a rule but they each had views on the current pickle and they aired them. Alec and I withdrew, fixed smiles upon our faces, and went in search of the library.

A housemaid was sweeping out the fireplace in the large hall we traversed. Although she was properly dressed in black with a canvas apron, there was something about her shining curls and the way her stockings clung about her neat little ankles without sagging.

'Are you Gilly?' I asked her. She jumped up, bobbed and blushed. She was indeed the girl we had seen the evening before.

'Madam,' she said. 'Sir.'

'Two questions, Gilly,' I said. 'We shan't keep you from your work. Where is the library? And do you know how long each of the staff has been in service here?'

Gilly pointed straight up at the arched ceiling high above our heads. 'The master's book room is right over this,' she said. 'It's not really a library but it's the closest thing we've got. Take any staircase and just keep walking till the red gate is right opposite out the back windows.'

She was, I decided, a sensible girl: these were excellent directions for two strangers in such a jumble of a house.

'And as for seniority,' she said. 'Pugh's been here thirty years. Mrs Ellen the same. And the cook. I'm ten years coming in the autumn. There's a gardener was here when I came.'

'Anyone here longer than the cook?' said Alec.

Gilly shook her head. 'There was a big change for Mrs Minnie coming,' she said. 'New butler, new housekeeper, new kitchen staff. Mr Bewer's nanny was still here, they say, and she was thinking of hanging on till she was needed, which would have been Miss Penny, but Mrs Bewer put her out to a cottage in the village there and she never came back.'

'Wonderful,' I said. 'I like to hear of servants retiring comfortably.'

Gilly was too well trained to say whatever it was she was thinking, but she was clearly thinking something. She gave me a small and sickly smile and then glanced back at her fireplace and its bucket.

'We shan't keep you,' I offered dutifully.

When we were a little way off, I said: 'A clean sweep of staff for the new bride.'

'That strikes me as very interesting,' said Alec.

'On two counts,' I agreed. 'Did they offload the old staff because they suspected one of theft?'

'Or?' said Alec. To be fair, he thinks less about housekeeping than do I and could not be expected to have landed on this theory.

'Or,' I said, 'while garnishing the castle to welcome Minnie, did one of the old staff happen upon the hidey-hole and therefore welcome the offered retirement. Imagine if Bluey's old nanny has been living in a free cottage for thirty years while spending the proceeds of selling the family treasure. Or perhaps there's a butler or cook who's now set up in a nice little business with no history of inheritance or nest-egg to explain it away.'

'Well, if it's so, the servants will know,' Alec said. 'Barrow knows the life history of a laundry woman who was long gone even before Mrs Lowie arrived. The legends seem to hang around the servants' hall for lifetimes.'

'No different with us,' I reminded him. 'We all know the gossip of our grandparents' youths, don't we? That's what

54

makes it so very odd that the story of the Cut Throat and the curse is news.'

'Let's keep the library for now, and try to find the kitchen,' Alec said. He nudged me and pointed along the latest stretch of passageway, which was just about to change from having paintings on the walls and carpet on the floor to being stone all around with plain tallow candles already replaced and waiting for later. At its end, a door was propped open with a lead stop and the unmistakable scent of boiling bones rolled out and came to meet us.

Our first glimpse of the cook was unfortunate. She was not a beauty, nor even a faded beauty grown into handsomeness. She was immensely tall and stooped and had a nose and chin striving to meet one another over a grim mouth. Still, had she not been stirring an elephantine stockpot with a wooden spoon roughly the size of a cricket bat and muttering, or had we not just been discussing the Scottish play, perhaps she would have made less of an impression. As it was, I stopped dead in the doorway and half thought of fleeing.

'Gosh,' said Alec softly at my side.

The cook's words, when we caught the gist of her mutters, did not improve matters.

'So much toil and trouble and for what?' she was saying.

I cleared my throat and she straightened as far as her spine would ever let her and looked over. 'Are you actors?' she said. 'Or carpenters? Carpenters I'll give a cup of tea to and a slice off the new loaf, for it's hard work. If you're actors, luncheon is at one and there's a bun shop in Annanbridge High Street'll take your penny.'

'We're neither,' Alec said. 'Mrs . . . ?'

'Porteous,' she said.

'We, Mrs Porteous, are the detectives,' Alec told her. 'We're here to find the Cut Throat at last.'

'Before the old master's hundredth birthday,' she said,

nodding. 'Last day of October he was born, in eighteen thirty-four.'

'You are very well informed,' I said. Then, regretting how clipped I sounded, I tried to turn it into a compliment. 'It's marvellous when a household endures without change down the years.'

'The family's dates are written in the Bible for all to see,' said Mrs Porteous, loftily. As though a cook reading her master's Bible was any less peculiar. 'And Mrs Bewer has always been a nice, warm, chatty lady,' she added. She did not say 'unlike you, madam', but I heard it faintly.

'Speaking of the family Bible,' said Alec, 'we are bound for the library this very morning to search out floor plans and make our task methodical.'

'But we shall also need to interview everyone, at some point,' I said. 'It's astonishing what people sometimes know and yet don't think is worth repeating. You might have seen something that could lead us right to the hiding place.'

She gave me a long steady look across the steam coiling up from her pot. Then, as the liquid in it belched threateningly, she reapplied her spoon and withdrew her gaze. 'I wasn't here when the ruby vanished,' she said.

'So Gilly has just been telling us,' said Alec. 'There was a changing of the guard. Retirements all round and new blood for a new mistress.'

I thought the same look that had flitted over Gilly's face now crossed this woman's, leaving a shadow.

'Were the old staff really all of an age?' I said. 'That's quite remarkable. I remember my childhood being an endless upheaval of servants leaving and arriving. My mother always blamed the remote location of our house. But that corner of Northamptonshire is Piccadilly Circus compared with Castle Bewer.'

'Nanny retired,' the cook said, fixing on this one just as Gilly had. She set a lid at a jaunty angle across the top of her pot, wrapped her hands in cloths and heaved it to the back of the range, where its bubbling slowed to occasional dull splats. She stowed the two cloths in her belt and turned to face us.

'And the others?' I asked her.

'They weren't of an age for retiring,' she said. 'They were sacked. Butler to boot boy, they were sacked. Well, they were given good characters but it was a clean sweep.'

'Why?' I asked.

'They were no loss,' she said crisply. 'The castle was in uproar. Master ill, mistress beside herself and that lazy lot had let the place go to rack and ruin. I've never seen a kitchen the like and if you ask Mrs Ellen about the state of the linen cupboards . . . '

'And yet Mrs Bewer gave them good references?' Alec said.

'Glowing, they were. One even went along the road. A fine step up.'

'Along the road?' I said. 'To Mespring?' If so it certainly *was* a step up.

'He'd been the master's valet here,' said Mrs Porteous, 'and went to be a footman for the Annandales.'

'Is he still there, do you know?' Alec asked, but Mrs Porteous only shrugged. I supposed the frosty relations between the two houses accounted for that.

'And what of the others who left?' I said. 'Did any of them keep in touch?'

This second shrug had a shake in it too. 'It led to a bad taste,' she said. 'All of them out to let us in. And it got in the way of the usual overlap, if you see what I mean.'

Alec nodded. It was what he had just been speaking of. The servants' hall letters, letters by which youngsters come to know strangers long gone before, had never been shared around the supper table at Castle Bewer. The clearing of the ranks had made a sharp, effective breach between old and new.

'And why was such a swingeing clear-out put into action?'
I said.

'It was part of Mrs Bewer's plan to put an end to tales of
the curse and let Mrs Bluey have a normal, happy life,' said
Mrs Porteous.

'It doesn't seem to have worked particularly,' I pointed out.
'Everyone knows about the curse anyway. Butler to boot boy,
as you said.'

'Well, as I said too, Mrs Bewer is a friendly sort of a
mistress. And besides, when the master leaves as suddenly
as all that you can't expect a staff not to notice something's
wrong. And then, of course, the burglaries began when we'd
been here but a year. So, you're right about us all knowing
the tale.'

'And yet you all stayed?' said Alec. 'Despite burglaries?' I
joined him in his astonishment.

'Some of the youngsters took off,' said the cook. 'But the
way I saw it, it wasn't the mistress's fault her husband was
such a queer one. It wasn't her fault he abandoned her either.
And as long as the Cut Throat is safely hidden here there's
no harm coming to anyone.'

'So you believe in the curse then?' I said, trying to speak
levelly.

'I think you can't be too careful with such things,' she said
stoutly.

'And so what do you make of us?' I asked her. 'Coming
to unearth it after all these years?'

'And put it safe where none will find it,' Mrs Porteous
said, not quite asking but not exactly stating either. 'That's
what you're at, is it not? Making sure none of the guests find
it and takes it away before you can find it and put it safe
forever.'

'Put it safe?' said Alec.

'Under a floor or bricked up in a wall,' said Mrs Porteous.

'Who told you that?' I asked her.

'No one told me,' she said, 'but what else would you do? When the master's hundred comes round and there's death duties to pay, the family might be asked to sell it if it's anywhere to be found. So they must hide it safely. And you're here to help them.'

'Oh dear,' said Alec as we left by a side door a few minutes later, stepping out into the new-washed sunshine and the cheerful shouts of carpenters busy moving long planks of white wood into place at the far end of the courtyard. 'Oh dear, oh dear.'

'Indeed,' I said. 'The staff think the ruby's sought only to be better hidden from the taxman. Ottoline thinks the ruby's sought to be given to Penny as a trinket. And all the time Minnie and Bluey are trying to find the thing and sell it on the quiet before Halloween.'

'Halloween?' Alec said.

'Richard Bewer's hundredth birthday. Mrs Porteous just said so.'

'Good grief,' said Alec. 'This case didn't need any extra dramatic shading really. Are there any more horrors to be unveiled? *Macbeth* instead of the *Dream*, a family divided by secrets and lies, and a cook who boils bones and calls it stock. I shall be pushing away my soup at dinner tonight, shan't you Dandy?'

'We still have occupation and diversion before us,' I reminded him. 'The castle plans await. Imagine if we find it!'

'Mrs Porteous will be thinking up new curses for us.'

'But after a couple of years,' I reminded him, 'when everyone is fine and the curse has been shown to be nonsense. When the society pages show the Cut Throat on the neck of some financier's wife at the Lord Mayor's ball and she's as healthy as a horse. They'll thank us then, won't they?'

'To the book room in the meantime,' Alec said.

We soon found a stairway; we could hardly help it, for Castle Bewer had more of them, twisted tight like sticks of barley sugar, than any house I had ever known. At the head of this one was the first really bright apartment we had come across yet, an airy gallery, much encrusted with the kind of plasterwork that kept tradesmen busy throughout the Regency. As usual, it was thoroughly picked-out in various colours, changing whenever a ridge or dip or corner gave the slightest excuse to switch brushes, every bump and bulge daubed with gold.

The portraits hanging over the panelling were as dour as those of any other Scottish family, a parade of mirthless patriarchs, mulish brides and sulky children, but at least, since the tall windows were unshuttered, the sunlight poured in and bounced off the glass, hiding most of them.

'Behold the red gate,' said Alec, pointing out of a window when we were halfway down the gallery's length. 'So this must be the book room. I hope it's orderly. Or has a catalogue. I suppose a librarian's too much to hope for.'

Since sacking the librarian seemed an easier saving than dispensing with one's privacy and filling the house with strangers, I expected any Bewer archivist was long gone – if he had ever existed at all – and so I entered the book room without knocking and without any attempt to appear guest-like. I simply strode in, unfolding my reading spectacles and settling them upon my face as I advanced, disturbing Bluey Bewer, who was standing by the window, leafing through an elderly volume. 'I was just having a look at my Shakespeare,' he said. 'Reminding myself of the plays and checking if perhaps the cast of one would fit the other. But it's quite hopeless. And, by golly, *Macbeth* is torture. I'm very cross with Penny and simply aching for poor Minnie after all her hard work. We shall have to pay back all the people who don't want to sit through murder and misery instead of love and laughter and we'll be worse off than before.'

He had wandered over to a writing desk and now sank into the chair behind it, running his hands through his thin hair until it was quite disarranged and stuck out all around his head like thistledown.

'Well, now, I'm not so sure,' Alec said. 'The *Dream* could be a bit of a washout if the weather does its usual midsummer trick on us. But *Macbeth* is about as proof against inclement weather as an oilcloth coat, isn't it?'

'And people will eat more if they're cold,' I said.

'And I'll bet Americans would rather watch a play *about* a Scottish castle, *in* a Scottish castle, than sit in a Scottish castle and try to imagine Venetian glades. It might turn out to be a blessing.'

'And you could always do the *Dream* next year.'

Bluey shook off that last attempt at comfort, but he did at least smooth down his hair again. 'We shall be gone by next year,' he said. 'Haven't the ladies told you? We shall be gone by Christmas, if the lawyers get cracking bright and early on All Souls' Day.'

'Ah,' I said. 'Yes, your father's century. And the death duties. Yes, Minnie did bring us up to date with it all, as a matter of fact.'

'Rotten luck,' Alec said. I did not know whether he meant the death duties alone, or if his rather bluff comfort was to cover the missing father and the curse as well as the coming penury.

'Still,' I added. 'We haven't even started yet. It's far too early to give up. And that's what brings us here this morning, actually. I'm glad we happened to find you. We're after house plans, to organise the great search!'

'You are too kind,' Bluey said. 'It's marvellous of you to say you'll do it.'

'You give us too much credit,' said Alec. 'We're champing at the bit, aren't we Dandy? I feel like a small boy at a birthday party.'

Bluey regarded us both quizzically for a moment before he spoke. 'I fail to see what's fun about it,' he said. 'One dull meeting with what will undoubtedly be a rather dull man. It's a good idea to acquaint yourselves with the house, though, I must say. You could even mark the plans with a soft pencil, if you like, to convince him you've actually gone poking around.'

'Convince whom?' I said.

'The taxman,' said Bluey. 'You'll vouch that we're church mice, with no treasure to our name, won't you? You'll swear that we haven't got the thing squirreled away?'

'But we'll poke around too,' said Alec.

'Oh my dear chap,' said Bluey. 'And dearest Dandy. There's no point grubbing about getting dusty. The Cut Throat is gone – long, long, gone – and all we need from you is your word under oath that it's not in the castle. I have already made applications to all the London jewellers – Paris too – hoping to hear that it passed through reputable hands, but that looks a little like playing to the gallery.'

'You think it's gone?' I said, rather stupidly, even for me.

'I do,' Bluey said. 'And so in all conscience we can't really dupe people into hoping it's not.'

'What people?' I said.

'No one,' said Bluey. 'It's out of the question. I think we've finally agreed on that score. And I don't mind losing this place. Not really. Different if we'd had a son, but Penny will settle . . . I would have said at her husband's place, but I suppose I must face the possibility that she'll be in an Edinburgh tenement with Leonard, making supper for all the touring players who're put up on pallets in her sitting room.' He sighed and shook the thought away. 'And of course, I would have liked Mama to end her days here, but it's only the fact of her days being so many that put the kibosh on that. Looking on the bright side.' He gave us a brave grin.

'If you don't mind my asking,' I said, 'where and when do

62

you think it went? Your mother seems quite adamant that none of the burglaries was successful.'

'Ah yes,' said Bluey. 'The burglaries. My father's repeated attempts to snatch the ruby.'

I could not quite decide what his tone was supposed to convey.

'The thing is,' he went on, 'that none of the burglars knew where to look. If my father sent them he'd have sent them to the exact spot, wouldn't he? And if some rascal killed him for—'

'Killed him?' I said. 'You think someone *killed* your father, Bluey?'

'Well, I believe he's dead,' Bluey said, 'and people have killed for less, haven't they? I can imagine a disreputable gin-joint somewhere and some even more disreputable black-guard holding a knife to my father's throat. His letters certainly made it sound as though he had fallen in with some scoundrels.' He blinked. 'But where was I?'

'Surmising that if someone killed your father he'd get a proper treasure map out of his victim first,' said Alec.

'Exactly,' Bluey agreed. 'So I've always thought that if my father had a hand in it at all, it was only that he told the story – in a club in some far-flung enclave, over one too many brandies, or perhaps he muttered it in delirium from under his mosquito net as he lay dying.'

'Were the burglars foreign?' I asked, the question occurring to me suddenly.

Bluey twinkled at me. 'I had no idea you were such a clever girl,' he said.

'We had gormlessness dinned into us,' I said. 'But many have shaken it off since.'

'They were *not* foreign,' Bluey said. 'Nor even sunburned. So, all in all, I don't think my father had anything to do with it. But then I should remind myself he had certainly changed a great deal by then.'

63

'Oh?' said Alec. 'Changed how?'

'Well, this very mania about the Cut Throat,' Bluey said. 'He was never peculiar about it when I was a child. Or at least not out loud. It stayed locked in its cupboard and my mother wore it from time to time but I had no idea there was such dread festering in him. As long as my mother played along, he seemed quite sane about it. But by golly when she mentioned giving it to Minnie, he blew up like a barrel of dynamite.'

'Were you there?' I asked. 'Was poor *Minnie* there, hoping the floor would open up and swallow her?'

'Thankfully not,' Bluey said. 'Mama told me in a letter and warned me not to breathe a word when I brought Minnie to visit.'

'And did you?' said Alec.

'We were too late,' Bluey said. 'He took off before we arrived. The place was in uproar. Poor Minnie must have thought it was a madhouse! No father, no servants, my mother at her wits' end. I shouldn't have blamed her if she'd turned tail and run.' He took a deep gathering breath and smiled as he let it go. 'But she stayed and we have been happy.'

'And about those burglaries?' I said. 'Sorry to harp on them but if your father wasn't behind them, who was?'

'I did wonder,' said Bluey, 'if perhaps . . . but it's the purest speculation and probably slanderous.' Nothing could sound more enthralling; Alec and I waited hardly daring to breathe, and eventually Bluey went on. 'One of the sacked servants went to Mespring.' He stopped again.

'You suspect he – it was a footman, wasn't it? – sent pals back along to pinch it?' I said. 'That makes quite a lot of sense, actually. A servant might well know where your father had stashed the thing.'

'And if this footman nabbed it soon after his dismissal,' said Alec, 'that explains why none of the later burglars could ever find it.'

Bluey was looking most uncomfortable now.

'Forgive us,' I said. 'Conjecture is a large portion of detecting. I didn't mean to traduce the man.'

'Although,' Alec said, 'if he's still there, we'd dearly like to speak to him, wouldn't we Dandy.'

'Well,' Bluey said, 'if you're thinking of going along there, perhaps it's better if I say what's on my mind. By way of preparing you. For a start, I don't think one of our servants would have *tried* breaking into the castle. Because of the drawbridge.'

'But it's permanently down,' I said, remembering the rickety assemblage of pine planks we had driven over so tentatively the day before.

'It is now,' said Bluey. 'But that was Mama's doing. She thought it was the drawbridge – the fact of being able to shut oneself off from the world so effectively – that gave my father the start of his obsession. *No more!* she decreed. The draw-bridge was dismantled and a permanent bridge put in its place. But you see the problem?'

'The servants who'd left wouldn't know that,' I said. 'Yes, I do see. But the one at *Mespring* would surely hear about it, wouldn't he? The estate carpenter chatting over his glass of beer at the end of a busy day?'

Once again, Bluey looked ill at ease. I rather thought it was whenever Mespring House came up that he turned shifty. I gazed at him out of guileless eyes and at last he seemed to crack.

'Oh dash it all,' he said. 'I'm going to tell you. I think the Annandales themselves sent burglars along from Mespring to take it back. It was something between a tease and an insult when they originally gave it to my grandmother. It's hard to explain without being mean-spirited.'

'Your mother managed the task nevertheless,' I assured him. 'And I told Alec.'

'Ah,' said Bluey. 'Well, good. And, you see, the lady in

question never married. She stayed at Mespring her whole life through and was still alive at the time we're speaking of – just when my engagement to Minnie was announced. I think, if she got wind of my father leaving, she might have said to herself: they think my pretty necklace killed my usurper and now has ruined a marriage. Very well then, I shall have it back, for it never did me any harm. If you could . . . Oh, I don't know . . . inveigle your way in there and persuade the family to come clean about it, I'd be awfully grateful. It's not as if it's doing them much good: they can't sell it since they don't own it and the women of the family can't swank about in it for the same reason. If it's only embarrassment over the behaviour of a dotty aunt who's dead now . . . assure them we'll overlook the indiscretion. The hope of that rapprochement at last after all these years is, frankly, the only reason I agreed to your coming. That seems like a job worth doing compared with all Minnie's twaddle about some innocent American finding it under her mattress like the princess's pea.'

'Rather ticklish,' Alec said. At Bluey's frown he went on, 'but not beyond us. Heavens, no. We are more than equal to our brief, aren't we Dan?'

I was beginning to lose track of some of the fluttering pages of our brief, truth be told. We had a castle to search, a scattered staff to track down and grill, a missing husband – or his grave, at least – to locate, some snooty neighbours to offend. Not to mention the small matter of the Cut Throat: to find for Bluey, guard from the guests, sell for Minnie, hide for Mrs Porteous, present to Penny, and deny all knowledge of for the benefit of the taxman. I groaned, but inwardly.

7

The castle plans were everything we had hoped and more: centuries of the things, from ink-blotted fantasies one step removed from 'here be dragons' to the most modern of architect's sketches with ruled elevations and measurements plotted to the quarter inch. Every cupboard, every crevice, every conceivable hidey-hole, was depicted there.

It was rather heart-rending to see drawings of the castle's middle years, after the current structure replaced an earlier tower house. Its four sides were complete then and all six turrets – the four corners and the gatehouse too – were five storeys high and topped with pennants. Then Castle Bewer, as was the way of it in those days, was more like a little town than a single home, with huts and cotts and cattle pens beyond the moat. I imagined all the peasants fleeing their humble dwellings and herding their animals into the castle keep when their watchmen told them marauders were on the way. I should like to say I felt a twinge of fellow-feeling for them, rushing terrified into the protection of the great family's garrison, but really I thought how annoying to be one of the Bewers of the day and have frightened peasants and livestock packed into one's courtyard whenever the border grew lively.

If the early pictures of life at Castle Bewer were diverting, the plans and elevations of the lost drawbridge left me feeling irritated. Quite apart from the fact that it was a sturdy beast of oak and iron, with stout chains – far superior to what had replaced it, it also looked to be of an ingenious design I had not encountered elsewhere and I should have relished telling Hugh about it and having him envy me.

'Very clever,' Alec said, poring over the drawing of it.

'What do you suppose all those extra wheels and cogs are for?'

'To tip invaders into the moat should they be caught halfway across,' Alec said. 'If that's a pivoting fulcrum.'

'Perhaps that had something to do with Ottoline ripping it out, as well as her wanting to re-join the world. As Hugh always says: "the more there is to go right . . ." And anyway,' I went on, 'she didn't re-join the world, did she? She put it about that Richard was gravely ill and kept the world at the gate.'

'And the moat, therefore, is fathoms deep to allow for all the workings,' Alec said, barely listening. 'Aren't they usually just deep enough to make a loud splash?'

'It certainly must have taken some digging.'

'We can't roll these up and march about with them under our arms, you know,' said Alec. 'They're far too fragile and the drawbridge plan is a rarity. We must make copies.'

'If we're to do as Minnie bid us,' I said. 'And ignore Bluey.'

'Oh, I think we should, don't you?' Alec was trying to sound thorough and dutiful, for all the world as though permission to scamper about a castle was not a gift to the little boy still residing deep inside him. Were the castle empty, I thought, he might set out with a wooden sword in his belt and a dustbin lid over his arm, the way Donald and Teddy did when 'playing at knights'. I remembered buttering Donald's ears to prise off a fruit sieve he had decided made a perfect . . .

'What's the name of the face-covering on a suit of armour?' I said.

'A bascinet?' said Alec. 'Why?'

'Just maternal wool-gathering.'

'How should we proceed?' Alec asked, rightly ignoring me. 'Dungeons to attics? The other way?'

'Neither,' I said. 'We should search the rooms the actors are to occupy now, before they're here, then the rooms that are to be rented to guests; we certainly can't go poking about once the budget of Americans arrives. And we need to make sure we've searched the rooms the company might be filling with all their junk: costumes and props and the like. The uninhabited areas – the attics and dungeons, as you say – can wait.'

'Hmph,' said Alec. 'Makes a lot of sense. In which case, I think today's first job is to commune with one of the family and draw up search plans of the various areas on separate sheets. Keep things tidy. How about you?'

'I can't decide,' I said. 'I shall need to ask Ottoline to see those letters from Richard. I hope she's kept them. And the visit to Mespring to ask if the mad aunt pinched the ruby looms. But for now I think I shall track down Nanny, if she's still alive. Or see if her neighbours remember her saying anything enlightening. Shall I send Penny up here, if I run into her?'

For I had not been misled by that airy 'one of the family'; not in the least. And while I held no great hopes for the case as a whole, if I managed to detach Penny from Leonard and affix her to Alec, Bluey and Minnie would surely thank me. For myself, while Alec's inevitable marriage to someone or other would deal a blow to our friendship, I was beginning to yearn for it as for the second boot dropping.

Alec was right about being methodical. Nevertheless, as I passed through the castle's corridors, I could not help looking closely at the stones of the walls around me. One in particular seemed to have no mortar at all, just dark crevices at its edges, and I went so far as to dig my fingers in and give it a tug. Nothing happened except for a broken nail. I rubbed the ragged edge and imagined Grant tutting. Still, I refused to feel foolish: Mrs Porteous in this enlightened age still wanted the cursed object bricked up or buried and so it seemed quite easy to imagine that thirty years ago someone might have taken matters into his – or her – own hands and actually done so. Who . . . was another question.

'Bricked up or buried,' I repeated to myself. I stopped walking and stamped a heel down hard on the floor beneath my feet. It was made of solid slabs of the same grey stone that formed the castle walls. There were no bricks to be seen. Scotland as a rule does not go in for them; the loftiest bank headquarters to the lowliest coal shed at the bottom of a cottage garden being built from stone, as though to last millennia. If the lumps of stone underfoot were as thick as those forming the walls, nothing could be buried there. I stepped over to a window and bent close to the tiny panes to judge the depth of the wall into which they were set.

Movement below caught my eye. The company in its entirety had arrived. There were two carts and a motor van pulled up near my Cowley and swarms of young people were busily unpacking wicker trunks and cardboard suitcases and dumping them down on the cobbles with great thuds. The cobbles, I noted. There was no earth anywhere that would allow objects to be buried. At least, I concluded, that would make searching somewhat quicker. Then, as a dreadful thought occurred to me, I turned away from the windows and hurried towards the head of a nearby staircase, hoping to meet someone who could set my mind at rest.

The welcome sight of Minnie with Ottoline on her arm met me as I burst out of a door into the sunshine of the courtyard. They were evidently on their way to survey the great arrival and Minnie hailed me with delight and bade me take Ottoline's other arm to hasten their progress. Penny was standing up in one of the carts, dressed in breeches. She waved and hallooed as she caught sight of us advancing.

'I have a question, Minnie dear,' I said. There was plenty

time to ask it for Ottoline's progress was a kind of doddering shuffle and the bustle of unloading was still yards away. 'About the curse. A technical question, I suppose one would say. What exactly counts as the castle, in your opinion? I was looking at some plans and saw that there was a village all around in what's now the . . . park,' I selected as a description, in case 'field' would hurt her feelings. 'Does the site of all those former buildings constitute part of the homestead still? Or does the castle start once you cross the moat? Or even at some mid-riparian *point* of the moat? For, if we're to dig up the fiel— park in case the Cut Throat is buried there, I don't think we can do it discreetly and certainly not if the ground is covered in motorcars, dogcarts and charabancs.'

Ottoline had ground to a halt completely and was staring aghast at me, breathless and pale. Had she forgotten that she was supposed to be as deaf as a post, I wondered. She ought not to have heard a word of what I had said so softly to Minnie.

'Good grief, that's a horrid thought,' Minnie said, stretching up to look over the open end of the courtyard towards the field rolling away behind the castle to some quite distant bushes at its edge. 'But put it from your mind. I am not well versed in the . . . might one call it the *theology* of curses or is that blasphemous? . . . Well, anyway, I think it's safe to say "the castle" means the walls. Starting on the inside edge of the moat. It was centuries before the ruby came to us that the field was covered in hovels and pigpens and—' She broke off. '*Mama*,' she yelled, close to Ottoline's ear, '*do you need to rest?*'

Ottoline was leaning heavily on me and, from the white marks on Minnie's arm where her fingers were digging in, was leaning no less heavily on that side either. But at least she was breathing again and her cheeks had a little colour back in them. Perhaps a little too much colour, actually; two spots of deep pink. I squeezed her arm in an attempt at a friendly reminder of her deafness, even while I wondered which of my words had unnerved her so.

Then as she pattered on a few more steps, all the glorious commotion surrounded us and distracted me.

'Meet my mother and my grandmother, everyone!' Penny shouted, still standing on the cart. 'Mother, that's Julian – Malcolm and second murderer – just squeezing past you there. Granny, those are Francis, who's Angus and a doctor, and George, who's Lennox and a king. And those are – Oh well, thanes and kings. You'll get to know everyone soon.'

She was wrong, of course. Most of the players remained a sea of names and a separate sea of faces throughout The Cut Throat Affair, only a few ever rising to prominence.

Minnie was in mid-nod to the first of the young men, who was indeed sidling by with his arms full of bundles of velvet, when she froze. 'Malcolm's not the second murderer!' she cried. 'Now, Penny, I really must put my foot down. It's bad enough that the play has changed but if Leonard's going to turn all modern and peculiar—'

There was a ripple of laughter among the gathered actors, but it was not unkind and a tiny little sprite of a woman trotted forward to explain.

'Lady MacDuff,' she said. 'Or Pauline, if you'd rather.'

'I'd rather Miss Something,' said Minnie, prissily for her.

'Really?' said Pauline. 'Miss Tavelock, in that case. How odd. But don't worry about the play. Leonard is very strict about "text".' She groaned. 'Don't ask why unless you've got an hour to spare.'

Penny gave a sour look. Leonard, I gathered, was not to be laughed at. 'We double up, Mother,' she said. 'It keeps down the wage bill. Julian plays Malcom and he also plays second murderer and Menteith, I think.'

'No, Miles is Menteith,' said one of the young men. 'And Donalbain, a doctor, first murderer, a lord and a king.'

'But how is it possible?' Minnie said. 'Doesn't it turn the play into a farce?'

'Not at all,' said Penny. 'Leonard has put it together exquisitely, like a watchmaker.'

'I'm not just Lady Macduff,' said Pauline Tavelock, cutting in on the paean, which was indeed rather sickening. 'I'm also the first witch and Fleance with my hair tucked in a cap.' She pointed over to a hoydenish young woman standing up in the back of the other cart. 'Tansy there is third witch, the boy Siward, MacDuff's son, and a servant. And Roger over *there*,' she hailed a rather barrel-like young man who was hefting trunks like a navvy, 'is MacDuff, a sergeant, a Scottish doctor, a king and an apparition.'

Nothing less like an apparition could ever be imagined; Roger was red faced and shining from his exertions and his waistcoat buttons strained over his middle in a testament to his tailor. As he let the last of the trunks drop to the cobbles he wiped his neck with a red-spotted handkerchief and then shook us all vigorously by the hand. Even Ottoline, who looked astonished by the impertinence.

'Thank you for letting us invade your castle,' he said, in an unexpectedly sweet voice. When he spoke, at last one could believe he was a stage actor. 'It's perfect for us, Mrs Bewer, and we shall do our best to make it profitable for you.'

Despite the bald reference to money the speech was so nicely turned that Minnie merely smiled. As the actors moved off, dragging trunks towards an open door, and Penny busied herself coiling up the ropes that had held them in place on the carts, Minnie murmured: 'Why couldn't she fall for him? He's obviously been properly brought up. And heaven knows he looks to be good stock.'

'I'm glad to see such thrift in the company,' I said hastily as Penny jumped down and joined us. 'One does wonder about actors, doesn't one? That they might be grand and

starry and ask for oysters at breakfast. But this lot seem very
. . . ' I drifted into silence at the sound of a motorcar trundling over the rickety bridge and through the gatehouse arch.
It was an elderly but well-cared-for Daimler and as it drew
to a stop, out of it stepped two equally elderly but almost as
well-cared-for actors of the very grandest type I could
imagine.

They were the very starry oyster-eaters I had just been
congratulating Minnie on avoiding. The gentleman, who had
been driving, wore a soft hat of a pale camel colour and had
a light mackintosh draped about his shoulders like an opera
cloak. Add the mauve handkerchief that foamed out of his
top pocket in artfully careless trails and the outfit of a dandy
was complete. I decided that he had been such a dandy in
his dreamy youth and had never updated his wardrobe. These
days, he was a mountain of a man – he would have made
even the navvy Roger look willowy, if standing by his side
– and his hair, eyebrows and moustaches were dyed the harsh
black of a dead crow, which clashed nastily with the
complexion of a lifelong bon viveur.

His companion stood in the shade of his hat, and looked
like a pixie sheltering from raindrops under a toadstool. She
was barely five feet tall and as slim as a boy. She was, truth
be told, rather too slim for her advanced years, the lack of
flesh beneath her skin making her look dried out and rather
raddled. Her hands, one of which was held aloft by the large
man, as if he thought they were about to dance a minuet,
were skeletal, liver-spotted and trembling.

Then she smiled and one could see the point finally. Her
face lit up, eyes shining, cheeks gleaming, teeth twinkling and
even her hair, unlikely loops of bright yellow, turning to gold.

'Reporting for duty,' the grand man said, sweeping his soft
hat from his black hair and bowing low.

'Welcome to Castle Bewer,' Penny said. 'Mother these are
Mr and Mrs Dunstane.'

'Now, now,' said the elderly lady, 'I'm Sarah Byrne when I'm working, Penny. I'm only Mrs Moray Dunstane when I'm bent over my mending basket.' She simpered up at her husband, who crooned down at her and stroked her hand. I turned slightly away; I have never been able to bear married people flirting.

'And besides, we are more properly Duncan and Lady M,' her husband said.

'Duncan, Old Siward, an old man, Third Murderer and a King!' said Penny. 'I've just been explaining how clever Leonard has been. And Lady Macbeth is a king too, Mrs Gilver. In the procession. Because of Queen Mary. Do you see?'

Sarah Byrne had, however, drawn herself up to her full, if rather negligible, height and was staring haughtily at Penny. 'Never,' she said. 'I am Lady Macbeth and Moray is Duncan. We are not dogsbodies.'

'I think the contracts—' Penny began.

'My contract is with the bard,' said Mr Dunstane in a voice quaking with emotion. 'I give my Duncan!' He paused. 'And Siward.'

'Hmph,' said Penny softly. 'Contract with the bard, my eye. Siward has a speech on the last page and Duncan's dead by the end of Act I!'

I had to look down at my feet to make sure of not giggling.

'Although the Old Man is too important to leave to chance,' Dunstane went on, stroking his moustaches. I was half-surprised not to see the extraordinary black come off on his fingers.

'Middle of Act II,' Penny murmured from the side of her mouth. 'The thing is, Moray,' she said at normal volume, 'that this parsimonious casting doesn't allow for any further switches. Leonard has it worked out to the last little scene, quick changes and everything.'

'I change in my dressing room,' said Sarah. 'With my dresser.'

'Well, as to dressers,' said Penny doubtfully.

Then the day was saved. Grant and Alec – very much Grant and Alec; that billing – made themselves known from where they had been lounging behind a stout buttress.

'There's no need to worry,' Grant said. 'I can be Bloody Mary in the procession of kings. It won't be the first time. And what is it you need by way of a gentleman, Miss Bewer? Another king?' she displayed Alec as though he were a side of salmon on the fishmonger's slab. He lifted his chin regally.

'And third murderer,' Penny said.

Alec rounded his shoulders and narrowed his eyes.

'And I'll very happily dress you, Miss Byrne,' Grant went on. 'There's a whole act between the kings and when you need to be back on in your nightgown.'

She had not sounded happier since the days we used to go to Paris to look at the new season's modes. I was ready to step in as her second should Sarah Byrne cavil, but the arrangement seemed to meet with guarded approval from the great actress.

'Your name, child?' she said.

'Cordelia Grant,' came the reply. It is always a surprise when I am reminded of Grant's Christian name and I think it was Alec's first hearing, for he opened his eyes very wide. 'My parents' company did not *only* do Shakespeare, but my father's Lear was the jewel of the repertoire. I got to shake the thunder sheet if I'd been a good girl.'

The approval was not even guarded now. Grant's credentials had been presented and were given the seal of approval. Miss Byrne put out a hand and Grant managed something between a shake and a curtsey without making it seem the least bit awkward.

Muttering that she would need Leonard's blessing, Penny hurried away.

'Well now, Miss Byrne,' said Minnie, 'now that that's all taken care of, I shall summon Pugh to show you to your quarters. Dandy, if you would just give Mama your arm to her sitting room.'

'No need, Mrs Bewer,' said Grant. 'I had a quick look at the players' rooms first thing, just to check them over – actors need good air moving through and couldn't settle with a smoky chimney. It's the voice, you see. They must protect the voice at all costs at the start of a run. Isn't that so? So I can show the Dunstanes to their room.'

I thought I saw Sarah open her mouth again to insist on 'Miss Byrne' but since the topic at hand was her sharing a bedroom with Mr Dunstane, decency prevailed and she merely inclined her head. Minnie, though, had reached her limits. My maid might have burst into the breakfast room with fairy wings and might have cast herself in a play and inspected the castle's appointments but she was not to show distinguished guests to their quarters. The four of them moved off together, leaving Alec, Ottoline and me.

'That girl will go far,' Ottoline said. 'And how are you two getting on?'

'*We've been making sketches of the castle,*' Alec thundered. 'No don't worry, Dandy. I must try to get into the habit of projecting before opening night. *And we're going to search*—'

'I'm not deaf,' Ottoline said. 'I heard everything except whatever Penny was muttering. I'm glad to think someone is going to constitute a proper search at long last.'

'Has no one *ever* mounted a search?' I said. Alec was clearing his throat; if he were going to 'project' for eight performances a week he would need Grant to coach him in the technique.

'I didn't care where the bally thing had got to,' Ottoline said. 'Bluey was too superstitious to want it for Minnie and I think Minnie didn't like to appear too avaricious. Penny used to amuse herself with it when she was a child. Hunt the ruby is a lot more fun than hunt the thimble, at least until it begins to dawn that one's never going to find it. But unless the servants have gone rootling, I'd say no.'

It was hard to believe. A priceless jewel had been lost for thirty years and no one had looked for it? I was sorry I had announced aloud my plan to go bothering retired servants. Alec's fingers twitched.

'I think I'll just shoot off then,' he said. 'As you pointed out, Dandy, the bedrooms of the players should be searched first and then the guest rooms..'

'And I'm off to the village, Ottoline,' I said. 'But when I return, I'd like to look at Richard's letters to you from all those years ago. Assuming you kept them.'

'His letters? Why?' Ottoline said.

'Oh, we always like to have a good look at everything,' I assured her.

'Any letters at all, to get his measure? Or just the last ones from abroad, to . . . ?'

'Ideally, the ones from abroad,' I said. 'Could you lay your hands on them easily?'

'I don't have them tied in a pink ribbon under my pillow,' she said. 'But yes, I daresay I could find them if I hunt through my belongings.' She looked troubled and I hastened to reassure her.

'I shan't mind a scrap what's in them, if he said mean things to you. We very often catch people at their worst moments, you know.' But still she looked worried. 'It's more the postmarks and any hints of his whereabouts that interest me. If we could find out through friends of friends – consulates or embassies, even – that he ended his days in comfort we might conclude that the sale of the ruby provided it.'

'Hmm,' said Ottoline. 'Well, there might have been a consulate at his first stop, but when he got as far as Zanzibar . . .'

'It's worth trying,' Alec chimed in. 'If we could find out that he actually showed someone the ruby, then we can all stop worrying about the curse falling, the taxman grasping and the lodgers stumbling on the thing.'

Ottoline's brow twitched at the word 'lodgers' but then

cleared. Her smile to me was wide with relief. 'I don't see what harm could come from any of that,' she said. 'Although success seems unlikely.' She turned to Alec. 'Young man, if you would escort me to my sitting room, I shall start searching for the letters right now.'

My heart was touched to see Alec so solicitous, slowing his pace and bending to catch her feeble voice, and I stood staring after them until the door was shut at their backs. I was not wool-gathering now. I was troubled: I was experiencing that oh-so familiar and oh-so unwelcome sensation that I had missed a turning on the path already. Someone had told me something, deliberately or not, that I should have noted. I drew out the little notebook and propelling pencil, beloved of me and scorned by Alec, and made in it the very first of a great many scribblings.

'Letters? Cast? Multiple roles? Dresser? Floor plan? Hunt the thimble? PIP!'

The last of these was my own personal code telling me to find the tiny nugget that mattered amid an ocean of senseless chatter. I knew better than to rush after it. I simply put it out of my mind and took myself off to visit Nanny.

8

Castle Bewer's pension cottages lay a pleasant half-mile along the lane from the field-gate and a lane in June is a pleasant thing indeed, when the rain stops. The meadowsweet waved in the light breeze, releasing its pungency, and red butterflies dotted here and there between the cornflowers and purple vetch. If I had ever met this Nanny I might have picked her a posy but – not knowing whether she'd welcome them or whether she, like my Nanny Palmer, would rather have a neat bunch of dahlias well-shaken out by the gardener to remove the earwigs – I held myself in check.

The cottages were built after the fashion of alms houses, I noted as I drew near, with more of a view to the pride of the benefactor than to the comfort of the residents, since they bristled with picturesque details – the middle one in the row had a clock tower on top of it – but were truly tiny. Even if Nanny herself proved too loyal to be indiscreet, no one living at such close quarters with her neighbours could be much of an enigma.

The front gardens were a picture. I rather thought, as I looked over the hedge, that a gardener must have retired here and set himself up as the commander of the entire row, for the same effusion of roses was rioting in every little patch, with the same carpet of columbine below, the same musky currant bushes at each gate and the same lavender lining each path. It was delightful to the eye, if rather overwhelming to the nose, and I paused at the gate of number three to drink it in.

Nanny, as a result, got the chance to take a good look at me through her lace curtains and then stump to her door on two sticks and throw it wide. She was an ancient woman, or at least appeared so. Bent like a crochet hook and with a face lined in stripes like mattress ticking from brow to collar. Her hair was no more than a few wisps peeping out from under a limp cap and the rest of her costume was a black garment that skimmed the floor as she walked and a blue cambric apron on top, the like of which I had not seen since my mother's maidservants turned out whole rooms in their great spring cleaning. She took a long moment to see if there was any way she could slam the door without speaking and failing to find one, she hailed me.

'Are you an actor?' she said in a voice, somewhat gruff from age but still not one with which I would trifle. I wondered briefly if something about me suggested it, since this was the second enquiry on those lines today, but I answered genially.

'I'm a friend of Mrs Minnie, Nanny. I'd like to beg a little of your time, please?'

It was a message in code and she swiftly deciphered it. A woman in her forties calling a perfect stranger by what amounted to a pet name and referring to a third party by another was really saying: I am one of the club. I am something you understand. You have no reason to fear me.

Nanny gave a thoughtful nod then, after a final swift look up and down, deemed me acceptable and waved me in the gate with one of her sticks.

Once I had jostled myself into the cottage, negotiating a hallway – so small with its three doors that it was more like the way into a sheep pen than the anteroom to a human dwelling – I settled in the little room that served as parlour, dining room and kitchen combined. I congratulated myself on eschewing the hedgerow posy. Nanny's cottage was a testament to orderliness, the only flowers being made of folded coloured paper and stuck into a cork dome like hatpins. My blowsy meadowsweet would not have been welcome here.

I sat down, while Nanny pegged out to the scullery on her sticks with an enormous black kettle under her arm, pish-poshing vehemently my mild suggestion that I might help her. Clearly, I would make some unbearable mess of her household if I were to attempt anything so ambitious as turning on a tap and holding a kettle spout under it. It was hard to believe that this woman had ever watched a household fall into disorder simply because its mistress had stopped paying attention.

There were two armchairs in the little living room, one either side of the range and each with a baggy crocheted slipcover tied on top of its original leatherette. They were terrifically slippery as a result and one had to brace one's feet against the floor to save from shooting right off and landing on the hearthrug with a wallop. This curtailed quite a bit of my attempt to twist around and make a proper survey. I had to settle for a close scrutiny of the high mantel where, as I had expected, I saw photographs of Minnie and Bluey, another of an infant Penny on a donkey and one of her in her coming-out dress.

There was, as well, a framed telegram; that same, framed, black-edged telegram that adorned so many cottage mantels still. If Hugh was right, I thought, and trouble really was brewing again from the same quarter, future generations would not even bother to keep the two wars apart in their minds and we – our lives, lived after 1918 and before what-ever was coming – would be a forgotten interlude. I turned my thoughts as resolutely from these notions as I turned my eyes to the table by Nanny's chair. My sons were twenty-one and twenty-two and there could not be a war until they were each safely forty. I would not countenance it.

The little table containing the requisite items for Nanny's quiet fireside days was very revealing. There was no Bible upon it, but there was the latest issue of *Picture Show* and two earlier issues lower down in the pile like the kind of evidence archaeologists use to establish early history. I used *these* to establish Nanny's character as open to the entertainments of melodrama, should any be in the offing. It was possible, of course, that the magazine was an unwanted gift subscription. It is the fate of us all to be a burden to our loved ones when it comes to the choosing of gifts. Donald and Teddy, once they were past the age of offering taper boxes they had made themselves in the nursery, racked their brains each birthday and again at Christmas and never managed to think of a single desired item to wrap in crepe paper and present to me. I thanked them for handkerchief cases, china models of Dalmatians and more writing paper than I could use if I were exiled to Alba for the rest of my days, then quietly bought my own little treats. As for Hugh, he took my hints about sapphire earrings and emerald bracelets as jests, smiled grimly, and on Christmas mornings spent so much time explaining the wonders of the new telescopic toasting fork or self-replenishing blotter he had found for me that my disappointment had gone by the time he was done and I always managed to thank him nicely.

But Nanny's *Picture Show* looked well thumbed. I had my opening. I would try to get her to talk about being given this cottage with no say in its position.

As she returned with a tea tray, balanced miraculously on her knuckles since she was still gripping the sticks, I smiled brightly and began.

'It's a pretty spot this, isn't it?' I said. 'But rather far from town.'

'We have two butchers with vans and a fishmonger with a cold cart,' she said. 'And the baker delivers to me because I trained his mother and she brought him up well.'

'Oh gosh, well of course, for a pillar of the community it makes no odds,' I said, retreating. 'I was thinking about the visitors to Mespring and Castle Bewer, really. Wishing the Annandales and Miss Penny success with their ventures, you know.'

Nanny nodded. 'She's always been the same,' she said. 'Of course, I wasn't her nanny, but she always included me in her capers. Many and many's the time I went along to her nursery to sit and clap at the latest of her shows. I was sorry she was an only one for it would have been ever so much more fun for her with sisters and brothers to direct. As it stood, she was everything but the wardrobe mistress and a cast of one puts a stop on what you can bring off, be it in the West End or in the night nursery with a painted sheet behind you.'

'Indeed,' I said. 'I met this Cousin Leonard today. Have you come across him?'

It was the very outer edge of what a loyal family retainer could stand, but so tempting that with a vague look on her face, as if to say: *I am not aware of what is passing; I am not responsible*, she replied: 'I daresay Miss Penny will bring him along for me to inspect. In time.'

'How lovely. Even though, as you said, you were never her nanny. You surely retired very young.'

She was not to be flattered. 'I retired at sixty,' she said. 'I'm ninety on my next birthday and I don't care who knows it.'

'Had you had enough of babies and tiny children?' I said, hoping that this time she would let me lead her where I wanted to go. 'I can understand that.'

Nanny's kettle was beginning to chirp on the gas ring out in the scullery and she lumbered off to deal with it. I felt my shoulders slump. How was I ever to bring her round to the question of her retirement and the reason for it and any possible contact she had with Richard after the changing of the guard?

Thankfully, she used the time away from me to make a

decision as well as a pot of tea. When she came back, on one stick and with a heavy brown china teapot wavering in her grasp, she had a determined set to her face. She banged the pot down and dropped back into her chair. 'You can pour,' she said. 'But mind and not drip. Not yet, girl! It'll hardly have started mashing.'

I withdrew my hand and braced myself for a cup of teak-coloured tar whenever Nanny decreed the pot was ready.

'I would have happily tended to Mr Bluey's little ones,' she said. 'We didn't know it would be Miss Penny alone away back then. But I retired instead. I retired very happily. It was the right thing. A clean sweep.' They were the same words Mrs Porteous had used too. 'The castle was no place for a bride and a staff can get set in its ways.' I waited in silence, hoping she would continue to enlighten me. 'We'd all have been too gloomy and sad for a honeymoon pair, missing our master and wondering what had become of him. It was better to have all the nasty old things swept right away and start afresh.'

'Nasty old . . . ?' I said, wondering what on earth she meant.

'Mercy, I don't mean the servants,' she said, clapping a hand to her mouth and then dragging it round to cup her cheek in an expression of horror. 'I meant the castle itself. It was a dreich place. Dark and dingy. Displays of swords and muskets on the walls of the great hall, suits of armour hanging about like murderers waiting to snatch at you. Those tapestries were like a zoological garden, seething with slaters and clipshears. And then there was Old Mr Bewer's specimens. They were none too lovely by the time Mr Bluey was grown. So Mrs Bewer turned the whole lot out and had the place as pretty as pretty for Miss Minnie. And a new staff too who wouldn't be harking back and making her droop.'

I cast my mind over the castle I had just left. Fresh and pretty were not the first words to spring to mind, but I could see that thirty years ago the cream distemper and printed curtains might have been charming and it was true that there were no mouldering tapestries or rusting muskets around.

'Healthier too,' Nanny was saying when I started paying attention again. 'Mr Richard was so terribly ill before he left to take his cure and you can't tell me those hangings were wholesome. Traps for germs of all sorts. No, she was right. It was better.'

'It must have been a shock to you that he left,' I said. I was pouring the tea. She had not instructed me that it was ready but she did not stop me. 'I hope he kept in touch with you from his stations abroad,' I added, as I handed her her cup and proffered the milk jug.

'He did not,' Nanny said. 'I was sadly taken in by Mr Richard, or so I came to see. He was a lovely daddy to my sunny little boy Bluey. He changed. Well, we all change; life changes us, but most stay the same at the core, I always say. Not Mr Richard. He changed at his heart. And he did it without me ever seeing it happen. So you see when it all came out it was like something had been stolen from me. All the long happy years of my life, stolen away from me.' She took a sip of her tea, drawing it over pursed lips in a rasping gurgle to cool it as it passed.

'How awful,' I murmured.

'Ocht, Mrs Bewer was trying to do right by him,' she said. She selected a biscuit from the plateful on the tray, hard little quoits of biscuits beloved of nannies everywhere, who do not believe that treats should be too delicious lest they spoil us. But she dipped it into her tea to soften it for her old gums. 'I think . . . ' she drifted into silence and then gave me a sharp look. 'You'll be keeping all of this to yourself,' she told me. I nodded. 'I think the illness was nothing to do with his lungs and the mouldy curtains at all, for taking himself off to Aleppo wouldn't help clear that up, would it?'

'Aleppo?'

'I had never heard of it in my life. Have you?'

I shrugged, which seemed to satisfy her. 'No,' she said, sucking her teeth, 'I think it was up here.' She tapped her temple with a crooked finger. 'Because all of that about the Curse that was supposed to have come to him from his father after his mother died? Supposed to have been festering in him all through his boyhood and came to a head at last?' I nodded again. 'Never!' she declared. 'Of course old Mr Bewer put the thing away when he had no wife to wear it. But he didn't turn his son against it with wild stories. I'm sorry to have to say it of a man I knew when he was young and strong and healthy, but that came out of Mr Richard's own fancy, did that. A curse! That was his own weak head. I could scarcely credit it when I heard it. And it took time, mind you! Mrs Richard stayed loyal as long as she could.'

'And then told you because you knew him best?' I asked.

Nanny, to give her credit, blushed a little, which told me that she had got the gossip at second hand. She changed the subject with a sniff. 'If he had had more occupation,' she said. 'If he had taken a proper interest in the farm or even gone in for beetles or butterflies like his father before him. Or more children. A nice family round him. Stop him brooding.'

I smiled at her and there was real affection in the smile. She might have been my very own Nanny Palmer come to life again, opining that no ailment of mind or body could withstand outdoor occupations and settled healthy habits.

'So he never wrote to you?' I said. 'You have no letters that might help us trace him.' She shook her head as she let her eyes pass along the collection of photographs upon her mantel, pausing as she got to the telegram and reading it with her lips moving. She sighed. 'And one last question, Nanny,' I went on. 'Do you have any idea – any suspicion at all – where the Cut Throat might be?'

'Cut Throat?' she said. 'Who's this?' I simply gazed at her.

87

'Oh!' she said. 'You mean the ruby necklace, don't you? Yes, the cook told me about that silly name he gave it. See, this is what I'm saying. He was not himself. His father never called it that. And Mrs Bewer never called it that or she wouldn't have posed for her pretty picture in it, now would she? Would *you*? It was the Judas Jewel in my day.'

That, I thought to myself, was not much of an improvement when it came to putting the thing round one's neck, but I said nothing.

'And you're asking me where I think it is?' she went on. She had finished her biscuit and now took a huge draught of her cooling tea. 'Well, I think he took it with him. Oh, it would have been so much easier if poor Mrs Bewer hadn't been trying to save face. Saying he was ill and then he was away for his health. And so she said he left the jewel behind too, did she? She thinks it's in the castle?'

'They all do,' I said. 'At least partly. And Minnie and Bluey have engaged me to find it.'

'Engaged you?' Nanny echoed.

'I'm a detective,' I said.

She put her cup down so smartly it rattled in its saucer. 'Here's me thought you were a lady!'

'I am a lady,' I assured her. 'Lady enough to know that nannies have all the best hidey-holes. From playing hunt the thimble and stashing Easter eggs. Is there anywhere in Castle Bewer that Mr Richard might know about but everyone else would overlook?'

'All these years?' she said. 'And while the place was turned out and done over and everything?' She shook her head as though the very question was folly. 'And we rolled our eggs down the hill like Christians. We didn't hide them.'

'Well, but is there anywhere even worth checking?' I asked. 'My own childhood home had a mouse house in the nursery staircase. A little door in one of the risers and behind it a mouse's parlour with doll's house furniture and a family of stuffed mice sitting down to their tea. My brother forgot about it and when I visited and told his children I became their favourite aunt forever. Nothing like that at the castle that you can remember?'

She shook her head even more decidedly. 'There was a little box with a hinged lid under the saddle of Master Bluey's rocking horse. He hid a broken inkwell there to stay out of trouble but the ink stained through and he had to take the slipper for clumsiness and for sneaking too. But I can't think on any hidey-holes in the castle itself. In the . . . how would you say it?'

'The fabric of it?' I suggested.

'The fabric of it, just so. It's a lump of a place. Everything stone and slab. Nowhere hollow. Now if it was Mespring House! Have you seen Mespring?'

'Not yet,' I admitted.

'I'll be along there with my shilling when they throw open the doors,' Nanny said. 'I can get my neighbour's niece to push me in a chair. I'll not miss it.'

'And shall you come to the play at Castle Bewer?' I asked, but her look spoke volumes.

'Sit in that draughty courtyard and watch that nasty play full of evil deeds and foul language?' she said. 'Not I. I'll leave that to them as have a taste for it.'

I was interested to reflect, as I made my farewell and headed back to the castle, that she knew already it was *Macbeth* and not the *Dream* that was afoot and I wondered if someone who lived in this row still worked for the Bewers, or if it was the usual tale of the housemaid's brother stepping out with the baker's sister. It really had been silly of Ottoline to believe that she could keep quiet a juicy tale like the Cut Throat curse simply by sacking a few servants and saying her husband was ill.

★   ★   ★

The bustle had become a frenzy by the time I returned. The carpenters were hammering in the very last nails in the transformed courtyard and one of them waved cheerfully at me, inviting me to climb the steps that formed the central aisle of the auditorium and try out one of the benches in the back row. I sat gingerly for there was nothing but my own vigilance to stop me from toppling backwards and, although the rake was shallow and there were only ten rows, still the plummet from the tenth could easily end in broken bones and an abrupt halt to my detecting.

'Aye, we'll pit oan a backrest,' the carpenter called up, seeing my discomfiture, 'but we'll have to sand it right well, case it rips the nice frocks and best coats.'

Penny was on the stage, anticipating one of the later scenes of the play by shoving around enormous pots full of greenery. I put a hand up to shade my brow and guessed at azaleas, which were certainly decorative but hard to work into one's usual picture of *Macbeth*. When she heard the carpenter she stood up and hailed him.

'Will it be extra?' she said. 'We've budgeted for this load of wood and no more.'

'Doctor's bill for folk falling off'll be steeper,' the carpenter called back.

'How about a rope?' said Penny. 'Bang some posts in and string a stout rope between them.'

The carpenter, just like a salesgirl in the dress department of a grand London store, curled his lip at the thought of his customer's budget being finite, but Penny's attention had been hooked away anyway. Leonard was striding down the aisle. He was still in the ancient flannels but his cotton square had been discarded and instead around his neck he now wore a long piece of silk chiffon, which fluttered behind him as he thundered forward.

'No!' he cried. 'No, no, no! What the hell is that, Penny?'

I felt a sudden need for the rough plank or the stout rope.

As I reeled backwards in shock at his words I could easily have toppled.

Penny did not blush, flounce off or burst into tears at being sworn at by her fiancé in front of half a dozen workmen and others. She put her hands on her hips and stared down at him. 'Now, don't be unreasonable,' she said. 'We got these to decorate the wings for the *Dream* and it's too late to change them now.'

'Flower bushes?' said Leonard. He leapt up onto the stage with a show of vigour that at last gave some clue as to what Penny might conceivably see in him. He was a healthy specimen, if nothing else. 'Pink fl— Oh, they're paper.'

'Of course they're paper,' Penny said. 'Good grief, Leonard, have you any idea how much enormous great shrubs like this would have cost if they were real? We don't have a gardener toiling away in a hothouse, you know. We would have had to go to a nursery and buy them!'

'Well, at least take the pink bits off,' said Leonard, descending on the nearest pot and snatching at the 'blooms' until the bush was ragged and the stage floor littered.

'Stop!' said Penny. 'Stop it! Oh, what a mess!'

But help was at hand. Grant, like all three apparitions rolled into one, suddenly materialised and laid a hand on Penny's arm.

'I can make cobwebs,' she said. 'Draped in gauzy cobwebs, these won't even look like shrubs. They'll just be nameless humps. Perfect for the heath and fine for the castle.'

'Won't it take a lot of . . . whatever it is you need?' said Penny, unconvinced.

'Wool,' said Grant. 'I brought a load of old shawls to unravel. I meant to wind it round the trees to make dawn mist in the *Dream*, but it'll do cobwebs just as well.'

'She's a marvel, isn't she?' said Alec, who had joined me while all my attention was onstage.

'And she knows it,' I said. 'She's talking far too loud for

just Penny and Leonard. She means it for me and will want praise later.'

'Nonsense,' Alec said. He was still so thrilled at the thought of his acting debut that he would not hear a word against Grant, even spoken in the mildest jest. 'She's projecting. She gave me a lesson in it. You speak from your kneecaps and deafen everyone. Why are you scowling, Dandy? Is it envy? I daresay Leonard would let you walk on if you ask nicely.'

'I can't say I care for our friend Leonard,' I said. 'He was just absolutely foul to Penny and given her lack of surprise I gather that's his usual way with her. I wonder if Minnie and Bluey know what a churl he is.'

'Dandy, you can't cause ripples,' Alec said. 'Two days before the first curtain goes up is no time to insist on tea-party manners. Actors are not held to the same niceties as others.'

'They are by me,' I said grimly. 'And he hasn't shown a moment's interest or an ounce of courtesy to Ottoline either. The matriarch of his own family after all.'

'Not really,' Alec said. 'She married into quite another branch of the family tree, didn't she?'

I turned the conversation to safer ground. 'How did you get on in the billets? Find anything?'

'Most definitely no,' said Alec. 'Which is a satisfactory end to a morning's work in its way.'

'Agreed, but why so very definite?'

'Simply this. The castle as a whole was given a great turnout for Minnie and Bluey's nuptials, as we know, but the cadets' quarters that I've been pawing over this morning didn't see so much as a lick of the paint. They've been as they are today since before Ottoline and Richard married. No floorboards have been lifted, no plaster pulled away and patched and there's not a single suspiciously light or dark line of grout in any of the stone walls. I would swear on a stack of Bibles that nothing is hidden anywhere.' He had been rummaging in his coat pocket and now drew out a sheaf of his floor plans. 'Pencil, Dandy!' he said, and proceeded to score Xs over all the rooms in the West Lodging before folding the plans in three and replacing them.

'This afternoon will be rather more tricky,' he said, 'because the best rooms – soon to be filled with Roosebilts and Vanderfeldts – were scraped back to the stone and titivated around the time of the putative stashing. And actually, it occurs to me now that that might explain the procession of bewildered burglars. If Richard put the thing in a cache that could only be found by looking for the join, as it were, and then the join was papered over with Morris's best squashed frogs – that's about the right vintage, isn't it? – well then, poor puzzled burglars, trailing about hopelessly.'

'*Are* there squashed frogs?' I said, for the rooms I had seen so far had escaped that particular element of Victoriana.

'I spoke generally,' said Alec.

'Anyway, Nanny reckons Richard didn't *have* any caches,' I said. 'Not in what we've agreed to call "the fabric of the castle" itself anyway. There was a rocking horse with a hollow back, though. Let's ask Minnie if it was dragged out and put in Penny's nursery or if it's languished in an attic all these years.'

'Or if it was tossed on a bonfire, hollow back and all,' said Alec.

'That's a nasty thought.'

'One thing though, Dan. Would Nanny necessarily know about "the fabric"?'

'This one would,' I said. 'She's a tartar who knows everything. So there's our afternoon. Search the attics for a rocking horse. And we might as well search them completely and only get filthy once, wouldn't you say?'

'Perhaps Grant can lift the cobwebs off us without breaking them and turn them to use,' Alec said. 'Did Nanny have anything else to add, since she's so well informed?'

I shook my head. 'A lot of gossip of the personal sort,' I

told him. 'She took rather a starry-eyed view of Richard– 'my sunny boy Bluey's lovely daddy' she said – and had trouble incorporating his latter behaviour into the picture. Oh, but she did say this: the Cut Throat wasn't always called the Cut Throat. It's first name was the Judas Jewel, apparently.'

'It doesn't get any more appealing the more we learn,' said Alec and despite the warm sun and the sheltered courtyard both of us shivered briefly.

9

Luncheon crackled with tension. Leonard was mulish, despite Grant's innovations, and Penny, it transpired, was one of those annoying individuals who becomes more and more cheerful and chatty when someone is cross with her. She prattled on about costumes and scenery, reminisced about earlier productions and kept putting a hand on Leonard's arm to draw him into the conversation. Minnie was a-flutter because of a telegram that had just been delivered announcing the early arrival of one of the guests – the Vanderfeldts and Roosebilts, as Alec called them.

Moray Dunstane and Sarah Byrne were stony-faced. Perhaps they had seen their quarters and found them wanting, or perhaps they were unused to not being the centre of attention at every party. After Bluey had enquired about counties of birth, school and regiments and got nowhere, he retired to his inner thoughts and Sarah spent the rest of the meal looking as though she were sucking a lemon rather than consuming a well-cooked piece of white fish and some cold lamb with rice and mint jelly.

Ottoline did not help matters any when she suddenly asked in her 'downstairs voice', the foghorn blare of a deaf old lady: 'How was Nanny?'

'*Oh, tremendous!*' I bellowed back at her. '*Full of good ideas.*'

Ottoline stared at me. 'About Richard's whereabouts?' she said.

'*Hidey-holes,*' I yelled, feeling rather foolish, for it is not a word suited for yelling. 'Which reminds me, Minnie. Did

Penny have the family rocking horse in her nursery as a child?'

Moray frowned with a great show of puzzlement as well he might. Sarah was still too annoyed to pay attention.

'Good Lord,' said Bluey. 'Stumpy? I had forgotten all about Stumpy. No, he went up into the farthest reaches when I went off to school and has been there ever since. Why?'

'Ah,' I said, with a single flicked glance at the actors. 'No particular reason, just something Nanny said.'

'About Stumpy?' said Ottoline. 'What were you *asking*? Oh! Oh my! The hollow—'

'*Mama*,' bellowed Bluey. '*Pas devant.*'

Sarah looked about her to left and right, and seeing no servants that Bluey might be referring to, correctly deduced his meaning. '*Pas devant moi?*' she demanded. 'Would you rather we took our meals in the kitchen? Or perhaps the carpenters could set up a trestle in the courtyard and we needn't come inside at all.'

'My dear lady,' said Bluey, 'I could cut out my tongue. I am writhing with misery to have upset you.' Sarah inclined her head, mollified, but Bluey kept talking. 'So they taught you French at . . . what was it? Bethnal Green Girls', did they?'

'Oh Bluey,' said Minnie. 'Dandy, do kick him if you can reach. Mrs Dunstane, ignore my goose of a husband, won't you?'

'Miss Byrne,' Sarah hissed. 'Since I'm not to be in on the "Dandys" and "Blueys" apparently.' She stood and swept towards the door, then as she realised that she was sweeping alone she turned and skewered Moray with an evil glare. 'Are you just going to sit there?' she said.

'Till I've finished my lamb, my lamb,' Moray said. 'Yes, I rather think so.'

'Well!' said Sarah and, as she flounced out, she somehow managed to give the impression of a great many bouncing petticoats and even nodding feathers, like something from the court of George III, even though she was dressed in tweed and jersey. It made me look forward to seeing her act, even while it made me determined to keep out of her way generally. I was glad Alec had searched her room already, for Lord knows what she would make of it if she were in residence while it happened. I would be interested to see her have the vapours but not if I had caused them.

'I rather think we should get round the guest quarters first, darling,' I said to Alec as we left the dining room at last. We had refused coffee and forgone our usual cigarettes to be away from the atmosphere that Moray, Ottoline and Penny had produced between them. 'Before the paying guests pole up, you know.'

'There's plenty of time,' said Alec. 'Let's do the rocking horse. Don't say you're as cold as all that? I mean I know little girls grow up to be women and little boys grow up to be bigger boys, but come on!'

'Oh, very well, since you insist,' I said. 'I shall force myself.' And we broke into quite a steady trot.

'I can't think why no one's checked before,' said Alec when we were round the first bend in the nearest stair.

'I think Ottoline simply forgot about it,' I said. 'And judging by his puzzlement just now, Bluey too.'

In a house where the principal rooms were crooked and vaulted and reached by struggling through stone warrens and bobbing up and down pointless little stairways, it was to be expected that the path to the attics would be a torturous one. Even at that, Alec and I considered trails of breadcrumbs or at least chalked arrows on the floor as we passed. At long last, though, we came to the head of a particularly steep and uneven spiral with a stout arched door set across the top, quite without any kind of landing, and a lock which looked the equal of the key – as large as a pantomime prop – which Pugh had entrusted to us.

Alec fitted it, turned it with both hands and a grimace, and stumbled down a step as the door swung outwards, creaking so very ominously that both of us were nudged beyond what my sons call 'the creeps' and started to giggle.

'Oh, let's get it over with,' Alec said. 'This is ridiculous and highly unlikely to yield fruit.'

I turned up the flame on the lantern Pugh had unearthed for us and raised it above my head as we passed through the doorway into a long narrow attic populated by stacked trunks and shrouded lumps. There was a little scuttling, but no more than happens when one opens a boathouse in spring and, if anything, there was less dust here than in the attics at Gilverton, for there were no windows to let it in and no wood to be nibbled by mice and moths and turned to gritty mounds. There were, on the other hand, more cobwebs of more distinct kinds than I had ever encountered. Swaying ropes of it eddied in the draught we made by opening the door, and trembling lacy spans of it stretched across every corner and joined each object to the next. Worst of all were the single invisible threads of it that caressed our faces every time we moved.

'Ugh,' Alec said. 'And what on earth is that *smell*?'

'Mushrooms of some kind, I expect,' I said. 'Hugh took me to a lecture in London once on the composition of medi-aeval wattle – or do I mean daub? – and there is a great deal of flora and fauna in the recipe as well as clay. A perfect breeding ground for mushrooms, I daresay, once a few slates slip and let the rain in.'

'I shall steam my head over mentholated crystals later,' Alec said. 'The spores from any mushroom that raises that stink could surely carry one off. For now . . . ' He shook out his handkerchief and held it to his face. I sniffed, and decided to risk it. The air was close and foetid enough without trying to breathe it through a mask of cotton.

'A rocking horse should be easy to spot,' I said. 'At least if it's a decent size and isn't draped in a dust shee— Oh!'

'What?' said Alec. I had stopped dead and he clutched at my shoulders to keep from toppling me.

'Ssh!' I hissed. 'Alec, there's someone up here.'

'Where?' he whispered back. 'Who?'

I nodded over into the far corner where a man was standing stock-still, presumably hoping we would leave without seeing him.

'Hie there!' Alec said. 'Who is it?'

The figure remained absolutely as still as a stone and I was aware of a crawling sensation climbing the back of my neck.

'Don't worry,' I called. 'We shan't get you in trouble. Did you hear about the rocking horse and come to look for yourself?'

Again the figure did not speak or move.

'Well, answer, can't you?' Alec said, seizing the lantern and beginning to pick his way towards the stranger. 'What's that you're holding?' He stopped short. 'Dandy, stay back! He's armed.'

My mind flooded with wild fears. Was it yet another burglar, come so many years after the last of his predecessors, meeting us here by the merest, blackest chance? Or was it— Alec laughing intruded upon my thoughts.

'It's a suit of armour!' he cried. 'What ninnies we are! It's a suit of armour on a stand with a pair of lances.'

'If you'd said he was armed with lances, I might have guessed as much,' I said, the humiliation of having been so foolish making me grumble. I squeezed past a hillock of elderly suitcases and joined Alec at the knight's side. 'Nanny did say that they scrapped suits of armour and took down collections of swords to pretty up the castle for Minnie coming. My heart is still hammering.' I took a deep breath. 'What's that he's holding? Not the pair of jousting sticks. I mean what's that bundle he's got under his arm?'

It looked like a parcel of sacking and it smelled like a parcel of sacking that had been home to many mice over long, quiet years. Alec poked it gingerly and stepped back as it disintegrated into a shower of foul-smelling scraps.

'I think that might have been the under-suit,' Alec said. 'The canvas long johns worn underneath the plate, you know.'

'No,' I said. 'He's still wearing his "winter underclothes" – I refuse to use that expression. Or he was until they rotted away. Look at his knees and around his feet.' Alec bent over and peered. More of the same mouse-nibbled and moth-eaten scraps had fallen out of the joints of the suit over the years so that the knight stood in a patch of sackcloth confetti.

'The set under his arm must have been a spare,' Alec said. 'He seems very well-equipped, with a change of drawers and two javelins, doesn't he?'

'Poor old thing,' I said. Alec was scrutinising the helmet and visor. He whistled softly.

'Poor old thing indeed,' he said. 'One gets so used to seeing pairs of these things guarding staircases one forgets they were soldiers' uniforms once. This one had a pretty rough time of it in some battle or other. Look at the dents in the back plate and look at that crushed place on the helmet where someone clonked him on the head. Those came from spikes, Dandy. Can you imagine it? Someone swung a mace and caught this chap right on the bean. I thought we had it bad in the trenches but this makes me shudder.'

'Come away,' I said gently. 'Come and find a rocking horse. That's much more pleasant work.'

It did not take much finding. Even with a dust sheet thrown over it, there is no mistaking the outline of a little horse and this one was not, in fact, all that little. I pulled the sheet off, holding my breath against yet more of the mice and mushrooms, and found myself face to face with a rather beautiful carving. It was not painted; instead the wood was varnished and made a good effort at looking like the burnished coat of a well-groomed chestnut pony. The mane was no more than a brush and the tail was close to gone, leaving only a sprout of stiff black hairs like a besom. I wondered if perhaps this was how 'Stumpy' had got his name.

'The buckles on the saddle have rusted to nothing,' Alec said, handing me the lantern to begin attacking them. 'I wonder if they'll even open. Oh!' At his touch, just as the knight's underclothes had, the rotted saddle leathers on Stumpy's back gave way and his stirrups dropped to the floor with a dull clank. Alec lifted the saddle clear and put it down on a nearby trunk top. I held the lantern over the broad brown back, seeing quite clearly the square shape of a lid set in there.

Alec's eyes danced. In the light thrown upwards from the lantern he looked like a gleeful goblin.

'What's the bet?' he said. 'Cut Throat or no Cut Throat? For a fiver.'

'No Cut Throat,' I replied. 'Something even better!'

Alec put his finger into the little scooped-out place that had been carved into Stumpy's back to allow the lid to open and lifted it gently.

I gasped.

In the square hollow, there sat a velvet box, unmistakably a jewel-box, rounded and gilded and not even faded, so tightly had the wooden lid fitted over it all these years.

'I'll take a cheque but I prefer cash,' Alec said, reaching in and drawing the box out. 'Oh and there's an envelope too! Sealed, no less. What a turn-up.'

He lifted the lid of the jewel box and held it out so that the lantern light could shine in.

'Huh,' he said.

Inside, resting upon the usual pleated satin, was a three-strand pearl choker with a diamond clasp. And in the cushioned-satin centre a pair of rings had been affixed with dressmaker's pins. There was a diamond cluster in an old-fashioned and barnacle-like setting and a hoop of what might have been rubies in dire need of cleaning, but which I rather suspected were garnets.

'I insist on cash, I'm afraid,' I said.

'What?' said Alec. 'How can you claim this is "better"?'

'Oh now come on!' I said. 'Of course this is better. We knew there was a ruby necklace missing and finding it would have been lovely. But we didn't even know about this lot! And we've found a hidden letter too. Who's it from?'

'Let's take it downstairs,' Alec said. 'If it falls to bits when we try to open it – a hat-trick of disintegration – I don't want to be grubbing about trying to pick it all up again.'

Alec spread a large handkerchief on a table under his bedroom window and set the jewel box and the envelope down in the middle of it. We both stared at the direction on the yellowed paper.

To my granddaughter

'Who had a granddaughter who lived in this house?' I said. 'Bluey was an only son and Richard was an only son. But it's modern writing and this paper is Victorian. No older, I'm sure. Open it Alec and see if there's a letter.'

'You seem more interested in the letter than the jewels,' Alec grumbled, but he did as I bade him and even he looked avid when he drew out a single folded sheet and opened it. It crackled but did not break. Alec placed it carefully back on the handkerchief and we both bent to read the few words written there.

Precious Child, May trinkets decorate your life but never change it for good or ill.

I opened the velvet box and we both stared into it.

We were still staring when Grant, with a peremptory rap, strode in.

'I thought I'd find you here, madam,' she said, 'when I couldn't run you to ground anywhere else. And I needed Mr Osborne for a fitting. Mr Dunstane is twice his size and the third murderer's leggings will sag if I don't take them in. Are you still thinking of searching the best rooms? Could you manage it without us this afternoon? There's a guest on her way from Carlisle in a taxi, by the way. Can you imagine? All the way from Carlisle in a taxi! If she keeps spending at that rate she'll be an answer to everyone's prayers.'

'Grant,' I said, as much to break into her bumptiousness as anything; she really was getting beyond belief. 'Come over here and tell me what you make of these, please. First impression.' I closed the sheet into its fold again but left the box open.

Grant joined us, pulled the table smartly away from the window, stepped behind it – the better to see in the stronger light – and bent close.

'What about them, madam?' she said.

'Mid-Victorian?'

Grant shook her head. 'Earlier than that. That clasp is a copy of the clasp on Her Majesty's wedding choker from the King and Queen of Denmark. See how pretty it is, the way it looks like a tiny pair of hands folded in prayer?'

I had not noticed more than that the clasp was set with diamonds but she was right.

'But doesn't that mean simply that it was made after the wedding?' I said.

How silly of me to think I could catch Grant out. She tutted briskly and enlightened me.

'No, indeed, madam, because only a few years later the double safety clasp was invented and no one in his right mind would risk a nice string of pearls on one of these after that. You had to keep checking that they were still round your neck. Don't you remember? You had a jet and emerald collar from Mr Gilver's grandmother that gave you no end of trouble till we had it updated.'

I did remember and it still had the power to make me blush decades later. It was rather a dashing object, more of a bib than a necklace and it filled up a décolletage nicely when necklines were so very low. But the catch had unhooked itself one night at a dull dinner and, when I stood up with the ladies to withdraw, the thing slithered free and plummeted down inside my dress. It would have been mildly embarrassing if it had stopped somewhere in the middle and somewhat more embarrassing if it had dropped straight through and hit the floor. What happened was worse than both: it went halfway and then the hook end of the fastening caught on part of my underclothes so that the necklace could clearly be seen dangling below my daring hemline. Of course, everyone pretended not to notice but, as I stalked awkwardly away to the stairs to take refuge in my bedroom and unhook the dratted thing, a great helpless gale of laughter broke out from the gaggle of wives I left behind me.

'Eighteen-thirty-seven-ish then,' Alec said. 'So these must have belonged to Richard's mother. Only that makes no sense because she had no granddaughters. Just Bluey.'

'And she died before he was born,' I reminded him. 'On Boxing Day, when Richard was a baby.'

'What do you mean about granddaughters?' said Grant and was duly shown the note, which she scrutinised very closely. 'She might have written this to future baby girls,' she said.

'But only if she had reason to believe she would not live to see them,' I pointed out.

'A premonition of her death?' said Grant, saucer-eyed. 'Is that what you mean?' She had picked up the rings and was turning them in her hands. She frowned and looked down. 'Oh,' she said. 'No, these didn't belong to Beulah.'

'How on earth can you tell?' Alec said.

'Because she died very young when she was practically a bride,' said Grant. 'And these rings were worn for years. Look at them.'

She was right. The band on the diamond cluster was worn thin at the back and the hoop of garnets had been mended with coarser gold at some point over its lifetime.

'Well, that's a puzzle,' I said. 'Luckily, it's one the Bewers will no doubt be able to help solve. I would have preferred to go to them with answers rather than questions, but no matter.'

'Meantime,' Alec said, taking out his watch and glancing at it. 'Shall we search a few rooms before tea?'

Grant cleared her throat.

'*I* shall,' I said. 'You have a costume fitting. Just point me in the right direction and leave me to it.'

In the end though we all went, many hands making light work and Grant being reluctant to miss out on the fun.

The Bower Lodging comprised four further apartments, besides my 'plague chamber' and Alec's 'dead man's drop'. I daresay if one had a romantic bent they were quite delightful, filled as they were with the kind of furniture our grandmothers threw onto middens or chopped up for firewood and which was just now being put in the windows of London antique shops and even reproduced to adorn what I believe are known as 'Tudorbethan villas' in Surrey. It was dreadful stuff: as black as treacle, roughly hewn as though wrought by lumberjacks rather than cabinet makers, and bristling with knobs and bumps that would catch one's clothes and ruin them. But the chairs had been covered in light cotton slips, and floral-printed cushions abounded. Besides, there is always something appealing about a very high, very mounded, snowy-white bed. There were, as well, jars of the very wildflowers I had admired that morning, standing in the open windows so that the breeze sent their sweetness through the air. I dared to hope that the American guests would not mind too much the washstands with jugs and basins and the long trip to the nearest actual bathroom. They might take it as part and parcel of the quaintness and might even – with Shakespeare in their minds – be grateful that the castle was not even more primitive. They might think of *Macbeth* and then look around and see only modernity and convenience.

The searches themselves did not take too long for it was true what Alec had said. Looking around these rooms one could not think for a single moment that anyone had hacked a hole in a wall or floor and then patched it up again. The broad black boards had impeccable patina, the wax and wear of decades upon them with not a single raw edge or new nail to be found. And the plastered walls were a perfect smoky ochre, the result of new distemper for Minnie and Bluey's wedding and then thirty years of wood fires and candles since. The furniture too was hardly a challenge. The beds were made of slatted boards, the mattresses visible in strips if one lay down and squinted, and the chairs under their cotton coats were simple wood. There were no chests of any kind, only cupboards set into the thickness of the walls and they did not seem to have any nooks and crannies about them anywhere. We even lifted the lining paper from the shelves and peered underneath it.

I stood in the centre of my second room once the search was over and looked up at the ceiling. It too looked solid, unblemished, unbroken and impossible. Gilverton would have taken a crack team weeks on end to search, for its panelling and its fussiness could conceal any number of secret compartments, but life in the fourteenth century when the Bewers built their stronghold was so very much simpler. I consoled myself that we were at least meeting Bluey's expectations, if not Minnie's or Ottoline's, and was turning to go at last when I heard a blood-curdling scream from the room next door.

I raced out into the passageway and swung round to see

Pugh standing in the corridor with two suitcases dangling from his hands, apparently rooting him to the spot. The scream had come from the bedroom he was just about to enter. I dashed in just as a tremendously solid woman dashed out and we made what is called in cricket matches a good contact. I was bounced back into the passageway where I made a second contact, not so good but much more unwelcome, with Pugh's frontage.

I came to a standstill just as Alec appeared at the solid woman's back and Grant popped up around Pugh's far side.

'My dear lady,' Alec said. 'I cannot begin to apologise to you.'

'What happened?' I said.

'I went into my room!' the woman said. She had the refined quack of a Bostonite. 'I opened a door and found a strange man in my room!'

'Ah,' I said.

'I've only got two hands,' said Pugh. 'I can't be carrying bags and opening doors both.'

'What is going *on*?' said the woman. Her outrage did not seem to be lessening any. Her black brows were drawn down in a deep frown and this, added to a pursed mouth and a rather definite kind of nose, made her look quite a bit like an eagle. The white hair, which contrasted sharply with her blackened brows, finished the effect to a T. She could not have been any other nationality on earth except American. A rich American lady from the north-east – just the prize trout Minnie was baiting her hook to land – and I recognised this as the disaster it was.

'Mrs Rynsburger,' said Grant, and how she knew the woman's name was anyone's guess, 'Mr Osborne here is a member of the household and the company and he was just leaving.'

'He's moving out as I'm moving *in*?' Mrs Rynsburger said.

'No, no,' said Alec. 'I was just . . . '

'Yes, we were just . . . ' I said. But nothing even slightly sensible sprang to mind.

'But you were in my *closet*!' said Mrs Rynsburger.

'Most unfortunate,' said Alec.

'With the door closed?' I asked.

'I suddenly remembered reading something once about a secret passageway that only opened up once the cupboard door was closed,' Alec said. 'You'd never see it if you simply opened the door and glanced in. It was done with pulleys, you see. You had to go right into the cupboard and close the door on yourself and then the floor fell away and revealed a staircase. I thought it was worth checking.'

I had been shaking my head as discreetly as I could while he got through all of this, imagining Mrs Rynsburger taking off to the nearest commercial hotel in Annan and telegraphing her friends to warn them, but to my amazement she dropped the hand she had pressed to her bosom and smiled for the first time.

'A secret passageway?' she said.

'We're doing a survey of the castle for the Bewers,' I put in. 'And we did hope to have these rooms ticked off our list before you arrived. I'm terribly sorry we overlapped and startled you.'

But Mrs Rynsburger was quite recovered now. She jostled Alec aside and hurried back into her bedroom gazing around herself.

'A secret passageway?' she said again, turning around in the middle of the floor and drinking in what she saw.

'Indeed,' came Minnie's voice from the stair head. She swept past us into the room and took Mrs Rynsburger by the hand. 'One of the many secrets of Castle Bewer. Do forgive me for not welcoming you in person. I was talking to the cook about dinner and I didn't expect you quite yet.'

'I'm early,' the lady said with a wave of her hand. 'I was sick of that ramshackle train and I got off a few stops before

Carlisle and shifted to a taxicab. So did you find it?' She swung back to Alec.

'Not yet,' he replied, taking his cue from Minnie.

'And what *kind* of secrets?' said Mrs Rynsburger.

'Oh, the usual,' said Minnie. 'There's a legend about lost treasure and somewhere in the castle is the entrance to the place it's hidden.'

'Really?'

'I'm afraid no one who comes to stay can ever quite resist the temptation to have a go,' Minnie said. 'You are naughty, Alec. Mrs Rynsburger, I shall make sure he doesn't come back and disturb you.'

'Oh, pish,' said Mrs Rynsburger. She had quite recovered her sangfroid and had plunged straight into her own search. She was over at the mantel, pressing and twisting all the protruding pieces of carving she found there and casting her eye around greedily when she was done. 'And is this room really where the passageway begins?'

'We have no idea,' Minnie said. 'The plans are lost.' I would have to ask Bluey to lock his map cabinet to bolster this lie, I thought to myself. 'But this room has always been known as the Gateway Chamber, so it seems quite likely.'

'The Gateway Chamber,' said Mrs Rynsburger. 'Now isn't that enchanting? We have a lovely home, even if I say it myself. It's comfortable and filled with beautiful things and in such a genteel neighbourhood of the city. But none of our rooms have names and we certainly have no lost plans and secrets. Oh, I think I'm going to be very happy here.' With that she drew an enormous pin from amongst the lavender netting that adorned her hat, took it off and fluffed her white hair. Clearly she was beguiled and meant to stay. Almost as clearly we now had someone helping to unearth the long-kept secrets of Castle Bewer.

10

Since Mrs Rynsburger needed to rest before tea, the taxi having been not that much more plush than the train compared with what she was used to in Boston, I took the opportunity to draw Minnie away, show her our find and ask for her thoughts regarding this mysterious grandmother.

'I don't know whether I'm more impressed or bewildered,' she said, turning the rings over in her hands. 'These are hideous. Hardly worth resetting.' She picked up the pearls and let them run through her fingers. 'But this is lovely. Smack back in fashion too. I can't wait to show Penny.' Then her face clouded. 'So long as Leonard doesn't make her sell them to help pay for his everlasting theatre. Oh, Dandy, why could you not have married out of your season like the rest of us? Donald and Teddy would be just right for Penny now and so much more suitable.'

'We really meant you to see if you recognised the handwriting,' Alec said, driving Minnie away from maternal daydreams and back to the point.

'I hadn't met Hugh by then,' I said. 'So any children I'd had wouldn't be Donald and Teddy. They might even have been girls, competing with Penny for the same beaus.'

Minnie gave me a startled look. She had known me as a deb, conventional and feather-headed, and was not inured to the way I now considered competing hypothetical states of affairs as easily as potential luncheon menus. Alec looked no less astonished, for I did not generally edge quite as close to the biological underpinnings of marriage and family as I had just done. I had even surprised myself, and rather unpleas-antly. Had I married at twenty, I realised, my daughter would now be a suitable match for Alec. That truth was most unwelcome.

So it was that all three of us bent closely over the note and gave it our full attention. At last I began to see what it meant.

'The slight warning only makes sense to someone who knows the story of the Cut Throat,' I said. 'Wouldn't you agree? Decorate your life but not change it – for good or ill? Rather an ominous tone unless the curse is in the background.'

'So, it was Ottoline,' Alec said. 'She has a granddaughter, after all.'

'Do you mean she stashed the jewels and wrote the note and . . . forgot?' I said. 'That doesn't seem very likely. On the other hand, she was flabbergasted to be reminded of the rocking horse, wasn't she?'

'It's not her handwriting,' Minnie said.

'And why wouldn't she have mentioned all of this when reminded?' Alec added. 'Minnie, would you ask her? It might be kinder coming from you. Less of an interrogation.'

Minnie was nodding doubtfully and I took the chance of her doubt to sweep in, for Ottoline was a witness, present in the castle before and after Richard's departure, and anything that an unexpected questioning would shake out of her was something Alec and I needed to know.

'Leave her to me,' I said, hoping I sounded helpful, not bossy. Minnie smiled her thanks and left us, hurrying away along the passage with a distracted air.

Outside in the courtyard, of which Alec's tower room had a bird's-eye view, two rattly motor cabs had rumbled through the gatehouse arch and squeezed themselves into what small spaces were left by the Bewers' motor, the vans and carts of the company, the trunks and boxes and endless bundles that seemed to grow like toadstools wherever the stage hands passed, and of course the arc of seats.

'It's turning into a bit of a circus,' Alec said, coming to stand beside me.

'And I'm beginning to think we're part of the show,' I said. 'After Ottoline, why don't we take ourselves off to Mespring and see how many rings are under the big top there?'

'The challenge being to dream up an excuse to go bothering them,' Alec said.

But Ottoline was just about to take care of that for us, and in the most unexpected way.

She was resting, as might fairly be expected of any ninety-year-old woman whose house is in uproar and whose life is under scrutiny, but she welcomed me cheerfully enough and took the idea of Alec joining me in good spirit, only going so far as to sigh with some gentle regret that a young man in her bedroom was unproblematic for her and un-noteworthy for him.

'Ah me,' she said, as she sent me off to fetch him. 'Of all the reasons I have to be bitter at Richard the one that troubles me most is this, Dandy. Everyone currently in my life met me when I was already past my prime. Minnie knows me as Bluey's mother, the entire household thinks of me as Old Mrs Bewer. Only Richard, were he here, might look at me and see a girl still. I should have liked to grow old with someone whose eyes grew kind as my face changed.' She heaved another sigh and turned her head away.

'You are welcome to join us,' I told Alec, pausing just outside her door. 'But try to be gallant. She's feeling old. And that's troubling her.'

Alec looked just about as keen on this brief as any man would be, but he set his jaw and accompanied me back into Ottoline's boudoir.

'Thank you for giving us an audience, Mrs Bewer,' he said. 'It's rather an unconventional moment, but we needed to catch you "between engagements". I believe there's a cocktail party for your new guests this evening and then dinner?'

'Minnie's guests, not mine,' said Ottoline, but she did not completely reject the compliment. She raised herself up a little and tucked a strand into her cap, ready to hold court.

'And I had to visit this room some time,' Alec added. 'Might I go over and inspect the portrait, please?'

Ottoline waved him on. The light on the Cut Throat painting was a great deal better during the day and I joined him, marvelling even more now at the indisputable quality of the thing. The winking rubies were not the half of it: the dewy skin of the bride, pink on her cheeks and cream on her shoulders, a delicate bluish tint in the fragile angles of her neck and jaw, made one want to reach out and touch her. As well, the satin gown of the young Ottoline gleamed on its planes and spangled in its folds, making me remember my own presentation and my days as a bride when pale satin became me. How I fretted that it would crease if I sat down and that the men would think me a sloven and decline to dance with me. How little I understood men. Now I knew it was the ranks of mamas in front of whom we were actually parading and it was our mamas in turn, and our maids and nannies, who were being judged on the strength of wrinkled gloves, drooping curls, and those creases in our satin.

'Where did you sit for your portrait, Mrs Bewer?' Alec asked, making me consider the background of the painting for the first time. It was definitely a castle and one would have assumed it was this castle except that through the window behind Ottoline's head was a view of turrets and snapping pennants and a hill rising up like a great black pyramid.

'Oh, the landscape is the work of the painter's imagining,' Ottoline said. 'Richard always said it was meant as a snub but if so, it was too subtle a snub to hurt my feelings. But that's why it's always hung in here instead of down where guests might titter.'

I stepped closer and tried to see more clearly. The hill, so dark and so very conical, was cruder than the rest of the painting at a distance but when one peered from six inches away as I was now, one could see a great deal of unexpected detail: glints and flecks of reflected light and darts of shadow as though the hill was actually made of tiny lumps of . . .

'Coal?' I said.

'Indeed,' said Ottoline. 'A reference to how my father made his money.' She had given up claiming that the nature of the snub was beyond her.

'And actually,' Alec added softly, fishing in his pocket for the sheaf of castle plans, 'I think the painter has included the parts of the house that were gone by then, hasn't he? What a cheek! No doubt he was paid his due for his work and yet he makes a sly dig at the state of the castle and sneers at "new money". I wish I could make out the signature so I could properly despise him, don't you?'

He turned away and went to sit at Ottoline's bedside. 'Very illuminating,' he said. 'But I can't believe the picture did you justice, Mrs Bewer. It barely does you justice now that you have added wisdom to your beauty.'

'Good grief,' Ottoline rasped at him. 'If you're going to flirt like that, young man, you had better call me Otto.'

'Well then, Otto,' Alec said, 'we have something to show you and something to ask. We found the rocking horse, you see, and in it we found this.'

Ottoline leaned forward as Alec fished in his pipe pocket. Her wrap fell open a little and revealed the top edge of her camisole but she did not seem to notice and I did not alert her. Her eyes, so wide open they were slightly protuberant, were fixed on the velvet box.

She gasped and the slight flush that Alec's gallantry had put in her cheeks drained away, leaving her waxen. 'You . . . You found it?' she whispered. 'I don't . . . How . . . You *found* it?'

'It's not the ruby,' I said.

'Well, no!' she retorted, sitting back as a flush much ruddier than the first suffused her. 'How could it be? In Bluey's rocking horse. So what is it?'

Alec opened the box and showed it to her. She turned her head a little to one side and then to the other, looking like a jackdaw, and said: 'I sacked a maid for stealing that. She swore on her Bible she hadn't and I showed her the door.'

'So they were yours,' I said. 'We thought they must be.'

'Not mine!' said Otto. 'They were family pieces. There's a portrait of Richard's aunt wearing the pearls, if not the rings.'

'His aunt?' I said. 'Would you recognise her handwriting, by any chance?' I had been guardian of the note and I now drew it out of my bag where it had been pressed between the pages of my little notebook. 'Did her granddaughter – that would be Bluey's third cousin, or is it cousin twice-removed; I never know – but did her granddaughter play here as a child? Share Bluey's nursery, perhaps?'

'Her granddaughter?' said Ottoline. 'Dorothy was Richard's *maiden* aunt. She had no children of her own. She lived quietly here, did good works in the village, was a boon to our neighbours. And took herself off not long after I arrived.'

'So I don't suppose you corresponded enough to know her hand,' I said.

'I don't think we corresponded at all,' said Ottoline. 'A note on my engagement perhaps, but nothing more.'

'So, if not Aunt Dorothy,' said Alec, taking the paper to show to Ottoline, 'who wrote this? Do you know? Minnie didn't when we showed her.'

Ottoline unfolded her lorgnette, raised it to her eyes and made a lengthy show of looking at the letter, but I was watching her very closely and I saw the flash of recognition, instant and sure, at her first glance. There was a flickering at her throat and her hand shook, so that the paper fluttered like the wing of a hovering bird.

'Oh dear,' she said. 'Oh dear me. I fear no good will come of this.'

We waited a polite interval and then Alec glared at me and tipped his head towards the old lady. I cleared my throat and spoke very gently.

'Would you say a little more? It's all such a long time ago, surely?'

She sharpened a bit at that, almost to bristling. 'How do you know how long ago it was?' she demanded. 'It's my lifetime, not ancient history.' Then she sat back.

'So . . . ' I said, trying furiously to decipher her words, 'the granddaughter is Penny and the woman who wrote these words was . . . surely not Minnie's mother? How could Minnie's mother gain access to a rocking horse in the attics of Castle Bewer?'

Ottoline's chest was rising and falling rapidly, making the lace edge to her wrap flutter as fast as the little piece of yellowed writing paper. 'There was no granddaughter,' she blurted out. 'Good heavens, the way you two build castles in the air! You'd have us all hanged on a fairy tale.' She gave a stern look at Alec and then at me and when she spoke again she sounded more her own mistress again. 'The direction on the note made an assumption about a baby yet to be born,' she said. 'Sometimes people can be very sure they know what's coming. It's a little too like witchcraft for my taste and in this case it was wrong. Because the baby – when it came – was Bluey.'

'But Bluey's grandmother was long dead,' I said. 'Killed on Boxing Day by a briar rose when Richard was a baby.'

'Yes, yes,' Ottoline said, 'but . . . Oh, it's all so very tawdry.' Alec sat back sharply at the word. I am ashamed to say I edged forward. I have no taste for salaciousness but what is tawdry is exactly what people will work hard to keep quiet and so is often exactly what we are listening for.

'I said, just now,' Otto went on, 'that Aunt Dorothy had been a good neighbour. Do you remember?' Alec and I nodded. 'And it was poor Anne Annandale she was a good neighbour *to.*'

'Anne Annandale?' I said. 'That's a thoughtless burden to hand to a child.'

'I daresay,' said Otto, 'they didn't think she'd have it long. She was to be Anne Bewer as soon as she turned eighteen, you see.'

'Oh,' said Alec. 'This was the rejected match for Richard's father, was it?'

'And Dorothy's great chum,' said Otto. 'Dorothy's bosom pal. Her *very* dear friend. I do hope you catch my drift for I am not willing to say more.'

'Gosh,' I said.

'Quite,' said Ottoline. 'She was a very strange woman, even besides that. And she grew more peculiar as the years rolled by. Eventually, her peculiarities began to tell on poor Dorothy. She got a quite ludicrous notion in her head towards the end. It wasn't the jilting, not even the Cut Throat, that finally quashed the friendship between our two houses.'

This time when we waited we were rewarded. With a look of some distaste on her face, Otto resumed speaking.

'After Beulah – Richard's mother – died, Anne started a sort of campaign to replace her. To become the second wife and thereby Richard's stepmother.'

'But I didn't think she was the marrying kind,' said Alec.

'Well no,' Otto said. 'That's the point. She really wanted to come here to live with Dorothy. And she thought since there was a son already and Richard's father didn't need any more there was no reason she couldn't do just that.'

'Hardly enticing,' Alec said. 'Although Richard's father *didn't* marry again, did he?'

'And after she saw that was a bust,' Otto went on, ignoring him, 'then she got really strange. She said Richard should have been hers. If his father hadn't jilted her, he would have been hers. She actually for a while nagged to have the little boy go and live with her at Mespring instead of here with his father and aunt.'

'How odd,' I said. 'One doesn't think of confirmed spinsters as being maternal.'

'She *was* odd,' said Otto. 'Just once, when I was expecting Bluey any minute, she came to visit. Dorothy brought her.'

'Dorothy?' I said. 'I thought Dorothy died just after your wedding.'

'No,' said Ottoline, frowning. 'She didn't die. I never said that. As I was saying, she brought Anne. And the woman rambled on and on about her imagined connection to the family and how much she looked forward to her granddaughter's birth. It was excruciating. I was furious with Dorothy. I told her to make her choice: the Annandales or me. Her mad friend or her nephew and his wife. She chose the friend. She took herself off to Mespring the next day and never came back. They lived out their days there two dotty old ladies together. The Annandales sulked at being landed with Dorothy, of course, and we've not been so much as nodding acquaintances since. It seems rather silly now.'

I agreed, but then a question occurred to me. 'How do you know so much about what happened when Richard was a child?' I asked. 'Anne's campaign to be the second Mrs Bewer, I mean.'

'Hm?' said Ottoline. 'Oh! Richard told me.'

'Who told *him*?' said Alec.

'Dorothy herself,' Ottoline said. 'They were very close and she was . . . well, as I said . . . rather unconventional. She regaled him with the whole story: the curse, the Cut Throat, the accident that dreadful Boxing Day, how Anne wanted to take his mother's place.'

'That ties up quite neatly,' I said. 'You didn't mention, the first time we spoke, who it was who poured it all in Richard's ear and I rather assumed it was his father. Mourning widower, you know.'

'Didn't I?' said Ottoline vaguely. 'Well, one would have liked to keep some of the family skeletons locked in their cupboards, you know.' Her airy voice dried up rather in the course of this speech and by the end of it she looked rather ghastly.

'Very understandable,' Alec said. 'But much to be resisted, Otto, if you can manage it. It's considerably easier for us to work out what's what if we have all the facts and can shuffle them like a deck of cards, put all four suits in order. We're only interested in a very few of them and, hard as it might be to believe, the others simply pass us by. We have forgotten more scandals than you'd find in a Sunday paper. Haven't we, Dandy?'

'Pretty much unshockable now,' I agreed. 'My husband laments it. He thinks I'm getting coarse and worries about my influence on our sons.'

In such a way we managed to lighten the atmosphere again and soon she was smiling, laughing along with us as we shared some of the more ludicrous highlights of our shared detecting past: the time we had to jump into the cold plunging pool of a Turkish bath as a fire raged in the rafters; the time we joined a village wedding as worst maid and man in tramp's clothes and odd boots; the memory – hazy for me but regrettably sharp for Alec – of my only and inadvertent brush with opium one night that I am glad I cannot quite remember. We entertained her until we saw her start to flag and then we withdrew to let her nap before dressing.

'One last thing,' I said from the door, 'where in the house is the portrait of Aunt Dorothy in the pearls?'

'It's not in the house,' Otto said, her voice low and thick with advancing sleep. 'It's at Mespring. A picture of Anne and her in the garden as girls. When they thought they'd be sisters one day.'

★   ★   ★

'Hmph,' I said as we walked away with the door shut behind us. 'It just goes to show you the dangers of social niceties. If we hadn't kept digging, we'd never have heard any of that. By the way, darling, what are you planning to do with the pearls and rings? The letter we can certainly keep in evidence but . . . ?'

'Oh quite,' said Alec. 'I shall hand over the actual loot to Minnie and lock the letter in my writing case. But as to social niceties; I should have welcomed some. I was blushing to my boot soles in there. Nothing was left unsaid.'

'Yes, but when Otto first mentioned the jilted Annandale girl she didn't say anything about her being uninterested in marriage and I jumped to the conclusion that she was plain or perhaps stupid. That it was Richard's father who baulked.'

'You think too highly of men if you think stupidity would be a bar,' said Alec. 'Some of my old chums, I wonder how they bear the mindless prattle of the women they've married, but they've only themselves to blame.'

I knew I would regret it but I could not resist; he had so very nearly raised the subject. 'I imagine it's getting easier to find a clever wife with something to say,' I murmured. 'Now that girls are being educated.' Alec did not answer, so I said a little more. 'Look at Penny.'

'Huh!' said Alec. 'Look at Penny indeed. Much good educating girls does if they throw themselves away on fools like Leonard.' He became utterly silent after this outburst – for I think it could fairly be described as an outburst – but I felt a spring in my step as we made our way back to the Bower Lodging and our own rooms.

Grant was in ebullient spirits. 'I think this play's going to be quite something,' she said. 'They were rehearsing – just the principals, without the lords and attendants – and they're grand actors, all of them. Mr Dunstane has a presence I've not seen since my own father was in his prime and Miss

Byrne – you'll excuse me speaking freely, madam – but twenty years dropped off her when she was up on the stage. I had thought she would make a sight of herself as Lady M, but they dropped away. She'll be fine. And as for the man himself!'

'Macbeth?' I said.

'Ssh,' said Grant. 'Don't tempt the fates, madam. When the stage is out in an open courtyard, who knows what counts as the theatre. Don't tempt them.'

I changed the subject, for I have little patience with superstition and there were far fewer things in heaven and earth than Grant included in her personal philosophy. 'When do the full rehearsals start?' I said. 'With all the lords and attendants, as you say?'

'Tomorrow,' said Grant. 'So if I can leave you to shift for yourself tonight, madam, I'd be very grateful. I've got some sewing I want to do. I think I've got enough of that iridescent gauze to make beautiful costumes for the apparitions. There are only three after all.'

'But one of them's Roger,' I pointed out. Grant pursed her lips. Her loyalties were no longer mine. She was a member of the company of players and they could do no wrong.

In the great hall, the only room in the castle that would not have been turned into a crush by the assembled number, Grant's ebullience met its match amongst the newly arrived paying guests and the yet further swollen band of players. Mrs Rynsburger, having beat the other guests by a mere half day, was nevertheless lording it over them shamelessly, calling Pugh and Gilly by name as they passed with trays and making sure the newcomers were aware of the age of the castle and that this chamber was in its oldest surviving wing.

The newcomers, as might fairly be imagined, were disgusted to have such a notable new experience as a Scotch castle on the far side of the Atlantic presented to them as something already picked over and chewed into palatable titbits for them by an advance party. They deserted Mrs Rynsburger the way a flock of skittish sheep will desert an ill-trained collie, rushing in a solid block to the other end of the paddock – in this case to the far end of the hall – and sticking there glowering. I bore down on them, partly because Pugh was up that end with cocktails so cold the glasses were beaded with condensation, but also, partly, early training. This was a party and Minnie was a pal. If guests were glowering it was my job to make them smile again.

'Mrs Gilver,' I said, offering the nearest lady the hand that was not firmly wrapped around the stem of an icy-cold glass of something pink-coloured and fragrant.

'Are you an actress?' she said, predictably. She was quite as old as Mrs Rynsburger but put together along very different lines, with a cloud of yellow curls and a sweet dimpled face.

'Surely not, Trixie,' said another of the group, a tiny woman with a tight cap of white frizz on top of a face either suntanned or weather-beaten but certainly vastly different from 'Trixie's' pampered peaches and cream. 'She would be Miss if she were an actress.'

'Well,' said a third, this one very glamorous, although not actually pretty, 'there's Mrs Patrick Campbell.'

'I am not an actress,' I said. 'I'm a fellow guest. A friend of Minnie's. But I can introduce you to some of them.' I was aware that they were all looking beyond me now, to Moray Dunstane, Miss Byrne and a new arrival so dashing one almost believed he had a spotlight trained on him even in the murk of this gloomy chamber.

'Minnie is Mrs Bewer, isn't that right?' said the glamorous woman. 'Such extraordinary names these Brits go in for. I'm Mrs Jonathan Cornelius, Mrs Gilver. Clotilde Cornelius, of New York.'

'Trixie Westhousen,' said the dimpling woman with a shy dip of her head. 'Mrs Linus Westhousen. New York.'

'And I'm Mrs Schichtler,' said the tiny woman. 'But I

answer to Shichter, Shicker, Shiltzer, Schinkler . . . Call me Jesamond. It's easier.'

'Well, let me take you over and . . . ' I stopped dead. I was carefully brought up and beautifully finished off. I could introduce an under-ambassador to the widower of an earl's daughter without blinking, but I had no idea – given a band of travelling troubadours, there because the balcony dropped out of their theatre, and a gaggle of what were in essence, lodgers – who I should be presenting to whom.

Minnie was evidently in the same quandary but had solved it in the most remarkable way. Pugh padded to the middle of the floor with a little glockenspiel, such as one sees in opera house bars at the interval, which I thought was a nice touch on someone's part, and banged upon it until the chatter died to be replaced by an expectant hush.

'Ladies and gentlemen,' Bluey said, 'distinguished guests, acclaimed thespians, and gentlemen of the press, welcome to Castle Bewer.'

Alec caught my eye at his words and we both frowned. Right enough, though, there were a couple of slightly louche individuals skulking around the drinks table whom I had taken to be stagehands but who might well be newspapermen.

'Although this little party,' Bluey went on, 'is merely intended to show how thrilled Minnie and I are to have you here, we thought we might steal a march and make our introductions. Penny? If you're ready.'

I have never attended a Brownie Guide meeting, although I got close early in my marriage, when the village still believed I might be that kind of woman. On one occasion I only outwitted the local Brown Owl by hiding in a stable until she had given up and gone home. Nevertheless I imagined a gathering of the troupe would be something like this: everyone standing around in a ring while someone tried, in hearty tones, to make all believe that they were having tremendous fun.

Penny gave it her very best. She noted earlier triumphs for every one of the actors, even if some of them were the lowliest triumphs imaginable: our third witch had once played Miss Prism at Pitlochry, a man by the rather marvellous name of Paddy Ramekin, currently Banquo, Caithness and Seyton, had once reached the heights of Falstaff in Aberdeen; and both Max Moore, the dazzling individual who was Macbeth himself, and a girl who looked far too young and sweet to be Hecate, had appeared in the West End, plays and parts unnamed. It worked too; this flurry of accolades. I never did quite learn who everyone was and the honours just floated around the company in general, adding a little sparkle to all.

When every last thane had been awarded his polite round of applause, Minnie took over and gave the American ladies a tremendous fanfare, making New York sound like the seat of a cultural empire, with Boston not far behind, and conveying the distinct impression that Rynsburgers, Corneliuses, Westhousens and even Schichtlers – she managed the name without *quite* sounding as though she had swallowed a fly while bicycling – were responsible for most of the delights to be found there.

'And finally,' she rounded off, 'my dearest Penny, and my dearest Bluey will be your lecturers for the morning programmes, starting off tomorrow with "Castle Bewer and the Family Bewer through the Ages".' The visitors twittered with delight. Perhaps New York and Boston really are a great deal more cultured than London and Edinburgh, for I am sure none of my set could have greeted that announcement with anything but a long groan and a hasty excuse for absence.

'And we have one final introduction to make,' Minnie said. She had a fixed look upon her face and a slight heightening of her usual bonny colour across her cheeks. 'We are delighted to have with us Mrs Gilver and Mr Osborne, of Gilver and Osborne Investigations.' All four of the ladies swung round and stared at us, just as we swung and stared at Minnie. 'Mrs Gilver and Mr Osborne are here to oversee a very special treat we have laid on for you all.' Sweet Mrs Westhousen clapped her hands with a childlike glee, already thrilled, even before she knew what the treat was. My mind went briefly back to Alec's words about rich men and silly women, for Mrs Westhousen was a goose but the rings that twinkled on her hands as she clapped them spoke volumes about the absent Linus Westhousen of New York.

Minnie now strode over to a dark corner beyond the enormous fireplace where I had not noticed a cloth draped over an easel. 'Castle Bewer, like so many houses that have stood for centuries and seen their fortunes rise and fall, has its share of secrets,' she said. There was a strained quality to her voice.

'She's going to do it,' I murmured to Alec. 'Whatever it is they've been hemming and hawing about, they've hemmed their last haw. Here it comes.'

'And the greatest of these is . . . ' Minnie paused and grabbed a handful of the cloth in one hand '. . . the Briar Rose!' With a sharp tug, the cloth fell away to reveal a portrait. It was not Ottoline, but it was certainly the Cut Throat or Judas Jewel, now evidently rechristened yet again. The four ladies gathered in front of it, the overbearing Mrs Rynsburger forgiven and quite one of the flock again. The five ladies gathered, I should properly say, for I jostled right in beside them, craning for a look.

It was, at a guess, Richard's mother, sometime between her hasty marriage, ill-timed child, and untimely death. She sat in a chair so ornate I would have thought it a throne if I had seen this picture in some European musée. Her gown was of bottle-green velvet with a deep froth of creamy lace at the shoulders and it was the perfect foil for that lustrous cascade of blood red jewels. One of the newspapermen rushed over to the corner of the room where he had left his Box

Brownie and then fairly cantered to stand in front of the picture and begin snapping.

'Who was she? Briar Rose,' said Mrs Cornelius, her voice throaty as she drank in the beauty before her eyes.

'She was the doyenne of Castle Bewer,' Minnie said. 'My grandmother-in-law, although I never met her. Her name was Beulah and she was, as you can all see, a great beauty. She was also – and I think you can almost see this if you look very closely – quite, quite mad. Our very own Lady Macbeth, if you will.'

'Does she rest in peace?' said Mrs Rynsburger. I had to hand it to her; not many people could have heaped any more Gothic atmosphere on top of what Minnie was shovelling, but Mrs Rynsburger had managed it. Mrs Westhousen, her dimples quite gone, edged a little closer to her friends.

'She looks down on us all and laughs,' Minnie said. 'Because the secret of Castle Bewer, my dear ladies, is that naughty Beulah Bewer hid the Briar Rose and no one has ever found it.'

The actors, perhaps inured to dramatic effect, had been paying only the most desultory attention to Minnie's pronouncements so far but, at these words, all of them seemed to grow still and were suddenly as attentive as a litter of kittens watching a piece of string.

'We have searched over the years, of course,' Minnie said. 'We have knocked on walls and tapped on floors, we have pushed and pressed every bump and notch in the castle's carvings and now, this year, to celebrate the opening of our first summer of Shakespeare . . . we give up and declare open season.'

There was a stunned silence throughout the room. The company – guests and actors – stood frozen. The only things that moved were their eyes, but their eyes moved like a shoal of sardines scattering under a shark's shadow; darting and flashing into every corner, flitting back to the portrait and then whisking off again as each individual in the room took in the news. There was a fabulous treasure and its finder was its keeper.

'It's an unorthodox move,' said Bluey, with considerable understatement even for a Scottish gentleman, 'but to be frank we shan't be any worse off once some lucky treasure seeker has found it and borne it away.'

The other newspaperman was scribbling furiously in his shorthand notebook, a shine on his brow that was surely not only caused by the cocktails. He had come along to the castle to cover a very dull little affair and take no more exciting a snap than that of four middle-aged American ladies. He was going back to his office with a story he could send down the wire to Glasgow, Edinburgh, London and beyond.

'Mr Bewer,' said Mrs Cornelius. 'Do you really mean to tell us that you are opening a treasure hunt for this ruby necklace and whoever finds it is its new owner?'

'Exactly,' said Bluey. 'I couldn't have put it better myself. Anyone who buys a ticket to see the play is free to search.'

'Free to search anywhere?' said Mrs Westhousen. 'What about our bedrooms?'

'Your rooms have been searched already,' Bluey said. 'And will be under lock and key. Lock, key and patrol by the reputable firm of Gilver and Osborne. You have no need to worry.'

'It's true, Trixie,' said Mrs Rynsburger. 'That nice young man was in the closet when I arrived. I nearly jumped out of my skin and his explanation seemed unconvincing but it all makes sense now.'

'And you're happy to give up your inheritance?' said Mrs Cornelius, turning to Penny.

'I've never seen it,' Penny said. 'It's been lost since before I was born so I'm not giving up that much really.'

'Another round of cocktails, Pugh,' Minnie said. 'Please, everyone, carry on and enjoy the party.' The newspapermen sped off as soon as the words had left her lips, jamming into the doorway together in a dead heat, but everyone else was delighted to accept another of the pink-coloured drinks and flutter about like budgerigars, twittering and chattering, as though some director had given them moves and lines and rehearsed them for weeks on end to perform the perfect successful cocktail party. I had seen nothing like it for at least ten years.

While it fizzed and buzzed all around I bore down on Minnie, meeting Alec, who was arriving at her other side.

'Well?' she said. 'Is it our masterstroke or evidence that we have lost our senses?'

'Both,' Alec said. 'It's mad and you'll be overrun.'

Minnie gave a great gusting sigh as the fretting of weeks and months finally left her. 'Oh!' she said. 'We did hope so. We just didn't quite dare to believe so. But look at them all, They're enchanted. We'll be a smash hit. Even with gloomy *Macbeth* instead of magical *Midsummer*. We'll be turning them away at the gate.'

'And what does Ottoline think?' I said, the cold spoon in the soufflé.

Minnie's smile dimmed a little. 'Yes, Ottoline,' she said. 'But we can't just sit by and do nothing while it all falls apart, can we? I'm afraid the cost of living so long is that one sees the world change around one. I hope to get to her age and be undone by the dreadful things Penny gets up to. What else can any of us hope for, really?'

'Where is Otto, anyway?' I said. 'I thought she was coming down for the party.'

'Oh, she's here somewhere,' Minnie said, waving a vague hand. 'But it's one of the boons of her deafness. She can be in the room and one never has to be worried about what one says.'

Alec and I shared a stricken look and, at that moment, as a clutch of young actresses – witches I rather thought, from

Penny's introductions – moved out of the way, we all saw Ottoline, sitting in a chair against the wall, the very chair, or its twin, that had been rendered in oils in Beulah's wedding portrait. Her head was resting against the high back and could not be comfortable with all that carving. Her mouth had dropped open. I hoped she was sleeping but I feared, hurrying forwards, that she had fainted. I prayed, as I drew close to her, that she had not died.

II

She had *not* died. Nor had she fainted or fallen asleep. She had simply closed her eyes in disbelief and let her reeling head fall back for a moment until it stilled again. She stood up as soon as I reached her side and bade me in a hissed whisper to take her to her room and tell Minnie she would dine off a tray there.

'Unspeakable!' she spat out as we stalked away through the passages back to her quarters. The stalking of a ninety-year-old woman is no less furious for being rather slow-paced and so she was leaning heavily upon me. 'Unspeakable!' she repeated. 'What is Minnie thinking?'

'I'd say it's a bit of a brainwave,' I told her. 'Especially if the Cut-Jud-Bri- . . . if the necklace is long gone. No one will find it and spoil the fun.'

'But you didn't hear them!' Otto insisted. 'Not the American visitors. They are wealthy and bejewelled enough already. Besides being stout and unwilling to besmirch themselves with castle dust. But those girls – penniless actresses all – they mean to make a job of it! They'll pull the place down around our ears. I heard one of them talk of hollow pockets in the joints of the roof timbers. And another said that chimney bricks as old as ours are never mortared. They'll *burn* the place down if they start knocking out chimney bricks. Or they'll bring it tumbling down like Jericho. Oh, what is she thinking?'

'Now, Ottoline please,' I said, stroking her arm and finding a soothing voice from who knows where for, in all honesty, I agreed with her. 'Of course the actresses are excited and a-twitter. But they will be far too busy to go dismantling roofs and draining the moat. They'll be pre-occupied with the play. It'll be a ten-minute wonder with them. Just you wait and see. As soon as the second or third batch of day-trippers is in here the players will want to be above it all – drawling about what a bore it all is and how gullible the paying public are. I promise you. Just wait and see.'

If anything, though, my words produced an even greater state of alarm than she had reached already. Perhaps she had not considered that wave upon wave of treasure seekers would be bearing down. She looked at me with trembling lips and stark eyes and said in a tiny voice: 'You won't help them, will you? You won't actually make suggestions and pass on tips?'

'Heavens no,' I assured her. 'One wouldn't want to make later arrivals feel the lake had been fished out. In fact, I think I shall say to Minnie that the hunters should be sworn to secrecy.'

'Will you keep searching as well?' said Ottoline. 'Or will you leave it to the . . . what did you call them? Treasure seekers.'

I considered it for a minute as we arrived at her door and she toddled over to her customary chair and footstool, drop-ping into it with a great groan of relief. 'I need to examine my conflicting sets of orders,' I said at last, 'but I rather think I shall carry on. I need to be able to say hand on heart to His Majesty's exchequer that I've looked and, apart from anything else . . . imagine if I found it!'

'It would spoil Minnie's plan,' Otto said, rather sourly.

'But if Minnie and Bluey had that fabulous jewel to sell they could afford a few trinkets to stash here and there just to keep the seekers keen. In fact, I think I'll suggest that anyway. A little silver locket with something mysterious and ancient inside. It doesn't have to be precious. A scrap of cloth from an old . . . I say, you don't still have trunks of clothes in the attic from the times these portraits were painted, do you? Beulah's and your own. A scrap of the pink satin or the green velvet in a silver locket would make a nice find.'

Otto's look had soured even more until she seemed, sitting there, like the very last of a bad batch of prunes. 'Of course not,' she said. 'Those frocks were turned and turned again, re-trimmed and handed on, then they went for petticoats and bed jackets when they were done. I thought you were brought up well enough to know that.'

'Of course,' I said, deflated but unchastened. 'Of course I was. I can't say I mourn those days, but you're right about them.'

I had *loathed* those days; walking into a dance in a gown 'turned and turned again and re-trimmed' and knowing that everyone knew. My mother had always claimed otherwise but by the time I was eighteen I could tell a new gown from an old faithful and so could every other girl in the room. Grant was the only one I knew who mourned the practice; for it was a great test of a maid's ingenuity and it was responsible for quite a chunk of a lady's maid's high wage, back in the old days. I smiled to think of her delight at turning the planned fairy wings into apparitions' weeds overnight in time for the dress rehearsal tomorrow.

'What are you grinning about?' said Ottoline. 'What are you plotting *now* and smirking so slyly about?'

I simply helped her off with her high-heeled shoes and put her stockinged feet up on their hassock. She was not really being disagreeable to me, I knew. She was merely tired and old and had had a new fright on top of a few days of too many surprises.

'I'll send Mrs Ellen up, shall I?' I said.

'Gilly!' said Ottoline. 'Send the girl.'

I supposed Mrs Ellen with her gloomy voice and her love of gossip would not be as soothing even if she was a family retainer of long years. I closed the door softly and went to fetch 'the girl'.

Dinner should have been entertaining, with all the excitement of the treasure hunt still at work in the company, but I had the great misfortune to be seated between two of the lesser actors. The American guests were given the plums, of course: Bluey, grand old Moray Dunstane and dashing Max Moore. I was left with George Bull and Robert Roberts who were exactly as thrilling as their names suggested. They spoke at length about their parts in the play, which were Lennox and Ross. These were two characters regarding whom I could not have dredged up a single word if my life depended upon it, but Mr Bull and Mr Roberts waxed on as though they had taken to the stage purely in hopes that one day they would get to sink their teeth into those very roles. Oh, the exquisite challenge of bringing these vital men to life! The length of Lennox's longest speech, upon which the play – it seemed – was to pivot! The mystery of Ross's scene with the Old Man upon which the play – it seemed – was to pivot again! The very precise challenge to an actor's diction of delivering such lines as 'Thence I go thither' and 'Hence I come hither' effectively.

'Without making anyone lau—?' I said, before I managed to stop myself. 'Or do you mean they're a tongue twister? But surely Macbeth's "with his surcease success" is the worst trap waiting for anyone in any play ever? She sells seashells, practically.'

Roberts and Bull treated me to a pair of withering looks and I gathered that when one is conversing with lowly lords and messengers one is expected to pretend the Macbeths and the rest do not exist, or only to provide a setting.

With my brick dropped, the two men proceeded to talk across me, showing off their superior knowledge of 'the play', 'the bard', 'the folio' and making chortling references to 'notorious' scholarly questions I had never heard of and did not care to.

It was utter tedium to my ears and only when Leonard shouted down half the length of the table and across the centrepiece too did I pay a scrap of attention to it.

'We are not changing the words of the greatest dramatist who ever lived!' he thundered. 'And poet,' he added, taking away quite a bit of the force of his words and, in my opinion, proving that he was neither. 'He is a man for all time and his words will be spoken as he wrote them this summer in Scotland as they were during the first season in London in 1606!' He tossed his hair back and stared down his nose at the two men, his eyes cold and glassy.

'But that's the whole point,' said George Bull, doggedly. 'They're not. They weren't. They can't be. The words we use were written after his death and not until 1623. We should go *back* to his own true words if he's the greatest—'

'What's this about?' I asked Miss Tavelock, leaning around Mr Robert's back, since he was leaning so far forward to shout up to Leonard. Manners had been suspended, clearly.

'Oh,' she said, flapping a weary hand at me. 'Don't get me started. Leonard is mad for his precious first folio. The first collected works,' she added, at my blank look. 'And George is quite right about it. It's pretty good on most of the plays but *Macbeth* is a mess. It's got songs added that hadn't even been written when Shakespeare dreamed up this play and I think they dropped the pages and bundled them back together in haste. Lady Macduff is straightforward enough, thank heavens, but some of the men's lines are . . . Oh, Lord it's too dull for words but someone talks about something before it's happened and no one can ever work out if the battle's been or is still to come.'

'Ah,' I said. 'Well, yes, it does seem rather silly not to tidy things up if they're in a muddle.'

Miss Tavelock smirked. '*I* think so. But don't ask me to

agree with you if Leonard's listening. Penny will back me up.' She leaned across and hailed her. 'Penny? Isn't Leonard peculiar about his "texts"?'

Penny gave her mouth a rueful twist. 'Men *can* be fierce about such silly things sometimes. But what harm does it do?'

I wiggled my eyebrows at her in what I hoped was a diplomatic but unmistakable reply and, once again, I wondered to myself how firmly stuck on Leonard she really was. She spoke of him with the exasperation of a wife not the adoration of a fiancée. And she spoke with just that practical, sensible air Alec always claims he is looking for in a woman. I turned to see if he was, by any chance, watching her – for she was very pretty in the candlelight and although we had not changed and her shoulders were hidden, her hair unornamented and her face shining with soap instead of gleaming with clever swipes of subtle colour the way girls' faces are at dinner now – she was still rather beguiling.

Alec, however, was sitting quite still and straight, looking neither to right nor to left; not even entertaining his neighbours, who were talking round him. He was certainly not craning up the table to drink in the sight of Miss Bewer.

'What was wrong with you at dinner?' I said, once the gentlemen had joined the ladies in the drawing room again. They had come swiftly, Bluey perhaps fearing for his cellars if the company of players spent too long over the port. 'You looked as though you'd seen a ghost. Or bitten down on a piece of shot.'

'Yes,' said Alec. 'I was chasing a wisp.'

I took in a sharp breath. 'Did you catch it?'

'Does one ever?' he said, and I groaned. There is much of the detective life that I enjoy, such as righting wrongs, and much that I abhor, such as fielding untruths and batting them back to their tellers who are invariably belligerent at being caught. There is just one aspect of our trade that I find in-furiating and that is when one knows – knows without doubt – that one has missed something. I do my very best to avoid the sensation by feverishly writing down every word spoken, every look thrown, every move made and unmade, every smile and frown and scowl that flits like a cloud across every face. I record all in my little notebook and am roundly scoffed at for my troubles. Yet still I manage to miss things and so am condemned to the limbo state that Alec found himself in now: knowing that somewhere there is a loose thread and that I have smoothed it instead of tugging.

Alec screwed his face up in a grimace. 'It was something someone did, or words someone spoke perhaps, that seemed like nothing, until someone else said something else and it struck me as a kind of echo.'

'Let it go and it will pop into your head unbidden,' I advised. Alec stood and went to fetch himself another drink from Pugh, who was presiding over the decanters and glower-ing at the actors and actresses as if with every drop of whisky they were taking food from the mouth of a starving babe. He managed to clear the drawing room by ten o'clock and I am sure I saw Bluey shoot him a grateful look as the last of them trailed away.

'I'm just going to look in on Mama,' Minnie said, standing. 'I felt a sweep for tiring her with that party, but I hope dinner in her room has left her feeling a little better.'

'She was quite a bit brighter already when I stopped in on the way down,' Bluey said. 'But she did say quite firmly that she wasn't to be disturbed again. So I would leave it, Min. Pop in before breakfast instead, eh?'

Penny, to my astonishment, was tidying the drawing room, gathering glasses and tipping ashtrays into the dying fire, before stacking them near the door.

'If my mother could see you, Penny darling,' Minnie said, 'she'd have twenty fits. Dandy, do your boys . . . what's equivalent for boys of my daughter acting like a nippy at the end of her shift?'

'Oh, Mother,' Penny said. 'Gilly and Mrs Ellen have enough to do.'

'Absolutely,' I said. 'I saw Donald in the stable yard busy filling up the petrol tank of his motorcar with a can and a funnel just the other day. And Teddy can iron a shirt. He's been on the wrong side of his scout so many times over parties and what have you that he's had to learn or go around crumpled. Mind you, it's an electric iron and I try not to think about it for I'm sure he might just as easily burn down the college as not.'

'Ironing!' said Minnie. 'What next?'

'I can iron,' Penny said. 'I can iron a Tudor ruff made of nasty artificial wool and starch it stiff enough for five acts of *Henry VIII*.'

'And one notable day,' I said, butting in before Minnie started nagging Penny again, 'he ironed the frock of one of his chums' sisters who was up on a visit without her maid.' I frowned, remembering. 'Rather a worrying lot of postcards went back and forth after that as I remember, but then she met a guardsman and ironing went out the window.'

Alec was staring at me slack-jawed. I would have liked to believe he was chasing another wisp, but I suspected he was marvelling at my inanity.

I raised my stock a little by letting him overhear me telling Minnie my brainwave about the silver lockets and scraps of stuff inside them. She leapt on it and immediately improved it, which pleased Alec even more. Really, our rivalry outdoes even that of my sons when they were little; and, once, they competed in the matter of who could consume more hard-boiled eggs on a picnic, which ended the picnic abruptly as I recall.

'Oh, yes, Dandy!' Minnie said. 'But instead of scraps of satin and velvet – for that's almost misleading, wouldn't you say? – what about dried wildflowers? A little cornflower or a single rosebud in a locket would appeal to the romantic in us all.'

'Can you dry some in time?' I asked.

Minnie gave me a sheepish grin. 'I have drawers full from when Penny was little,' she told me. 'She was a great drier and presser of flowers and never tired of presenting them to me. We can rummage out some of the less mouldy ones, can't we Penny darling?'

With that they were chums again and I took myself off to bed, unable to face another chapter in the day's events, should the chumminess prove unlasting.

Grant, as she had forewarned me, was not in evidence and so I bumbled around on my own, tangling my bracelets and scraping my scalp, once quite badly, as I tried to affix my pins for the night. Soon enough though I was tucked up with the curtains open to the moonlight and applied myself to missing Bunty for a minute or two before I felt sleep steal over me.

My dreams were disordered, as always when a case starts to knit itself around me. I dreamed of Leonard marching about a stage with a sheaf of letters in his hands, bellowing at the actors to stop reordering the words of the great man. Minnie was there, cutting little squares of canvas out of Beulah's portrait and poking them into lockets which creaked open and snapped shut like the visors of armoured knights. I was hauling myself around in that dreadful treacly attempt at rushing, where the world has turned to quicksand and one cannot get where one is trying to go. 'No!' I cried out. 'Stop it!' quite without knowing what it was they were doing that had to be stopped. When the screaming started it was a relief to waken.

I knew at once who it was, not only from the direction of the noise but also because only one person in the whole of the Bower Lodging had the stature to produce such a resonant and lusty bellow. Mrs Rynsburger, out of her corsets and able, therefore, to fill her deep chest to its pit, was screaming holy murder and seemed disinclined to stop. I leapt out of bed and, snatching at my wrap, thundered barefoot along the passageway to her bedroom.

She was sitting up in bed, the bedclothes clutched at her chin and one finger pointing wildly into a dark corner.

'A ghost, a ghost, a ghost!' she sang out at the top of her lungs. It was operatic in tone and in the rising pitch of each repetition, but it sounded quite sincere.

I rounded to face the corner but saw nothing. There was a door, locked up tight although no key or bolt could be seen on this side, and not so much as a billowing curtain or patch of reflected moonlight to explain her fright.

'It's gone now, Mrs Rynsburger,' I said. 'Can I fetch you a glass of water?'

She looked almost as aghast at my inadequate response as she had been at her vision, but thankfully at that moment the other three arrived: little Mrs Schichtler in just a white nightgown and bed cap, looking like Clara in Act I of *The Nutcracker*, dashing Mrs Cornelius in a black satin dressing gown with a dragon on the back, and sweet Mrs Westhousen in quilted pink with matching slippers and, surprisingly, a poker in her hands. She was holding it like a baseball bat, which is to say much like a cricket bat but with greater determination.

'What happened, Hetty?' demanded Mrs Cornelius. 'You look terrible!'

'I saw a ghost,' said Mrs Rynsburger. 'In that corner over there.' Again she pointed. The three women huddled a little closer to her bedside, a little further away from the shadowy corner.

'Oh Hetty,' said Mrs Schichtler. 'Come away with us in case it comes back.'

I suddenly felt I might swoon. The three women, gathered

139

together, and Mrs Rynsburger regaling them suddenly brought the play to mind. Hecate and her visions. Her three weird sisters beckoning her to come away, come away. A shudder strong enough to make me take a balancing step passed through me.

'What did it look like, Mrs Rynsburger, and what did it do?' I asked. If she had said it looked 'vaporous' or that it hung in the air and then vanished I think I might have fainted dead away. She did not.

'It looked like a ghost,' she said. 'A shining ghost, lurching about like Frankenstein's monster.'

'Shining?' I said, a dreadful notion beginning to creep up on me.

'Shining as bright as the moon,' said Mrs Rynsburger. 'And lurching.'

I rattled the door again and felt high and low for a bolt. Then a soft cough came from just outside the room in the passageway.

'Do I have your permission to enter, Mrs Rynsburger?' Alec said.

'The more the merrier,' the lady cried. She had recovered her good spirits now, surrounded by her friends and being the centre of attention. Alec's arrival was a delight to her. He sidled in, rather hilariously gave a small bow to the four ladies – as though very stiff manners could offset the dressing gowns – and then joined me.

'What's on the other side of this door?' I asked him. 'Can you remember, from your sketch plans?'

'A staircase that leads from the kitchen corridor up to the far end of the book room,' Alec said. 'Don't you remember? There's a door set into the wall halfway up a flight.'

'And where's the key? Presumably not on the other side? Perhaps Pugh keeps it.'

'Key?' said Mrs Rynsburger. 'It was a ghost, I tell you. It had no need of keys.'

140

'It had no need of doors, come to that,' Alec pointed out.

'But if the person lived here in his life he would always have used that door and be in the habit,' she countered.

'Do you think he was showing you the way to the treasure?' said Mrs Cornelius, and now she too came to give the door a good shove and a rattle of its handle.

'Was it definitely a man?' I asked. Mrs Rynsburger frowned with her eyes closed for a moment and then nodded.

'Most definitely,' she said. 'A shining, lurching man.'

Her companions shuddered at the words and to be fair she did give them a sepulchral swoop as she spoke them but I had made my mind up and was feeling grim. 'Where shall you spend the rest of the night, Mrs Rynsburger?' I said. 'Do you want to swap with me?'

'You can't—' she began, but Mrs Westhousen interrupted her.

'You stay put, Hetty,' she said, 'but let me join you.' She twirled the poker and her sweet face was even grimmer than mine. 'I didn't always live in New York City,' she said. 'And I married very well.'

She looked so determined that I felt safe to leave Mrs Rynsburger in her hands and, as Alec and I made our way out, the others were fussing over both of them, offering to fetch flasks 'for the shock' and plumping pillows.

'What I'd like to know is where the devil are the Bewers?' Alec said. 'Or can't they hear what goes on in this wing from theirs?'

'And what *I'd* like to know is whether Penny colluded with whoever it was and, if not, how he got the key.'

'*What?*' Alec said.

'If I find out Grant's in on it, I shall send her home and dock her wages,' I said. 'Unforgivable.'

'Dandy, what are you talking about?'

'Oh this place!' I cried out. 'What's the quickest way down to the kitchen from here?' Alec put a hand under my elbow and ushered me through a series of anterooms and across one corner of the great hall to a short straight staircase that led down to the passageway we had entered on our first day. 'What I'm talking about is Grant's iridescent gauze for the apparitions' costumes. She was working on it tonight and I gather she's had a fitting. When Mrs Rynsburger said she saw a ghost, she was speaking the truth, you see.'

There was a bright light showing around the edges of the kitchen door and I sprang forward and threw it open, striding into the room and crying out, 'Aha! Red-handed.'

12

My entrance revealed a gaggle of players lounging up and down both sides of the long kitchen table, which bore many stone bottles of beer and several stout brown pots of tea as well as a good new loaf, badly hacked into rough slices, and a pot of jam with the breadknife sticking up out of it. None of the principal actors was there, but Leonard sat at the head of the long board, in what I took to be Pugh's Windsor chair, with Penny on his lap. Despite that, my eyes were all for the tableau on the hearthrug: Grant on her knees with a mouthful of pins and Roger, boots off and trousers rolled to the knees, swathed in gauze. Hardly ghostly but certainly shining.

'Where are the other two apparitions?' I said. 'I take it you've finished with them, Grant, have you?'

'Miles and Tansy?' said Leonard.

'I don't know their names,' I snapped.

'Is something amiss, madam?' said Grant, infuriatingly. I ignored her.

'And Penny, do you know where the keys are to the unused doors in the castle? Are they all kept together?'

'What's happened, Mrs Gilver?' Penny said, sliding from her perch.

'Mischief,' I said. 'I assume you don't know about it? Weren't part of the planning of it?'

Penny gave me a look of wide-eyed innocence, but I did not forget that she had theatrical training.

'Someone entered the bedroom of one of the paying guests

and pretended to haunt her,' I said. Leonard chuckled but I was pleased to see a frown on Penny's face.

'One of the Americans?' she said. 'Is she kicking up a ruckus? Do the others know? Oh Lord, is she *leaving*?'

'She kicked up a terrific ruckus and yes the others know,' I said crisply, 'but thankfully no. She is not leaving. She has decided she believes in it and thinks it came to show her where the treasure was hidden. Now, the keys?'

There was a board in Pugh's pantry, Penny told me, and a set of spares locked away in her father's book room. Beyond that, Pugh had what he needed by way of cellar, silver store and jewellery safe; Mrs Ellen kept her own selection handy for the store rooms; and Mrs Porteous was in charge of the larders and icehouse.

As Alec went off to check on the whereabouts of the Second Apparition and Penny to see if the Third Apparition had gone straight to bed after her fitting as she had announced, I was pantry bound.

Thankfully, Pugh was still up, sitting looking fairly orderly except for his feet being eased out of his shoes and his collar being unbuttoned with his tie pulled a little way down.

'Pugh,' I said, 'I think someone might be scampering about where they shouldn't be.'

He turned down his mouth at the corners, as though his face needed any more lugubriousness, and shrugged. 'House parties for you,' he said.

'Good grief,' I said, 'I don't mean— No, but I think one of the actors was in the guest wing. The Bower Lodging.'

Again, Pugh shrugged. 'They're all guests,' he said. 'If they want to go a-wandering I can hardly stop them.'

I tried a third time. 'I rather think,' I said, 'that someone has pilfered one of your master keys.'

That did the trick. Pugh rose up like a whale breaking the waters and, shoving his feet back into his shoes and yanking his tie back up his neck, he bustled over to his locked key board. It took less than the blink of an eye before he fell back again – actually fell back – and leaned against the wall with relief.

'All present and correct,' he said. 'Going worrying me like that!'

'Are you sure?' I said. 'Do you know the keys off by heart then? Which one fits the door between the staircase and the Gateway Chamber? You know the door I mean; halfway round one of the spiral flights where one would have to take a hop, skip and jump to get through it.'

Pugh was frowning at me. 'That door's never used,' he said.

'And the key?' I asked him, hiding my exasperation.

Pugh put his finger on it without a second's hesitation. It was a large iron affair hanging with two more of similar age and size and, even without close examination, I could tell that all three had been there undisturbed for quite some time. There was a layer of dust on them and the barrels were dull and dark, not a single bright scratch to show recent employment.

'Can you tell me where in Mr Bewer's book room the other key to that door is kept?' I said.

Pugh emanated grievance and outrage better than any butler I had ever come across, and it is one of a butler's special talents to do so.

'There's another board like this one here, isn't there?' he said, huffily. 'At the back of the last bay with the Romans and Greeks.'

'And the keys are in the same arrangement?' I said, counting two down and three along to fix it in my brain where I should be looking.

'Exactly,' said Pugh. 'This is an orderly house we run here. But Mr Bewer's book room will be locked up for the night, madam, if Mr Bewer has gone up. It'll be locked tight.' He could not have sounded more pleased to be thwarting me.

I simply gave him what I hoped was a withering look and helped myself to the small key, plainly marked 'book room', from three pegs down on the board.

Pugh insisted on accompanying me. His dour presence at my side, his plodding gait, and his utter lack of a single word of conversation meant that I was soon sunk in a gloom to match his own. Even if I solved this little puzzle of Mrs Rynsburger's ghost, I thought to myself, it would not help me with the overarching mystery. It would only turn the players against me for spoiling their fun and that would make my task harder still.

So I was looking at the floor as we arrived on the library corridor and would have missed the sight if Pugh, beside me, had not drawn in a sharp gasp. When he did so, I glanced up just in time to catch a glimpse of someone disappearing around the far end and making towards the gallery. Mrs Rynsburger was exactly right: the figure was shining as it lurched away.

'Hey,' I said. 'You there. Stop!' I gave chase, calling over my shoulder to Pugh to check the keys, for it seemed to me that this 'shining ghost' might well have just left the book room after returning one.

When I reached the gallery door there was no sight of him anywhere in the huge empty room and I stood still for a moment watching the shadows from the dying fire leap and dance across the portraits, seeming to make expressions cross those flat painted faces for the first time in centuries. I padded to the centre of the room, still listening, and was rewarded with three little sounds in quick succession: a door let bang, a whispered shush and a smothered giggle. I took off again, slipping through an archway into a corridor I had not entered before and following the source of the sound, which I thought had come from above me. I rounded a turn in the stairway and ducked, sure that something was about to hit me. When nothing did, I straightened and then immediately ducked again as once more a black shape seemed to come straight at me. It happened a third time and now, emboldened, I stood tall and tried to decide what the strange flit of shadow was. Then I had it. Someone was racing up the stairs and every time he passed a candle sconce his shadow was thrown back down to taunt me. I gathered up the skirts of my dressing gown and set off after him.

The stair narrowed and the steps grew more and more bowed and slippery the further up we flew, until at last the stones were so close around us that I could hear his ragged breath and I am sure he could mine. I was just beginning to wonder where he was going and to ask myself if it really could be one of the actors, who had been here only a day and could not have memorised the layout of this turret, so far from his own lodgings, when there was a knocking sound above and then a gasp and, before I could brace myself, a bundle of shining tatters and flags came plunging towards me. I caught it in my arms, teetered, put one foot down one stair, teetered again, then somehow we managed to find our four feet and stand steady.

'It's you, Mrs Gilver,' the bundle said, panting a little as she spoke.

'And it's you too, Tansy,' I said, recognising the apparition as one of the witches. 'What are you doing?'

'Running away from whoever was chasing me,' she said. 'If I'd known it was you I wouldn't have given myself such a stitch.' As if to lend credence to her claim she pressed a hand to her side and bent over awkwardly, there on the shallow, bowed stairs.

'I called out,' I said to her. 'I don't have the most mellifluous voice ever but I surely don't sound like some kind of ruffian, do I?'

'I didn't hear you calling,' she said. She stared at me out of her large eyes, her face like that of a choirboy: perfectly solemn and fooling no one. Choirboys are notorious for hi-jinks in their stalls while they sing like angels.

147

'But what are you *doing*?' I said again.

'Going to bed after my fitting,' she said. 'Why?'

'From the kitchen to the players' lodging via the book room?'

'Book room?' she said. Her eyes were so wide that even in the very dim light of this turret top I could see the whites all around.

'Well, gallery corridor anyway,' I said, flustered. For of course it was true that she had been a long way from the book room when I saw her. 'Look, let's get down from this eyrie before one of us falls to our death, shall we?'

She made her light-footed way, leaving me to pick my rather more ponderous way down after her.

'Did you want to see me for some reason, Mrs Gilver?' she said when we were one landing down, onto better steps and could make faster progress.

'I wanted to catch whoever was dashing about dressed as an apparition,' I said, wondering if her act of innocence could possibly be sincere.

'To ask me something?'

I hesitated. I did not want to appear foolish, accusing her of mischief when I had no proof. Gratifyingly, my hesitation bore fruit. As I followed her down a further turn in the stairs a voice hallooed from a fair distance off.

'There you are! I thought you'd fallen down an oubliette or something. Look, let's call it a night, shall we? They're all abed and it's no fun haunting if there's no one to scare.'

Tansy made some kind of furious gesture that was hard to interpret from behind but which I guessed was an attempt to shut the man up. I came around the corner of the staircase and into the light while he was still talking.

'Mr . . . ' I said.

'McEwan,' he said. 'Miles McEwan. Donalbain, Menteith, Murderer, and Apparition. At your service.' He executed a bow with a heel click, the sharp movement making his shimmering costume dazzle in the candlelight.

148

'Now look, you two,' I said. 'I am going to have to insist on complete candour. Tansy, you're not in trouble but you must come clean.' It was like talking to a small child and, like a small child, Tansy scowled and drew her brows down. I waited in silence and eventually she puffed out a sigh.

'Oh very well then,' she said. 'Yes, when Delia finished us off we decided to have a bit of fun on the way to the wardrobe room. Why be in a castle in the dead of night dressed as a ghost and not do a bit of flitting about and moaning?'

'And the key?' I said.

Mr McEwan and Miss Bell exchanged a look and somehow came to the agreement that Mr McEwan was to be the spokesman.

'What key?' he said.

'The key kept in the book room that opens the unused door halfway up the stair to the Bower Lodging,' I said.

'What?' McEwan said, giving me a look of deep puzzlement. I was not to be caught with the same trick twice in such quick succession, however, and I took them each firmly under the elbow and marched them to where Pugh stood waiting in the open book-room door. He had a large key in his hand, held aloft like a torch. As I drew near I could see from the fresh, silvery marks on its barrel that it had been used very recently, that it had been scraped and scratched while turning a stiff lock. Just the sort of lock – unoiled and dusty – one would expect in a seldom-opened door.

'Aha!' I said. 'Did you find it back on the key board, Pugh?'

'I did, madam,' Pugh said. 'And I took it to the door in question and checked that it was working. It turned as nice as nice and back again, not so much as a squeak.'

'Oh,' I said. 'You did, did you? I don't suppose you gave it a close look, beforehand by any chance?'

'Close look?' said Pugh. 'What for? Best way to try out a key is to stick it in the lock, madam. No point just gawping at it, is there?'

No *more* point berating him for his dull wits, I thought to myself, especially since I had not mentioned the need to study the key while we were plodding through the house towards it.

'Very good, Pugh,' I said. He recognised the dismissal and took himself off. Tansy and Miles were close to giggles. I was not entirely sure what was entertaining them so – their ghostly garb, the solemn Pugh with his hangdog look, or the thought that they had got away with something. But I am sure that my matronly 'very good, Pugh' was part of the fun and it made my heart sink a little to be old enough to give young-sters giggling fits the way drawing masters used to dissolve my brother, my sister and me.

'Do I have your word,' I said to them, 'that you did not open a door into Mrs Rynsburger's bedroom and go in to frighten her?'

'I didn't,' Miles said. 'Go into a lady's bedroom who hadn't asked me?'

'Stop being silly,' I said and was gratified that his face straightened and his next words were sincere.

'I mean it, Mrs Gilver,' he said. 'I need this job. I wouldn't risk getting the sack bothering the guests of honour like that.'

I turned to Tansy. 'What about you?'

'I might have if I'd thought of it,' she said, 'but I didn't know where the keys were kept till you and Mr Pugh told us both just then.' She gave me an impish look, but as I drew breath to reprimand her we all heard something, faint but unmistakable, that put thoughts of mischief out of our minds.

'Help,' came the voice. 'Minnie! Bluey! Help.'

It was impossible to tell from where in the castle the feeble cry came – whether up chimney or down slop chute, in or out of open windows or across rooftops – but there was only one person within these walls, besides Alec and me, who called Minnie and Bluey 'Minnie' and 'Bluey'.

'Ottoline!' I cried and took off at a run.

Alec and Penny got there just before Tansy, Miles and me.

I arrived in time to see Alec shove Penny behind him quite roughly and burst into Otto's bedroom.

'I'm here, Mrs Bewer,' he said. 'Help is at hand. What's the matter?'

'Isn't he decisive?' Penny said. I could not tell if her tone was wry or enraptured. I gave a quick knock on the half-open door and strode in. The room was in darkness except for the embers of a very smoky fire.

'Just me,' I said. 'What is it, Otto? Have you seen something?'

'Someone was in here!' Ottoline said. She was standing by her bedside, evidently having leapt out in fright, and she looked terribly wobbly and frail. As I gave her my arm to help her back in, I cast my eye around wondering if there were unused doors in this room too. I saw none but even still I turned to Penny and said in a low voice, 'Find Roger, please. I want to know where he is and if he's still got his apparition costume on.'

'Roger?' said Penny. 'Why?'

'Ottoline,' I said. 'Did you see something you thought was a ghost? It was probably just one of the company playing a trick on you.'

'*Was it a ghost, Granny?*' shouted Penny.

'A ghost?' said Ottoline. 'Fiddlesticks to ghosts. I'm talking about a burglar. Penny, go and tell Pugh to shut the gatehouse door. Someone was in my room and has stolen away my reticule. My little evening bag. It's gone.'

'I'll go with you,' said Mr McEwan. 'You shouldn't be racing about this place on your own, Penny, if there's someone on the prowl.'

'And I'll come too, I think,' said Tansy, who I am sure wanted only to escape me and any further scolding.

'Oh stuff!' said Penny. 'I think Mrs Gilver's probably right and it was Roger having fun in his wraith's wrappings. *Granny, the actors have been larking about a bit.*'

'It was a burglar!' said Ottoline again. 'Tell Pugh to shut the gatehouse door and tell your parents to telephone the police.'

'Raise the drawbridge!' McEwan cried.

Otto started speaking then coughed and coughed and finally said, in a ragged voice: 'The bridge doesn't draw. Hasn't for years. Penny, why are you still standing there like a lump? Go!'

Penny gave me a panicked look and I tried, although my lack of theatrical training was a handicap, to gesture to her that her grandmother was upset and must be soothed, but that the police could wait awhile until we were sure what had happened. I am not certain how much of my mugging and grimacing Penny could decipher but she left, taking Tansy and Miles with her.

'What exactly did you see, Ottoline?' I asked once the three of us were alone.

'A strange man in my bedroom,' Otto snapped. 'Aren't you listening?'

'Did he climb in the window?' Alec said, going over to the casement which stood wide open with the curtains pushed back.

'What? No. How? *What?*' said Ottoline, irritable now that the danger was gone. I guessed that she was embarrassed to have cried out in such a dramatic way, for she was brought up on the same repressive principles as me, even more so because a generation earlier.

'Why isn't it fastened?' Alec said. I joined him and looked out. A sheer wall stretched down to the moat below, without a single ledge or anywhere that could serve as a foothold.

'Ha,' Ottoline said. 'It's standing wide open because that stupid girl made a mess of my fire and I had to stop myself choking on the smoke.' She gave another little cough in emphasis to her words. 'And a very good thing, as it turned out, because if I had been more comfortable I would have been fast asleep and I'd never have known he was here.'

'And you say he took your evening bag?' I said. 'That's all?'

'Isn't that enough?' Ottoline demanded.

'Where was it?' I asked her. Alec was busy lighting lamps and when he turned up the gas I saw that Ottoline was quite right to deplore the fire Gilly had laid, for wisps of smoke were drifting lazily across the room on the shifting air and even I coughed a little, from sheer suggestibility.

'It was on my dressing table there,' Ottoline said, pointing. 'I had set it there to take down before I decided to dine in my room.'

I checked down each side of the table and then in the small space between its glass top and the bottom of the mirror, but there was nothing.

'Are you sure Gilly didn't take it away to sponge or mend?' I said.

'It was on my dressing table when I closed my eyes to sleep,' Ottoline said stoutly. 'I could see its sequins and spangles winking in the firelight but only very faintly because of all the smoke because of that *stupid* girl.'

'Perhaps he thought it was jewellery,' Alec said. 'If he saw something glittering on a dressing table, that wouldn't be an unlikely conclusion to jump to.'

I considered it for a minute and it appeared sensible enough. In fact, after Minnie and Bluey's invitation to a houseful of strangers to search for trinkets and keep what they found, it seemed quite likely.

'Much better than *actually* having your jewels stolen,' I said. I cleared my throat but it only made me cough even harder. 'Ugh, I think the breeze is whipping the smoke up instead of clearing it.' I turned to the hearth and tutted. Gilly had laid the fire far too far forward into the hearth. It is an irritating habit the maids at Gilverton have caught too. They do not want to lean in far enough to make sure the chimney draws properly, for that way they might soil the sleeves of their frocks with soot. And heaven forbid they should roll them and don canvas cuffs the way the maids did in my youth. 'I have exactly the same problem with the girls at home, Otto,' I said.

She did not answer.

I glanced at her and then rushed back to her bedside, for she was trembling.

'Ottoline?' I said. 'What is it?'

'I've only just remembered,' she said. She put a hand over her eyes and pressed it down hard. When she took it away again there were tears on her lashes. 'My bag. I did as you asked.'

'What do you mean?' said Alec.

'Richard's letters!' she said and passed her hand over her eyes again. 'I looked them out and put them in my evening bag to give to you at dinner but then I was so upset by that silliness about the treasure hunt I stayed up here and forgot all about them. They've gone. Oh! The last thing he ever gave me! His last words to me all those years ago and I've lost them.'

Alec gave me a sickly grin and then melted away, as unwilling as any man would be to mop the tears of a ninety-year-old wife mourning the scoundrel husband who had deserted her decades ago. I am not a romantic sort, but I am a woman, and I understood that her brave words from earlier had been taken over by sentiment now that – as she said – the last wisp of him was gone. And so I took her hand and made soothing murmurs.

When I left her a few minutes later I had the sudden urge to write to Hugh, if I should ever find my way back to my own room at the end of this interminable night. In the meantime, I trailed downstairs, wondering where the Bewers would be gathered to take stock of events so far. I eventually tracked them to the little sitting room where they had greeted us on our first afternoon. It was, granted, a long way from Otto's bedroom and explained why they had not heard her crying out. It did not explain why they had not rushed to her side once they heard about the upset either from Penny or from Alec, who were both now with them. I gave Bluey a sharp look as I made my report.

'Your mother is settled and calm,' I said. 'And Mrs Rynsburger has the surprisingly belligerent Mrs Westhousen tucked up in bed with her, wielding a poker. The three players who've been scampering about dressed as ghosts are dispatched – I hope – and I assume Pugh has locked us up. Are the police coming?'

'I rather think not,' Bluey said. 'We've decided we don't believe in this burglar, you see.'

'But your mother's evening bag is definitely missing,' I said.

'Hmm, well, I'll ask Gilly to search for it tomorrow,' said Minnie. 'I daresay it'll turn up.'

'She seemed very definite, didn't she Alec?' I said.

'And the windows were wide open?' Bluey said. 'Oh poor Mama. She really is beginning to get quite childlike in some ways.'

'I don't understand your meaning,' I said.

'We think she dropped it,' Minnie said. 'Either by accident, if she wrestled with the window catch while she still had it hooked over her arm . . .'

'Why not pick it up?' I said.

'When I say she dropped it,' Minnie went on, 'I mean in the moat.'

'That doesn't seem likely.'

'Well, there was that time she got into her bath,' said Penny. 'Poor Granny. She was in a hotel in Glasgow and she had rather a lot of banknotes in her purse so she was hanging onto her good brown leather handbag like a limpet. She took it to the bathroom with her instead of leaving it in her room and then she actually—' She sat back and giggled. 'Oh *poor*

Granny. She was terribly flustered. She had to dry out the money between two bath towels, and then ask the hotel maids to iron it. So if she was trying to keep it quiet that she had all that lolly with her it was a bit of a bust.'

Minnie and Bluey were giggling too now. But Bluey sobered rather abruptly and shook his head fondly. 'Or,' he said, 'there's just a chance that she . . . oh, it's terrible to tell tales out of school on one's own mother but she does have rather a habit of dropping things in the moat, doesn't she, Min?'

'What sort of things?' Alec said.

'Coins,' said Bluey. 'For luck. And sometimes pebbles. Well, quite big stones. She likes the plunking sound they make, she says. But there was a time recently, she was terribly anxious – about money, of course, as usual, as we all are and . . . Well, I'm afraid we caught her making a sort of sacrifice, I suppose you'd say. She dropped a—'

'Bluey, please,' Minnie said, flashing a look at Penny who was staring open-mouthed.

'A sacrifice?' she said. 'Granny? You make her sound absolutely gaga.'

'Old age comes to us all and earns us the right to be a little odd sometimes,' Minnie said, but it did not seem to placate Penny much.

'Dropped a "what" anyway?' she said. 'A goat? Chicken's entrails? Good grief! Don't let Leonard hear about it or he'll add it to the scene on the blasted heath.'

'Leonard will only hear of it if you tell him,' Minnie said. 'So there's no need to worry.'

'And we'll search for the bag in the morning,' I added. 'We particularly want to find it, Minnie, because it had in it some letters from Richard that Ottoline was going to show us. The letters from years ago, just after he left.'

'What do you want with them?' said Bluey.

'Just in the name of completeness,' Alec said. 'To see if there are any hints in any of them that might help us track your father's movements and find his place of . . . Well, wherever he ended up.'

'Very thorough,' said Bluey, vaguely. 'Very commendable. Not sure what it would get us, mind you.'

I opened my mouth to tell him, then closed it again. I was not sure what the point of the letters was either, now I came to think of it. In fact, I was less sure all the time what the point of any of it was, not sure what Gilver and Osborne were doing here at all.

That is why, when I sat down at the little table in my bedroom to write to Hugh, it was not the billet-doux Otto's tears had suggested to me – just as well, for Hugh would have been perplexed to receive such a thing and would have taken months to forgive me – nor the humdrum little reminder that Teddy would be home in two days and the maids were planning to take down the drawing-room curtains to remove the winter linings. Instead it was the most honest communication I had ever written to my husband in all the years of our marriage. I knew he would barely skim it but the writing of it helped me, nevertheless.

Minnie and Bluey got us here under false pretences,' I scribbled. 'Minnie didn't want us forewarned of our brief in case she changed her mind about it or in case we demurred. But in any case, we are not really to find the necklace, or not primarily. We are to oversee a great public treasure hunt, which you will have read about in the *Scotsman* before this letter reaches you, I daresay. Beulah and the ruby and the Boxing Day mishap. Old Mrs Bewer is horrified by the whole thing and is getting quite dotty from all the upset, beginning to jettison her possessions into the moat (we are told this is a favourite habit of hers when she is terribly anxious about something). A secondary task, tertiary perhaps now I think of it, because Bluey wants us to act as character witnesses in the face of the taxman, assuring His Majesty's exchequer that the Bewers don't have the thing stashed away. Where was I? Our tertiary task is to try to establish the movements and fate of Richard Bewer, Bluey's father, probably long deceased but about to be incontrovertibly deceased in the eyes of the law upon his hundredth birthday. If we could find some evidence that he took the thing with him all those years ago and sold it in Aleppo, then His Majesty would have to lump it regarding the death duties. So, dearest Hugh, I don't suppose you, in any of your extensive correspondence, ever heard that a Richard Bewer left his wife and travelled the globe. No one met him in the British Bar in Cairo and told the story? Ask George at the club if you run into him, would you? George knows everything and will always tell it. A side-note, while I think of it, is: can you believe they hushed it up? Can you credit that a chap left his wife and grown-up child thirty years ago and, with a quiet wedding for the child, a change of staff in the house, and a vague tale of some distressing illness, they got away with it? But then the stories from the generation *before* would make your hair curl. I know you didn't read *The Well of Loneliness*, Hugh, but you'll have heard of it. Yes, well, besides the unfortunate Beulah, there was also a dotty aunt who spent a happy spinster life with her dear friend at Mespring. This dear friend was supposed to be delivered to Harold Bewer as his bride, until Beulah scooped him in the time-honoured way, walking down the aisle with a large bouquet held very close. This spurned friend got quite peculiar after Beulah died and I am Mespring-bound tomorrow to see if any of the peculiarity is pertinent to our concerns. But fear not. I shall not be dropping bricks in the drawing room and disgracing you. It's really a servant I want to grill: there is a servant there who used to be here. Used, in fact, to be Richard's valet. He might be able to shed some light on Richard's last days in the castle, don't you think?

I signed my name, added a postscript instructing him to scratch Bunty's ears for me, then blotted the paper and sat back.

There was no way to know whether Hugh would be more horrified by my grammar, my indiscretion, my reference to 'that novel' or my plan to sit, yet again, in a servants' hall. It was probably a dead heat.

So, since the chances of Hugh or even George knowing anything about Richard Bewer seemed quite remote, I tore up the letter and tossed the scraps of paper in the fire, stirring it with the poker until it was quite gone.

Then ignoring that damned wisp, which Alec had passed to me, or its cousin which I had just somehow spun for myself perhaps, I took myself to bed and dreamless sleep.

13

By eight the next morning, when I came downstairs, Castle Bewer was a perfect hive of anticipatory coming and going. I hung out of a landing window to watch it, in a manner that would have seen Nanny Palmer take the vapours. The actors were up and already out on the stage engaged upon vocal exercises or mysterious silent trampings about and squintings, looking for the best spots to stand upon during the play I supposed. Leonard was shouting and waving his arms like a windmill, presumably determined that they would stand where he told them and like it. The American guests, too excited by the treasure hunt to stay in their seats until breakfast was done, were actually drinking cups of coffee as they stood in the courtyard pointing up at windows and arguing. Alec, I thought, could have sold them copies of his sketch plans at a pound apiece to help them organise their searching. The carpenters were back and, aided by Bess, the still mysterious 'ASM', were now knocking together crude trees and battlements. Minnie and Bluey had won that skirmish apparently. There was to be scenery, to please the conventional tastes of the locals.

Busiest of all, as I saw when at last I drew in my head and carried on to the ground floor, the family and servants were flying around with armfuls of unearthed crockery and even Bluey was tramping hither and yon with spare tablecloths.

'For the teas!' Minnie shouted over her shoulder. 'You should see *The Scotsman*, Dandy. Top of page five. We're going to be inundated. Mrs Porteous is on her fourth batch of scones and she says we're going to need more jam too. Such a terrible time of year for fruit! Would you be a dear and pop into the greengrocers in the village and—'

'You can't serve grocers' jam!' I said.

'*Green*grocers,' Minnie repeated, 'and pick up as much as you can lay hands on – gooseberries, I expect.'

'Doesn't he deliver?' I said.

'Ah, but we don't want spies,' Minnie said. 'Castle Bewer is a stronghold fast again. Just for today to help excitement build.'

'Very well,' I agreed. 'I was going out anyway.' Then I bit my lip for I did not want her to ask where I was headed. Luckily, she was far too busy and simply smiled her thanks and dashed off in pursuit of Bluey, shouting after him. 'They don't need to be pressed, dearest. Mrs Ellen doesn't have time and Gilly is sulking. We'll sprinkle drops and put lots of plates on them and they'll be flat by tomorrow.'

Gilly was indeed sulking. She was standing mulishly at Alec's elbow in the breakfast room, willing him silently to hurry up and let her clear. She did not know the strength of her opponent. I have never seen Alec either hurry a meal or stop eating a moment before he was stuffed to the gunnels. His few hints have led me to blame the trenches and the many days and nights of gnawing hunger he spent in extremis there and so I cannot scorn him or even call him greedy. Thankfully, he is blessed with a constitution that seems to absorb the enormous meals without it showing, although it does occur to me now and then that such constitutions do not last but rather turn on one and take the upper hand when one's youth is gone. I hoped he would finally settle on a wife before he was transformed into Henry VIII as he surely would be if this morning's work was anything to go by: a porridge plate, smeared with cream, and another bearing the unmistakable remains of kedgeree and five – five! – bacon rinds sat at his elbow, while he was engaged upon what looked –

from the emptiness of rack, butter dish and marmalade pot – to be his seventh or eighth slice of rather thick toast.

'How is Mrs Bewer this morning?' I asked Gilly, pointedly.

I was rewarded with an impressive scowl. 'She's fine,' Gilly said. 'If she'd leave it be and ring for me, she'd always be fine. I've never known such a meddler. Why employ a maid at all, if you're going to live like a . . . like a . . . frontiers-woman in a cabin on the prairie!'

With that, her patience deserted her, and she flounced off, no more than a 'ring the bell if you *ever* stop eating!' thrown over her shoulder.

'Golly, she's impertinent,' I said. 'Even for nowadays. I hope Grant doesn't study at her elbow – I'm not sure I'd put up with that.'

'Hm?' said Alec. 'Try the kedge, Dan. It's bliss.'

It was harder than I would have expected to drag myself away from the castle an hour later, after the kedgeree had been finished, coffee drunk, first cigarettes smoked and the results of our night's musings shared. The stage, even in plain daylight, was beginning to be transformed and to exert its particular magic. The setting was, as all the Bewers had proclaimed, quite intoxicating and my scepticism was done away, chased off by a little dance in my innards. It was the same dance as used to be danced there when I was taken to ballet matinees as a child and the first few times I had sat myself down in a darkened picture house too. When Sarah Byrne walked onstage in a long red velvet dress with trailing sleeves and her bright hair flowing loose down her back, I actually caught my breath.

'She's going to be marvellous, isn't she?' I said to Alec who was standing at my side.

'I don't know whether to be glad I shan't be upstaged by her or sorry I shan't get the chance to act with her,' Alec said.

'Are you busy rehearsing all day? Or can you come with me to Mespring.'

'Not a chance,' Alec said. 'Two roles, Dandy. Murderer and king. I'll be running lines even when not actually rehearsing.'

'Do the kings *have* li—?' I began but swallowed it out of kindness and instead asked the question that had been troubling me since I first heard of Leonard's thrifty casting. 'Won't everyone recognise you? All this doubling up: doctors, kings, murderers and what have you?'

Alec stared at me a good long time before he answered. 'No,' he said coldly at last. 'The performance of a lord or a gentlewoman is quite distinct from the performance of a murderer or witch, Dandy. And we have hats.'

I nodded solemnly and managed not to let out a single giggle or even allow my lips to twitch until I was alone in my little motorcar, trundling over the rickety bridge and across the field to the gate, taking wide swerves around Pugh and a lad I did not recognise but took to be the hall boy, who were pounding pennants on stout sticks into the ground, presumably preparing for the 'traffic jam'.

Mespring House was not quite three miles away but it occupied a very different world. The rough hedges bordering on the lane gave way first to trimmer hedges and then to high stone walls with iron fleurs-de-lis atop them then finally, at a curve in the wall, to angel-crowned gateposts. Behind these, a pair of storybook lodge cottages, with low eaves, latticed windows and ornamentally crooked chimneys, announced the entrance to the park. And what a park it was: not for the Annandales the straggle of fading rhododendrons and a monkey puzzle tree brought back by an errant uncle and plonked on a lawn to kill the grass and concuss garden boys. Here the drive was lined with yew, clipped every so often into the fantastical shapes of dragons, lions and serpents and, in between, clipped no less skilfully – and rather more impressively to my mind for its very understatement – into an endless undulation like a rough sea or like what one is told about clouds viewed from above by adventurous friends who have taken to the skies in aeroplanes. Beyond this hedge, if it were not a calumny to call it by the same name as the thickets of hawthorn and bramble around the castle, there was an expanse of soft green velvet studded with those conspicuously interesting trees, which have bright or shining or papery, peeling bark, enormous girth or height or etiolation, lime green leaves or flowers upon bare branches. Everywhere – as I could see quite clearly because they had been recently polished – there were little brass plaques stuck in the ground, no doubt telling the trees' Latin names. I remembered Pugh and the hall boy banging in pennants to organise the motorcars and my heart bled for the Bewers and hardened against these Annandales before I had clapped eyes upon any of them.

Were I the jealous type, my heart would have hardened even further – or soured anyway – when, after a long drive through this horticultural vulgarity, I rounded a little hill and gazed across a valley at Mespring. Of course, I knew what it looked like; pictures of it were reproduced in every book on Scottish architectural history ever written and Hugh likes nothing more than reading books on Scottish architecture unless it is to foist them upon me. Besides, I was sure I had been to a party here once or twice in my girlhood. I should not have paid any attention to it then, of course, for there was no young man to whom the house was an accompanying element in the decision we girls were ever encouraged to be making, and I was particularly prone to being dragged along wherever my mother sent me and Nanny took me, paying no attention and barely knowing in which of the kingdoms the train had stopped. I assumed back then that I would spend my life in soft Northamptonshire or another of its neighbouring counties and that the great houses of the

Scottish Lowlands would be no more to me than Venetian palazzos or the ruins of Rome.

Now, though, seeing the house anew after decades in Perthshire and a couple of nights in the higgledy-piggle of Minnie and Bluey's domain, it took my breath away. Some of that was trickery, for it stood just beyond an artificial lake and its Palladian front was reflected and therefore doubled. Even without the mirrored Mespring in the still water though, the place was quite something. There were three banks of three windows in three storeys and the depth of the shadows to either side told me that this was the narrow end.

At least Pugh's pennants would have helped me decide where to leave the motorcar. As I drew closer to the great house I found myself unaccountably dithering about whether to carry on round and try to find the kitchen door to beard the valet, late of Castle Bewer, or to sweep up to the front steps and ascend, reminding the family of our acquaintance and forcing a cup of coffee out of them in a morning room. I could, I supposed, find a middle ground; ringing a bell, presenting my Gilver and Osborne card and hoping against hope that no one remembered me.

The decision was taken out of my hands by the fact of a lowly door opening under the mobile steps as my wheels crunched on the gravel. A young man came pattering out, waving his hands. He was dressed in shirtsleeves and braces but was clearly not a footman caught without his livery, for everything about him, from his floppy hair to his cigarette holder to the cut of his ludicrously high-waisted trousers, which, if they had been taken in, could have made a sail for a decent-sized dinghy, screamed that this was a sprig of the family tree. I sent up a prayer that Teddy was not, this moment, wearing such bags and sucking on such a cigarette holder, making some other woman my age want to groan.

'Next week! Next week!' shouted the sprig, in a friendly but firm way, still advancing and still shaking his hands. 'Sorry and all that. Hope you haven't made a long trip.' He stopped in front of the Cowley and put his hands on his hips.

'Oh,' I said, stepping down. 'No, I'm not a visitor. Gosh, I wish I were. It's tremendously grand, isn't it? No, I'm from Castle Bewer.'

He asked, just before I realised that of course he was going to: 'Are you an actress?'

'Friend of the family,' I said and then, judging his instant reaction, which was a downward droop of boredom in the haughty eyes, I added: 'although currently employed by them as a detective.' The eyelids lifted again, taking the arched brows with them.

'Detective?' he said. 'Are they in some kind of trouble? Nothing trivial, I hope.'

I could not help laughing. 'Dandy Gilver,' I said. 'Gilverton, Perthshire as the family friend and Gilver and Osborne with my detective's hat on.'

'Ah,' said the sprig, shifting the cigarette holder to the side of his mouth like a pipe – I noted in passing that it was made of jade with a gold tip. 'Hugh Gilver? Friend of Silas Esslemont? And Gilver and Osborne? Well, yes, indeed. Quite. Golly. Can you tell me about the trouble or is it hush-hush?'

'There's no trouble,' I said, 'or it would be completely hush-hush, because we guarantee discretion.' I spoke as archly as he was, the annoying habit of the young these days being to say everything with a veneer of insincerity. I have even heard wedding vows exchanged that way and it made me want to smack bride and groom. 'Just an enterprise in need of an overseer. Perhaps you haven't—'

'Heard?' said the sprig. 'Haven't *heard*? It's all over *The Times* and since it's all over the *Record* too, our maids are like a flock of budgies with it, just when we need them concentrating. I am livid. And Mummy is absolutely beside herself. Of course, we knew about the *Dream* and we were pig sick enough about not having had the idea ourselves, but the ruby! A treasure hunt? Pchah!' He tore his cigarette out of its holder, threw it down and ground it to shreds under his elegant leather heel. Then, with an even greater cry of frustration, he crouched down and picked it all up again. 'We've got to keep the place pristine,' he said. 'You wouldn't believe what we're charging them to shuffle round and gawp at a few Holbeins, a bloody awful Titian from before he learned to paint and a deeply disputed Rembrandt we keep in a dark corner or it would fool no one. Billy Annandale, by the way,' he said, straightening. He tipped the crumbled tobacco and paper into his left hand, wiped his right thoroughly on his trousers and shook mine.

'Well now,' I said. 'Funny you should mention pictures, because one of my reasons for popping along this morning is that I very much wanted to see the painting of Anne Annandale and Dorothy Bewer.'

'Oh Lord, not Aunt Nancy!' said Billy Annandale. 'Mespring's great scandal of 1834. Have you heard?'

'I've heard murmurs,' I said, quietly hoping for better.

'Come and see her if you really want to,' he said, stepping back into the shadow of the stairs.

'Oh I do!' This was rot, of course. The only reason I had come was to mention the ruby and see if I could tell – from guilty looks and blushes – whether they really had pinched it back again.

'And you can be a guinea pig too,' he went on. 'We're all sick of the sight of every last sketch and footstool but if you could ooh and aah a bit we might get our spirits back up in the face of the betrayal. It is a bit of a cheek, isn't it? Those Bewers on our coat-tails?'

He ushered me into a low passageway. It was not quite sumptuous but not quite plain, dating from the days before the fashion for showing off turned great houses into the burdensome white elephants they have become; that same fashion that had started the journey towards *this* day, when palaces and castles were opening to day-trippers, laying on teas and putting up plays.

'You could out-do them,' I said, feeling disloyal to Minnie but unable to help myself. 'Stage an opera on your terrace and knock them into a cocked hat.'

'Opera?' said Billy. 'I thought they were pushing it with Shakespeare, if I'm honest.'

'Oscar Wilde then,' I said, teasing now.

'My mother would drop,' Billy said. 'Do you know her?'

We traced acquaintance in a desultory fashion as we made our way up a set of back stairs to the entrance hall. When we emerged through a door in the panelling I stopped speaking from sheer awe.

Mespring was, quite simply, staggering. A game of rugby football could have taken place in this hall and still left room for the household to have tea undisturbed by the fire. It was enormous, like a cathedral, and stuffed to its waistline with marble in every conceivable shade. The floor was mustard with green veins, the fireplace ginger with pink, and the pillars were the nasty brown of chocolate ice-cream. The statues were good plain white but they were dwarfed by what was above them. Surely, I thought, this hallway had been raised at some time in its long life. Surely no architect had planned all of this at once. For on top of the green, brown and pink marble excesses was another room entirely, as though its floor had fallen through and they had simply left it hovering there. The upper room was a riot of painted frescos, crawling over walls and ceiling. Literally crawling in most instances, I noted, since the tableaux – as such tableaux tend to – suggested that people do not walk around or sit down but that instead they drape themselves on couches if mortal or clouds if not, so that a crowd of them painted on a grand scale is simply a tangle of arms and legs and the odd bit of floating drapery. Gods, cherubs, graces, nymphs and putti rolled about from the top of the hideous marble on one wall all the way across to the top of the hideous marble on the other, eyes beseeching, limbs waving and clothes mostly falling off.

'It's—' I said.

Billy Annandale guffawed. 'It certainly is. Let's keep walking. I'm afraid there's a lot more of it before we get to the long gallery.' He cleared his throat modestly, an impeccable imitation of a very correct footman, or perhaps a clerk in a rather staid bank. 'This, as you see, is the great hall and if we ascend the great stairs' – he waved to both sides, pointing out the disputed Rembrandt on the way – 'we arrive at the great drawing room.' Here, in a chamber forty feet long if it was an inch, as well as marble and tapestries and a fresco of the birth of Venus with a great many more flailing arms and legs and even less clothing, there was also a quantity of veneered wood in that very intricate parquetry that I am afraid makes me think of dartboards. Add the fact that the carpet was Victorian and so had not yet begun to fade the way that older carpets do – so kind to their surroundings – and the fact that the curtains were set about with tassels and tucks and looked like the costumes of a battalion of pantomime dames, and the drawing room was worse than the hall.

'And now the great dining room,' Billy said, flinging open one of a pair of doors.

'What on earth is that?' I asked, stepping through into an even longer room, which seemed to have been afflicted with some kind of fungus.

'It's leather wallpaper,' Billy said. 'Stamped, silvered and gilded. Do you like it?'

'Uh,' I said. 'It's ingenious.'

Again Billy only laughed and said, 'If you're wondering how much better it would look with more gilding covering the leather . . . Behold the great music room.'

'Oof,' I said, for here the gilt was dazzling and the marble border above it – quite ten feet deep – had even more naked nymphs, all managing to play violins, pipes and lutes while rolling on their backs.

'We did think of redoing the chairs,' said Billy, waving at the rows of those uncomfortable little gilt and velvet affairs one sits on during music recitals. They are wonderful at keeping one awake even after a solid dinner, but most unfortunately in this case they had been covered in what I can only call orange. It was not the gold of the leather walls nor even the cream of the damask curtains. It was an unrepentant orange. 'But really,' Billy went on, 'what's the use? If we actually started to look at any of it with the eye of taste we would curl up in little balls and weep, wouldn't we? Anyway, finally the ordeal is over and we have arrived at . . . the great gallery.'

We passed through another tall door and it was a testament to the garish nature of the rooms behind us that this – a sixty-foot gallery with red walls, red carpet and gargantuan portraits in those gold encrusted frames that look as though they have been overrun by barnacles – seemed almost soothing.

'God knows what the trippers will make of it all,' Billy said.

'I think,' I told him, quite honestly, 'they will be overawed and delighted but, because not everything is exactly in accordance with modern tastes, they won't be quite so covetous and dissatisfied with their own little villas and flats as they might be otherwise.'

Billy stared at me. 'What a nice woman you are,' he said. 'They'll be happy to have paid their sixpence to see this ugly barn of a place and they'll go home to cream paint and plain rugs quite content?'

'Exactly. Tell me though, are you really going to call everything "great" as you lead people around?'

'*I'm* not leading people around,' he said. 'Good God, no. But yes the guides are thus instructed. It's inarguable for one thing. They are great rooms even if hideous, and besides that, if people ask about the ordinary rooms – the dining rooms and drawing rooms that are actually habitable – we have an answer.'

'They can see them for a modest extra fee?' I guessed and was rewarded with a smirk and a waggled eyebrow.

'We'll go through for coffee after this and I'll show you. But first . . . ' I looked with interest up and down the walls of portraits and then hurried over to where he was pointing.

14

'John Watson Gordon,' I said, as I approached. John Watson Gordon was responsible for a fair few of the gloomiest portraits of Hugh's ancestors. I spent every evening at home facing a picture of his grandfather glaring down at me and despising me for sins unknown and, as a result, I would recognise the painter's work anywhere. Even when painting girls and therefore deprived of mutton-chop sideburns and round spectacles, there were still clothes so dark as to be invisible and that same background of sepia landscape that did for everyone. He was only any good at faces really. 'It's rather unusual for him to paint a pair of young ladies, isn't it?' I said.

'Yes, indeed,' Billy said. 'Provosts of far-flung burghs and elderly ministers are more his thing. But as you see, Nancy and Dot didn't go in for frills.'

I looked again. The portrait was clearly from the 1830s, when gigot sleeves reached their zenith, rather as Billy's trouser legs had today, and necklines were at their very lowest and widest too. The girls' snowy shoulders, bedecked with pearls, rose out of what looked rather like a molehill of cloth. And that molehill was grey and black in the case of one sitter and brown and black in the case of the other. Their hair too was in the unfortunate style of the day. For this the blame was to be laid at the tiny feet of the new young queen, who had been very badly advised by her lady's maid into believing that pouched cheeks and a needle nose would be set off by lank loops of hair echoing the pouches on either side of a sharp parting. At least, Anne Annandale and Dorothy Bewer had better bones and the loops and molehills did not make them look quite as comical as the same fashions had rendered Victoria in her youth.

'The Bewers said they were . . . very close friends,' I murmured.

Billy nodded. 'Devoted to one another,' he said. I glanced at the pearls, wondering if an expert would be able to tell if they really were a depiction of the strand I had just found. I should have said they were a little shorter but that might have been because the dress's neckline left such an expanse below them. Next I studied the rings, noticing that the girls wore one each on their intertwined fingers. Mostly, however, I was mesmerised, as one often is, by the frank gaze of these painted strangers who died so long ago. Anne's light, sparkling eyes held mine and the slight purse to her decided mouth made me wish I could hear what she was thinking. Dorothy was the milder of the pair and, although she too looked out of the picture at me, the tilt of her head suggested that either she had just turned from gazing at the other girl or was just about to.

'Anne was very much the boss of the outfit then,' I said.

'Now how clever of you to see that,' said Billy. 'It's true, from what the stories have told us anyway. She was rather wild and headstrong, and in latter years even more than headstrong. Quite peculiar. Dorothy was the peacemaker, the good listener, the patient one. But, how did you know which was which?'

I blinked in surprise for the question had caught me out. Then I laughed. 'Simply that Penny Bewer is her Great-Aunt Dorothy's double,' I said.

Billy subjected the portrait to a moment's close study. 'Well, as far as I know I've never met Miss Bewer,' he said. 'Because of the feud, you know. It was set in stone before I was born. But even if I had, I daresay I'd take your word for it. Women are always finding family resemblance. From the day a child is born, a howling pink monkey of a thing, women are always telling the doting parents that it looks like one or the other granny or someone. I would take it as an insult but no one else ever seems to.'

I found it rather rude the way this young man was pronouncing on the habits of 'women' as he called them, and I wondered if his coarse manners meant that I could simply plunge in with both feet and ask about the nasty wedding gift. Before I had made my mind up, though, he took the matter out of my hands.

'I suppose you've heard that this marvellous necklace the Bewers have been advertising actually used to be ours,' he said.

'I've heard so many different things about the necklace that I can't keep them straight,' I said. 'I can't keep up with what it's called from day to day for a start.'

'Yes, Briar Rose is a bit more enticing than Judas Jewel, isn't it?' said Billy.

'Or Cut Throat,' I added.

'That's a new one,' he said. 'Where did that come from, I wonder.'

His ignorance was rather puzzling but then, from the breezy way he spoke of its being 'women' who cooed over babies, I supposed he was also above remembering the gossip of his grandmother's day. Except that he had rather delighted in the 'great scandal of 1834'.

'Come and ask Mother if she can enlighten you,' he said. 'Tell her what you told me about the ugliness of this place being a boon and she'll adore you. She should just about be sitting down for her coffee about now.'

He swept me away through another of the panelled doors but this time we emerged into a long plain passageway with a fine carpet runner, polished edges to the floor, pale blue walls and some soothing landscapes. There was no furniture except for the odd half-moon table here and there and upon them some bowls of roses.

'I'm glad to see you really don't live against those backdrops we've just seen,' I said. 'I should have worried for your sanity.'

Billy laughed and ushered me into a sitting room where the current Lady Annandale was just being served with a laden silver tray of coffee and plain biscuits by a maid in black serge and white apron. The settled domesticity of the scene was delightful and Lady Annandale herself, coolly dressed in angora the same shade as her corridor walls and with a sleek little greyhound or some such leaning calmly against her still-shapely legs, was quite a contrast with poor Minnie, harassed and frazzled and running about with armloads of tablecloths the day before the opening of her home. Lady Annandale was so far from frazzled that, when her son burst into her morning room with a stranger in tow, she did not even blink but just murmured to the maid to bring another cup and beckoned me to sit.

'This is Mrs Gilver, Mother,' Billy said. 'Hugh Gilver's wife.'

'Dandy,' said Lady Annandale. 'Of course. How kind of you to drop in while you were in the area.'

I was horrified. I could not have produced this woman's name if I were dangling from a rope over an abyss and it was the password to secure my release. But I summoned the spirit of Nanny Palmer, Mlle Toulemonde and the entire staff of my finishing school and dug deep down into my memory.

So, I had definitely been here before then. Perhaps I stopped off on my way north, on the very trip during which I met Hugh. I kept digging. If so, I was here with Daisy and her mother and *they* were here because Daisy's mother had been on a crossing to New York with the new wife of Lord Annandale who, oddly enough, had honeymooned on an island off the Massachusetts coastline, even though the wife was not an aluminium heiress or anything of that nature. She was a perfectly ordinary English girl and her name was . . .

'Winifred,' I said. 'Of course. I should have telephoned to you but the line seemed always to be engaged so I popped along on the off-chance.'

'I should have been hurt if you hadn't,' Lady Annandale said. 'When I read that you were here I was a little hurt I hadn't seen you already.'

She was pouting and my memories of her were solidifying nicely. She was just as big a ninny now as she had been thirty years ago. Back then she had a kitten with a bow on its head instead of the whippet or Italian greyhound or whatever it was and she had made a terrific fuss about it scratching her when she tickled it. She had wrapped her finger in a hand-kerchief and gone to the nursery to have it bathed and smeared with ointment. Remembering this, I had to concentrate to keep smiling. So it took me a moment until her words went in.

'You've read about me?' I said. 'In the newspaper?'

'Quite a long write-up,' she said, as if that would please me. 'The real-life Lady Macbeth, they called you.'

'What?' I said. 'Why?'

'I have no idea,' said Lady Annandale. 'The notion of a gentlewoman plotting and planning, perhaps?'

'But it's Minnie who's . . . ' I said, then shook the words away. That did not matter. 'Was it in the *Scotsman*?' I said knowing my voice had dried out a little. She heard it and hastened to pour me a cup of coffee.

'Only the *Mail*,' she said. 'It's my little treat, I'm ashamed to say.'

I sat back and took a draught of the coffee in my relief. Hugh would not have the rag in his part of the house and none of the servants would be so disloyal as to enlighten him. I ran over them all quickly, paused a moment at Pallister, but then told myself that even Pallister had a heart.

'Mother,' said Billy, sitting down and slinging one long leg over the other, making Winifred frown at the billowing swathes of his trousers, I am sure. 'Mrs Gilver has something to ask you.'

He spoke with an innocent air but, having two sons of my own, I was not to be taken in by it. For some reason, Billy Annandale was toying with me. I thought about it for a moment while drinking my coffee and eating my biscuit. Both were excellent, the coffee piping hot and very strong without being the least bit muddy and the biscuit fresh and short, probably made that morning and only just cooled in time to be crisp for her Ladyship's morning refreshment. Mespring House struck me as the sort of ordered place where everything is just so.

'It's about the ruby necklace,' I said at last. Winifred Annandale dropped a hand on to her dog's head and stroked its ears. I wondered if the gesture was meant to soothe her and, if so, why she needed soothing. 'The Bewers seem to have rechristened it the Briar Rose and I've heard it called the Cut Throat as well as the Judas Jewel.'

'Briar Rose and Cut Throat?' she said. 'I imagine those were dreamed up in the Bewers' sitting room about a week ago to make it sound romantic to the romantic and exciting to the ghoulish. And one can see the sense in Cut Throat – it does look rather ghastly against a white neck. Briar Rose is a little fanciful, for aren't they usually white? Or the palest pink? But I can certainly account for Judas Jewel. That name was given to it by my late husband's Aunt Anne to mark what she saw as a betrayal by the House of Bewer.' Winifred was staring distractedly at the dog's ears as she fondled them and her pretty face had come as close to a scowl as I supposed it ever did. It did not look like discomfort; it looked like displeasure. 'I wonder what they would say if we went along there and joined in,' she said. 'Found the thing and brought it back where it belongs.'

'Do you have any idea where it is?' I said. Surely they would squirm now if the necklace was already here in their own safe. 'Do you know the castle well?' I added innocently.

Lady Annandale blinked and came out of her reverie, with a tinkling little laugh. 'Heavens, no!' she said. 'I tried several times to mend fences and put things right between the two houses, but years go by, don't they? My last attempt was just before Bluey and Minnie's wedding and . . . Well, let's say it wasn't entirely successful and leave it at that. As to my knowing the castle, I've never been there actually. I was musing, that's all. It rankles a bit that someone might carry it off. If it weren't so unseemly I might even check with a solicitor to see if the Bewers have the right to give it away. It might still be ours.'

'Not if Anne gave it in a gift,' I said.

'Anne?' said Lady Annandale. 'How could she? It was to be part of her dowry when she married, but she didn't marry.'

'So I heard,' I said. 'Dorothy and Anne – devoted friends right to the end. Despite everything.'

'Despite what?' said Lady Annandale.

'Well, the curse for one thing,' I said.

Lady Annandale put her cup down and stared at me. 'Curse?' she said. 'What on earth do you mean? I've never heard tell of any curse.'

'You've really never heard about the curse of the ruby necklace?' I said.

'Have another cup of coffee and tell me now,' said Lady Annandale. Again her breeding, the long years of being a delicate and decorative ornament to the family she had married into and the house over which she presided, stopped her from sounding the least bit grim. Her voice was light and her face wore its perpetual slight smile, but I would not have thwarted her with an army to help me.

'The story I heard,' I said, 'was that Beulah died in a hunting accident on Boxing Day.'

'Yes, that's true,' Billy said, and when his mother flicked a look at him he added, 'Father told me to make me stop jumping the paddock gate.'

'But the reason she died, was that she took the necklace away to the house party with her instead of keeping it within the castle walls,' I went on, speaking quite fast and trying to ignore their blank faces. 'That was a problem because when it was given, she was told it was to adorn her neck throughout her life in the castle – I forget the exact wording – but it wasn't to be taken away. And so when she took it away, she died.'

Billy and his mother were staring at me open-mouthed. Winifred gathered herself first.

'Beulah,' she said, 'Bluey's grandmother, wore the ruby necklace?' It seemed an odd point to get stuck on.

'And the story goes on even further,' I said, in for a penny in for a pound, 'that when she was lifted out of the ditch she had thirteen droplets of blood on her neck where the vine – a briar rose as a matter of fact – had garrotted her.'

'And *why* was it cursed?' Winifred asked, rather faintly.

'Because Harold Bewer was supposed to marry Anne Annandale. But he jilted her. And so she gave his bride a poisoned chalice of a wedding gift.'

Winifred Annandale put her cup back into its saucer. It did not rattle. I daresay she had never rattled a cup and saucer since she was first taught to use them in her nursery many years ago, but the putting down hinted that she did not feel able to hold it safely. I ploughed on.

'That is why the necklace was never worn again. Richard's father believed it had killed his wife.'

'And how exactly did you come to hear this wild tale?' Winifred said.

'Dorothy told Richard, Richard told Otto and Otto told me,' I said, wondering again what was puzzling her. How else could the story have come to my ears after all?

'Richard's father having told Dorothy initially?' she added.

'Presumably,' I agreed.

'It's a good account,' Winifred said. 'It explains a lot. Does Otto believe it?'

'Oh no,' I said. 'Otto never believed a word of the curse. She had her portrait painted wearing the necklace and she would quite happily have put the thing in her jewel case and taken it wherever she went. But she wasn't troubled by living under its yoke either. It wasn't until Minnie came on the scene that it started to annoy her. She wished Richard would stop being silly and just let Minnie have the pretty necklace. That's when he left.'

'At last,' said Winifred. 'A matter of plain fact. Richard left. But can you believe it took us almost two years to find out? I was here by then and all I knew was that one of our neighbours was in very poor health. My mother-in-law told me that much and no more.'

'Your footman didn't tell you?' I said. Both of them stared. One could see the family resemblance when their expressions chimed in that way, although ordinarily Billy's twinkling and Lady Annandale's serenity got in the way. 'I mean, didn't your footman regale the servants' hall and didn't your own maid then tell you?' Still they stared. 'Your footman,' I repeated. 'He used to be a valet for the Bewers and then he came here when Otto changed the staff in honour of Minnie's arrival. But perhaps he left quickly and never got chummy with the rest of the servants. Funny, though, I rather got the impression from Nanny that he had stayed and risen. How odd.'

'Our *butler* came here thirty years ago,' Lady Annandale said. 'Do you mean him? Gunn? I have no idea where he came *from*. Except that I guessed he had been with the family since before the flood and done someone a great service sometime. But while my father- and mother-in-law were alive I took no part in running the house. Is it Gunn you mean, Dandy?'

180

'I can't tell you,' I said, 'but if I could speak to him perhaps?'

Lady Annandale was visibly shocked. 'Have him up here telling tales?'

'Not here,' I hastened to make clear. 'And not with you in attendance. I am quite used to going below stairs and talking to servants on their level.'

This did nothing to lessen her shock, but she did not speak.

It was Billy who stepped in. 'You want to interview our butler to see what he knows about a scandal in our family and why he didn't tell us anything about it?'

'No!' I shot back, before I had had a chance to think about it, for it sounded monstrous. 'I want to interview your butler – if he's the man I mean – to see what he remembers about a different household from decades ago and the particulars of Richard Bewer's flight. Nothing to do with your family at all, I assure you. Nothing more than that you have an interest in the jewel Richard either hid in the house or took away with him when he left.'

'Well, of course he took it with him when he left!' said Billy. 'This treasure hunt is a piece of trickery. Obviously the thing is long gone.'

'I think so,' I said. 'And so does Bluey. And so does Otto too, deep down. But . . . ' I realised I could not say any more without compromising my client's privacy rather badly. I could not talk about the fact that Richard had never been declared dead or that he was just about to be, once and for all. I could not mention the death duties hanging over the Bewers' heads, even though such considerations were surely behind the Annandales' decision to open up their house and let the great unwashed troop through it.

'I just can't believe you didn't know the story,' I said. 'If Dorothy came here every day until her death and actually lived here latterly. Or was it Anne who died first? How could such a story be kept from your ears? From everyone's?'

'The story that Harold jilted Anne, who gave a cursed gift

to his chosen bride, who promptly died?' said Winifred. 'That's the sort of thing any family would keep quiet.'

'No,' I said. 'Not that bit. The story that Richard believed the curse and Otto didn't and the ruby vanished when he left her. Thank you for letting me go and grill the butler about that end of it. He was right there on the spot when the events took place. He must know something.'

Thus I managed to sweep past the fact that they had not actually agreed at all. I stood, left them sitting there in stunned silence and went on my way.

15

Below stairs at Mespring was a little more bustling than above them, but there was still nothing like the frantic careening around that was the order of the day at Castle Bewer. Black-clad maids and under-footmen in shirtsleeves were abroad in the warren of passages and gave me no attention as I prowled around looking for the headquarters. I wondered a little at that. Had they been warned not to pay attention to strangers in the house now that there were to be so many? But surely the visitors would not be down here in the ser-vants' passages. Or perhaps they took me to be someone who had legitimate and unremarkable business here. Perhaps I looked like a seamstress or a friend of the housekeeper. It was not a gratifying thought and I determined to speak to Grant about my clothes when we were home again. I am so used to resisting her every suggestion that it was possible I had drifted imperceptibly away from simple tidiness in my zeal to avoid fashion.

Before I could ponder it further, I turned a corner and knew that I was reaching my destination. Here were coat pegs where those footmen had left their livery and here were baskets and parcels awaiting attention. Somewhere near here, the housekeeper, cook and butler – that triumvirate of power in these parts – would be going about their business. At that moment a door just ahead of me swung open and a maid in blue cotton backed out with a wooden tray in her arms. Upon the tray were a single cup, a tiny coffee pot and two biscuits on a plate. It could have been for the housekeeper but the tray cloth was without any lace at its edge and the china was very plain.

'Is that for Gunn?' I asked the maid. She started, but well trained as she was, not a drop of coffee was spilled on the snowy cloth.

'Aye,' she said.

'I'll take it in.'

Her quick glance showed me which of the closed doors was his pantry.

'Who—?' she began. 'I mean, is Mr Gunn expecting you, madam?'

'Don't worry about that,' I told her crisply and took the tray from her hands. 'Open the door for me though, would you?'

She knocked and unlatched the door before beetling off back to the kitchen to regale her workmates about the happenings. I entered the little room and cleared my throat politely.

Mr Gunn, the Mespring butler, was not at all what I had been expecting. Pallister, our butler at Gilverton, is a good example of the type, being portly in his bearing and possessing a face apparently carved from granite. Even Pugh along at Castle Bewer was snooty and unbending in his own peculiar way. Gunn, as he looked up from his wine ledger, could have been a park keeper, a bus driver or a schoolmaster. He did not have a butler's bearing at all. He did not even glower at the intrusion.

'Can I help you?' he said mildly.

'I've intercepted your maid and brought your coffee, Mr Gunn,' I told him. 'I've come to interview you, with Lady Annandale's permission, about the goings on along at the Bewers'. Rather neat timing if you were stopping for a little break, don't you think?'

Gunn had some butler's instinct after all. At my words he turned as still as a deer in a clearing when it hears a stick break nearby, and he stayed that way until I began to feel every bit of the tray's weight and glanced at his table top to see if there was room to set it down there.

'Goings on?' he said.

'You must have heard about the play and the treasure hunt,' I said. 'I'm staying there at the moment to help.'

'Are you an actress?' he said, inevitably.

'I'm a detective,' I told him. 'I'm interested in what happened all those years ago. What happened to Mr Bewer when he left. Where he went. When he died. That kind of thing.'

'Does Mrs Bewer know you're here?' he said. 'Mrs Richard Bewer?'

I thought about it before answering. Did Ottoline know that I was interviewing the discarded servants? No. Did it matter whether I told this man the truth on that score? Not a bit. But which answer would help me more? That mattered a great deal and I was not sure.

'Of course,' I said, in the end, judging that less likely to shut him like a tapped oyster. 'She sent me along here to talk to you. Practically,' I added, with a burst of honesty.

'Why?' said the butler. 'Is she ailing? She's a grand age but I never heard she was starting to fade. Why now?'

'It's *Mr* Bewer's grand age that's the salient fact,' I said. 'Mr Richard Bewer. He turns a hundred at Halloween.'

'Turns a hundred?' came the echo. I wondered if the chap could really have blanched and if he had, why that might be.

'Have your coffee,' I said, sitting down.

Gunn poured a cup and drank thirstily from it. He broke one of the biscuits too but only stared at it and put the two pieces down without eating a crumb.

'Has he written again?' he said at last and, whether or not I had imagined the blanching, I did not imagine the note of strain. 'Is he really still alive?'

'I shouldn't think so,' I said. 'It would be notable enough had he lived quietly at home. Spending his golden years and

185

dotage traipsing around the Empire isn't the surest way to reach a century. It would be more accurate to say that the hundredth anniversary of his birth is coming and with that milestone comes his legal death, no more shilly-shallying.'

'And – if you don't mind me asking – why does that need a detective?'

It was a good question from a butler's point of view, I daresay. As long as a man like Gunn had a little pot of cash somewhere to cover the expense of his funeral he could afford to die whenever he chose. He would never feel the cold shadow of what hung over Bluey's head.

'Well, Mr Gunn,' I said, 'it's about what Mr Bewer might have taken with him when he left the castle, you see. Or where he might have put something if he left it behind.'

'The Cut Throat,' said Gunn, and he sounded like a man who had just given up on a long-held dream. I had no idea why the mention of it should take him that way. 'Why does that suddenly matter after all these years?'

'The Cut Throat indeed,' I said. 'As to why it matters. Well, if he took it with him then it is not part of the estate and the Bewers will not have to pay tax on it after All Souls' Day when the dust settles. And if he hid it in the castle and it is found, well, at least its sale will provide the funds to *pay* the tax bill.'

'But it said in the paper they were giving it away to anyone who laid hands on it,' said Gunn.

'Proving, if you ask me, that they know it's long gone.'

The butler nodded slowly, considering the point. 'And – pardon my impertinence – but how can *I* help you?' he said after a silent moment. 'It's a long time since I had any doings with the Bewer family. Or any of the household at all.'

'Thirty years,' I said. 'Quite. I understand that there was a wholesale change of personnel after Mr Bewer left.'

'A clean sweep,' Gunn agreed. 'For the wedding. Blow the cobwebs away.'

'The words Nanny used,' I said. 'A clean sweep. And the new servants – well, hardly new any more, but you know what I mean – did mention that the castle had rather got away from you all.'

'Got away?' said Gunn.

'Wasn't exactly bowling along like a hoop,' I said. 'Disarray' was the word Mrs Porteous had used but it would be rude to repeat it. I changed the subject. 'It was jolly accommodating of you all to take it in such good spirit, I must say.'

'I landed on my feet,' said Gunn. 'I was valet to Mr Bewer along the road and I came here as a footman and rose and rose until you see me now.'

I took a look around his pantry and I did not have to try to seem impressed. It really was pretty impressive. The glass-fronted cases were filled with ledgers ranging back for hundreds of years, all stamped with the date on their spines. The watercolour of the house on the wall above his fireplace was fine enough that it might have graced the morning room or breakfast parlour at Gilverton.

'So,' I said, 'if you cast your mind back across those thirty years, what can you tell me about Mr Bewer's last days and his departure?'

'He wasn't himself,' Gunn said. 'Not at all. He had never been a difficult man and no one knows a gentleman better than his valet. When he started on about the necklace it was quite out of character.'

'He spoke to you about it?'

'Muttered,' said Gunn, 'and I heard him.' He looked as uncomfortable as he might, admitting that he listened to mutters and remembered them. 'The curse, the death of his mother, his terror that his daughter-in-law would die before an heir had come along. He was never a man to be so fanciful. I think he was ill, if I'm to be honest. Not – I don't mean lumbago or headaches. I mean I think his nerves were strained until they snapped. I think he was ill in that way.'

I nodded my understanding. It was a terrible betrayal for a valet to suggest such a thing as mental weakness in his master and I liked to hear Gunn so troubled by it. If he was not a gossip or a man who revelled in scandal, I could take anything else he told me that much more seriously.

'Did you witness any of the terrible final quarrel between him and Mrs Bewer?' I said.

Gunn was still again at that. He might have been reliving the memory, or perhaps he was just casting himself back over the years, tide after tide, until he remembered it: the scenes he must have tried so hard to put away from him.

'The quarrel?' he said, and he spoke haltingly. 'The night that Mrs Bewer threatened to go out with the ruby on?'

'That's it,' I said. 'Were you there?'

'He snatched it off her neck,' he said. 'I saw the weals. I went to help him dress and I heard her crying through the dressing-room door.'

I tutted. 'And it was shortly after that he left for good?'

'I helped him,' Gunn said even more haltingly. Each word seemed as though it were being wrung out of him. 'I packed.'

This case had been regrettably free of such moments but, as he spoke, I knew that finally some part of it was going to loosen. My excitement was like a little fish leaping inside me, flicking itself free with a shower of droplets and then plonking heavily down again. It was not exactly a pleasant sensation but since the thoughts accompanying it were so welcome and so overdue I almost enjoyed it.

'You packed everything?' I said. He nodded glumly, as if he knew what was coming and did not relish it. 'And I take it you did not pack the Cut Throat?' I said. He shook his head, just as glumly. 'But did you pack anything big enough to contain it?' I persisted. Another shake.

'I don't suppose you know of any favourite hiding place where he might have stashed it?' I asked him, hope fading fast. 'We know it's not in the rocking horse because we looked and what we found there was nothing to do with Richard. It was a note to Bluey from his . . . Well, *not* his grandmother, actually, but it's all rather a tangle and since it was written before he was born . . . Is something the matter, Mr Gunn?'

'Not a thing,' he said. He roused himself and said, more stoutly. 'Not one single thing. Why?'

The honest answer would be that he looked as sick as a child swallowing castor oil, but no one wants to hear that of himself and so much of interviewing reluctant witnesses is buttering up, I have found. 'Have you remembered a hidey-hole?' I said. 'Are you tussling with your conscience?'

'My conscience?' he said, ringingly enough for it to make a tiny echo. 'My conscience is quite clear. I sleep the sleep of the just every night. I've nothing on my conscience.'

'I only meant,' I said, 'that if you had remembered a likely spot you would have to choose between telling me or joining the treasure hunt and winning it for your own.'

'I know of no likely spots,' he said. 'There are no hidey-holes in the castle that I ever heard of. Mr Bewer was bad with his nerves and then he left his house and abandoned his family and travelled all over the place. He sent letters, you know: Zanzibar and Aleppo and Beirut and—'

'And?' I said. 'Aleppo, Zanzibar and Beirut we have heard of. Is there another place you'd rather not mention, Mr Gunn? Do you know for sure that the place you won't mention is one we'd like to know about? What exactly are you hiding?'

'Hiding?' he said. 'I – hiding? I'm not hiding anything. It's not me who lost it. It's not me who squirreled away a treasure. I'm hiding not one single thing. I was a young man in a household with many troubles. I witnessed distressing scenes. I helped my master pack and then I left there and came here and had no more dealings with any of them.' He shut his mouth very firmly and crossed his arms over his chest as punctuation.

I let myself out, judging that nothing would open those

lips again, and met the same little maid only now coming back with the extra coffee cup.

'Too late,' I said. 'Not to worry. But you might fetch Mr Gunn a glass of brandy.'

'Is he ill?' said the maid. Behind her the kitchen door nudged open and I saw a cook in the same blue cotton as the girl, with a capacious apron tied over it, and a housekeeper in strict black with a bunch of keys at her waist. They had been listening and were clearly agog.

'He's not ill,' I said.

'Did you bring bad news?' said the cook.

'Unwelcome memories,' I said.

'And who exactly are you?' the housekeeper put in, as well she might.

'I'm . . . helping out along at Castle Bewer,' I said. 'With their new venture.'

'Oho,' said the housekeeper. 'That would do it. Mr Gunn doesn't care to be reminded of those days.'

'Yes,' I said. 'I do appear to have rattled him.'

'Good!' said the cook. 'Whether you meant to or not, if you've lit a fire under Mr Gunn you've done the house a favour.'

I thought about her words all the way home. Gunn knew something about Richard Bewer's disappearance, that was for sure. He knew that there was one place on the grand tour, besides Aleppo, Beirut and Zanzibar, that he should be careful not to name. And he was not a good enough butler to be the butler at Mespring House. The housekeeper had almost said as much to a perfect stranger and Lady Annandale had hinted that his rise was in payment for some mysterious good deed done in the distant past. And despite what he had said about not knowing a thing about any hidey-hole, he had gone the colour of milk when I mentioned it.

I was still puzzling when I tramped across the bridge and through the gatehouse arch, interrupting the technical rehearsal at a very tricky moment and being glared at from the stage by both Macbeths, a couple of lords and all three murderers; the third murderer, on his first day as a thespian, just as withering of my faux pas as any of them.

'Let's stop now for luncheon,' Leonard shouted from his perch halfway up the rake of wooden seats. 'Since we've been so roundly knocked out of our concentration anyway.' He stood and passed a weary hand over his brow. 'We shall start again in one hour exactly. From right there. Act III, scene 3, "Alight, alight."' He gave me one final scowl and then took himself away, dragging his feet like the loser of the men's doubles after forty games in the last set on a hot day. It was a bit much, in my opinion, since he had only been sitting there watching others working.

Alec, after some important-looking conversation with the other two murderers, jumped down from the stage and strolled towards me. He was wearing a soft-collared shirt of heaven knew what provenance, for I was sure Barrow would have given notice if Alec had tried to introduce such a garment into his wardrobe at home. What is more, the top button of the soft collar was open and the sleeves were rolled to the elbow. His ordinary country tweed trousers did not look quite as peculiar as Leonard's flannels or indeed as Billy Annandale's bags, but otherwise he had dressed as one of them. I even thought his hair was flopping a little.

'Any luck?' he said. 'Any answers?'

'Lots of luck,' I said, 'but only questions.' And I laid it out to him, as succinct a report as I had ever delivered, perhaps to remind him by my very briskness that he might be a bright young thing of the theatrical sort suddenly, but I was still me.

'I just don't know what any of it means,' I concluded.

'Really?' Alec said. 'I think it's quite straightforward.' I waited. Alec looked ostentatiously over each shoulder before he spoke again, like the baddie in a picture show. 'Gunn took the ruby back to the Annandales,' he said. 'That bought him his start and secured him his advancement. They've had it all along. Lady Annandale's protestations of ignorance are hard to swallow. Don't you think?'

'I don't know about that. She seemed truly astonished by the tale of the curse and she is not one to let her mouth hang open easily. And what about the burglars?'

'The Annandales sent them to throw the Bewers off the scent,' Alec said. 'That makes a lot more sense than Richard pulling strings from the farthest reaches of Empire, when you actually think about it.'

'And speaking of the farthest reaches,' I said. 'Here's a strange thing. Why did Gunn gobble the name he found himself almost saying? Aleppo, Zanzibar, Beirut and . . . he stopped himself saying a fourth one.'

'Lisbon,' Alec said. 'That's the other place that was spoken of in my hearing.'

'Why would he get tongue-tied about mentioning Lisbon?'

'Perhaps that's where Richard died and he didn't want to mention the fact.'

'But how on earth would the ex-valet know where Richard died?' I said. 'And in fact—'

Alec interrupted me. 'If he died in Lisbon, he was on his way back, wouldn't you say?'

I knotted my brow and tried to bring to mind the globe I had spun for Donald and Teddy when they were small, as they planned their life's adventures. We had not known then that none of us would be taking the tours our parents had enjoyed. 'It does seem like a round trip, actually,' I said. 'When you really think of it. To Lisbon and then either to Beirut or Aleppo, then down to Zanzibar, and back to either Aleppo or Beirut and then Lisbon again. One way by sea and one way by land it makes a nice little tootle. But if we imagine him on one long outward journey, it's a bit of a mess.'

'But why would Gunn fear to mention it?'

'I don't know,' I said. 'I have no idea. And there's no need to look at me like that. Let's hear *your* brilliant explanation for Gunn suddenly clamming up, if they're so easily to hand.'

Alec glared at me for a moment and I daresay my tone had invited it. I was unrepentant. It is far easier to listen and carp than endlessly to volunteer ideas to be carped at and Alec, in my estimation, took that easy path every time. As I watched him, though, an even less welcome expression than the glare spread over his face. He beamed at me with eyes twinkling and began patting his pockets. I groaned. Alec smug and patronising is bad enough, but Alec smug, patronising and talking at a snail's pace in between fussing with his interminable pipe is just about unbearable.

'What is it?' I said.

'Can't you guess?' he said. He had his baccy pouch out and was knocking his pipe against the wood of the bench so smartly that I hoped he would break it. 'I'll give you a clue. Who knew Otto was planning to hand over the letters from Richard to you?'

'No one,' I said. 'And I don't see how that's a clue.'

'Think about it, Dandy. Why should someone break into Otto's room and steal her evening whatsit rather than her jewels?'

'They were after the *letters*?' I said. 'But what does that have to do with Richard dying in Lisbon?'

'And his itinerary not making much sense as a single journey,' Alec said. He waited. 'Oh come on! I'm practically handing it to you.'

'Enlighten me,' I replied, hoping that I spoke drily enough to take the joy out of it for him.

'He went to Lisbon and died there. Aleppo, Beirut and Zanzibar were tarradiddles and the letters he supposedly sent home were fakes.'

I opened my mouth to pooh-pooh his words but realised that, as theories go, it was an excellent one. 'But then who stole the letters last night?' I asked instead.

Alec shrugged. 'We must try to find out,' he told me. 'Does it make more sense to think that someone broke in or that someone already in the castle did it? There's the question of the keys and how an outsider would know where to find them.'

'Gunn knows the house,' I pointed out. 'Oh and actually – the very first night we were here Grant and I thought we saw lights in the lane. That would fit with someone creeping along from Mespring to . . . Hmm, but that was before we asked Otto for the letters.'

'Perhaps, as soon as detectives were known to have arrived, it seemed inevitable that the letters would be subjected to scrutiny.'

I nodded uncertainly. 'But I don't think anyone at Mespring knew we had arrived until the piece in the newspaper this morning'.

'Oh come now!' said Alec. 'Not upstairs perhaps. But don't tell me there's not fraternising between the servants. You've talked about it yourself. How the attempt to keep the story of the Cut Throat curse quiet by a change of staff failed so miserably because they all visit one another.'

That was not quite what I had said but I could not put my finger on why the discrepancy bothered me. I was too taken up with another problem. 'Wouldn't Otto have noticed that it was different writing?' I said. 'If someone faked letters from her husband after the first one from Lisbon?'

'Now you're just being disagreeable because I thought of it before you!' Alec said.

'I'm simply being thorough,' I answered, grandly. 'But very well, let's accept your idea and take a good look at it from every angle. Richard left. The butler helped him pack. The staff was being sacked anyway, so Gunn secured a good position at Mespring by pinching their ruby and taking it back to them. Richard wrote from Lisbon before he died there. To cover up his death until the question of the ruby was too far back in time to be easily answered, someone –

one of the Annandales, I presume – had friends who were travelling send back more letters to Ottoline to make her believe her husband was still alive. And they organised burglars to come and pretend to search for the jewel.'

'Tell me what's wrong with any of that!' Alec said. 'Except for the nitpicking point about handwriting. And anyway, I bet Richard went to the same prep school and public school as Annandale and was taught to write by the same masters. There'll be nothing in it between their two hands.'

'Annandale?' I said. '*Lord* Annandale, you mean? You think he was behind all of this?'

'Who else?' Alec said.

'It strikes me as a woman's crime,' I told him. 'Domestic in scale, concerned with baubles, not to mention scandals. I'd be very surprised to find a man behind it, if I'm honest.'

Alec, reluctant to let go of his brilliant idea and needing Lord Annandale's masculine penmanship to make it hold together, saw off my hunch with no more than a desultory wave of his pipe hand and so, as we set to, trying to think how to prove it, we left my hunch behind.

16

'Minnie,' I called, as she shot across my field of view minutes later, this time with an armful of cushions so high they almost obscured her face and put her in real danger of tripping over the dog at her heels. She could not possibly see where she was going. 'Minnie, I need a quick word but let me help you.'

'Oh, thank you,' she said, dropping the lot on the passage floor and kicking some towards me. 'I told myself if I tripped I'd have a soft landing, but yes please, Dandy. You take half.'

'Where are we taking them?'

'The chapel,' Minnie said. 'We're going to have the lectures in there. It's quite plain and there are no saints or anything so with luck the attendees will think it's a schoolroom.'

'Why are—?'

But Minnie was at that pitch of busyness and preparedness where she could not listen to an unnecessary word and she cut across me.

'Between the teas, the need for the Americans to have a quiet sitting room to get away from the day-trippers and the need for Ottoline to have a quiet sitting room to get away from the Americans, this is the only place left. But the pews are torture so I'm grabbing cushions from everywhere and squashing pillows into cushion covers too, hoping no one notices.'

I had picked up the five or so that she had kicked towards me and we set off.

'What I wanted to ask was if you had a telephone in a quiet room where I would be unlikely to be disturbed. Or rather to bother anyone.'

'Only one phone,' Minnie said. 'And it's in Bluey's book room, where we've stuffed the ladies to get them away from the hurly-burly. But they won't mind. Is it anything they shouldn't overhear?'

Just, I thought, me telephoning the embassy in Portugal to ask about suspicious deaths thirty years ago. 'How is Mrs Rynsburger after her ordeal?' I said.

'Oh in great spirits,' said Minnie. 'They've decided they would have been disappointed *without* a ghost. They rather suspect me of laying it on for them.'

'You didn't, did you?' I asked, then I laughed to show I was joking as she gave me an old-fashioned look. 'Well, in that case, I do want to ask about the keys in Pugh's pantry and in Bluey's room. Have they always been there, exactly where they are now? If someone came back who hadn't been in the house for decades could he lay his hands on them?'

'Back?' said Minnie. We were at what I guessed to be the chapel door, an arched affair with no lock, I noticed, keys being on my mind. Minnie opened it simply by turning round and leaning against it, since her arms were full. 'You think my father-in-law has come back? You actually think he might still be alive?'

'Not a chance,' I said. 'And I don't think his ghost has come back either. And if it did, ghosts don't need keys.' Thus I threw her off the scent and the sight of Grant busy in one of the pews halfway forward did the rest of the job.

'Delia?' she said. I surmised that Grant's shift from lady's maid to member of the players was complete.

'I thought I'd just run up some bolsters to soften these hard benches,' Grant said. 'There was a trunk full of mattress ticking in the attic – I found it when I was searching for set dressing. We got a good lot of that too, by the way.'

Minnie and I feasted our eyes. Every pew was covered with a plump bolster of unbleached striped ticking. They looked a little like sacks of meal but a lot more inviting than the hard wood designed to keep servants alert during a sermon.

'What are they stuffed with?' said Minnie.

'Clean straw,' said Grant, 'as they would have been in Shakespeare's own time. Miss Penny is adding a line at the top of her lecture about you trying to recreate the atmosphere down to the last little detail. We were thinking of nosegays on the benches during the play. They would have had nosegays at the Globe.'

'What will I do with these?' said Minnie, nodding her chin at her armload of cushions.

'They're rather modern,' Grant said. 'I'll take care of them for you.'

Minnie, for the second time, let the cushions drop and started hurrying out again, her little dog torn between his love for his mistress and the reappearance of this pile of bedding at his feet.

'Early dinner,' Minnie said. 'Patch! Leave those be. Come here, you brigand! Six o'clock if you can believe it, but the dress needs to start at seven to make sure there's time. Leonard tells me all sorts of things can go wrong during "the dress". They last all night sometimes.' And the door closed behind her.

'You're getting very keen on all of this,' I said to Grant. She simpered, taking it as a compliment.

'Grant, I give you my word that I shan't be cross, but did you encourage one of your apparitions to do a little extra haunting last night?'

'In Mrs Rynsburger's bedroom?' said Grant. 'Of course not. I would never go along with anything so unprofessional.'

'That is not the word I'd have chosen.'

'Oh, but it's extremely unprofessional to go larking about in a costume offstage,' Grant said. 'I told them to get straight to the wardrobe room and hang them up properly. I worked quickly on them but that's not to say I didn't work hard.'

'You are certainly working hard,' I agreed. 'Do you think a nice walk would do you good this afternoon?'

'A walk?' she said, making a kind of screech out of the word. 'I don't have time for a nice walk. I'll barely have time between the tech and the dress to swallow a bite of supper, madam. Walk where?' she added, which rather spoiled the effect. I was sure that if the destination had offered any scope for drama Grant would have fitted it in.

'Just to the Post Office to send a telegram to Gilverton,' I said. 'But no matter. I'll go.'

It was what I needed. A stroll down the lanes to the little sub-Post Office at Annanbridge would have given me just the time required to sort through the deluge of snippets and stories and start to see the pattern that was in there. Somewhere. But it was not to be. Alec sat down next to me at the scratch luncheon Minnie had laid out in the great hall and whispered urgently in my ear, putting his lips so close to my head that his breath tickled.

'Come to the rehearsal after lunch, Dandy, and watch me until I go off for the last time and after the rehearsal come to my room and . . . help me. I don't think I can do it. I think I'll forget my lines, or fall over my feet or perhaps just faint dead away. I don't know what I was thinking.'

'Oh, you'll be fine,' I said. 'Once the audience is in and the stars are shining down and the footlights up.'

'Audience?' said Alec, paling. 'Promise me you'll watch. I'm on right after lunch and the very next line is mine, then I'm a king in that dratted procession of dead kings that makes me want to scream, then third murderer again in Act IV, scene 2, then nothing but lurking about as a soldier with a bough in front of my face and even I can't muck that up surely, so you don't need to watch till the bitter end.'

'Good,' I said. 'Because we actually have a job to do, beyond swanning about in doublet and hose, Alec. And I was planning to get on with it.' His face beseeched me silently although he did not speak. 'Oh all right then. When exactly can I duck away?'

'At *Exit Lady Macduff pursued by murderers*,' Alec said.

'Poor thing,' I said. 'Now let go of my arm so I can eat some luncheon, would you?'

The soup was tasty but terribly hearty with it and the slices of buttered bread piled high on platters all up and down the table were such as would fill a ploughman at noon with a jug of beer to wash it down. I wished I had had the forethought to join the American ladies in Bluey's book room, for surely they were not spooning up this broth – so thick it was more of a stew really – nor tearing into these hunks of bread. The players did not seem to mind. Even the grand Miss Byrne made a good effort and did not push back her chair and light a cigarette until she had scraped the bottom of her bowl and consumed the crust, which had defeated me.

Leonard and Alec alone seemed too nervy to apply themselves. Leonard kept hopping up to look out of the window and Alec simply sat and stared at some of the young actors – thanes and the like – who were chatting in an easy way on the other side of the long board. Perhaps he thought he could absorb their training, or at least their years of calm experience, if he watched them closely. Of course they saw him at it and that only made them loll further back and speak in lazier drawls, as though they felt not a whit of anxiety about the opening night soon to be upon them.

Moray Dunstane and Max Moore – Duncan and Macbeth themselves – sat at head and foot and silently regarded one another. Perhaps they could not shake off the mantle of King and Pretender and prattle about shaving strops and railway tickets the way the youngsters were.

'There won't be enough,' Leonard said to the company at large as he sat down again after one of his trips to the window.

No one answered and so I took pity on him. 'Enough what, Mr . . . ? Enough what?'

'Branches,' he said. 'Boughs. Greenery. I've sent a couple of lads to hack some branches off those trees at the edge of the field. I thought it would be much better than the card and wool affairs we brought with us, but there's too much branch per leaf and they're going to be too heavy.'

'Did Bluey give his permission?' I said mildly. I did not know if Bluey was as peculiar as Hugh about the pruning, thinning, pollarding and coppicing of his trees, but if anyone had taken an axe to the edge of the park at Gilverton to make Birnam Wood out of it, Hugh would have set about the man with a horsewhip.

'He didn't mind as long as it's the lane side and doesn't leave bare patches visible from the house,' Leonard said. 'But they're making a mess of it!' He hopped up again and went to lean out of the casement, where this time I joined him.

It was easy to diagnose the problem as I squinted across the breadth of the field at the two young men in shirtsleeves who were grappling with some large branches of elm. They were actors, not farmhands, and they had no idea until they started whacking, just how solid a real branch is compared with what Leonard had called the 'card and wool affairs'. They were struggling to get them across the top of the gate and, even when the heftier of the two lads managed to pivot his over and send it into the field, it landed so heavily that it crushed and snapped all the little leafy twigs. They were left behind when he started dragging and what remained was no cover at all for a soldier on the move.

'Paddy! Francis! Open the gate, you fools!' Leonard yelled out of the window and once again I had cause to note that the training of the theatrical voice is a wonder. 'Why on earth are you trying to seesaw them over? Use the *gate*!' High above us another window opened and Ottoline's voice, querulous and thin, came wafting down.

'Who is shouting so?' she said. 'And what are those ruffians doing?'

'Ottoline?' I called, leaning out and craning up. I could not see her but I thought I knew roughly where she must be. 'It's Birnam Wood, coming to Castle Bewer in readiness for Dunsinane. Bluey has given permission, I believe. There's no need to worry.'

Leonard's yelling had finally attracted the attention of the lunching players and a few of the young men and girls were now at the other open windows along the length of the hall, jeering and catcalling. It was the strangest jeering I had ever heard though, being completely couched in the words of the play.

'Your leafy screens throw down and show like those you are!' yelled Robert.

'Ring the alarum bell,' cried George. 'Blow wind, come wrack.'

'Though Birnam Wood be come to Dunsinane, and thou opposed being of no woman born!'

'What?' came the cry from above. 'What are you shouting out of the windows for all the world to hear?'

'Otto,' I called again. 'Close your casement and don't worry about it. They won't be long.'

'She's deaf,' said Leonard. 'She won't hear you.'

'Macduff was from—' shouted Roger, who had the lustiest voice of all.

'Stop it!' I told him, pulling my head in and going over to where he stood.

'Macduff was from his mother's—'

'You're being naughty and childish,' I said and I went so far as to wag my finger.

'Macduff was from his mother's *womb* untimely ripped!' Roger finally managed to get out, louder than ever despite the fact that he was giggling. I heard, from above, Ottoline's window slamming shut.

'That's not even anything to do with the branches!' I said. 'And Mrs Bewer should not have to listen to such puerile nonsense.'

'She's as deaf as a post,' Leonard said again. 'I'm surprised she heard a thing.'

'And,' said Roger, 'the Bard's timeless—'

'Don't give me that,' I said. 'It was pure mischief.'

The whole company was giggling now, even Moray and Sarah were smiling, although they were too dignified to be throwing lines around.

Then Leonard, practically falling out the window, started yelling again. 'Paddy, look! Stop! Look behind you! Francis, it's going to go!' I turned back to see what was happening. Even Alec was roused from his meditations by the new note in Leonard's voice.

One of the two young men, sweating and struggling like a plough ox on a steep field, had dragged an enormous bough all the way to the drawbridge. It began to skew as he slowed and then to teeter on the edge of the outermost planks, before the inevitable happened and it fell with an almighty splash into the green water. The players gathered above hooted and clapped and Leonard screamed down at the boy with all restraint gone, his pale face turned a blotchy red and a hank of hair falling over his eyes as he shook his fists. 'Get it out! Get it out and get it dried!'

The two lads looked at one another and then coming to a silent agreement they jumped in.

Then all hell broke loose. One of them came up spluttering and swearing about the cold of the water, whipping his hair out of his eyes and laughing as he cursed. He looked around for his mate, still laughing at first and then with growing alarm on his face.

'Oh God,' I said. 'I forgot! It's deep. It's not an ornament. It's ten feet deep and more.'

Finally, the lad came up, coughing and retching and

only managing to say 'I can't swim!' before he went down again.

Otto was screaming and wailing up at her window, sounding utterly panicked now, as the first lad took a deep breath and, with a kick like a fish, plunged under the water.

Penny came into view across the bridge from under the gatehouse arch, picking her way between the branches abandoned there and turning to look up at us.

'What's going on?' she shouted.

'He's drowning!' Tansy Bell shouted down. 'Francis is drowning.'

Penny kicked off her shoes without another thought. She ignored her grandmother's voice from above begging: 'Penny, no! No! Everyone stop. It has to stop!' and Alec's voice from beside me shouting: 'No, Penny. Use a branch or fetch help!' But just as she took a little run backwards, ready to dive, Paddy Ramekin's head came up again and, with it this time, Francis too, retching and spluttering, to a great cheer from the players.

'Don't jump in,' Paddy told Penny. 'Here, help me get him on the bank.'

Ottoline was still screaming like a kettle up in her room. She sounded hysterical and, even though I shouted up with my familiar voice and Roger shouted too with his tremendous bellow: 'He's not drowned, Mrs Bewer, He's fine,' it just carried on and on as if she would never cease.

Down by the moat, Francis had been hauled on to the bank. The next order of business was to eject all the water he had consumed. This filled the watching players with hilarity but did not strike me as a spectacle I wished to witness.

'I better go up and see if Ottoline is all right,' I said.

I met Bluey on my way. He cut an odd figure, drifting along the gallery outside his book room with a clutch of silver lockets swinging from one fist and a faraway look in his eye.

'Was that my mother yelling?' he said as he saw me. 'What's the matter?'

204

'*Everyone* was yelling,' I said. 'Ottoline was screeching. She thought one of the actors had drowned, jumping into the moat after an elm branch.'

Bluey blinked and frowned, as who could not, for the tale made no sense to anyone who had not seen it happen. But he was consumed with the question of where to hide the trinkets and he did not pursue it beyond saying: 'Ah. Well, Mama doesn't think much of the moat water, you know. At least for swimming. She forbade Penny from it when she was a child. Never did me any harm, I must say, and I spent most of my summers in there, like a tadpole.'

'Hang one on Beulah's picture frame,' I said nodding at the lockets. 'It's got lots of knobs and twiddles, hasn't it? And the silver won't be visible against the gilt unless one looks for it. I think it would be a neat trick to hide one where everyone will look but no one will see. Adds to the fun.'

'Do you think we're mad, Dandy?' Bluey asked, giving me a frank look. 'Do you think there's any chance it'll work?'

He spoke so honestly that I wanted to give an honest reply, rather than reassurances. But even when I thought about it coldly I found myself nodding. 'I think it *will* work,' I said. 'The lunches, teas and suppers, the lectures, the play itself. I was down on the idea of *Macbeth* as much as you when Leonard first revealed the truth but it seems very fitting somehow.'

'That's hardly an endorsement of one's home!' said Bluey. 'That *Macbeth* fits in nicely.'

'Would it help to know the Annandales are envious of your originality?' I said. 'I mean, of course, Mespring is pretty swish, but a castle is a castle is a castle. A moat and a drawbridge and stone spiral staircases have their own romance. And there's going to be so much more for everyone to do here than just shuffle around and feel awed by the Old Masters. I think it's going to be marvellous, actually.'

I was soon to wish I had not used up so much of my cheer on him, for when I knocked gently and entered Ottoline's bedroom I saw that I would need it all.

She was lying down on her chaise with a handkerchief pressed to her mouth and was a very peculiar colour, rather yellow in streaks but with hectic patches under her eyes. I hurried over and laid a hand on her forehead.

'You're ice cold,' I said. 'Let me ring—' I remembered that there were no bells, 'Well, let me run and fetch some tea and a hot bottle for you. He's fine, Ottoline. They fished him out and he's quite fine.'

'What?' she said, struggling to sit up. 'What's happening?'

'I think his name is Francis,' I told her. 'He plays one of the minor lords – or are they all thanes? I never know. And probably a porter, doctor and king too. Shall I go and fetch Patch for you to hug? Nothing like a dog to warm one up.' I was chafing her hands and I thought I could feel a little life come back into them. 'I don't know how they keep it all straight in their heads, do you?'

Only then did I remember that I was supposed to be in quite another room, chafing other hands, and offering assurances that it was easy, not doubts that it was possible. Well, Alec would just have to do without me in the face of Otto's greater need.

'No need for that,' she said. 'I'm feeling a little better now.'

'Excellent.'

'I got the wind up.' She did sound more like her old self. 'Watching those silly boys racketing about.'

'It was very foolish of him to jump in without knowing how deep it was. It's extremely deep, isn't it? Bluey said he was forbidden it when he was a child.'

'Very deep,' Otto agreed. 'But Bluey is swaggering. He always hated cold water anyway. He wouldn't swim at the seaside either. Or not until the first time we went all the way to Eastbourne anyway. Oh, I would have loved to move to

Eastbourne, Dandy. Sea breezes and warm sunshine and never dark at teatime the way it is here in the winter.'

'Perhaps,' I began, then I thought the better of it. The chances of Alec or me finding the Cut Throat now that the great treasure hunt was splashed all over the press seemed vanishingly thin. Minnie's dream of selling it and furnishing a quiet little life in Edinburgh for her and Bluey was fading fast. Ottoline in rooms in Eastbourne with a companion seemed even less likely. As I looked at her lying there, however, at least it appeared that her remaining days would be without upheaval, for she could surely not last until after Richard's century and the time it would take for the bills to arrive and their due date fall for paying.

She was snoring now. I pulled a rug up over her shoulders and left quietly.

17

The book room had been turned into quite an organised head-quarters and the four ladies – Mrs Rynsburger, Mrs Westhousen, Mrs Cornelius and Mrs Schichtler – looked like four generals planning to take a city. They had cleared Bluey's desk of all his possessions and spread there the architect's drawings of the house, held down at the corners by inkpots and the like. Besides, they were almost in uniform, each of them in a long sturdy skirt and a crisp white shirt of plain design. Mrs Cornelius even had her cuffs unbuttoned and her sleeves folded back to the elbow.

'Ah, Mrs Gilver,' Mrs Rynsburger said. 'Are you here to help? We're not to be disturbed otherwise. We only have tonight to find the prize before everyone else gets here.'

'I'd rather watch the dress rehearsal,' said Mrs Westhousen, patting her golden curls. 'Rubies don't suit my complexion.'

'I thought you were attending the first lecture this after-noon,' I said.

'Oh, we came to an agreement,' said Mrs Cornelius, sounding more hard-bitten than ever. 'We're happy to hunt treasure and Penny and Mr Bewer are needed for last-minute panics. They don't have nearly enough servants to run this place, in my opinion.'

She spoke as though budgetary concerns were quite unknown to her and it was simply some quaint quirk of Minnie and Bluey's that they were rushing about with piles of cushions and fistfuls of lockets.

'Well, I'm afraid I must disturb you for just a minute,' I said. 'I want to use the telephone.'

'Go ahead,' said Mrs Schichtler, waving at where it was holding down one of the curlier plans at the far end of the table.

'Oh,' I said. 'Well, I have something rather private to say.'

'You've found it!' said Mrs Rynsburger. 'Oh, phooey! You've found it, haven't you?'

'I have not found it, I assure you. It's my husband I'm ringing and . . . ' I ran dry. What could I say to them that would explain my bundling them out of their base camp?

To my surprise, I did not need to say anything.

'Well, of course,' said Mrs Westhousen. 'You've been here for days now. You must be missing him.'

It seemed utterly preposterous to me, but the other three all put their heads on one side and grew misty-eyed.

'Of course we'll clear off while you talk sweet nothings to your dear one,' said Mrs Rynsburger. Even that did not cause a single one of them to curl a lip, although I had to concentrate hard on mine. They stood and gathered a few pens and sheets of scrap and then, with more fond smiles, they left me. I listened for the sound of guffaws when they were outside, for I was sure it must be a tease, but there was nothing but the sound of their sensible shoes on the stone floor as they marched off in pursuit of the ruby.

When Pallister answered the telephone a devil on my shoulder told me to ask for my dear one, but reason prevailed. 'Is Mr Gilver at home, Pallister?' I said instead.

'Of *course*, madam,' Pallister said, managing to wedge in a little disapproval of my wanderings in comparison to Hugh's quiet ways.

'Please fetch him.'

There followed a long stretch of silence and then the sound of Hugh's pack of terriers and hounds approaching, heralding Hugh himself.

'Dandy,' he said, his usual greeting.

'Hugh,' I agreed. 'Is Bunty there with the others?'

'She is,' said Hugh and I took the earpiece away from my head and stared at it. That had sounded awfully like affection. I surmised that, with my absence, Bunty's own sweet nature had got round Hugh at last. I decided not to spoil it by letting him know it was showing.

'Very well,' I said, with not a scrap of interest. 'Hugh, I'm ringing up to ask you a favour.'

'There already, eh?' Hugh said. He harbours a belief that when a case really hots up Alec and I have to call him in to do some essential piece of reasoning. I see no downside to letting him think that way.

'Hardly,' I said. 'I don't think we've made much headway at all, but there's a particular task I need you to carry out for me if it's not too much of a bore. Do you know anyone in Lisbon?'

'Lisbon?' said Hugh. 'Portugal?'

'Exactly. Do you know anyone who lives there or anyone at the consulate? Embassy? I never know the difference.'

'A consulate,' Hugh began, inevitably, 'is a—'

'Yes, but do you? Or can you think of any other way to find out about something that happened there thirty years ago? Wasn't one of the Carnegie boys there for a while?'

'Not thirty years ago,' said Hugh. 'What sort of something? A crime?'

'Well, a death,' I said. 'The death of a man of seventy, unidentified I daresay. A stranger in the place.'

'What on earth is this about?' said Hugh. 'I thought you were trying to find a diamond.'

'Ruby. Yes. But we think it's a wild goose chase. We rather think it was taken away thirty years ago by this chap who we rather think might have died in Lisbon. Do you know anyone there who could slip along to the police station after the siesta and pour a . . . ? What do they drink in Lisbon? Pernod? Absinthe?'

'Port, of course,' said Hugh, 'but not policemen in the

middle of the afternoon on a working day with a British ambassador in the office.'

'Well, a cup of tea then; it's hardly the point. We need someone to go and ask about a sudden death where the chap couldn't be identified, some time just short of thirty years ago. He would have been a well-to-do sort – a gentleman – passing through.'

'And might *I* just ask, Dandy?' said Hugh. 'If no one in Lisbon knew who he was, how did someone in Scotland find out that he might have died there?'

I drew breath to answer and then let it all go again. 'That's a very good point,' I said. 'That is an excellent point. It makes no sense, does it?'

'I'm glad I could help after my usual fashion,' said Hugh, unbearably smug. 'If you get into any more tangles, do ring back.'

I crashed the earpiece down and set the whole thing back on top of the curling floor plan, fuming, just as the four ladies reappeared, offering profuse apologies but quite firm that there was not another moment to lose. I turned to face them.

'Why you're quite flushed, Mrs Gilver,' Mrs Cornelius said. 'How charming.'

'How long have you been married to your sweetheart?' said Mrs Westhousen.

'And they say the English are cold!' said Mrs Schichtler.

'It's not that,' I said. 'Good grief.'

'Oh!' said Mrs Rynsburger. 'What have you seen? You saw something on the plans, didn't you? You've had an idea about where the Briar Rose is hidden.'

'But you'll tell *us*, won't you?' said Mrs Schichtler, coming close and looking up into my face. 'I mean to say, you'll be paid your wage no matter what. There's no need for you to have all the fun as well, when you're doing your job, no more and no less. But if we find it, it will be the crowning glory to our trip. We'll dine out on it all winter.'

There it was again: the disregard for money, the absolute lack of any sense that Bluey and Minnie would not want to give the Cut Throat away if they could help it. And there was something else bothering me too. I left as quickly as I could extricate myself, hoping that some solitary pondering might bring it into focus.

Why, I asked myself as I stood looking out of the window in the passageway, did it bother me so much that they misread the flush in my cheeks? That they thought it was ardour when it was irritation? It was slightly embarrassing but only slightly after all. Did I really care so much about any emotion being witnessed? No, that was not it either. Maybe Alec could help me, I thought, and then with a guilty start I hurried off to the courtyard and the rehearsal hoping that I had not missed his scenes completely.

I had missed his scenes completely. I sidled in beside him on one of the lower wooden benches and mimed apology.

Burly Roger was on the stage with a young man I was almost sure was called Julian, and was belting out a speech at the top of his capacious lungs and at top speed too. 'Thy Royal father was a most sainted king,' he said and the very walls of the castle echoed it back at him. 'The queen that bore thee oftener upon her knees than on her feet.'

'Is he hoping to catch last orders at the local pub?' I asked Alec.

'Sssh,' Alec said, but his lips twitched. 'I was just thinking that it was going to be jolly good actually, in the gloaming, with lights in the castle windows.'

Leonard, who was a couple of rows in front, turned round and shushed us.

Julian was speaking now. 'This noble passion, child of integrity, hath from my soul wiped the black scruples, reconciled my thoughts to thy good truth and honour.'

'Hmph,' I said. 'I can't agree with Mr Shakespeare there.'

Leonard swung round again and actually shook his fist at me.

'Let's go,' Alec breathed in my ear. 'I'm not doing Birnam Wood anyway unless they get more branches.'

We sidled out and away, tiptoeing so that our shoes would not ring out on the cobbles and give poor Leonard apoplexy. When we were inside the castle walls and could talk freely again I apologised properly for my absence, but Alec waved my regrets away. I was already forgiven.

'Will the leaves dry out in time to be used in the dress rehearsal?' I said.

'The branch that went in is hanging on the clothes airer in Mrs Porteous's kitchen,' Alec said. 'She is most displeased and one can hardly blame her. She's trying to bake for the multitudes tomorrow and it's dripping on her head. Is Otto recovered?'

'She is,' I said. 'She's sleeping. Aha!' Alec started. 'Sorry. But that's what's been troubling me. Mrs Rynsburger and the rest of them caught me red-faced and panting after a telephone conversation with Hugh.'

'What did he say to incense you this time?'

I laughed. 'Exactly! Because you know us both you know what my red face meant. But those women seemed to think they had interrupted a tryst. They knew it was Hugh on the telephone and concluded that we were one of those sickening couples still cooing in our dotage. Ugh.'

'But what did he say?'

'I'll get to that,' I insisted. 'The misunderstanding made me feel troubled and I think it's because I had just done the same to Otto.'

'The same in what way?' said Alec. 'Did you catch her fluttering her eyelashes at Pugh?'

'Don't be revolting,' I said. 'No, I assumed that her squealing like a kettle was because she feared Francis Whatsisname might drown. But she was already upset, don't you see? She was yelling and weeping before they jumped in.'

'She *was* making quite a racket,' Alec agreed.

'And why would that be?'

'Because,' Alec began slowly. 'Hmm, yes. Why *would* that be? Where are we going by the way, Dandy?'

'Oh,' I said, looking around. 'Somewhere peaceful, please. The collective panic in this house is beginning to give me a headache. How about the chapel? We can sit side by side and stare into space without bothering anyone there. And I can explain about Lisbon too.'

The white chapel, stripped of its altar cloths and candlesticks, was restful to the eye and the straw-filled ticking was remarkably comfortable, its only drawback being our conviction that we should not enjoy a pipe or even a cigarette while perched upon it.

'Perhaps it was the trees,' Alec said. 'Perhaps Otto is fond of them and didn't like to see them hacked about by amateurs.'

'Fond of an ordinary row of elms bordering a lane?' I said. 'Different if it was a grove of mighty oaks lining a drive, darling. And she wasn't angry, she was rattled. Before the drowning, during the dragging.'

'Why not just go back and ask her,' said Alec, rather disagreeably. He does so hate to have his notions shot down.

'Darling, if you'd seen her. She was yellow and purple in patches and clammy to the touch. Terribly distressed.'

'A great perturbation, eh?' said Alec.

'What?'

'Lady Macbeth,' he said. 'But you could ask her gently.'

'She's asleep,' I told him.

'To her deaf pillow she will discharge her secrets.'

'*What?*'

'Lady Macbeth, I tell you.'

'Shakespeare should make his mind up,' I said. 'Malcolm just told Macduff that his passion was proof of his integrity. But Lady Macbeth being all riled up is supposed to prove her guilt? That's all very convenient, isn't it?'

Alec glared, but rather than argue he said, 'Tell me about Lisbon.'

'Oh, yes. Hugh, God rot him, pointed out that if people here knew that Richard died there then he can't have died incognito. Makes perfect sense, more's the pity.'

'Unless,' said Alec, 'someone went from here to kill him.'

'What motive?'

'We already think he was on his way home,' said Alec. 'Well, if he was supposed to have taken the Cut Throat away with him, or stashed it in the castle, the last thing its thief would want would be his coming back and revealing he did neither!'

'And who – in this outlandish theory of yours – is supposed to have killed him?' I said. 'Gunn might be the thief, but a footman can't take off across the seas suddenly.'

'One of the Annandales,' Alec said. 'I told you already.'

'Doing murder to cover theft? It makes no sense. It's easier to believe that Ottoline cares about a row of elm trees. And that makes no sense *at all*.'

'True,' Alec said. 'Unless, of course, the Cut Throat is buried in a casket at the foot of one of them.'

'And Ottoline knows that, does she?' I asked drily. Alec had the grace to look sheepish. 'Although, Grant and I did see lights in the lane just about there on our first night here. They didn't come any closer than those trees.'

'A maid with her sweetheart,' said Alec.

'There's only Gilly,' I said. 'Although I daresay Mrs Porteous would look at her best in a dark lane with only a match lit.' I sat and mused upon it all for a minute. 'There's something about the servants,' I said.

'There certainly is,' said Alec. 'I shall give Barrow a raise when we get home in case he ever leaves me and I'm reduced to the likes of Pugh.'

'No,' I persisted, 'there's something about the servants who left. Not only Gunn, although certainly Gunn. But Nanny too. I must review my notes and see if I wrote down whatever it is that's bothering me.'

Alec reacted as predictably as a clock striking the hour. Exit Dandy pursued by snorts.

When I emerged, blinking, from my room in time for the dress rehearsal at six, I did not have an answer but at least I thought I knew the question. It was the name of this bally jewel that was bothering me, I was almost sure. Why could no one agree what it was called or who had called it that or when they had started or why they had stopped?

I sat myself down in the middle of a bench all alone, studiously ignoring the four American ladies who were in a state of great excitement three rows in front of me. The stage looked marvellous, even in the rather blank light of a dull afternoon becoming evening, and it would only look better tomorrow at eight when the first performance began to a packed house. Even Minnie, Bluey and Ottoline, who arrived and sat down at one side on the front row, looked quite perky as they drank in the sight of their courtyard transformed.

'*Are you sure you want to stay, Mama?*' bellowed Bluey into Ottoline's ear. 'It'll be terribly dull for you not hearing anything.'

'I have a copy of the play to read along and I can enjoy the spectacle,' Ottoline retorted. 'I hope there's going to *be* a spectacle,' she went on, turning to look Leonard straight in the eye. 'For we shan't fill these seats night after night without one.'

'If everyone would do their jobs,' Leonard said, 'the spectacle would be beyond question already.'

Bess appeared at one wing with her hands on her wide

hips and her mop of hair wilder than ever, as though it was a hank of wool from some hardy breed of sheep, midway between the fleece and the spinning wheel. 'I can't be rummaging in attics for something that clearly doesn't exist *and* be nailing swords to boards,' she said.

'Of course, it exists!' said Leonard. 'This is an ordered household.'

'I shall have everything ready for tomorrow,' Bess said. She spoke, like an actor, with heightened emphasis but with a restraint suggesting that she could speak even louder and with stronger words still should the scene continue. Leonard, recognising as much, subsided. 'Once I've given up the wild goose chase and had time to attend to it,' Bess finished. She turned on her heel and swept offstage.

'Wild goose chase?' said Mrs Cornelius, from the fourth row. 'Mr Bewer, is that woman talking about our treasure? Why does she say it doesn't exist?'

'Not at all, Mrs umm . . . dear lady,' said Bluey, twisting round and hailing her. 'Quite another . . . Something to dress the set, was it, Leonard? Well, have at it. Anything you can find. Swords or whatever you think. Absolutely.'

'But don't take furnishings from out of the rooms them-selves, will you?' said Minnie. 'I've counted chairs and tables most precisely for the teas and suppe—'

'Quiet!' Leonard shouted. 'We are late. We have not yet begun and already we are late! Act I, scene one. Witches!'

They advanced onto the stage from left and right and from the back middle where a card and wool tree offered a third entrance. I knew that they were Penny, Miss Tavelock and another girl by the name of Elizabeth, but with their cloak hoods up and their backs hunched they made me shiver as they began to speak the familiar lines.

'They're jolly good,' I said to Grant, who was sliding into the seat beside me. She looked absolutely haggard with exhaustion and was wrapped in a blanket from neck to ankle.

'What on earth is wrong with you?' I blurted out. 'Are you ill? You can't go on like that. Have you got the flu?'

Grant gave me a look of incredulity and laughed loud enough to make Leonard turn again and swear this time. 'It's make-up, madam,' she said. 'I'm made up to play the ghost of Bloody Mary in the procession of kings. And if you think *I'm* bad!' She nodded beyond my shoulder. I turned and gasped. Alec had sidled in at my other side, dressed and made up as Third Murderer, with dishevelled hair, a stubbled jaw, blackened teeth and grimy nails. He was dressed in a worn-looking tunic tied at the waist with frayed rope and some greyish brown hose, bagged at the knees and holey along the hems above bare filthy feet.

'You look dreadful!' I said. 'You both look worse than the witches.'

'Exactly,' Grant said. 'I asked to do the make-up and Leonard said no. So I thought I'd show him what he's missing tonight and he'll change his mind by tomorrow.'

'Ah,' I said. 'And why the blanket?'

'Oh,' said Grant airily, 'just to keep my costume clean until my entrance.'

I had no idea what she was up to, but the dull speeches about battles had finished, the men were gone and the witches were back, as thrilling as a pantomime. When Banquo and Macbeth joined them, Paddy Ramekin none the worse that I could see for his dowsing, Leonard relaxed like a bag of meal with its string cut. He sat back and put his hands behind his head, lacing his fingers there, then stretched his feet out in front of him. It lasted for two lines until a speech by the third witch brought him snapping upright and scribbling in his script. Elizabeth, who had delivered the line, noticed – How could she not? – and her distraction distracted the other two. Max as Macbeth ploughed on with his next bit – 'Stay, you imperfect speakers' which drew a 'Ha!' from Leonard. It was so loud that even Macbeth stopped, befuddled, and looked out over the footlights with his hand above his brow.

'What?' he said.

'Keep going! Keep going!' said Leonard. 'For God's sake, this is a dress rehearsal. You keep going even if the whole set slides into the moat. I shall tell you all what I think of you at the interval.'

'But how of Cawdor?' said Max turning back to the witches. 'The Thane of Cawdor lives.'

What's wrong with *him*?' I whispered to Grant, nodding at Leonard's back.

'The third witch said "beget" instead of "get",' said Grant. 'Trying to make the prophecy about children a little clearer.'

'That seems a sensible idea,' I said. 'Anything to help the audience understand. Unless we give all of them a book, like Ottoline, and let them just enjoy the spectacle.' I gestured towards the front row but saw that, already, Otto had gone.

'Listen,' Grant said, holding up a finger just as Macbeth delivered the line 'your children shall be kings'. 'See?' she said. 'Half a page later and they sum it up nicely for everyone. There's no need to pander.'

'But in the interim people might get tired of being lost and just wander off like Mrs Bewer has,' I said.

'She didn't wander,' said Grant. 'She bolted. Before the play had even started. Perhaps she's not feeling well again.'

If so, I thought, Minnie and Bluey were being as callous as ever, for they were both just sitting there watching the rehearsal with every sign of enjoyment. I slipped past Grant and down to the ground level of the courtyard to follow Ottoline and make sure she was comfortable.

She was not in her room, nor in the sitting room, great hall, morning room nor book room. I was at a loss. I even went and stood listening outside the door of the nearest lavatory, hoping that I would not hear anything, then knocking to make doubly sure when indeed there was only silence from within. I set off for the kitchens next, thinking of Mrs Ellen and Ottoline had a close connection for mistress and servant and so perhaps Otto had gone there for succour if she was overcome by illness suddenly.

Then my footsteps stilled. There I was standing like a statue in the dark of the passageway as my thoughts raced. Close connections between mistress and servant, I thought to myself. Or master and servant anyway. Gunn, Nanny, Gilly, Pugh. I had missed something.

At last I started moving again, surprising myself with how I could so assuredly find my way through this warren of stone passages. I rapped on the door to alert Mrs Porteous to my presence and, when I entered, it was to see the bright room transformed by the leafy bough slung over the airer, filtering the sunlight from the high windows so that it seemed we were in a glade, as though it were the *Dream* after all that had stormed the castle. It was also to see a huddled figure, sitting with a blanket pulled right over its head, on a stool drawn close to the fire.

'Otto?' I said. 'Are you ill?'

'I'm ill,' said the figure, pushing the blanket back and turning to me. 'But I'm not Otto.' It was Francis Mowatt, shivering and glassy-eyed. Mrs Porteous came in from the scullery with a basin and dropped it at his feet.

'A mustard scald'll see you to rights,' she said, sounding more like one of the witches than ever and looking so unfortunately like one too. Francis's reply was a huge sneeze that left him shuddering and brought more tears to his eyes.

'You caught a chill in the moat then?' I said.

'I caught more than a chill,' said Francis. 'I've had a premonition of my death.'

The chill seemed more to the point right at that moment, but I did not want to appear rude.

'How so?'

'I thought I was drowning,' said Francis. His voice had

shrunk to a croak and he coughed piteously. 'I saw visions and almost swooned before Paddy snatched me back up again.'

'Are you able to go on?'

'I've been on,' Francis told me. 'I'm Angus. I've just come off. Angus isn't back until Birnam Wood in Act V but I'm the porter at the start of Act II as well and I need to get changed soon.'

'If you take your clothes off in that howling draughty passage they've got fitted up as a dressing room you'll catch your death,' said Mrs Porteous. 'They'll have to get someone else to do it.' She was back with a kettle and she proceeded to fill the basin with hot water.

'Oh, oh, oh!' said Francis. 'It's too hot! There *is* no one else. Leonard has us down to the bone already.'

'It's a scald,' said Mrs Porteous witheringly. 'Of course it's hot. And as for no one else? The castle is fair lowping with actors. There must be one. I'll get the mustard pot,' she added and left again.

'I don't have to take anything off for the porter,' Francis said. 'Good God, look at my skin!' He lifted one foot out of the basin and indeed it was as pink as a piglet and seemed to pulse with heat. 'I just have to put a nightshirt and nightcap on and roll my hose up to look bare-legged. And I need this job and the show must—' Then he fired off five sneezes in rapid succession. Tears were streaming down his face when he was done.

'Alec could do it,' I said. 'He's made up as a ghost though, and he doesn't know the lines.'

'Take him the book,' said Francis, pointing to where a script lay on the table. 'It doesn't matter that he's reading. Just take him the book and the cap and gown. As long as we don't stop the dress. If we stop the dress Leonard will sack me and find a new Angus by tomorrow. This is my first proper job all year. Please, Mrs Gilver. Hurry.'

I snatched up the script and the bundle of linen that was sitting beside it and made my way at a trot to the door leading into the makeshift wings. 'Where are we?' I whispered to Bess who was in the prompt corner with a tungsten torch, following the lines with her finger. She did not turn, even for an instant, but just tapped the page with her finger. 'Macbeth doth murder sleep,' I read over her shoulder just as the same words came in a terrified, quaking voice from Max upon the stage:

'Macbeth doth murder sleep, the innocent sleep, sleep that knits up the ravelled sleave of care.'

I fluttered the pages forward, muttering 'porter, porter', then finding nothing started to flutter them back again almost all the way to where I had started. I gasped.

'Sssh,' said Bess, again without looking up.

'It's the next page!' I whispered. 'How can I get Alec round here by the next page?'

'Will you shut up!' said Bess, bending low over her book.

I peeped out of the wing to where Alec and Grant were sitting and waved madly. They did not see me. Then, at a tug on my arm, I turned to see that Tansy was reading the script over Bess's shoulder and Bess was glaring at me.

'Where's that bloody Francis?' she said, whispering so furiously it was more intimidating than if she had bellowed. 'He's on and he's nowhere to be found. Have *you* seen him?'

'I?' I said, planning to lie to her in case she boxed my ears for being the bearer of bad tidings.

'Is that the porter's costume?' she said. 'What are *you* doing with it?'

'Here!' I said, shoving it at her. 'He's in the kitchen with his feet in a mustard scald, shivering and sneezing. You'll have to go on. Here's a script too.'

'I can't go on!' said Bess. 'I'm on the book.'

'Well, Tansy then,' I said.

'I'm on soon,' said Tansy without looking up. 'And I've got

222

Lady M's quick change coming. She'll never manage it herself. In fact, Bess, I need to step away.'

Bess looked down as Tansy disappeared.

'Enter Porter,' she said in an insufferable, told-you-so kind of a voice. And she knocked hard on the beam beside her little chair.

'Porter!' screamed Leonard from the front. 'Where's Francis? PORTER!'

'Nothing else for it,' said Bess. She seized the bundle of linen, shook the cap free of the nightgown, jammed it onto my head, turned the book back at the right page and, with both hands in the small of my back, shoved me onto the stage so firmly I stumbled and almost fell.

18

Seven o'clock on a midsummer evening in Scotland is not dark by any means, but the high castle walls to the west, the lights shining up from our feet and the fact, it must be said, that my eyes misted over with the kind of greyness that usually precedes a faint, meant that I could not see anything beyond the edge of the stage. Far from that reducing my state of utter panic, it increased it, for I could not look out and confirm for my reeling head and banging heart that only Leonard, the Bewers, Alec, Grant and the four American ladies were watching me. And since I was upon a stage, my flustered imagination filled in what is usually on the other side of those dazzling lights, what has been on the other side of them every time I have been in a theatre; namely, a packed audience of my peers, some of them exacting, half of them bored and all of them watching.

Bess knocked again on the beam by her stool and hissed: 'Here's a knocking indeed.'

I stared helplessly into the wings, witless and unable to tell what she wanted.

'Get on with it!' Leonard bellowed to someone. I turned back to face the front and squinted, trying to see him.

Knock, knock went Bess. And again she hissed: 'Here's a knocking indeed!'

'Look at the bloody book!' bellowed Leonard. I understood then that he was speaking to me and bent my head, searching the swimming words for anything that might help me.

A third time, Bess knocked on the beam and my eyes

caught the words on the middle of the page. As she spoke so did I, so that we were in chorus.

'Here's a knocking indeed.'

Bess subsided and it was only me.

'If a man were porter of hell gate – oh my! – he should have old turning the key.' I had heard a soft giggle I was sure was Grant at my unintended 'Oh my!' and I gripped the book tighter.

Knock, knock, knock went Bess and this time I was ready for her.

'Knock, knock, knock,' I read. 'Who's there i' the name of Beelzebub?'

On we went, me standing stock-still in the middle of the yawning stage, rambling on about a farmer, an English tailor, geese and primroses and bonfires, and over and over again Bess knocked on the beam and I answered 'knock knock' until at last, after what felt like half an hour, at her umpteenth knock, I answered instead 'Anon!'

The stage direction told me to open the door. I went over to the prompt corner and mimed the action. Bess was so aghast she took her eyes off her precious book and stared at me.

'I swear you remember the porter,' I said, to thin air.

From the other side of the stage, George Bull and Roger appeared and I swung round and scampered over to them. It was not just Grant giggling now. I was sure I heard the sound of suppressed titters from the front row

George spoke and then I spoke and then George spoke again and if I had been hanging by my fingertips begging for a hand to safety I could not have told what any of the words were. Then George spoke again, but after his line he strode to the front of the stage and, shading his eyes, called up to Leonard, 'Let's skip the next speech.'

'This,' said Leonard with a quiet menace, 'is a dress rehearsal. We do not "skip" speeches. Porter, your cue is "what three things does drink especially provoke?"'

225

I had seen it and I had seen my answer. I swallowed hard. 'Marry, Sir,' hissed Bess.

'Marry, Sir,' I said. 'Nose-painting, sleep and . . . ' a long whinny of mirth came from the audience. I recognised it most definitely as Grant this time. 'Urine!' I cried. 'Lechery, sir, it provokes and unprovokes.' My voice was shaking and I thought I might cry. The American ladies were laughing too now, tittering, honking and choking as they tried to suppress it. 'It provokes the desire and takes away the performance,' I said. And on and on, my voice bleak with misery, while the lot of them collapsed into helpless gales of laughter, shaking with it, even George and Roger's lips twitching.

At last it was over.

'Is your master stirring?' George said. Then Max Moore entered.

Or rather Macbeth entered. If my voice was bleak, his was bleaker. If my face was stark, his was starker.

'Good morrow, both!' he said, with a dreadful empty cheerfulness. Bess was waving at me from the wings and, when she caught my attention, she swept her arms backwards, telling me to subside upstage and let the principals play the scene.

And so I did, watching Macduff go off on his doomed errand to fetch the king, while Lennox chatted and Macbeth stumbled over his words, desperately trying to chat too. Macduff ran back on, shaking and wild.

'Horror, horror, horror,' he said. 'Tongue nor heart cannot conceive nor name thee!'

I do not know what the porter is supposed to do while the unspeakable truth is coming to light of foul murder and black treason, but *this* porter was transfixed. When Lady Macbeth came on, perfectly bleary from sleep, croaky-voiced and halt-limbed, I truly believed Sarah had been napping.

'Woe, alas,' she said. 'What, in our house?' I could only marvel at it. In six little words she took in the dreadful news, displayed enough fright for the men to be fooled, but

226

with just enough missing for Banquo to wonder, and with a cold enough seam of evil underneath for the audience – or at least the porter – to shiver at her. How could one woman contain so many moods, cover so much and think so fast as to hoodwink everyone, all while her frailty tugged at our pity. Sarah Byrne, I decided on the spot, was welcome to her airs and graces for she was a great actress and deserved them.

At last the scene ended, the supposedly guilty guards tidily dead already, Lady Macbeth helped away, Macbeth and Macduff gone to dress in manly readiness, Malcolm and Donalbain fleeing the nation, twitching with suspicion. And the porter still standing there like a pillar of salt until Bess hissed one more time and cawed me off, to not a single smothered giggle.

'Ten-minute tea break,' Leonard shouted, 'and then all back on stage for notes.'

'How did they ever expect to get away with it!' I found myself saying to Alec who had 'come round', as the saying goes, to congratulate me on my performance and apologise for laughing. Unfortunately, as he tried to say sorry, he collapsed into giggles again.

'Of all the parts in all the plays!' he said. 'The porter in *Macbeth*. Oh Dandy, it was priceless. I shall go to my grave glad to have seen it. And as for Grant! She's had to go and repair her ghostly make-up because she cried it all down to her collar, weeping with laughter.' He sighed and sobered. 'How who got away with what?'

'The Macbeths!' I said. 'How they thought they would get away with murdering the king in their own house and just getting rid of the guards.'

Alec was laughing again. 'You were absolutely agog!' he said. 'Standing there pole-axed! Mrs Cornelius murmured that you must have had some dramatic training to be so realistic, but I knew it was all you. Have you never seen *Macbeth*, Dandy? How could the plot surprise you?'

'It wasn't the plot,' I said. 'It was the acting. Watching them at it up close, anyway. They're really very good. Sarah gave me goose pimples. And it made me think too.'

'Thank heavens you weren't shoved on stage with Sara Bernhardt and . . . '

'. . . Henry Thingamajig,' I said. 'Well yes, but I daresay they were never in productions where Angus and the porter were played by the same chap and he caught his death of cold jumping into a moat to drag bits of Birnam Wood back out the day before opening night. But I'm trying to tell you, darling, it got me thinking.'

'Is *that* what happened?' Alec said. 'And speaking of Francis, will he be back on or are you to be Angus later too?'

'He'll be back,' I said grimly. I ripped off my nightcap and set off towards the kitchen again to make sure of it.

'Hie, Dandy,' Alec said. 'You never told me *what* it all got you thinking.'

'What?'

'You said watching them act made you think something. Something about the case?'

I stopped and stared at him, trying to bring it back to mind. 'It's gone,' I said. 'If you would ever learn not to interrupt me. It's quite gone now.'

'Maybe it'll come back tomorrow in the same scene.' His eyes were dancing.

'Which I shall watch from out front,' I said firmly.

'Dandy,' said Alec. 'Am I imagining it or are there more of those little wisps this time than ever before?'

'Wisps?' I said. 'Little threads that don't weave in properly?'

'But can't quite be caught? It's worse this time than usual, isn't it?' I thought for a moment and then nodded. 'And why is that, would you say?'

'Well, for one thing, we are distracted by being actors as

well as detectives. I'm going to go right now to Francis and tell him I am no longer willing to be his understudy.'

Francis was where I had left him but looking a little perkier, with a hot toddy in his hand and his feet still in the basin of mustard water. Mrs Porteous was stirring cocoa on the range, with a cup warming.

'How did he do?' said Angus. 'Alec, I mean. Walking on for the porter. It's an entertaining scene if you're willing to surrender to it. I'm sorry to have missed it tonight.'

'It went past,' I said. 'And the play carried on. That's the main thing.' He would hear the worst soon enough and I was in no mood to be laughed at again, nor to shock Mrs Porteous. 'Once you've finished your toddy, had your cocoa and dried your feet you'll be fit for Act V, will you?'

'This isn't for him,' Mrs Porteous said. 'This is for Mrs Bewer. Gilly fetches a cup of cocoa up to her at bedtime.'

'I'll take it tonight,' I said. I wanted very much to see if Otto had surfaced and to hear where she had been.

She was in her room, tucked up in bed. Gilly was still there too, banging about as though not quite recovered from the scolding over last night's soot.

'Here's your cocoa, Ottoline,' I said. 'With Mrs Porteous's compliments. I happened to be in the kitchens and thought I'd save Gilly some steps.'

'Thank you, Dandy,' Otto said, reaching out a hand that trembled a little. 'I find myself in need of comfort tonight.'

'Oh?' I said. 'I noticed that you had left the rehearsal. Were you cold? Or is it the seats? Perhaps we could bring a comfortable chair for you to sit in tomorrow. It would be a shame for the play to be on right here in your own house and for you not to enjoy it.'

Otto's face twisted into a bitter little frown, most unlike her usual expression.

'You could watch the first half one night and the second the next if it's too much all at once,' I went on. 'Or a matinee perhaps. It's jolly good. I just . . . watched . . . the scene when the murder is discovered and I was riveted. Sarah Byrne was quite breathtaking in it.'

'Well, well, we shall see,' Ottoline said. 'I do so wish it was *A Midsummer Night's Dream*, though. I do so worry about it all.' She bent her head and took a tiny sip from her cup. I debated whether to reassure her how thrilling it was all going to be, for if she had fled the rehearsal before the murdering began, nothing about the rest of the play was likely to comfort her.

'What was it that made you leave tonight?' I said. 'The witches?'

There was that little twisted frown again. 'Oh no,' she said, 'nothing like that. I was just tired suddenly and came up to bed early.' She gave me a wan smile. Behind me, I heard a particularly loud bang from Gilly as she shut a deep drawer.

'Then I shall leave you,' I said. 'And I hope you sleep well.'

'That's me too, madam,' Gilly said in a loud voice. 'Unless there's anything else?'

Ottoline waved us both off and we left together.

'She did not,' said Gilly when we were a few feet along the corridor.

'Who did not what?' I asked, frostily. Of course, I knew but there should be a little decorum.

'Mrs Bewer did not come straight up to bed from the courtyard. That's another of her wee fairy tales, like being deaf.'

'What makes you so sure?'

'Look at the state of her frock and stockings.' Gilly displayed the clothes she held folded over her arm – a tea gown, since today was so disordered that we had not changed – and the stockings tucked discreetly under it. 'She's been somewhere she shouldn't have been, hasn't she?'

'They do look a little dusty,' I agreed. 'But then the castle has a great many nooks and crannies.'

'Excuse me!' Gilly said. 'But we keep this place spick and span, never mind that it nearly kills us between the cobbled floors and the high ceilings and those windows up top that are just grills over them and no glass at all, like an invitation to spiders to come in and take their rest.'

'Of course,' I said. 'Yes, of course you do. I didn't mean a thing by it.'

'And how I'm supposed to deal with clarty frocks and stockings tonight – or even tomorrow – on the biggest day the castle's ever seen!' she went on. 'But if I don't, it'll be the soot all over again. I get wrong like a bad bairn even when I've done nothing, so be sure I'll get wrong if I don't stay up all night sponging and rinsing.'

'Give them to me,' I said, before she could work herself up into a complete blue fit. 'Grant can take care of them for you. She won't mind.'

Gilly was reluctant to let go of her excuse to be in a foul temper but she was very keen to ditch the actual task and in the end the scales tipped that way. She shoved the clothes at me – it was my evening for having others' linens thrust into my arms – and took herself off at the next branch in the corridor.

'Tell her to iron the stockings straight, mind,' she said over her shoulder. 'Mrs Bewer won't wear a stocking with the press line not on the seam.'

I daydreamed briefly about what would happen if I tried to tell Grant how to press a stocking; whether she would hunt Gilly down and box her ears or take the quick way and simply box mine, then I went to my room to wait for her arrival. I was missing the rest of the rehearsal but, I told myself, it was unfair to the actors to distract people from their efforts by reminders of mine.

By eleven o'clock, Grant had not shown her face and I was irritated anew by the lack of bells anywhere in the castle.

231

How one was supposed to summon one's maid was beyond me. Then a thought struck me that softened the irritation: surely they were not still rehearsing? Surely nothing could have gone so badly wrong that a run through of Shakespeare's shortest tragedy had taken over four hours and counting? I had been resting on top of my bed, but I leapt up, put my outdoor shoes on again and went to look out of the nearest inner window.

The courtyard was in darkness and there was a silence that told me no one was there in the wings or backstage. Clearly the rehearsal had been over for some time. I checked the drawing room but there was no one there either and the fire was banked, although the lamps were still lit. The great hall was empty and set for the teas to be sold tomorrow, with little card menus propped up against pots of daisies and columbine and with a great array of very solid plain white china which Minnie had procured from heaven only knew where.

I was beginning to suspect that everyone but me was abed and that Grant had simply forgotten about her mistress in the face of such excitement as the play had brought her, when I heard the murmur of voices from above me and ducked into the nearest stairway to investigate. It led to the long gallery, which was also empty with only candles enough lit to show the way safely along its length, but around the edge of the book-room door there was a line of light and from inside there came a steady hubbub and the smell of tobacco. I had, at last, found someone, even if only the American guests. I hurried over and entered.

The four ladies were indeed there, in their war room, in their shirtsleeves again, but with them were the Bewers, Grant – who was absolutely resplendent in a Tudor costume more elaborate than many a leading lady had worn upon the West End stage, I am sure – and Alec, now crumpled and pale as well as made-up as an apparition, and looking simply ghastly. Leonard, Penny and most of the players were there, wrapped in robes or wearing jerseys and trousers, some with their hair still pushed back behind bands and faces still shining from the cold cream they had used to remove their make-up. Only Moray Dunstane, Sarah Byrne and Max Moore – the Macbeths and King Duncan – were missing. All who *were* there had been there for an age, to judge by the pall of smoke that rolled towards me as I let in a draught to suck it out.

'Has someone found the Cut Throat?' I said.

'No but someone's asking to have his throat cut!' said Leonard, shoving a heap of scribbled-upon papers away from him and putting his head in his hands. His voice was ragged with tobacco and exhaustion.

'Francis collapsed,' said Alec. 'He made it through his lines and then sank down on the stage and had to be carried off.'

'Oh well,' I said. 'Lots of people get carried off, dead and alive, towards the end, don't they?' There was a frozen silence and I gathered that I had dropped a bit of a brick.

'It's the curse,' said Tansy Bell, sepulchrally.

'Which one?' I asked, which did not raise my stock. 'The Scottish play or the Cut Throat. Because the curse of the Cut Throat only springs to life when it leaves the castle and the curse of *Macbeth*—'

'—is a lot of Victorian twaddle,' said Penny. 'We don't have time for either. If we concentrate on the job at hand, however, we do have time to save the production.'

'Won't he be better by tomorrow?' I said. 'Another mustard scald perhaps? A couple more toddies?'

'He's gone,' Penny said. 'He left a note and walked to the high road to catch the late bus to town and the train home to Glasgow.'

'Did *he* find the Cut Throat?' I said. 'Was it in the kitchen?'

'Dandy, for heaven's sake,' said Alec. 'Could you forget about the Cut Throat for a minute. Francis Mowatt, who

233

plays Angus, a doctor, the porter and a king has left and we open tomorrow.'

His defection from the role of my partner to being one of Leonard's players was, it seemed, complete.

'But how did he manage to walk to the high road if his chill was bad enough that he fainted on the stage?' I said. 'I don't understand. What did the note say?'

Minnie, who had been standing off to the side clutching it and therefore looking rather like Lady Macbeth in Act I with the battleground bulletin in her hand, now stalked forward and thrust it at me.

'I have seen my death foretold and I must fly,' it said, a declamation worthy of any bard. 'Help yourself to the rest of my beer,' it went on, with a considerable lurch towards the prosaic. 'I can't fit it in my knapsack.'

'We wondered if he was delirious,' said Tansy Bell. 'George and Bob went after him, checking in the hedgerows in case he was lying there, but they saw nothing and there's a little row of cottages just at the bus stop and one of the cottagers came out and . . . What was it she said, George?'

'Told us that a young man with a haversack had come along the lane at a fair clip and just caught the bus. She'd paid particular attention because he was in such a hurry she wondered if he had found the jewel and was rushing away with it.'

'So there we are,' said Leonard. 'Short four parts and there's no way to square it.'

A groan went up from several quarters at his words but it was Penny who sat down, took his hands in hers and spoke to him pleadingly. 'Leonard, please. The answer is there. Julian takes on Angus as well as Malcolm. Alec goes up to second murderer and Bob takes third murderer and porter.'

'Yes, yes, yes,' said Leonard, 'but that solves nothing.'

'I hadn't finished!' said Penny. She took a deep breath. 'We make the English doctor a nurse—'

'No,' said Leonard. 'Never.'

Another groan rang out around the room.

'Leonard, dearest, there's no need to—'

'Couldn't the English doctor and the Scottish doctor just be rolled into one?' I said. 'Even if they're onstage together, if they're both doctors, aren't they saying much the same sort of thing—'

'They're not onstage together,' said Leonard with a sort of dreadful patience that should have warned me to shut up and yet did not.

'Well, then there you are!' I said.

'They're not onstage together,' Leonard said in the same low menacing tone like a growling guard dog, always so much more effective than a barking one, 'because one is in Scotland and one is in England! How can it be the same doctor?'

'So,' said Penny with infinite patience, 'Miles takes the English doctor, George the Scottish doctor and we' – she was trying to sound gay and light but the fact that she had to pause for a breath before the next words ruined the effect completely – 'we cut Hecate out, which frees up me and the other witches to be servants and messengers.'

'I don't mind,' said one of the girls. Hecate herself, I guessed.

'The servants can't *all* be women!' said Leonard. 'And if *any* of the battlefield messengers are women the play will be a travesty.'

'Oh, for love of God above,' said Minnie. 'Leonard, I am not part of your theatrical world, but when was the last time you heard an actress say she was willing to have you cut her part – not cut it down but cut it out completely! – to save your production? Your production, which is in this muddle because you pared your cast back to the very rind to save money on wages? Hmm?'

'The servants in Macbeth's castle would be men apart from—'

'But who's going to know that?' said Bluey. 'Come on, old chap. Most audiences in the West End wouldn't put their chips down on it and none of the trippers who're coming along here to have a jolly night out and a poke around a castle will either know or care.'

'And I am not cutting out a whole character written by the greatest playwright of all time, just because Francis Mowatt has caught the last bus and gone home,' said Leonard. 'I might as well put on a nativity with two kings, one shepherd and twins in the manger because that's who I happened to have to hand!'

If he hoped to shock someone with his blasphemy, he was disappointed. Perhaps they were too tired, or perhaps the thought had simply loomed too large in the minds of all that, in less than twenty-four hours' time, buses and carts and motorcars were going to be parked in rows all over the field between Pugh's flags, and those wooden benches were going to be filled with paying customers waiting to see, amongst others, a porter who was not wearing her country tweeds and reading from a script.

'He didn't write Hecate,' one of the young men murmured.

'It was added in later,' another chipped in.

'Along with all the songs.'

'And you're not doing the songs.'

We all waited, with bated breath, still enough for the wraiths of tobacco smoke to stop shifting and just hang in the air. Alec was scribbling busily and Minnie was wringing her hands; actually wringing her hands, as though applying cream to them, or perhaps, I thought, as though trying to cleanse them with all the perfumes of Araby.

At last Leonard cleared his throat. 'No,' he said. This time the chorus of groans was more like shrieks: of frustration and despair.

'We could just sack you, you know,' Bluey said. 'What's a director for, once the play's up and running anyway? In

236

fact, yes, I think that's the answer. Leonard, old boy, you're sacked. Get your things and be ready to leave before breakfast and be thankful I don't just take you by the scruff of your neck and the seat of your pants and heave you out the window right now. I've never seen such silliness in a so-called grown man.'

'Daddy,' said Penny. 'I know you're angry but there's no need to rant at poor Leonard like that.'

'I'm not ranting, Penny,' Bluey said. 'I mean every word of it. I'm sick of him and he's sacked. Out you go, Leonard, cousin or no. Fiancé or no. You've tried my patience too far.'

Leonard looked about as rattled as a sloth hanging from a branch. 'Do you really think my company would stay without me?' he said.

'Of course, I do,' Bluey said. 'We'll pay them and they'll get to perform and, and, – we'll knock a bit off their room and board in thanks for their loyalty.'

Leonard nodded as though taking it all in very calmly. He cast his eye around the players who had sat up and started paying close attention. 'Who's staying?' he said.

They looked at one another but no one spoke until Roger cleared his throat and said, genially, 'The play's the thing, I suppose.'

'The show must go on,' agreed Paddy Ramekin.

'Indeed it must,' said Leonard smoothly. 'Very well, you all stay down here and put on *Macbeth* for trippers and curious locals and I'll go back to Edinburgh and start thinking about casting all the plays for the winter season.'

Roger froze and Paddy Ramekin looked as though he would like to stuff his words back into his mouth and swallow them. He actually reached forward and gobbled at the air like a goldfish.

'Of all the sly, creeping, unwholesome creatures who soil this earth,' said Bluey, 'a blackmailer is the worst of them.' He stood up. 'Be off before I pick you up and throw you out and don't look at me like that. I might be an old man but I was a soldier. And a boxer. In fact, yes! Let's settle this like men.'

To my astonishment he tore off his jacket and with shaking fingers began to work at his cufflinks as though to roll up his sleeves for fighting.

'Daddy!' said Penny. 'Please, don't. This won't get us anywhere.'

'Bluey, don't be an oaf,' said Minnie.

'Leonard?' It was Alec. He had not spoken for some time but now he looked up from his scribbles and addressed the man in a clear, calm voice. 'How about this? Two doctors, no nurse. All the messengers are men. The servants, I'm afraid, are women, but Hecate stays? Could you live with that?'

'It can't be done,' said Leonard.

'It *could* be done,' Alec countered.

'*If* it could be done,' said Leonard, and for the first time there was a hint of him softening.

'It *can* be done,' said Alec, 'if Mrs Cornelius, Mrs Westhousen, Mrs Schichtler and Mrs Rynsburger don't mind not getting to sit in the front row and enjoy the show. But instead . . . '

Which way would they jump, I wondered, turning to where the four of them were sitting. It is so hard to tell with American ladies: in some ways so prim and in some ways such hoydens.

'. . . instead be in the play?' said Mrs Rynsburger.

'Now, hold on!' said little Mrs Schichtler.

'Playing what?' said Mrs Cornelius.

Alec glanced down at his notes. 'A servant, an attendant, an apparition, and a king.'

'We've cast the only "king" that's a queen,' said Grant hastily.

'Yes, and that's another thing I need to talk to you about,' said Leonard. 'That costume is completely wrong. A white

238

robe like the others and plain gold coronet by tomorrow or you're out.'

Grant waved him away like a gnat and persisted, 'Who's the other queen?'

Alec shifted a little and gave a sickly smile to the statuesque Mrs Rynsburger. 'It's a lot to ask,' he said, 'and if you think it would be undignified, I shall understand completely . . . ', and at last I caught his meaning. Mrs Rynsburger was not only tall, she was also broad of shoulder and narrow of hip and her features were strong and definite.

'It won't be the first time,' she said with a good-natured sigh. 'I spent my girlhood in just the same way. Who am I?'

'James the Sixth and First,' Alec said. 'He wasn't a great hairy beast of a man by all accounts, if that's any comfort.'

'And who am I? Who am I?' said Mrs Westhousen, actually bouncing in her chair and clapping her hands.

'Take your pick,' Alec said. 'Although you're rather too bonny to make much of an apparition so a servant or an attendant, dear lady, as you will.'

'This servant's not the porter?' said Mrs Cornelius, provoking a general titter and a few sharp looks my way that flooded my cheeks again.

'Attendant!' said Mrs Westhousen. 'It doesn't sound quite so lowly. Is my dress pretty?'

'Your costume will be the male servant's costume with some kind of . . . ' He waved a hand and cast a look of supplication towards Grant.

'Headdress,' she said. 'I'll make it and an overskirt too.'

'But don't go mad,' said Leonard again, pointing at the silk-slashed sleeves, the satin petticoats and brocade overdress, the pearl embroidery and velvet trim she had donned to walk over the back of the dark stage for half a minute.

'Which makes me the apparition, does it?' said Mrs Cornelius. 'Well, my mother always said this face would be good for something.' We all murmured politely but she was right.

'And you're the servant, Jesamond,' said Mrs Westhousen to Mrs Schichtler. 'Oh what fun! How much more fun to be part of it all. One big happy band!' They looked so delighted, even the actors beginning to relax again, grinning and giving one another pointed looks as if to say it would be such a bore to be nannying amateurs on opening night. So soon after vowing I would never set foot on a stage again as long as I lived I actually felt a little left-out, a little crestfallen and wistful even. It had been fun, lavatorial lines aside.

'No,' said Mrs Schichtler.

'Oh Jesamond!' Mrs Rynsburger cried. 'You can't be a stick-in-the-mud when dear Alec has been so clever and saved the play. You can't be so mean, surely!'

'I can't do it,' said Mrs Schichtler. 'I tried as a schoolgirl and I disgraced myself. From nerves. I physically . . . disgraced myself. In front of everyone.'

'Oh, but you're older and wiser now,' said Mrs Westhousen. 'You speak in public all the time at the museum luncheons.'

'Well, I wouldn't be so hasty . . . ' said Leonard. 'If you mean you might actually . . . '

'To be honest, Mrs Schichtler,' said Alec. 'The servant's costume wouldn't fit you anyway. And I'm not sure Miss Grant has time to be taking in hose as well as everything else she needs to do by curtain up tomorrow.'

'Although,' said Leonard with another darted glance at the queenly Tudor gown, 'she is obviously a quick worker.'

'So can one of us three do two of the new roles?' said Mrs Westhousen.

'Or can I?' said Grant, not keen to relinquish higher billing without a fight.

'Or,' said Alec, with a grin spreading upon his face, 'we could give the little part to the only one who's out in the cold, couldn't we? We've seen what she can do with the part of a lowly servant after all, haven't we?' They were laughing again and I smiled politely until I realised that they were laughing at *me* and that Alec was grinning at me. I shot back like an arrow to my stout ambition never to tread the boards again, but it was no good. All the arguments that had fitted Mrs Schichtler fitted me too, as did the costume apparently, and that was that.

Leonard and Penny jotted down the dramatis personae to make up errata for the programmes and the rest of the company dispersed.

'You've got the plum of the new parts, Dan,' said Alec under his breath to me. 'Two lines and you share the stage with Sarah Byrne. Enter together and exit alone.'

'You are Machiavellian,' I said. 'I'd rather be an apparition, for I am sure I could go on without make-up. I'll be pure-white from nerves.'

'You're far too pretty to be an apparition,' he said casually as he surged ahead of me to catch George and Robert for a quick word. If he had not just used almost the same gallantry to Mrs Westhousen I would have hugged it to me. I hugged it a little anyway, until Minnie touched my arm and drew my attention.

'He's such a splendid young man,' she said.

'He's a good sort,' I agreed.

'Just a pal, though?' she said mildly.

'Of mine?' I said, feeling my cheeks, for the third time that evening, flush like dawn in the tropics. 'Good heavens, Minnie. I don't move in those circles. Gosh, who could be fagged with it, apart from anything?'

Minnie laughed. 'Excellent news,' she said. Then her face grew grim and her voice too. 'Penny cannot marry that blister. We must stop it somehow. I wouldn't put it past Bluey actually to throw him out a window if we can't persuade her to ditch him. He's awful.'

'He really is,' I said. 'And if he's this insufferable as a young man in courtship, just imagine what kind of husband he'll be as the long years begin to roll by.'

It was a depressing indictment of the differences between Minnie's life and mine that she seemed not to know what I meant. Thankfully, my agreement on the subject of the unsatisfactory Leonard was all she cared about. She squeezed my elbow and we went up to bed arm-in-arm, like girls again.

19

At six o'clock the next morning, as the blush of a midsummer daybreak faded and the pure-blue morning to come began to breathe warmth and birdsong in at my open window, I was sitting up in bed, stiff with terror. A knock came at my door and Alec sidled in.

'Ah good,' he said. 'You're awake. Is Banquo gone from court?'

I gave him a grateful smile and said: 'Aye, madam, but returns again tonight.'

'Say to the King I would attend his leisure for a few words,' said Alec.

'Madam, I will.'

'And then you go off, stage left, and you're done,' Alec said. 'You're going to be fine, Dandy.'

'But without any rehearsal at all!' I said. 'Surely one of the girls could do it. Penny or Tansy. Surely Bess could walk on for a minute and walk off again.'

'And risk upsetting Leonard afresh?'

'But no one is who they were this time yesterday anyway,' I said. 'What difference would one more tiny adjustment make now?'

'*A Midsummer Night's Dream* is where nothing is as it seems,' Alec said. 'Not *Macbeth*. This is all very straightforward, though rather ugly.' I stared at him. 'What?' he said, coming and sitting on the edge of my bed and taking one of my hands. 'What is it? Have I just started a hare running, saying that? Do you think someone truly isn't what he seems? Dandy? Say something.'

'What?' I said. 'No, no hares. I'm just sick with stage fright. I mightn't even be able to get myself on tonight. Sitting here, I feel as though my legs are paralysed and I've still got thirteen hours to go. I must try to think of something else or I'll go mad. And I must try to do something more than just read those two lines over and over again all day.'

'Forget the play,' Alec said. 'The case is the thing. We need to start with what we know and work out the rest. We can do it, Dandy.'

'What do we know?'

'Plenty! First, Richard didn't write the letters. They were fakes,' Alec said.

'Fakes,' I repeated dully. 'Oh, I wish Grant would come with my cup of tea. I can't think clever thoughts about fake letters without it.'

'I've just seen Grant already hard at work on the overskirts,' said Alec. 'Your best bet is to get up and go down.'

I heaved a sigh of self-pity for it really did seem a bit thick. 'Very well, then. I shall meet you in the breakfast room in half an hour to hear all about it.'

Since he did not offer to bring me a tea tray instead that is what I did, dry-mouthed and maid-less, and by the time I got downstairs my interest in the case was flagging, compared with my interest in coffee – I was far beyond tea – and breakfast. The others had been and gone, I surmised, and the sideboard was rather picked-over, but Alec looked so eager, perched on the edge of a chair with his first pipe, that I contented myself with the last of the scrambled eggs scraped from the bottom of the dish, two slices of barely warm toast and a cup of opaque coffee, got by upending the pot completely, and settled to listen.

'What makes you so sure—' I began. Then at his frown I amended it to, 'How did you deduce that the letters were fake?'

Alec settled back and, as I ate enough of the unsatisfactory breakfast to see me through to luncheon, he regaled me.

'Because, as we said, the itinerary makes no sense. One wouldn't go to Lisbon en route to any of the other places mentioned, either on the way there or on the way back. And also because Minnie and Bluey were so cavalier about Ottoline's ghost cum burglar. This explains it. One of them crept into Ottoline's room and took the bag containing the letters because they had heard us say we were going to read them. The story of her tipping things into the water never struck me as all that likely. Did it you?'

'She's never appeared gaga that I could see,' I agreed. 'How did Minnie and Bluey know the letters were fake, though?'

'Because they wrote them,' said Alec. 'Bluey wrote letters supposedly from his father and gave them to pals to post back from foreign lands, to make his mother believe . . . Well, whatever the letters said. That he was sorry, that he still loved her, that he was coming home.'

'But Otto said the letters were nasty. Filled with loathsome-ness.'

'Well, then Bluey wrote them to make her feel less sad over her abandonment.'

'But in either case if the letters fooled Ottoline why would Bluey and Minnie think they wouldn't fool us? And why does the question of Ottoline recognising Richard's writing ring such an alarm in me?'

'Hm,' said Alec. 'I don't know. And I don't know.'

'And what's it got to do with Gunn along at Mespring?'

Alec took a while to knock out and refill his pipe. I had given up on the rubbery eggs and chewy toast and had lit a cigarette of my own before he spoke again.

'Ha!' he said. 'I've got it. They were fake through and through. They weren't only forged by Bluey imitating his father's hand, they weren't even sent from Aleppo and the rest of it. The stamps were left over from someone's grand tour – Bluey's own, I expect – and the postmarks were fudged and smudged. Gunn helped them appear to arrive through the post so that Ottoline would believe the story.'

'That actually does make sense,' I said. 'And the burglars?'

'Again, Gunn and Bluey colluding to make his mother believe . . . '

'Yes, but in this case, believe what?'

'Believe . . . ' Alec said slowly, '. . . that the jewel was still in the house.'

'When, in fact . . . ?'

'Richard took it with him, of course. To fund his trip.'

'And why would it matter if Ottoline knew that? If her husband had left her, would the fact that he'd absconded with a necklace really make it so much worse? She doesn't believe in the curse, remember. She wanted the necklace to be a wedding present for Minnie.'

Alec puffed steadily for a minute and then took the pipe out of his mouth and said: 'The hypocrisy might hurt. If Richard trotted out the curse to keep it off Otto's neck all those years and then conveniently disregarded the curse when he needed a quick sale for cash.'

'So . . . ' I said, thinking furiously, 'Minnie and Bluey know very well that the Cut Throat is long gone, do they? And all of this treasure hunt is just flim-flam. And Ottoline thinks perhaps it really is still here.'

'Why didn't Minnie and Bluey just tell us the truth, though?' said Alec. 'I mean about the letters, even if they had to fib about the Cut Throat so we would collude in the treasure hunt with a straight face? I don't see what the problem would have been in their saying, "Oh, ignore the letters. We wrote them to spare Mother's hurt."'

'Let's ask,' I said, but to my surprise Alec frowned and shook his head.

'There's too much going on today,' he said. 'And it strikes me that it's probably not Minnie and Bluey at all, but Bluey

246

alone. After all, Minnie was a new bride when this happened. It's not likely that she'd join in with an elaborate plot to stop her new mother-in-law mourning the loss of her scoundrel husband. I can't see Bluey being quite so blasé as to rope her in. Can you?'

'But I'm sure Otto recognised Richard's writing,' I said. 'Her eyes flared with it in that unmistakable way.'

Alec nodded slowly and sucked on his pipe. Then suddenly he coughed. 'Hold on,' he said. 'We didn't see Otto with Richard's letters.'

'Oh! What an idiot,' I said. 'No, of course we didn't. We saw her with the note to the granddaughter that she said was written by the very peculiar Anne Annandale. But Ottoline shouldn't have recognised *that* writing at all, should she?'

'No, of course she shouldn't,' Alec said. 'Are you sure she did?'

'Absolutely certain,' I said. 'And that story struck me as most unlikely anyway. Even if the dotty Miss Annandale came to visit while Bluey was expected but not yet arrived, how would she lay her hands on the rocking horse to stuff Dorothy's pearls and rings in it? If two maiden ladies come for tea in your house you don't let them patter around in the attics.'

'Well,' said Alec, 'one of them had lived in the house for most of her life so she wasn't exactly a visitor. And perhaps since, as you say so coarsely – you are getting to be an absolute crone, Dandy; you shock me sometimes – but if, as you say, Bluey was soon expected, perhaps the rocking horse was down in the nursery and easily accessible. Perhaps Ottoline took the ladies to show them the cradle and all the rest of it. Isn't that the kind of cooing ladies like to do?'

I wanted to stick my tongue out at him, but since I had already been called coarse I refrained.

'We can ask her,' I said. 'Ottoline is not doing any of the

preparation for tonight and there's no reason she couldn't bear up under a couple of questions.' Then I felt the breath leave my body as the thought struck me anew. 'Oh, God,' I said. 'Tonight.'

'You'll be fine,' Alec said. 'It might even be fun.'

'Not what you were saying yesterday,' I reminded him. 'I could throttle Francis Mowatt for taking a fit of the willies and leaving us all in the lurch. How he thinks he'll ever get another job in theatre if this comes out! And I can't imagine Leonard keeping it quiet out of friendly feelings, can you?'

'It's for the best,' Alec said. 'The three other ladies couldn't be more thrilled.'

'I suppose I should try to be more sympathetic,' I said. 'He must have been truly rattled simply to leave a quick note and then take off into the night.'

'Truly,' Alec agreed. 'Right then. You for Otto and I for . . . Well, I promised Grant I would intervene on her behalf with Leonard and Bess regarding the make-up, but after last night's Queen Mary costume I'm not sure there's any point. She's getting worse instead of better, Dan.'

We left the breakfast room – it had not escaped my notice that Gilly had come to the door twice and sighed gustily to see us still in there – and went our separate ways. I do not know if my words echoed in Alec's head at precisely the same moment they echoed in mine, but I do know that, once I had gasped, clapped my hands and turned on my heel, we met back at the breakfast-room door.

'He left a hasty note and took off into the night!' Alec said.

'It was Richard who stashed the pearls and rings in the rocking horse for the granddaughter, as yet unborn, that he knew he'd never meet!' I said back.

Thankfully Gilly had finished her clearing and gone, for we made no attempt to moderate our voices and anyone nearby might easily have overheard.

'Otto recognised his writing!' said Alec.

'And Bluey knew the fake letters wouldn't pass muster if the two specimens were considered side by side!'

'Not by nasty, nosy suspicious detectives like us anyway.' We had finally managed to stop exclaiming at one another.

'So,' I said, 'he took the key and broke into his mother's room and stole them away, evening bag and all.'

'And I'll bet *Bluey* suggested to the youngsters that they should flit about the corridors in their diaphanous costumes. As decoys.'

'Of course,' I said. 'Well, then. I shall go and see Ottoline and charge her with it. And then where shall I meet you afterwards to tell you what happened? Unless you want to come with me. She didn't seem to mind you being in her bedroom that other time.'

'I minded,' Alec said with a shudder. 'And it makes more sense to divide and conquer. I shall meet you in the book room, to start proving that Richard wrote that note.'

'Proving it?' I said. 'How?'

'If you haven't worked out how by the time you get there, I'll tell you,' said Alec infuriatingly and, turning again, left me.

Ottoline was still abed, and I was happy to see that someone had brought *her* a cup of tea. It did not seem to be doing her much good, though. She appeared more shrunken even since the night before when she was none too bonny.

'Ottoline,' I said, bending to kiss her forehead. I had become fond of her in the few days of our acquaintance and I felt sorry for her to have all this upheaval in her house. She had not had a happy nor an easy life and she deserved more peace than this at its close. 'Might I sit and talk a while?'

'Certainly,' she said. 'What would you like to talk about? My thoughts run to my granddaughter this morning. That man is no match for her but I'd rather see her married than spurned.'

I was delighted to find the conversation turning so easily

to where I needed it. 'Speaking of granddaughters,' I began. 'And I agree about Leonard, by the way. He's not worthy of her. But speaking of granddaughters, we've worked out who wrote the note in the rocking horse.' Her eyelids fluttered and came to rest with her eyes closed. I lifted the teacup, almost empty, out of her hands. 'It was Richard, wasn't it?' I said gently.

'Everything I told you about Dorothy and Anne was true,' she said, rather querulously.

'Oh, I know,' I said. 'I heard enough to confirm it, along at Mespring.' Her eyes fluttered open again. 'I'm afraid there's a lot of snooping and checking in what Mr Osborne and I do. But back to the "Granddaughter" note: I'm afraid I shall have to press you. Richard wrote it before he left, didn't he?'

'Yes,' Ottoline said. 'I've been thinking of it – as you can imagine – since you brought it to me. And I think it shows that he was beginning to see sense. I think he had to go away to clear his head but he was certainly beginning to come out from under the spell of the curse even before he left. Do you see what I mean?'

I cast my mind back to the words and nodded. 'He knew he had been gripped by some kind of mania,' I said. 'And he wanted to make sure no one else in the family ever became so obsessed with baubles. Yes, that would have been cause for hope if you had seen it at the time.'

'But he died somewhere out there in one of those hot, unwholesome places, didn't he?' said Ottoline. 'And quite soon. The letters stopped within the year. Poor Richard.'

I had half-decided not to tell her what I suspected about those letters, but looking down at her wan face, her brows drawn up with anguish and her lower lip not quite steady, I thought I should bestow what comfort I could, for it was precious little.

'Ottoline,' I said, very softly. 'I don't think Richard sent those letters to you.' She stiffened, but said nothing. 'I think Bluey

– dear old Bluey – wanted you to feel some hope or at least no regret. Perhaps he was searching for his father, unbeknownst to you, and he wanted to . . . Well, keep the home fires burning, I suppose you'd say. So he forged them and then he pretended they'd come from overseas. But he did it to comfort you, not to trick you. Or only incidentally anyway.'

'Bluey?' said Ottoline. 'You think Bluey wrote those letters from his father to me?'

Her tone had me wondering what precisely was in them and reflecting how shocking it would be to write letters to one's mother that one might properly only write to one's wife. Her next words assured me.

'Bluey never had any talent for that kind of thing,' she said.

'He didn't do it all on his own,' I said. 'Gunn, his father's valet, helped him.'

Ottoline was now absolutely rigid in her bed. 'Gunn? The servant who went to Mespring?'

'It doesn't matter, does it?' I said. 'It's all a long time ago now.' Too late, I remembered that when I had said similar words before she had berated me for treating her lifetime as though it were a great sweep of history. This time, she did not even seem to notice, or perhaps she had come to agree, for all she said was: 'I have lived too long.'

I tried to shush her but she waved my words away. 'I have lived too long and now all I want is to die at home in peace. I wonder if I shall be permitted to.'

It was the sort of remark for which there is no adequate answer. I tried a kind of boisterous good cheer instead.

'Well, there won't be much peace today, certainly. Are you keeping to your room?'

Ottoline met my tone with a matching effort. 'I might toddle down later and see what sort of fist Penny makes of her lecture,' she said. 'Although if she sees me in the audience she'll bellow to make sure I hear and I don't suppose that would be very comfortable for the rest of them.'

'Why did you ever decide to play deaf?' I said. 'It must be extraordinarily inconvenient for you.'

'There was a moment when it seemed the best thing,' said Ottoline. 'All a long time ago now, of course.' Her eyelids were beginning to flutter again and so, with one last stroke of her cool brow – smooth in sleep – I left her.

20

Of course, Alec was delighted when I arrived in the book room looking just as mystified as ever. He did not know, though, that it was the moment when deafness seemed useful that was mystifying me, not his riddle.

'Do you give in?' he said, grinning like an imp.

'What?' I said. 'Oh! No. Although, of course you're right and you're very clever for seeing it before me. There must be more of Richard's writing somewhere amongst all these family books and papers, mustn't there? He lived here for seventy years, after all. Have you found any that looks like the granddaughter note yet?'

Alec tried to hide how miffed he felt with a long droning explanation of how he had divided the areas to be searched: estate ledgers, from when the Bewers owned more than the field in which the castle sat; albums and scrapbooks from foreign travel and special occasions – just the sort of thing letters were pasted into when Otto and Richard were young; and Bluey's desk.

'Bluey's desk?' I repeated, aghast. 'Have you asked him? You can't go poking around in someone's private papers?'

'You don't think employing us as detectives to search a castle for a hidden item pretty much buys us free entry to every receptacle in that castle?'

'No I do not,' I said. 'And nor do you, if you're honest. Of course we can feel around the backs of drawers for secret compartments and false bottoms but we can't open the drawers and read the documents inside them.'

'Very well,' said Alec. 'I shall take care of the desk on my own and you – cloaked in honour from head to toe – can tackle "Our Indian Journey" and the rest of the scrap books.'

It was supposed to chasten me, but Alec underestimated my appetite – the appetite of all females, I daresay – for looking at photographs of people, even strangers, even strangers long dead. I settled to my task quite happily.

'Our Indian Journey' had been pasted onto the board pages of a leather album by Ottoline, it soon became clear. 'Richard and I on elephants!' exclaimed one label. 'Richard and I with the Maharaja!' another, and the same hand was evident throughout. I checked the hand against the 'granddaughter note' as we seemed to be calling it, which Alec had placed handily between our two stations. They could hardly have been more different if one was Chinese. With reluctance, I closed the elephants and maharajas, and turned to the other, much thicker, record of the more humdrum days at home in Castle Bewer.

I began at the back, for it seemed sensible to start with people I knew and work my way down into the history of unfamiliar strangers. The last page was devoted to Penny's coming-out from five years previously. There she was in her pretty white dress with her long white gloves and those three ridiculous feathers, looking stiff and scared in a panelled anteroom. There was another of her at her own dance, standing between her parents at the head of a flight of stairs. How well I remembered that dreadful moment, standing at the top of the steps waiting to receive the guests at one's coming-out ball, hoping the room would fill, and becoming more and more sickeningly sure that no one at all would come and that one would be muttered about and shot kind looks for the rest of the season. I could still hear the sound of the first carriage wheels slowing and stopping outside the door and I could still feel the drop of my mother and father's shoulders on either side of me, for we were huddled together like orphaned lambs there. It was one of my first intimations that grown-ups felt just the same swoops and soars of emotion as did I and the disappointment was considerable. Up until that moment I had looked forward to the day when I should be beyond them.

There were pages on end of Penny. I was sure that my mother had not saved menus and dance cards from my own ball and invitations to other grander ones, nor the bread-and-butter letter from the debutante to her parents telling them how marvellous they were for putting on such a beautiful party. I was not sure I had ever thought to write that letter and I told myself it was peculiar, to avoid feeling churlish. At any rate, it was another hand to check against our note and discount.

'Penny didn't write it,' I said to Alec and got a withering look in reply. 'It's best to be thorough.'

The christening was just one double page. There was an invitation to it, an order of service for it and a photograph commemorating it: Minnie in a dining chair with Penny in a froth of lace and ribbon on her lap and Bluey, his hand on the chair back, bending over slightly and beaming at the baby. Ottoline, darker-haired and somewhat plumper but otherwise the same, was in another dining chair alongside and behind them were a handful of what I assumed to be godparents, all slightly dead-eyed in the usual way of those days, when photographs took so very long. A young slim nanny in a pale dress and a dark hat with a badge spoke of the family's correctness and prosperity.

The photograph just before that one spoke of it even more loudly still. It was Minnie and Bluey arriving at Castle Bewer after their honeymoon, as I surmised from the style of Minnie's travelling costume – those droopy crêpe coats that were crushed to rags as soon as one sat in them – and the high necks and fancy caps of the servants who had all gathered on the bridge, new and bright-looking, to welcome them.

There was Pugh with a shock of hair instead of the plastered strands he sported today. There was Mrs Porteous who looked entirely unchanged. I supposed it was one of the few benefits of true ugliness that one had no looks to lose. Mrs Ellen was there, stouter and more buoyant-looking than the heavy-legged woman who hauled herself around the castle, sighing and panting, these days. And there were a bevy of maids and boys, five in all, smiling shyly at Minnie, who was their contemporary but in every other way must have seemed a creature from another world. One of the maids was a mere child, looking far too young to be anywhere except at her mother's side. Just for a moment I felt a flash of that revolutionary spirit Hugh always suspects my detecting career will ignite in me and which I always stoutly deny. Minnie and I might lament the loss of the world we were born to and trained for, but I could not help thinking that little girls being at school instead of curtseying to the new mistress was not anything to sigh over.

Minnie's wedding, if one ignored the sagging frocks anyway, was beautiful. There was just one photograph pasted into the album: Minnie, her bridesmaids, and all the ladies in their finery. She smiled out of the picture as radiant as any bride I have ever seen. I was sure she was smiling at Bluey, banished along with the other gentlemen from this composition of lace, silk and covered buttons. I remembered how much they adored one another – that jolly Minerva Roll and young Bewer – the trouble they had got into for sitting so close together too, making chaperones frown even as they made the rest of us girls pine for someone to sit so close to *us*. Perhaps that whiff of scandal accounted for the look upon Ottoline's face in the wedding group, which was one of pure relief, more usually the expression of the bride's mother. I scanned the faces in the three rows of guests to see if I could spot such a person. But quite a few of the gathered relations were cut off at the nose by the hat feathers of a lady in front.

Hats were dreadful that year, as they are most years to anyone who is honest enough to say so.

'That's interesting,' I said, recognising a face at the edge of the second row. 'Things were friendly enough between Mespring and the Bewers for Anne Annandale to be at Minnie and Bluey's wedding, at least.'

'What?' said Alec.

'It's quite a testament to a portraitist's art if you can recognise a person from a painting, don't you think?'

'What does that have to do with Richard's handwriting?' said Alec.

'Although I can't pick Aunt Dorothy out from the crowd,' I added. 'So perhaps Anne just had one of those faces that's easy to capture. I'm forming a complete view of the case and the characters involved in it,' I added loftily as Alec gathered himself again to tell me I was wasting time.

I picked up a bit of speed anyway, eschewing the reading of the wedding breakfast menu and only glancing at the invitation which was pasted in beside it. Another page further back, though, were pictures impossible to resist: pictures of the castle interiors from the days of Bluey's childhood here. I gathered that his father had procured his first camera around about the time Bluey went off to Eton for, as well as a picture of the boy beaming in his tails before the fire in the morning room, there were a myriad more snaps of the castle's rooms, including two capturing each end of the very book room we were sitting in this morning. I could not help looking up and down and up and down, tracing the few changes and noting the many ways the room was just the same, for Bluey's retreat had escaped the wholesale overhaul of the castle I had been hearing about from everyone, when Ottoline – for Minnie – threw out the dark furniture and the memorials to the castle's past as a fort, painted every wall in pastel shades and covered every seat with roses. Gone were the suits of armour that used to guard either side of the entry to the great hall, gone were the displays of swords from claymore to dagger that had once adorned the walls as well as the current black iron sconces. Gone was some quite dreadful Tudor furniture almost as black as iron itself: those chairs it is torture to sit upon, beset with carving as they are; and those endless chests on little legs in which travellers used to haul their plate and coin around when roads were the workplace of highwaymen.

It occurred to me also, as I looked at a photograph of a long passageway, that the Castle Bewer of today had not a single stuffed and mounted head anywhere inside it. It was the first moment of my feeling anything but pity and sympathetic anger for Otto regarding her husband's flight. She had the worry and shame, to be sure, but she had been able to toss a bewildering array of stag, doe, bear and tiger heads onto the bonfire when Richard departed, as well as the zebra-skin rug Bluey stood on in his new finery and an elephant's foot umbrella stand that had once been filled with fishing rods by the gatehouse-passage door.

There was a photograph of the party responsible for one of the stags: seven men with pipes in their mouths and guns broken over their arms, standing in a chilly dawn, two of them with feet up on the flank of the great beast, all grinning.

'What's wrong?' said Alec. I had not been aware of sighing. I certainly had not realised that I was getting sentimental about stag in my advancing years.

'I wonder if Leonard knows there are cannons stashed away somewhere,' I said, to throw him off the scent. 'He'd surely want them for the stage, don't you think?'

'Cannon,' said Alec. 'The plural of cannon is—' but he stopped himself before he finished and had the grace to give me a sheepish look. 'Finding anything?'

I did not want to admit to barely thinking about the task in hand at all and so I concentrated hard and managed to make a point with a bit of stretching.

'If the Cut Throat is hidden in the castle,' I said, 'I bet it's in this room. This is the only room that wasn't gutted and painted over after Richard left.'

Alec sighed now. 'It seems a long time since we really believed the Cut Throat was hidden in the castle though, doesn't it?' I nodded and bent to my work once more.

Those *Homes and Gardens* pictures of the castle were the last of the photographs altogether. There was an invitation and an order of service for Bluey's christening, the same again for Richard and Otto's wedding, a terribly yellowed set of menus and invitations for Harold and Beulah's wedding and their engagement party, and every page before that was filled with watercolour sketches of the castle, faded invitations to yet more parties, and I had wasted twenty minutes and achieved absolutely nothing.

'Hmph,' said Alec.

'Hmph what?'

'Typical,' he added, unhelpfully. I waited. 'Penny inherits everything if they can keep hold of it,' he said at last.

'I don't know whether to be more shocked that you're reading Bluey's will or that he's got it there in his desk instead of safely with his solicitor.'

'Of course I'm not,' said Alec. 'It's a clerk's copy of the entailment on the estate.'

'Oh well then!' I offered, hoping he would catch the sarcasm. I wondered how he would feel if someone was poking around the entailments on his own estate and I did not see how its being a clerk's copy made any difference.

He flipped a page. 'Huh!' he said.

'Huh what?'

'*Typical.*' Again I waited. 'It used to be eldest legitimate male. When there were farms and forests and a moor to shoot over, it was male heir to male heir all the way. They changed it to general "legitimate issue" once it had gone down to this white elephant of a place and a row of pensioners' cottages. Penny only gets it because it's no longer worth getting.'

259

'Drat,' I said, the mention of cottages reminding me. 'I meant to go back to see Nanny today. See if I could shake loose that little thing that's bothering me. I could do it now and leave this to you.'

Alec groaned. 'Dandy, by this time in a case there are so many little things bothering you, you might as well be lying on a bed of nails. Much better to stay here and finish what we started.'

Because he had annoyed me, I said something then that I otherwise might have bitten my lip upon. 'So she's not an heiress, whatever her other charms.'

Alec bent lower over his papers and continued reading.

Then, because I felt a bit of a rotter, I redoubled my efforts to find Richard's writing. Therefore the question of what I wanted to ask Nanny, as well as all the other little worries, were set to one side and soon overwhelmed by the many events of the day.

And find Richard's writing we did. In the very place we should have guessed it would be found: the official record of all the events that the engraved invitations, be-tasselled menu cards and, latterly, photographs unofficially commemorated too. Mrs Porteous had even spoken of it to us. We were caught between patting ourselves on the backs and kicking ourselves for fools.

The first I knew was Alec leaping to his feet and snatching up the scrap of paper we had found with the pearls and rings.

'Aha!' he said. 'There's no way Anne Annandale would be recording Bluey's birth in the Bewer family Bible, now is there?'

'Oh jolly good!' I said, leaping to mine and joining him. 'Is it definitely the same hand?'

'No doubt about it,' Alec said, putting our little note down on the other side of the open flyleaf. I studied the long list of names and dates and the few words we had come to know so well and nodded.

'Not only the same hand,' I said, 'but the same ink. I'd bet it was the same pen.'

'No question at all,' said Alec. 'Richard Bewer wrote his son's birth into the Bible and Richard Bewer wrote a note to an unborn granddaughter and hid it in his old rocking horse, with a selection of his Aunt Dorothy's trinkets.'

He grimaced.

'Yes,' I said, agreeing with the grimace. I daresay I wore one of my own. 'That sounded more and more ridiculous as it went on. Why those trinkets, apart from anything else? Shouldn't it have been the Cut Throat?'

A moment of perfect silence settled over us. I gazed into space. Alec trained his eyes upon the open Bible.

'We've been fools,' he said, breaking the silence.

'Dolts,' I agreed.

'That note can't have been meant to accompany two worn-out rings and an indifferent strand of pearls.'

'It was madness to think so.'

'That note would only make sense if Richard was hiding the Cut Throat.'

'Yes,' I said. 'So someone swapped them. But why not just destroy the note?'

Alec, though, was not listening. He did not even glance at me jabbing the note with my finger to emphasise my point. He was still peering at the list of dates in the flyleaf.

'This isn't right,' he said. 'Harold and Beulah were married on the twenty-first of November in 1834. But, if Richard's hundred is coming on the thirty-first of October 1934, that means he was born before the wedding. That can't be right, can it Dandy?'

'It's a fraction disorganised if so,' I said. 'Unless the wedding was all set, a race between the vicar and the stork, and he really did come early and confound them.'

'But they were cutting it fine at that,' Alec said. 'If one's planning a wedding where time is of the essence, one doesn't leave it until the last minute, surely.'

'Perhaps she didn't let on,' I said. 'Perhaps she didn't know.'

'How could she not— No, don't tell me,' Alec said. 'I don't want to hear it.'

'What date's in the Bible for Richard's birth?' I said. 'Maybe they're miscounting.'

'None at all,' said Alec. 'They drew a veil.'

'Let me have another look at the scrapbook,' I said. 'See if perhaps any light can be shed there, by way of a christening invitation.' I turned a few of the heavy board pages and only then noticed something that had escaped me.

'Hmph,' I said. 'Nothing. A thick veil, as you say, firmly drawn over Richard's birth. Well, I suppose it would be, wouldn't it? No invitation, no order of service.'

'How strange,' said Alec.

'Well, yes but Richard was *there*. No one doubted it. It's not like all those terrible stillbirths in some family Bibles. Screeds of them sometimes all with the same name until one of them survives the cradle and the name sticks.' I shuddered.

'As you say,' said Alec, in a musing sort of voice. 'The record matters most if the child itself is gone. Without the child or the record then it's as if it never happened.'

I remained quiet, letting him think, for I knew he was thinking furiously. I could practically hear the cogs turning and see the thoughts spinning off the machinery to float free.

'We agree the note in the rocking horse was too portentous for Aunt Dorothy's rings,' he said at last. 'But don't you think it's odd that whoever found the hidey-hole swapped the trinkets instead of just getting rid of the note?'

'You know I do!' I said. 'I just said so.'

Alec blinked. 'Really? I wasn't listening. This is important, Dandy. If someone found the stash, why would not that someone simply rip the note up while taking the Cut Throat away?'

'I've just said all this!'

'Good,' said Alec. 'Because I think you're right. A birth recorded in a Bible is all the more essential if there's no lusty baby as independent evidence. In just the same way, the note was left as evidence . . . of something that would be less convincing in the note's absence. But what?'

'Depends on who,' I said.

'Not Ottoline,' said Alec. 'Unless you think she was acting when we showed her the granddaughter note.'

I cast my mind back and tried to think about exactly how Otto had reacted. 'She was surprised to be reminded about the hollow place in the rocking horse,' I said. 'I think she knew once but had genuinely forgotten about it. Which she would not have done if she'd made the switch.'

'And then afterwards,' Alec said, 'seeing the velvet box, she was truly astonished. She really thought we'd found the Cut Throat, didn't she?'

'So it can't have been Ottoline.'

'But why did she lie and say it wasn't Richard's writing?' said Alec.

'Protective habit? She's still fond of him after all these years. Perhaps she thought – since the note seemed so dotty – better lay it at the door of a dotty old lady whose reputation doesn't matter.'

'Not that Richard is exactly an advertisement for steadiness,' Alec said. 'So Bluey alone or Bluey and Minnie together?'

'Doing what?' I said.

'Making the swap, of course. I reckon they found the Cut Throat years ago, sold it and spent the proceeds and are trying to stop Ottoline finding out, with all this nonsense about a treasure hunt.'

I shook my head. 'She's been pretending to be deaf for

years so she can keep herself apprised of all the goings on,' I said. 'They'd have let something slip if they had secrets. And anyway, Bluey and Minnie had no reason I can imagine to leave the note and swap the trinkets. They'd have emptied the hollow and called it a day.'

'Are you sure?' Alec said. 'If Bluey was forging letters to soothe his mother perhaps, in the same vein of kindness, they left it as a treat for Penny.'

'And then forgot?' I countered. 'No. When we reminded Bluey about the rocking horse, he showed only a sort of nostalgic surprise.'

'As he would if he were trying to cover up his . . . Ach,' Alec said. 'I give up. I'm ready to go back to thinking Aunt Dorothy did it.'

'Or Anne Annandale,' I said.

'Or Mrs Porteous! Or Pugh!' said Alec.

'They weren't here when—'

'Dandy, for heaven's sake!' said Alec. 'Leonard's first drama master, Gilly's young man from the petrol garage. I'm trying to tell you I don't care and I want to stop talking about it before I run mad.'

'Very well,' I said. 'Let's stick to what we know. Richard left the Cut Throat behind for a future granddaughter. Bluey sent forged letters, as though from overseas, with Gunn's assistance, to help his mother find the abandonment a blessing. Someone found the ruby in Stumpy's back and put trinkets in its place. And the burglars . . . Are they real or are they fakes too?'

Alec groaned a groan so long I wondered if one of the actors had given him breathing lessons.

'Let's concentrate on the play until after tonight,' I said. 'Or see if we can offer any practical help to Minnie and Bluey. Sit in on Penny's lecture and make admiring noises. Eat the teas and call them delicious in ringing tones.'

'I'm not sitting on a straw-filled bolster, listening to a lecture,'

Alec said. 'I shall go and see if Bess needs help with the swords and these cannon that there are somewhere apparently.'

'Only if you're willing to help lug them up on to the stage.'

'She's a big strong girl,' said Alec. 'Besides, they roll.' And off he went to play at knights and soldiers.

21

There is a particular feel to the air, I learned that day at Castle Bewer, during the daylight hours preceding a first night. Although I have never been far enough up a mountainside to know the breathlessness of altitude, I imagine that is similar. And although I have never stood on a wooden floor with a wasps' nest under it, feeling the throb and thrum through the soles of my feet, I imagine it to be much the same too. Everyone in the castle could feel it that long midsummer's day. At first it lent a sense of cheerfulness and optimism to proceedings. Penny's lecture, on the true history behind the story of the play, was well attended and well received and the first of the teas laid out in the gallery was met with smacked lips and hardly a grumble about the cost at all. Mrs Porteous's scones were little clouds of buttery heaven – breaking open sweet and light – to murmurs of approval all round. And getting a Scotswoman to approve scones baked by another's hand is a feat. The sandwiches were meat paste but the bread white and fresh and the crusts long gone. The tea was best black Indian but piping hot and plenty of it and the little cakes were topped with blood red icing, which entranced everyone and led to much quotation. Even the treasure hunt went off better than anyone could have hoped: everywhere one looked there was another band of strangers, one of them clutching the little notice handed over with the tickets. They scuttled around the corridors, gawping and giggling, and enjoying themselves tremendously, without ever actually looking too hard, since none of them was quite sure it was truly allowed.

I watched a family of five – a clerk sort of a father, his tidy wife, their grown son and daughter and a chap who was either the son's friend or the daughter's follower – standing in front of Beulah's portrait in the great hall, studying the flyer and gazing at the painting.

'The Briar Rose,' read the father, 'was given as a wedding present and has been missing in the castle since Beulah Bewer's untimely death at Christmas in 1836.'

I stared along with them, wondering about this woman who had seduced Harold Bewer away from his intended bride, who had borne him a child mere weeks before she married him, who had died so wretchedly at the foot of a ditch, young and beautiful with all of her life ahead, leaving feuds and curses and heartbreak behind her.

'She doesn't look very happy,' said the clerk's daughter, and the young man who was not her brother put his arm around her and gave her a squeeze.

'If I find the ruby for you,' he said, 'promise me you won't wear it with that sulky look on your face!'

'If we find the ruby, it's a four-way split,' said the girl's father. They all laughed but the wife and daughter looked a little wistfully at the painted gems as they began to walk away.

'Ahem,' I said. I could not resist it. The mother, who was at the back of the group, turned with an enquiring glance. I raised my eyes and nodded at the top of the picture where one of the silver lockets hung, camouflaged against the ornate frame. She squinted then stood back, eyes wide and gasped.

'Cissie!' The daughter turned back. 'Dad! Read that bit off of the bottom again.'

'Several other necklaces are hidden around the house where a lucky treasure seeker might stumble across them, while on the trail of the Briar Rose,' he read. 'Happy hunting!'

'There's one right there,' said the wife. 'Look. Up there.'

Her daughter had both hands clasped under her chin and was bouncing up and down with glee.

'Well, now, Em,' said the man. 'How do we know that's one of the prizes and not someone's private property. We don't want to be thrown out before the play, do we? We don't want to be arrested for theft and get our names in the paper.'

'Oh, come on!' his daughter exclaimed. 'It's a necklace and it's hooked over the picture of the lady who owned the ruby. It couldn't be more clear.'

'Less of your cheek to your father,' her mother said, but it was too late. One of the young men had leapt onto the back of the other and was reaching up. He unhooked the necklace, jumped down, and handed it to the girl.

'Oh!' she said, with a soft cry of delight. It was a cheap little thing but even I had to admit that the moment had some charm. She opened the fastening and took out a tiny twist of rice paper which, when unfolded and held to the light, gave up the words: *congratulations on your find, from the Bewers.*

The note blew all their doubts away. No one, I thought to myself as I walked off to leave them to their wonderment, puts a note in a hidden place unless they want it to be found and read. No one forgets that they have planted such a thing. I did not know what any of it meant but I felt, somehow, that I was getting closer and closer to the moment when I would understand everything.

As I reached the head of the stairs, I could still hear the clerk's family regaling another band of treasure seekers and, by the time I had been to find Minnie and tell her the news, it had spread like a plague throughout the castle, now like a dovecot with all the flitting and twittering in it, as quite forty people dashed around, newly enthused. Only the clerk's family, whose day could not reach higher heights, sat relaxed in the gallery over cups of tea and told and retold their story to all comers, omitting – I was intrigued to hear – my part in the proceedings.

Things did not start to turn until the end of the afternoon, when the day should have been winding down into gentle evening: the last of the tea-takers not minding that Gilly was sweeping; the last of the lecture-attendees understanding that Penny had to leave the chapel and promising to send all remaining questions in a letter. The motors full of sightseers should have been pulling away across the field and leaving the Bewers to cocktails and ease. Instead, as the hour of the curtain approached, the thrum of the wasps under the floor and the crackle in the air around our heads became harder and harder to ignore and, by the time the first ticket-holders slid into the front row of wooden benches, the day had tipped from anticipation to something more like dread.

The weather was not helping. The clouds that had begun high and pale in the midsummer sky had lowered and darkened as the afternoon wore on and they trapped a close mugginess under them. There was not a breath of wind. The elms looked yellowish and unreal, paler than the clouds behind them, and the birds quieted hours early, taking shelter and leaving an uneasy silence.

'This is the first time I've been glad it's *Macbeth* and not the *Dream*,' Minnie said. 'This all helps rather and it would have been disastrous for the Athenian glade. Did you know we're sold out? And Mespring isn't even open yet. These are people who've come just for us alone. Now come to the dressing room, Dandy, and get your costume on.'

I had never seen the backstage properly before. Sarah Byrne had her own dressing room somewhere and I daresay that the men, of whom there were so many, were hugger-mugger in the little rooms that lined the passageway, erstwhile still rooms and game stores and the like. We ladies, from Lady Macduff down to the lowliest of the non-speaking parts, had been given a chamber which started life as a dairy, to judge from its slate floor and its many shelves, but which had been kitted up with getting on for a dozen dressing tables, ready to receive the fairies and their queen, and was blindingly bright from an electric lamp which had somehow been rigged up high in the arch of the ceiling and was beating down mercilessly upon us all. The witches looked utterly ghastly in its draining glare and Penny and Grant were engaged in a heated dispute when I entered.

'Leonard was quite clear about wanting subtle make-up, Delia!' Penny said.

'Leonard doesn't know the first thing about stage make-up,' Grant retorted.

'Leonard has had his own company for the last seven years,' Penny said.

'With not a dresser nor a maker-upper to its name,' Grant scoffed. 'Hecate told me they all just slap on whatever panstick comes to hand in the dressing room and extra rouge if they're playing a romantic lead. But when it comes to Shakespeare . . . '

'You can't seriously believe that you can teach Leonard anything about Shakespeare?' said Penny. She was laughing, but then she had never locked horns with Grant before and did not know any better. I turned away and considered the dressing tables still available. The plums had been plucked of course, by Lady Macduff, Hecate and her sisters, and the gentlewoman, as was only fitting, but also by Mrs Cornelius, Mrs Westhousen and Mrs Rynsburger because they had turned up before me and nabbed them. I slid onto a three-legged stool before what I was sure was a washstand with the bowl-hole covered up and peered at myself in the rather spotted glass.

Lady Macduff was staring at herself too and muttering lines, ignoring Penny and Grant completely.

'Aye, madam but returns again tonight,' I said to my reflection. 'Madam, I will.'

I was just beginning to wonder what to do to my face to turn it into that of Lady Macbeth's servant when Grant seized me by the shoulders and spun me round.

'Fine,' she said to Penny. 'Be like that, then. Far be it from me.' And, with a few brusque strokes around my eyes and some blows upon my cheeks with a round sponge, she used my face to tell Penny Bewer exactly what she thought of Leonard before flouncing off.

I turned back and jumped so badly the legs of my little milking stool screeched against the stone floor. I had been transformed into something from a Punch and Judy show: my brows black darts, my eyes larger by half than any eyes should be and my face a shade of orange unknown to nature.

'Lipstick?' I said faintly.

'Of course not,' said Penny. 'You're done. Do you need help with your headdress?'

I glanced at the coat hanger on the peg beside my table. I saw a dress, brown and baggy, and an apron too, but nothing like a hat. Penny sighed, twitched down a square of cloth I had not noticed and wound it into a turban, finishing it off at my nape.

'Good enough,' she said, looking at my reflection.

'Thank you,' I said, meekly, trying not to stare at Lady MacDuff's cone and veil – or at least not to covet it when I did so. 'When should I dress, to be ready for Act III?'

'Now!' said Penny. 'Now, of course. Act III? What are you—? Good God!'

Without questioning her outrage, I took down the baggy brown dress and wriggled into it. A pair of soft leather boots, more like stout socks really, and I was complete. For the first time in the case I wished Hugh were here. He is not given to fits of merriment; sometimes months go by without him actually laughing, beyond a gruff 'ha!' when some item of dire news he predicted is announced in *The Times*, but if he could see me now he would be helpless and weeping.

'Is it all right to stand in the wings until it's time to go on?' I asked Tansy Bell who was on my other side. 'Or should I keep out of the way in case someone trips over me.'

'You'd *better* be standing in the wings where Bess can see you,' said Tansy. 'If she has to come looking, she'll flay you alive. You're carrying on a plate of food in Act I.'

'What?' I said.

'Act I, scene 7,' Tansy said. 'Diverse servants.'

'But-But . . . ' I said, thoroughly rattled. 'No one told me. What plate? Where do I get it? Where shall I put it?'

'I'm telling you now,' said Tansy. 'Bess shoves it into your hands and you put it on the table. Where else?'

'And then I leave?' I said.

'No!' said Lady MacDuff, letting her concentration drop and becoming Miss Tavelock again. It was the first time she had acknowledged my presence. 'Good God, do you want your head cut off? If you go scampering about the stage during Moray's "if it were done when 'tis done" he'll come after all of us. You trot on, put the tray on the table and stand still till the exeunt.'

I nodded then looked back at myself in the mirror. I could carry a tray of food, so long as I did not have to speak at the same time. 'Aye, madam, but returns again tonight,' I said. It was becoming a sort of prayer. 'Madam, I will.'

'And you're on and off in a blink the second time,' said Penny.

'The second time?' I could feel my face blanch, even if my orange cheeks hid every trace of it.

'You come on with the murderers in Act III, scene 1,' said Penny, 'and then they say to go to the door till they call you back and you go. On and off, quick as a flash.'

'And *do* they call?' I said. 'Do they call me back?'

'No, that's it,' said Lady Macduff. 'Until you're back on with Lady M in scene 2.'

'Aye, madam, but returns again tonight. Madam, I will?'

'Word perfect,' said Tansy. Lady MacDuff smiled at me too, for encouragement, and all three of us pretended not to hear how badly my voice was shaking.

For a moment I considered going the way of Francis Mowatt and just walking out of the castle to catch a bus for town. It would have to be a bus, for my little Morris Cowley was trapped at the far end of Pugh's field by a charabanc that had brought a party of Rotarians up from Carlisle and the yellow sports car of some bright young things who had fetched up from heaven only knew where to have fun of the wrong kind, in Leonard's sour opinion.

But how could I escape to the bus stop? There was only one egress from the castle – through the gatehouse passage and across the bridge – and between me and it in one direction was a long corridor thronged with excited playgoers taking their seats. I could hear them. In the other direction were Leonard and Bess breathing fire in the wings. I was as completely trapped as if the ingenious drawbridge still pivoted on its hinge and had been brought smartly up to seal us all off from the world.

Besides, there was no more time. Even as I had the thought, Bess was making her way along the dressing rooms, rapping on doors and calling 'Act I beginners, please! Witches, Malcolm, Duncan, Captain, Lennox, Ross! Act I beginners, please!' She stuck her head into the ladies' dressing room. Her hair now had the wild look one associates with Bedlam inmates – just like the dreadful etching of Bertha in an illustrated *Jane Eyre* I had owned as a girl – and her eyes were stark and huge in her face, stretched wide with first-night panic. I would not have crossed her with a knife under my ribs.

'Act I beginners,' she bellowed at us, before she withdrew.

Lady Macduff threw a cloak over her shoulders and brought it up over her head, transforming herself into First Witch. She and the other two proceeded out, leaving the American ladies and me in awe of their calm expressions

273

and steady gait. Mrs Westhousen, in contrast looked rather sick, and Mrs Rynsburger had a high colour in her cheeks and on her neck that no amount of patting with more of the orange panstick could disguise.

I decided I would rather be in the wings watching the professionals prove it was possible to walk onstage without dropping dead from fright than sit here letting my fellow amateurs wind me up into a blue funk.

I missed the witches' first scene and the reports of battle and arrived just in time to hear the prophecies.

'Thou shall *get* kings,' said the third witch, almost yelling the word that had got her into such trouble with Leonard.

Bess, on the book, snorted. 'It's going to be that sort of first night then, is it?' said Sarah Byrne suddenly at my elbow. 'Terribly unprofessional.' She glanced at me and started. 'Mrs Gilver? Are you going on?'

'Didn't Leonard tell you?' I said. 'There's been quite an upheaval since yesterday.'

'You're not the porter, are you?' said Sarah and her lips twitched.

'Servant,' I said, my mouth drying again at the thought of it. '*Your* servant. Aye, madam, but returns tonight. I'm petri-fied.'

'Say to the king I would attend his leisure for a few words,' said Sarah.

'Madam, I will,' I said gratefully.

'You'll be fine,' said Sarah. 'But might I ask why the upheaval?'

'Francis Mowatt left,' I said. 'He's gone.'

'Angus?' she said, and swung round to look onstage. 'Why yes, I see Julian on there instead. But I don't believe Francis has really gone. Has one of those scamps not locked him in a broom cupboard for a joke? It's the sort of thing Roger would do. Poor Francis is probably beating on the door and wearing out his voice shouting for help.'

'No,' I said. 'He's really gone. He fell in the moat.'

Sarah shot out an arm and clutched me. 'You mean "gone"?' she said. 'Gone to his rest?'

'What?' I said. 'No. Gosh, no. He caught cold and had a fright and has gone . . . home, I suppose, to recuperate.'

'He'll never work again,' said Sarah. 'A cold? *A cold?* I went on as the Duchess of Malfi with a broken ankle when I was young. I didn't even limp. The only excuse for not going on and giving your all in a part is if you're actually dead. Quite dead and stiff.'

'And even then there's Yorrick,' came another voice. Moray Dunstane had arrived, dressed as King Duncan again and even grander somehow than he had been the day before at the dress rehearsal. Bess and Sarah tittered and I took it that this little exchange was a well-known routine.

'Snap an ankle, dearest,' said Sarah, as Moray gathered himself to enter.

'Shatter a kneecap, my love,' replied Moray over his shoulder. He swaggered onstage with his wife blowing kisses behind him and I considered how much nicer Sarah and Moray were when they were actually acting. All the grandeur and hauteur quite gone. Sarah was chatting again now, chummy as anything.

'—Duncan's not a great part, but combined with the Old Man it at least gives an evening's work. And of course he'll be in Duncan's crown again for the curtain and that always gets a cheer. I still remember the first time I saw the play. I was quite a young girl and very sheltered. I didn't believe he was dead. I sat waiting for him to come back and wreak revenge right up until the end. I wept with relief at the curtain.'

Her words made me think of Richard, long gone and surely dead by now, but everyone always wondering.

'I had been seeing so much of Oscar's oeuvre,' she went on. I could not help catching Bess's eye. Oscar Wilde was not writing plays when Sarah Byrne was a girl. We smirked but said nothing. 'And of course no one who is missing is actually dead in *those* plays. No one is ever even missing. They are all right there disguised as governesses and cousins. Does *anyone* actually die onstage in Wilde?'

'I haven't seen them al—' I said.

'There's something more honest about dying right there onstage where everyone can see it,' she said, talking over me. 'I wonder why Mr Shakespeare didn't let King Duncan have his death scene.' She tutted, then strode forward, taking a scrap of paper from her pocket as she went. I was so surprised that I almost reached out to grab at her, to warn her that she was walking onto the stage. But of course she knew that. Duncan and Macbeth had exited at the far side; this was a different scene; and Sarah Byrne, with barely a breath between, had left off chatting to me and was now acting. There was something marvellous about that to my mind, I decided. I was thoroughly glad I had spoken to her. I nodded. Thoroughly glad. Although, if I were honest, something she had said was, for some reason I could not fathom, troubling me.

I could see Duncan and Banquo in the wings on the far side waiting to come back on. And all around me other 'diverse servants' were beginning to gather. Tansy bent low over Bess's shoulder following the lines and then at the end of a speech she slid into the chair that Bess slid out of and bent still further.

'Plates,' said Bess. 'You, take the beef and put it in the middle.' She gave an oval of painted card with a lump on it to one of the men. 'You, maidservant, take the soup.' She nodded to me and I picked up a deep covered dish with a ladle. 'Put it on the far end of the board and stay o/p upstage of Moray.'

'What is o/p?' I asked.

'Opposite prompt,' she said. 'Other side of the stage. But

that doesn't really matter. Upstage of Moray does. Do you know what that means?'

'Don't get between him and—'

'Right,' said Bess. 'Now go.' And with another of the little shoves that had sent me flying onto the stage the night before I was on again.

22

It was darker tonight, the low clouds Minnie had lamented helping the courtyard feel more like a theatre than I would have imagined possible. It did not help me. Out beyond the footlights, I knew they were all there, hordes of them. I could hear them breathing.

Except I could not possibly hear them breathing, I told myself because I was a servant in Macbeth's castle. I looked around at the tall boards where Sarah and Bess had nailed swords to make a murderous display. A suit of armour stood in the shadows at the back of the stage and I saw, as I glanced towards the footlights, that they had found the cannon. Two of them sat at angles one to the other in the corners, like the arrangements of flowers that used to adorn every variety show.

But I should not be gawping at the fittings of this castle where I worked hard in the kitchens. I marched over to the far end of the table with my soup tureen held aloft the way I had seen Pallister hold aloft soup tureens down the years. I set it down, with a bit of a thump, for it was lighter than it should be and the table top was hollow despite its sturdy look, but apart from a glower from Moray at the thump interrupting his lines no one seemed to notice. I withdrew myself to the dark, back portion of the stage and stood listening to Macbeth lose heart and Lady Macbeth scoff at his cowardice and scorn him.

What a peculiar play it would be if Duncan really were hiding in a blanket box after his last exit, ready to jump out at any moment. But Sarah's point was well made as far as

Richard was concerned. If *he* were dead, as surely he must be, what a disastrous twist of fate it was for him to die somewhere no one knew him and without any papers upon him, so that word never reached home.

I had stopped listening to the actors altogether now. It was not just a disastrous twist; it was preposterous. He wasn't a desert tribesman dropping from thirst between watering holes, or a tramp expiring under a hedge on a country road, nor even a king in the days when life was brutish and deeds dark. He was a gentleman travelling with a trunk and writing case, not to mention a passport.

'If we should fail?' Macbeth was saying.

'We fail?' said Lady Macbeth, with a snort and a look of disdain.

It was a simple plan if one had the stomach for it: to kill the old king and then get rid of the guards and call the job done. What had happened at Castle Bewer all those years ago was considerably more devilish. A curse, a ruby, a feud. Burglars, letters, a note in a rocking horse. Pearls and diamonds, servants sacked and new ones—

There! There it was at last. *There* it was. It was not the name of the gem that had been troubling me at all, when I spoke to Nanny in her cottage. Oh, if only I had gone back and interviewed her properly! I should not be having these revelations when I was stuck onstage with a hundred strangers watching.

It was the timing. Richard's illness and disappearance and when one followed the other. That was what had been worrying away at me like one of those beetles that fell mighty trees with years of gnawing. Had Ottoline pasted a picture of ladies only into the scrapbook of her son's wedding because her husband was ill and spoiled the look of the group? Or was there no photograph of Richard because he was already gone?

When did his illness turn into his absence? The new servants had said the master was ill and left to go to the mountains for his lungs, and what a thing it was for him to leave before Minnie even arrived. But the old servants, Nanny and Gunn, said the master was ill and left to go to the mountains for his lungs and what a thing it was for him to go when Minnie had just arrived. So which was it? Whether he had left before Ottoline sacked the servants or after, whether he left before Minnie arrived or soon after she came, some of the servants – new or old – should have seen him go.

'What can you and I not perform on th'unguarded Duncan?' said Lady Macbeth.

And not a single one of them had seen him! But one of them claimed to. Gunn. Suddenly, I knew everything. Richard had not been ill at all, neither in his mind nor his body, and he had never left the castle. At least not on his own legs. Someone had killed him. Someone had killed him and sent fake letters back from distant ports and that same someone had found the ruby in the rocking horse and put some unwanted old baubles in there instead, so that when they were found, everyone would believe Richard knew he was leaving.

I was as sure as I had ever been of anything that Ottoline knew nothing about the rocking horse. Which left Bluey. With or without Minnie.

'. . . we shall make our griefs and clamour roar upon his death,' said Lady Macbeth.

Minnie had been filled with sorrow at the misfortune of never meeting her father-in-law. Could she have sounded so sincere if she had taken a hand in his killing? I remembered Sarah joking and gossiping with me and then striding forward and acting her relief about Macbeth's battle triumphs.

'False face must hide what the false heart doth know,' said Macbeth and the stage emptied around me as everyone swept away.

★ ★ ★

I did not even realise what had happened until Banquo and Fleance came on from opposite sides of the stage and huddled in the middle.

'How goes the night, boy?'

'The moon is down; I have not heard the clock.'

It was another scene. It was another room in the castle. It was the middle of the night after the setting of the moon and yet still I stood there. I took a step to the left just as Max Moore came striding back on, then halted. If I 'scampered about the stage' while Macbeth himself was speaking I shuddered to think what might befall me. As Banquo started up again I sidled back.

'The King's abed,' Paddy said and my knees turned to liquid. It was the very moment, solemn and dreadful, when Duncan was being murdered, and there I was, shuffling back and forth and distracting everyone. I was sure I could hear a few whispers from the wooden benches. I would have given anything to have been playing the porter again, giving those toe-curling speeches with my cheeks flaming. Anything but this. I looked around wildly and, at last, I saw an answer.

The suit of armour Bess had finally dragged down from the attics stood just to my right in the darkest upstage reaches. Slowly, I took three steps back until I stood beside it as though at the other edge of a door. I clamped my hands to my sides and, thanking Penny at last for the cloth that bound my head, I raised my chin and froze.

This time there was definitely a whisper, and a rush of smothered laughter, from out in the audience. I thought I heard a scuffle in the wings too, but I stared straight ahead. I could almost convince myself I was doing the production a great favour. For suits of armour, like cannon, come in pairs. A single suit of armour plonked on the stage just made Macbeth's castle look silly.

The air was still, in the shelter of the courtyard. Not a

breath of wind stirred. Yet, a shudder passed through me and left my skin crawling, as the dreadful revelation broke.

Suits of armour come in pairs. And yet there was just one in the attics of Castle Bewer. One suit of armour with two lances. One suit of armour with its own curious, canvas under-suit left inside it and rotted to shreds around its feet, and another canvas suit bundled up and shoved into its arms. One suit of armour left and its mate pressed into service again after hundreds of idle years.

It was when Leonard and Bess started arguing about dressing the stage with swords and cannon – and suits of armour – that Ottoline hurried away. She went to the attic and got her dress dusty and her stockings filthy. She was checking what she suspected and, once she knew it was true, she took to her bed, saying she had lived too long and wanted only to die. Her son and his bride had killed her husband and her life was now a hateful thing to her.

But why would one put a dead man inside a suit of armour, having killed him? Why make a body so heavy it was all but impossible to move?

I gave a start, but barely noticed the giggle that ran around the audience at it.

I could think of one excellent reason to weight a body and it made sense of many things. Francis said he had a vision when he plunged into the moat and sank to the bottom. Ottoline screamed holy murder when she saw him go in. Not in case he sank, but in fear of what was sunk already. I frowned. She had always suspected where Richard's body was, I realised. She did not let Penny swim in the moat although Bluey had swum there when he was a boy. The difference was that when Bluey was a boy there was nothing worse in the moat than a few tadpoles and perhaps a water rat. But by the time Penny was born, Ottoline dreaded it had a much more grisly resident, sunk to the bottom and slowly mouldering there.

A bell rang and I flinched again and looked around me. The scene was drawing to its close. Banquo and Fleance were gone and Macbeth stood alone.

'I go and it is done,' he said. 'Hear it not, Duncan, for it is a knell that summons thee to heaven, or to hell.' Then he marched upstage, grabbed me above my elbow, gave me a look that could freeze a cauldron of boiling oil and dragged me off with him.

Leonard was waiting. 'Get that costume off,' he said in a low mutter. 'You are a disgrace to the theatre. You are sacked.'

'Good,' I said. 'I've got other things to do.'

I left him spluttering, flew to the ladies' dressing room, stripped my servant's dress off, shrugged my own back on, and went to find Alec.

The first room I tried was clearly Sarah Byrne's little bolthole. There were flowers on her dressing table and a pink silk wrap pushed back on her chair where she had let it fall as she sat there. Next door again was Moray Dunstane's, with more flowers – I wondered if they sent them to each other – and a satin wrap hardly different, except for being quilted where Sarah's was sheer. He was already in there, his crown off and his kingly robe thrown on the floor, busy sticking grey wisps to his temples to become the old man.

'What the devil?' he said.

'Sorry, wrong door,' I told him and tried a third time. This room was even fuller than ours, simply stuffed with tables and stools and one-third full of actors, all throwing off soldiers' garb and donning servants' cloaks, or throwing off servants' cloaks and donning the ghosts' shrouds for later. Alec was halfway, standing in his summer vest with his trousers rolled up.

'Dandy?' he said. 'Wrong dressing room, darling.'

'He's dead,' I said.

Paddy Ramekin and Julian clutched one another.

'Who?' said Paddy.

'Onstage?' said Julian. 'It's the curse!'

'Moray? Or Max? If it's Max I could go on. I know the lines.'

'Are you sure?' said Alec, ignoring them.

'And I know where the body is too,' I said, which set Julian and Paddy all a-flutter and got Alec out into the corridor beside me, summer vest, rolled trousers and all.

'Where?' he said.

'I'll tell you, but come away from here,' I said. 'Leonard is probably hunting me down to cut out my heart. I made a bit of a mess of things, I'm afraid.'

'*Where?*' hissed Alec as we fled along the corridor to the safety – from Leonard, at least – of the kitchen passageway.

'In the moat,' I said. 'In a suit of armour.'

'Who did it?'

'Bluey. Or Minnie and Bluey together. Ottoline has long suspected and she finally worked it out yesterday.'

'How?'

'Same way I worked it out just now,' I said. 'Because there was only one suit of armour. And only one reason to put a corpse in the other one.'

Alec clutched me, just where Moray's fingers had bitten in deep to the flesh of my arm, making me yelp. 'Dandy, you don't think they *know* she knows, do you? You don't think she's in danger?'

I shook my head. 'No, not yet. They're still laughing at her. Saying she's gaga. Saying she's peculiar about the moat.' But, as I spoke, we both heard footsteps and, looking along to the end of the passageway, we saw Bluey striding with great purpose. He could have been going anywhere but his general compass looked to be set for the Gatehouse Lodging and Ottoline's bedroom there. Swift and quiet, we started moving.

Thinking there was no way we could have beaten the

castle's owner through its labyrinthine corridors when he had a head start, we slowed and listened as we reached Otto's door. Then with a soft knock we entered.

All was quiet darkness. The window was open to the night air but the hush in Ottoline's room was such as I had never heard and the inky blackness blinded us completely.

'Light the candle, Alec,' I said, my voice ragged.

As Alec fumbled for a match and struck it, I found the bed and Otto's hand upon the coverlet, icy and jagged. She had clutched at her bedclothes as she died.

'Long gone,' said Alec, raising the candle and looking down at her. 'Nothing to do with Bluey. Long, long, gone.'

'She got what she wanted,' I said. 'To die in her own bed in her own house. She said this afternoon she had lived too long. Oh, but it's hideous, Alec. What a pitiful end.'

Alec heaved a sigh up from his boots but, before he had quite huffed it all back out again, he stopped. 'Are you absolutely sure it was Bluey and Minnie, Dan?' he whispered. 'Because if – and I'm only suggesting it as a possibility but – *if* Otto had put her husband in the moat in a suit of armour, and he'd be found if the castle were sold and the new owners drained it, I should jolly well think she *would* want to die in her own house in her own bed. Wouldn't you?'

'Alec!' I said. 'We're standing at her deathbed. Have some—' Then I caught my breath.

'And,' Alec went on, 'if she knew that her husband's century meant a tax bill and the sale of the castle to pay it I should jolly well think she'd feel she'd lived too long too.'

'But she didn't know about the note!' I said. 'She didn't know about Stumpy . . . Ssh, someone's coming.'

We had just got ourselves out when Bluey appeared at the head of the staircase at a trot.

'Ah,' he said. 'Great minds.' Then, as he took a closer

look at Alec, he said 'Rather informal attire for visiting my mother, old chap.'

'Were you coming to see her?' I said.

'Actually, I left the play because it suddenly occurred to me I should replace that little locket on top of the picture. I've got the Speirs family sworn to secrecy about where they found it. Thank goodness, because we couldn't keep thinking up new places. And then I just thought to myself I'd see how Mama was poddling on. Is she sleeping? Has she had her cocoa.'

It was a masterful performance, if performance it was.

'Stashing bits of jewellery, eh?' I said, hoping my tone would unsettle his act, but he only frowned at me and asked again.

'Is Mama all right?'

'Bluey,' said Alec, suddenly. 'Why did you change the drawbridge from that feat of engineering to the one you've got now.'

Bluey groaned. 'I didn't,' he said. 'That was my mother and I was furious. She did it while I was away staying with Minnie's family just before our wedding and she's never really given me a proper reason for it. Why?'

Alec and I looked at one another. At least Alec stared at me beseechingly and I glared at him. It did no good, my glaring. The task was mine.

'Bluey, I'm afraid I have some bad news,' I said. 'Two pieces of bad news, actually. One recent and one rather old, at least for news anyway. I'm so sorry.'

'Old news?' said Bluey, 'Don't tell me you've unravelled it all! Is the ruby truly gone?'

'Never mind the ruby just now,' said Alec, in his kindest voice.

The kindness made Bluey blink. 'Oh,' he said. 'You've found out what happened to my father, have you? Well, out with it. It'll be a relief more than anything, finally to know.'

'It's not your father,' I said and perhaps I placed the emphasis oddly, for he blinked twice more.

'Oh,' he said again. 'Am I to take it that I am an orphan?' His lip wobbled. 'Let me get Min before you tell me, would you? I'm not sure I'm equal to it on my own.'

23

'But Ottoline couldn't possibly,' Minnie said. 'She's a— Was a— Oh, I can't believe she's gone! And all alone in a dark room too. My heart will break from it.'

I decided then and there never to tell Minnie I had suspected her of plotting to kill her mother-in-law to keep secret the fact that she had killed her father-in-law too. Some things are better left unsaid.

We were in the little sitting room we had been led into on the first day, all clutching brandy and sodas and all trying and failing to make much sense of it all.

'She was a willow wand,' Minnie managed to get out at last. 'Even if she somehow killed Richard, with poison or a pistol or something, she doesn't . . . didn't have the strength to put him in a suit of armour, carry him to a window and tip him out into the moat. She couldn't do it.'

'She didn't do it alone,' said Alec. He took a stiff swig of his brandy. 'She had help. From Gunn.'

Minnie and Bluey exchanged blank looks.

'Gunn, your father's valet,' I said. 'Now the butler at Mespring.'

'Why on earth would Gunn . . . ?' Bluey managed to get out before words failed him.

'For advancement,' Alec said. 'He was a lowly valet in a charming but rather lowly household, if you don't mind me putting it that way. And now he's a butler in one of the grandest houses in the land.'

'And my mother wrote him a glowing reference in return

288

for him helping dispose of my father's body, did she?' said Bluey, sounding bewildered. 'But why would a reference from such a "charming but lowly" individual have such an effect on people as "grand" as the Annandales? It's not as though there's friendship between the two houses.'

'He didn't go empty-handed,' I said. 'He took – at least we think he did – he took the Cut Throat with him.'

There was a silence so profound it almost seemed to ring.

'I was right about that then?' said Bluey.

'Yes, I think so,' I said gently. 'It's the only thing that makes any sense. It was Sarah who put all of this in my mind, really. She said when she was a child she never believed Duncan was dead, because no one saw it happen. And it struck me that all of the stories about the Cut Throat stemmed from after Richard was gone. Nanny didn't know anything about the curse and the obsession. Bluey, you said all that only came out afterwards and it wasn't part of your own childhood. No one saw it happening, you see, because it didn't happen. Ottoline made it all up. She made it up out of whole cloth to explain the absence of both her husband and the necklace. To cast herself as the voice of reason – saying she wanted to give it to you, Minnie, but Richard wouldn't hear of it. To cast herself as the victim of rather sordid circumstance – saying that her husband was mad and had abandoned her. To cast herself as heroic and loyal – saying she had kept his descent quiet from everyone. But she had to change the castle's staff. No one can keep a secret long in a house full of servants.'

'And the true story is simply that she had killed her husband and did not want to hang,' said Minnie. 'That was what underlay all her passion for keeping this place and living out her whole life here.'

'Exactly,' I said. 'As long as you owned the castle she was safe. If it changed hands, the new owners would no doubt make it their first priority to improve the drawbridge. That hasty affair thrown up after the murder has never been worthy of the place after all.'

'I'm not arguing,' Bluey said, 'because I never understood Mama's position on that gimcrack bridge, but why choose that side of the castle and cause the problem in the first place?'

'Ah,' said Alec. 'Of course. Because even a strapping young Gunn would be hard pressed to heave a knight in armour up over a windowsill. They must have dragged the body to the drawbridge, dressed it there and then simply rolled it.'

Bluey was staring aghast at him. Alec, carried away by the light shining on the puzzle at last, had forgotten he was talking about the man's father. Hastily, I changed the subject.

'She must have been horrified by the plans this summer.'

'Poor Mama,' said Bluey. 'All the visitors, the treasure hunt, you two crawling over the castle looking for clues, Dandy.'

'Did you know her hearing was perfect, by the way?' I said.

'We had our suspicions,' Bluey said. 'I thought perhaps she'd just got tired of taking part in things and that was the easiest way to remove herself. Poor thing. Poor Father too. Poor us, all round.'

Minnie stood, took the glass out of his hands and drew him up to standing. 'Let's go to bed and try to sleep for a few hours, dearest,' she said. 'I'll get Mrs Ellen to sit with Ottoline until morning and then we can telephone to the undertakers.'

'And the police?' I said.

'No,' said Minnie. 'Ottoline will be laid to rest with some respect and then – if we decide to drain the moat or work on the drawbridge and make a gruesome discovery – we shall deal with what comes.'

'Are you suggesting we just carry on?' said Bluey, swaying where he stood. 'The play and teas and luncheons. The treasure hunt?'

'Of course not,' said Minnie. 'We are a house of mourning.'

'And what are *we* to do?' I said. 'Alec and me? Stand by and say nothing? If there has been a crime we can't turn a blind eye.'

Minnie swung round to look at me. 'You, Dandy, are to go to Mespring and find out from Gunn what really happened. If it was perhaps an accident. Or if it was deliberate, why on earth she did it. It wasn't the nonsense about the necklace, clearly. So why did Otto kill him?'

We waited until a decent hour for visiting below stairs. It was seven o'clock in the morning when Alec, Grant and I, and Penny to represent the family, made the journey from Minnie and Bluey's field to the Annandales' magnificent park. We had not slept a wink. We had simply scraped off our stage make-up, dressed in less remarkable clothes and waited for sunrise.

'Why do wives murder their husbands?' Alec said by way of chat, once we were under way.

'Mariticide and uxoricide,' Grant said, 'are usually jealousy of a lover, discovery *with* a lover, inheritance, insurance or simple disaffection. Manslaughter could be discovery again or maybe they were arguing and she shoved him down one of those spiral staircases. That would do it.'

I tried hard not to be shocked. After all, it was Grant's clarity of thought that had made me invite her along with us in the first place.

'But don't you think it must be something to do with the Cut Throat?' Penny said. 'Why would Granny weave the curse into her story so tightly if it didn't belong there?'

'We think the curse was a fairy tale Otto herself made up,' said Alec.

'But how else could a necklace have caused a murder and got such a starring role in the drama invented to cover it up?' I said. 'If there wasn't a curse at the heart of it?'

'Perhaps Mr Bewer wanted to sell it and Mrs Bewer wanted to keep it,' said Grant.

'Or,' I said, 'perhaps Richard wanted to give it Minnie and Otto didn't want to let go. She did say that he snatched it off her neck during an argument. Perhaps there was a grain of truth in that.'

'Is it only because I'm a man,' Alec said, sounding rather hesitant, 'and so don't really care about such things that it all seems . . . Not that I'm suggesting ladies are silly about their jewels but . . . It doesn't seem *big* enough. A necklace? An argument about a necklace?'

'Once an argument about a necklace has caused a shove down the stairs and a death it becomes the matter of a noose,' said Grant.

'Poor Granny,' Penny said. 'Let's see what Gunn has to say.'

Gunn was just finishing breakfast when we arrived at the servants' door, our four faces so grim that the little housemaid hustled us straight into his pantry, terrified of she knew not what, and then scurried off to fetch him. He arrived, wiping his lips with a cotton napkin and looking equal to anything we might ask.

'Ottoline Bewer is dead,' Alec began. 'And we know the whole story.'

'The whole story?' said Gunn. 'Are you sure?'

'We might need your help to fill in a few of the details,' I admitted. 'But we know she killed Richard and you helped her weight the body and roll it into the moat. We don't know why she sent faked letters from all over the world but we suspect you helped her. You bit your tongue while you were listing the places they came from, you know.'

'I wondered if you'd noticed that,' Gunn said. 'How would a servant who'd left the household know where his old master was travelling? That was a bad slip.'

I groaned to myself. There was nothing special about Lisbon in the list of cities at all. Gunn had simply happened to stop talking just before he said its name.

'And what details would you need me to add?' he was saying now.

'A motive for one thing,' said Penny.

'And the reason behind the note and trinkets in the rocking horse,' I said.

'The truth about the burglaries that plagued the castle,' Grant added.

'A clue about why she destroyed the letters before we could see them would be nice,' Alec put in.

Gunn looked around us with a kind of amused twist to his mouth. 'She was such a clever woman,' he said. 'The cleverest I've ever known. And she wore it so lightly. Even I can't pick apart the threads she wove. I don't suppose anyone ever will.'

'Start with the Cut Throat,' I said. 'The Judas Jewel.'

Now Gunn actually laughed. 'Oh, if only it was a little later in the day. I want to raise a glass to her, really I do. "The Judas Jewel" was one of her early triumphs. A smidgen of fact – it came from the Annandales right enough – mixed in with such clever lies – Anne and Dorothy and the dark secret behind the so-called jilting – and all stirred up until there's no way to tell what the truth is.'

I remembered the conversations I had had with Ottoline about Dorothy and Anne and Richard's father and I knew exactly what Gunn meant. She changed her stories so gradually and with such deftness that one never quite knew where one stood.

'But now she is gone,' I said, 'if we give you our word, will you tell us, at least? What the truth is.'

Gunn laughed again. 'I'm trying to tell you, I don't *know!*'

'Tell us everything you *do* know,' I said. 'Let *us* find that smidgen of fact in the midst of the lies.'

'She had wheels within wheels,' Gunn said, his voice still filled with awe as he remembered. 'Fail-safes all over the place in case this or that happened, you know. She hid the note in the rocking horse so that it could one day be "found" – evidence, you see, that Richard planned to leave under his own steam. She put the trinkets in there – and trinkets is the word for them – to make it look as if the necklace had been there a while and then been taken away.'

'It's a bit elaborate,' Alec said, rather grudgingly considering he had drawn exactly those conclusions, just as Otto had planned.

'Exactly!' said Gunn. 'Who would do such a thing? And then she sent the letters to herself – I helped her – but it was her idea. Those letters did two things, two birds she caught with that wee stone. They sowed the idea of Richard travelling and the writing on them matched the writing on the note. And she got rid of every other piece of Richard's writing from dungeon to chimneys.'

'Except in the Bible,' I said. 'The family dates in the Bible flyleaf.'

'Ha! I forgot about the Bible,' said Gunn, with his eyes dancing. 'She wrote Bluey into the Bible. Oh, she was a marvel.'

'*She* wrote that?' I said. 'How can that be?'

But Alec spoke across me before Gunn could answer. 'Why did she destroy the letters the other night?'

'Well, there was nothing to be gained by you looking at them, was there?' Gunn said. 'Back in the early days, it was worth the chance of a bright bobby seeing the letters and smelling a rat. The other alternative, after all, was him smelling a bigger one. But what makes you think she destroyed them "the other night"?'

'She said she had them and then she said they'd gone. Blamed a burglar. And she'd burned something in her fire and made the room smoky.'

Gunn laughed. 'And you believed her? Those letters could have been gone for decades. The smoke could have been anything. Wheels within wheels, you see.'

'And what about the other burglaries?' said Grant. 'The earlier ones?'

'Did she make them up?' Penny said. 'Or did you help out there too?'

'I did, Miss Penny,' he said. I was glad to hear he had some respect left in him, even if he spoke of 'Richard' in that impertinent way. 'That was more dust she kicked up. More shadows where the truth could hide. She could have written Gothic novels if she'd a mind to. What better way to make it seem that Richard was alive and well and wanted his ruby necklace back than to have a whole staff of servants swearing to the fact of burglars? So she paid me and a couple of my most discreet pals to black our faces and creep in around the castle, making sure to leave tracks behind us. The last one – the one that was caught at the gate – was my cousin up from Devon for my auntie's funeral. No one knew him and his voice has a twang it's hard to place if you don't know that part of the world.'

'I see,' Alec said. 'The same again. So madly elaborate it must be true?'

'Exactly,' said Gunn again. 'There. I've answered all your questions.' He shook his head and laughed softly. 'But you haven't asked the biggest question of all.' He laughed louder at our blank faces. 'The biggest question of all is: where's the ruby?'

'What?' I said. 'You brought it back, didn't you? You bought your way back into Mespring and assured your rise through the household by returning the lost treasure. *Didn't* you?'

'No,' said Gunn. 'That ruby is lost. The mistress turned the castle upside down and inside out, looking for it. It's gone.'

'But then how *did* you get your job here?' I asked. 'Unless you brought something along with you?'

'Oh I brought something all right, but not a necklace. I brought a secret. And I kept it too.'

'What secret?' Alec said.

'Didn't you see the portrait?' said Gunn. 'I mean, didn't you look at it?'

'Which portrait?' I asked, looking at Alec and Grant to see if they understood. Mystified looks came back at me from both of them.

'The painting of Beulah in the velvet gown?' said Grant.

'Or Ottoline in her satin?' Alec added.

'Or,' said Penny, 'do you mean the portrait of Anne and Dorothy. I've always wanted to see that one.'

'I think a good look at all three would be worth your while,' said Gunn.

'But you're wrong about what's the biggest question,' Penny said. 'The only question that really matters at all is "why?" Why did she do it? Why did Granny kill him?'

'She didn't mean to,' said Gunn. 'She only meant to stop him. He had just told her he was marching off along here to bring her life tumbling about her ears. She went for him, right enough. She was in a rage. She shoved him. But she didn't mean to kill him. She mourned, you know. Even while she kicked over her traces and laid her false scents, she was grieving.'

'That's all lovely, I'm sure,' said Penny and there was a steely sound to her voice. 'But *why* did she shove him? *What* enraged her?'

'The portrait'll tell you that too,' said Gunn. 'But you didn't hear it from me.'

It was a new experience for me to begin a visit to comparative strangers by coming in at the servants' part of the house and then simply passing through the green baize door to the grand hall. That is what the four of us did that morning.

'Blimey,' said Alec, as we emerged into the marble and gilt, the naked hordes frolicking in oil paint far above us.

'Indeed,' I said. 'Now then, the portrait gallery is this way.'

'It's not exactly . . . ' said Penny as we trooped through the rooms. 'I mean, it's certainly . . . But it's not . . . '

'No, it's not,' I agreed. 'Now then, here they are.'

We stood in front of the portrait of the two girls and stared.

'What did he mean?' said Alec. 'What is there in this portrait that will help us unravel Ottoline's web?'

'And whatever it is, how does Gunn know about it?' I added.

We stood in silence like a row of dunces for a few minutes more, without answers to any of the questions arising in our feeble minds, and then were interrupted by a polite cough.

Billy Annandale was standing behind us, wearing pyjamas and a dressing gown as well as the carpet slippers which accounted for his silent approach.

'Not that it's not lovely to see you again, Mrs Gilver,' he said, 'but might one just casually enquire . . . ?'

'We honestly wouldn't know where to start,' said Penny. Billy gave her a mildly curious look, then he blinked and looked up at the picture and back to Penny again.

'I don't believe we've met,' he said.

'Penny Bewer.'

Billy looked up at the canvas and down into Penny's eyes one more time.

'Oh Lord!' I said. 'Billy, the last time I was here, the first time I saw the portrait of Anne and Dorothy, I said Penny bore an extraordinary resemblance to her great-aunt. But I think I made a mistake.'

'Ah!' said Alec. 'That explains why "Anne Annandale" was at Otto and Richard's wedding but "Aunt Dorothy" wasn't.'

'What is everyone talking about?' said Penny.

'The Great Scandal of 1834, you called it,' I said to Billy. 'And you very politely didn't say any more. But perhaps you'd say a little more now.'

Billy shot an uncomfortable look at Penny and muttered: 'I'd rather not, if it's all the same.'

'Very well,' I said. 'But tell me this at least. The nature of the scandal. It wasn't just the closeness of Anne and Dorothy, was it? Anne didn't give the ruby out of spite. She wanted the girls in the Bewer family to wear it, didn't she? The daughters, or even the granddaughters.'

'Nonsense!' came a voice so sharp it was almost a bark. I would never have imagined such a sound could come from Winifred Annandale's lips. 'How could a slip of a girl give away a chunk of the family's wealth? Exactly what's going on here? Gunn told me you'd practically broken in, Dandy. What's happening?'

'A great light is dawning,' I said. 'And a great many chickens are about to come home to roost.'

'Not before time,' said Lady Annandale, still sounding crisper than I had ever heard her. 'It's gone on long enough but it was hardly our place to end it. Penny my dear, it's wonderful to meet you at long last. I'm glad Ottoline has come to her senses. I look forward to getting to know her better. Life is too short for these feuds, you know.'

Penny tried to speak but the tears gathered in her eyes and she gave a sob instead, so it was up to me to break the news of Ottoline's death and then, promising more later, to put an arm round Penny and take her home.

'You had them the wrong way round,' said Alec, when we were back in Bluey's book room alone again. Minnie had taken a great deal of unwelcome and startling information on the chin, with no more than a nod to show that she had understood it all, and then had turned her mind from it and towards her child. Penny was now tucked up in bed and close to dozing.

'I had a great many things the wrong way round,' I said. 'That was a very good point Lady Annandale made, you know. How *could* the unmarried daughter of a family have enough clout to give away a treasure like the Judas Jewel. We are allowed to wear them but they never actually belong to us.'

'Ahh!' Alec said. 'The ruby came to the castle not as a *wedding* gift at all.'

'Exactly,' I said. 'Do you know, Alec, Lady Annandale *told* me she had tried to mend fences before Bluey and Minnie's wedding as her mother had before Otto and Richard's wedding. If I had asked her what she meant I might have solved this days ago.'

'Huh,' said Alec. 'She might call it mending fences, I'd call it dropping a bomb.'

'Me too,' I agreed. 'It certainly landed like a bomb on Otto. But I think Winifred Annandale spoke honestly. The Annandales had no intention to strip the Bewers of everything and boot them out of the castle. It was the shame Ottoline couldn't face. Nothing more than that. Just the shame.'

'So,' said Alec. 'Just to be clear I've got this right. Anne Annandale, the jilted fianc—'

'There was no jilting,' I said. 'Otto made that up. And there was no more between Anne and Dorothy than a friendship. Otto made *that* up too.'

'So what . . . ?' Alec began. '*What?*'

'Harold Bewer had a by-blow,' I said. 'By the Annandale girl. But for some reason we shall probably never know, he didn't marry her. Perhaps he scorned her for her loose morals. It wouldn't be the first time.'

'Don't scowl at *me*,' said Alec. 'I've never done such a thing. Perhaps he simply preferred Beulah. Or perhaps she was rich. Perhaps he didn't know about the baby until it was too late.'

'For whatever reason,' I said, 'Harold married Beulah. When Beulah died without providing an heir, he was persuaded by the Annandales to take the child, Richard, and give it his name and his payment was in rubies.'

'And that's why Richard's birth date wasn't recorded!' Alec exclaimed. 'Harold took him in but he wouldn't write a lie in a Bible.'

'It also explains why Bluey wasn't in there when Otto started her schemes. Why it was up to her to add him.'

'Does it?'

'If Richard wasn't really a Bewer – not a legitimate Bewer, anyway – then neither is Bluey. I'll bet Harold was still alive when Bluey was born and I'll bet he said he'd make the entry of his grandson's birth. Paterfamilias and all that.'

'What a sorry mess,' Alec said, then he sat up sharply. 'Oh! This means that when Anne started saying she was Bluey's grandmother, she was speaking the truth.' He scratched his head. '*Did* she put the note in Stumpy for her granddaughter then?'

'No,' I said. 'Actually she might not have made the claims either. Otto might have made *both* little stories up for our benefit and woven them together to make them hold. An inch of fact and a yard of fantasy. No wonder we thought there were more wisps than usual!'

'But if Otto was weaving tales,' Alec said, 'why didn't she weave better ones? If Beulah didn't walk down the aisle weeks after a confinement, why didn't Otto put a more believable date in the Bible?'

I laughed. 'Exactly. If you make up a date, you make up a good one, don't you? We questioned many things, after we found the Bible: why didn't they shift the wedding; did the poor girl even know the baby was coming . . . But we didn't doubt the date for a minute, did we?'

'I bet it was Richard's birthdate Otto made up,' Alec said. 'Halloween. Just for sheer mischief. Oh, how I wish we had worked all of this out while she was alive. There's so much only she could tell us. For instance, I still don't think I see why she was angry enough to shove Richard down the stairs. Gunn's so-called explanation doesn't actually explain much.

He was "going to Mespring to bring her world down around her ears"? Does that make sense to you, Dandy?'

'Yes, it does,' I said. 'We can talk it over with Winifred to make doubly sure, but I imagine that, when she tried to untangle it all before Bluey and Minnie's wedding, she met with a measure of success. She persuaded Richard that it was time to stop the nonsense and admit that the Bewers had died out. I think he was probably going to Mespring to begin to put matters straight and end the secrecy. Names would be changed, for one thing. Richard was the son of a Mespring spinster. His name would be Annandale. And *his* son might not be an acceptable match for Minnie any more. Certainly his wife . . . '

'Ah,' Alec said. 'Otto couldn't bear the world at large knowing she had married into cousins on the wrong side of the blanket.'

'To put it bluntly,' I said.

'Although, given what she did afterwards, it is odd. Rolling his body into the moat, paying off an accomplice and living in the castle for fifty years while it mouldered feet from her bedroom window? Couldn't the woman who did that manage the shame of a story two generations old? You said yourself the Annandales had no plans to turn her out.'

'Winifred would never do anything so unseemly,' I said. 'Not that it was up to Winifred alone.' Then a terrible thought struck me. 'Oh Lord, Alec, that's the whole point! It wasn't up to Winifred. It's not "up to" anyone. And it's *not* about "shame". If Richard wasn't a Bewer then Bluey isn't a Bewer and Castle Bewer doesn't belong to them. Legitimate male issue! You read it with your own eyes.'

Alec whistled. 'The entail,' he said.

'It's the same as a spinster not being able to give away a necklace. The *Annandales* can't decree that they don't mind the Bewers staying on! Somewhere out there is the legitimate male heir to all of this – the castle and the almshouses and the family portraits – even if the ownership of the ruby is hard to determine, should it ever actually turn up.'

'You don't think it's Leonard, do you?' Alec said. 'I do hope so. He'll have about three months to swank about and get even more insufferable before he gets his tax bill. Ha!'

'You've recovered from your love affair with the theatre, then?'

'I don't imagine I'm alone in that,' Alec said. 'Minnie and Bluey are no doubt very sad that Otto died, but they must be relieved to shut the doors and have done with it.'

'And do you really think they mean not to tell the authorities about Richard's resting place?' I said. Then I turned my head at a distant sound. A police klaxon was coming along the lane.

'There's your answer, Dan,' said Alec. 'I expected as much. He's been down there for thirty years, but it's different once you know.'

'Unless you're Ottoline,' I said. 'What an interesting character she was. I'm sorry she died before we ever got the chance to talk honestly.'

Unbeknownst to me, Bluey had put his head round the door as I was speaking. Alec flashed his eyes and I turned. 'Thank you for those few kind words, Dandy,' he said. 'I think we shall be needing that kind of sanguinity for a while. Gosh, my mother dead and my father in the moat for decades? The newspapers are going to have a field day.'

He did not know the half of it, I thought, and with a deep breath I began to tell him.

Postscript

The newspapers had not just a field day, but a festival that lasted for months on end. Every morning, and especially on Sundays, there seemed to be more to say about the long and tortured history of the Annandales and Bewers.

By the time Alec and I returned, it had begun to settle down a little, but the reason for our visit was sure to set it off again.

No one could blame the press for their paroxysms when the frogmen brought Richard's body up from its watery grave. It was indeed encased in armour. Inside the armour, his clothes had rotted away to no more than a few horn buttons from his tweed coat and a few rusty studs from his collar and links from his cuffs. His breast pocket had gone, of course. But the ruby necklace he had tucked in there before he set off to Mespring had survived, as sunken treasure will. The newspapermen even managed to spare a little pity for Ottoline, since it truly was pitiful to think of her ransacking the castle for the rubies she herself had just tipped into the moat.

'To think of it,' as Grant said. 'All of that scheming and all those stories and yet she didn't check his pockets. Easy to see she'd never done a day's laundrywork.'

The next chapter in the sordid history soon put the piteous Ottoline out of the minds of the great reading public anyway. The disinheritance of Bluey and the installation of Cousin Leonard, the rightful heir to the Bewer fortune, the very man who had brought the *Tragedy of Macbeth* inside the castle walls, just as all the heinous deeds came to light? It was too delicious for words.

Francis Mowatt sold his story, of course. He was a nine-days wonder with his tale of falling down through the green water and seeing the knight's helmet in its murky depths.

Mrs Rynsburger chipped in with her tale of the 'shining ghost', although I remained convinced that Miles and Tansy, freshly costumed in Grant's iridescent gauze, had been responsible for that particular piece of mischief.

There was one more revelation still to come. As we were welcomed to the long gallery at Mespring and offered cocktails by a new and properly granite-faced butler, Billy Annandale waved at the far wall. 'Did you notice our acquisitions? We bought them from Leonard.'

I glanced over, behind the long sofa where Minnie, Bluey and Penny were all drinking their cocktails thirstily, and was astonished to see, hanging side by side, Ottoline and Beulah, each with the ruby around her neck.

'Wait a minute!' I said, putting my drink down and stepping closer.

'I told you she'd see it, Mother,' Billy said. 'It's unmissable when you put them side by side.'

Indeed it was. These were not two portraits painted of two women who wore the same ruby for their sitting. The necklace in the picture of Ottoline had been copied, stroke for stroke, bead for bead of reflected light, and simply added to the portrait of Beulah. It was the same size in both pictures, even though the pictures themselves were not, and so it was much bigger on the neck of the one than of the other.

'We think whoever added it used tracing paper,' said Penny, ruefully.

'And this was why Mama was always so careful to keep the two pictures apart,' Bluey said. 'Her own in her bedroom and Beulah sewn up in sacking and tucked away. All the talk of luck and curses!'

'I had been wondering about that,' said Alec. 'Gunn told us there was something to learn from all three portraits, not just the picture of Anne and Dorothy. This is what he meant, is it?'

'Of course!' I said. 'There couldn't *really* have been a portrait of Beulah wearing the Cut Throat, because it wasn't until *after* her death that it came into the family.'

'And speaking of Gunn,' said Alec. 'What of him? That's one angle the papers seem to have missed.'

'When the docs said Richard's death was probably an accident,' said Billy, with a wary look at Penny, 'we thought it best to let all that side of it die down. We've pensioned him off and he's gone to live in Alnwick.'

'He's got off very lightly,' I said.

'Oh well, you know,' said Lady Annandale. I was not sure I did.

'And have the lawyers managed to work out who owns the Cut Throat?' I said.

'It's ours, all right,' said Billy. 'Even Anne's father didn't have the right to give it away, actually. It was part of the entailment. So, I suppose you'd say it's mine.'

'But Minnie and I think – we really do,' said Bluey, 'that it should be in a case in front of the two portraits when the house opens up again next spring. When it's not being worn to parties anyway.'

I could not help raising my eyebrows at the interested way he spoke and in such detail.

'Oh yes, indeed,' said Lady Annandale to my eyebrows. 'We've roped our cousins in. I have no talent for that sort of thing at all. We were hopeless at it all compared with Minnie and Bluey. Gosh, the very week we were supposed to open up last time we almost threw ourselves on their mercy and begged to pool resources.'

'We got as far as the castle gate one night, before we funked it and slunk off home again,' Billy said.

'The lights in the lane!' I exclaimed, sitting upright. 'That was you?'

'That was us,' said Winifred. 'I wanted to come clean, tell all, and beg for help.'

'We got there in the end,' said Bluey. 'We are all aboard for the great adventure now.'

'The great adventure?' I said.

'This pile of a place on the one hand and the Bewer way with talks and teas and plays on the other,' said Billy. 'We might just break even. Worth a try.'

'And thanks to Cousin Winifred we've got rather a lovely dower house to live in, at least for a while,' said Minnie. 'Much more comfy than the castle any day.'

'Yes, I hope Leonard gets consumption before he has to sell up,' Penny said.

I was glad to hear her speak of it so openly, for I had found it shocking. The loathsome Leonard, if you please, had decided that a man of his stature – the owner of a castle and the latest in a long and illustrious line that could trace its roots back to the Conqueror – needed a more respectable wife than Penny to support him in his new role. And a rich one too. I hoped against hope that he would not be able to cast this individual, but I could not be sorry that Penny had lost the part. I glanced at Alec to see if the news struck him as interesting. But I had missed a hint. Lady Annandale threw it again.

'Oh, I don't think I'll be moving into the dower house, Minnie. Once this place is off my hands, I intend to do a great deal of travelling and in between times I shall take up residence in the north lodge and wave my walking stick at villagers who step on the grass.'

'Off your hands?' said Alec. He had missed the hint even at its second pitching, but I smiled at Penny who blushed and gave Billy a shy look.

She had found herself another cousin, it seemed. And a considerably broader canvas than a shabby theatre in which to put on her next show.

'Ah,' I said. 'All's well that ends well, wouldn't you say?'

Facts and Fictions

Castle Bewer's location and lay-out owes something to Caerlaverock Castle and anyone who makes an excursion to it will recognise some features. Mespring House does not exist, in Dumfriesshire or anywhere else, but some of its decorative excesses will be familiar to anyone who has visited enough major historic piles. The characters here are all fictitious, although Sarah Byrne is so named thanks to the real Sarah Byrne's winning bid in an auction for a very good cause.